AF228403

SOULS OF FIRE & STEEL

SOULS OF FIRE & STEEL

JILL CRISWELL

BLACK
STONE
PUBLISHING

Printed in the United States of America

First edition: 2021
ISBN 978-1-9825-5629-7
Young Adult Fiction / Fantasy / General

1 3 5 7 9 10 8 6 4 2

CIP data for this book is available
from the Library of Congress

Blackstone Publishing
31 Mistletoe Rd.
Ashland, OR 97520

www.BlackstonePublishing.com

RUINS OF
DRAGON'S LAIR
SJOGLEN
LAVALANDS
GYLDENHRING
VAKNAVANGUR
STREAMLA
N
W
E
S

ISENELD
HIDDEN FALLS
HIGHLANDS
MEAD HOUSE
DRAGON'S DOMAIN
TEMPLE OF THE MOUNTAIN
FJORDLANDS
UNTAIN OF FIRE
HAUNTED ISLES
SJAF'S STAIRCASE
NEW FJULLTHORP
VOLVA ISLE

PART ONE
THE DEATH-BRINGER
AND
THE WOLF LORD

PROLOGUE

In the time before time, when what would become the mortal realm was nothing but violent seas broken by chunks of rock, a goddess made of living fire emerged from a crack in the earth and gazed upon the untouched wilderness with bright eyes.

A revelation took shape within her. A hunger awoke.

She called upon her fellow gods from the immortal realms—her brother, Gwylor, who ruled over an empty palace; her sister, Eyvor, who frolicked alone in a giant meadow; her cousin Veronis, who wandered and mused, seeking solace he could never find. Ildja explained her epiphany: power would taste far sweeter if it could be wielded over those who did not possess it.

The gods traveled from island to island, populating the realm with beings. Veronis gave fragments of himself to create creatures he could look after, from the huge and lumbering to the tiny and scampering, filling land and sea with all manner of beasts. Gwylor breathed life into the first mortals, and Eyvor gave each one a spark—an essence that made every mortal unique, a piece of them that would live on after their lives flickered and faded: a mortal soul. When their time in the earthly realm ended, these souls would fill Gwylor's palace and Eyvor's meadow.

Ildja saw what her siblings and cousin had made, and she twisted their designs to fit her own vision. What she birthed from her mind was dark and tainted—monsters that could survive even in her home of shadow and fire. She filled them with a hunger to match her own, and they devoured what Gwylor and Veronis had created. She looked at the monsters, smiled, and said, "I will call them Destroyers."

More of their kin joined the gods and goddesses, adding their own touches to this realm, their own iterations of human and beast. Together, they watched their creations: the mortals lorded over the animals, but the Destroyers terrorized them all, tearing apart anything they could to sate their hunger. The other gods were displeased by the wreckage Ildja's demons caused, and they exiled the Destroyers to the nether realms.

Ildja burned as she never had before, with the fury of a mother whose children had been scorned, but she was outnumbered. She bit her tongue.

She bided her time.

The gods continued to observe their creations. Ildja joined them, fascinated by the lowly creatures in spite of herself.

When the mortals weren't struggling to stay alive, they turned to one another for comfort and amusement, and in their search for meaning in their brief existences, they found ways to meld their bodies together that the gods had never dreamed of. The mortals gave names to these frivolities: lust, adoration, love.

It stoked a new sort of fire in Ildja. A desire for something she'd never had.

Veronis felt it too—Ildja could see it when she stared at her cousin, becoming increasingly aware of every inch of his divine beauty. He created worlds, created life, and yet he had always seemed incomplete, as if some vital part of him was missing. He wanted more than a deity's existence provided, and Ildja wondered if she could be his missing piece. So the goddess of fire went to the god of beasts, offering him what the mortals gave to one another.

But Veronis spurned her. *Her*—strongest and most beautiful of all the gods.

Because Veronis loved another. A mortal. A girl with a spark so bright all the gods crowded around to watch her.

Veronis was smitten with a fragile sack of bones who would live and die and rot. The girl was nothing. But that spark . . . it was a thing Ildja did not possess, a thing she should not need to compete with.

A thing her sister had created.

In a rage, Ildja tore a hole between Eyvor's light-filled meadow and her own boiling realm of shadow. Where the two worlds met, mist formed, thick and cloying. Ildja marched through the mist, into the meadow, with her Destroyers at her back.

"You have no right to trespass in my home, sister," Eyvor said. "Your children are not welcome here."

"My children long for company." Ildja glanced at the sun-drenched fields. At the beings inhabiting Eyvor's lands—the remaining essence of dead mortals. "Those who belong in the light may remain. But any with shadows in their souls belong with me."

The Destroyers dove through the meadow, snatching up every soul with a hint of shadow inside them, dragging them beyond the mist. The souls cried out to Eyvor, and the soul-keeper ran after them, but she did not make it past the wall of mist. A being of light—even an immortal one—could not penetrate that realm of endless night. She shouted at Ildja about the souls' worthiness, about redemption, but Ildja ignored her. "From now on, my Destroyers will be waiting and watching the souls that enter your meadow. All those touched by darkness will be brought to me."

"I am the soul-keeper, and I will not abandon them," Eyvor said. "This is not over."

"You rallied the gods against us, didn't you?" Mist wreathed Ildja, clinging to her like a shawl. "You led the charge to have my children exiled to keep your precious mortals safe."

"They had to be stopped before they ruined everything the rest of us built," Eyvor said.

"What you built. You mean *this*." A Destroyer flew past Ildja with a soul in its talons. Ildja took hold of the soul, glaring at the scintillant blob. She wanted to sink her teeth into it. She wanted to annihilate it.

And so she did, biting it, chewing it, just as her Destroyers did to beasts and mortals. She swallowed. The texture, the taste—it was like eating starlight, airy and luminescent, and it filled her with warmth.

She quite liked it.

Eyvor pressed her hands to her lips. "How dare you," she hissed. "And you wonder why Veronis doesn't love you, why he will *never* love you. You are obscene."

"I don't need his love!" Ildja roared. "These realms are full of gods and mortals that wish to offer me their love. But you, sister. You call me obscene? For how you've wronged me, I will make certain no one ever loves you."

Veronis was the god of beasts, but at Ildja's behest, he had gifted her command over the serpents—the lowliest of all creatures, poisonous and ill-tempered—to be companions for her Destroyers. Ildja flicked her fingers at Eyvor, and the soul-keeper fell to the ground. Eyvor's body lengthened and fattened, her milky skin growing scales. Her lovely face stretched out, fangs jutting from her gums, blue eyes protruding from her head and narrowing to slits. Her legs fused into a twitching tail.

"I will silence your insults and judgments," Ildja said, circling her hand. Eyvor's body curled in on itself, still growing, elongating, until her mouth and tail came together. Until she was an unbroken loop, consuming herself. "I exile you to the mortal realm. I sentence you to guard the island above your meadow, and the mortals on it whom you care for more than your own kind."

Ildja drew a line with her finger, slicing a rift between her sister's realm and the ocean on the other side. Atop the ocean was an icy rock where groups of mortals had made their home. With a final twist of her hands, Ildja shoved Eyvor through the rift, and the soul-keeper was sucked into the sea.

"Good riddance, sister." Ildja dusted off her hands and strolled out of the meadow, back into the fire and steam that was her home.

The goddess was still quite hungry, and there were many souls waiting to be devoured.

CHAPTER 1

LIRA

With a whisper into its mind, my horse trotted steadily across the field between opposing armies, trampling wildflowers under its hooves. The Auk Isles were beautiful, blanketed with heather-strewn meadows, burbling streams, blue-tinged mountain ranges. It reminded me of Glasnith, but the land was less rugged and weather-worn, not unlike its people. Even its soldiers.

It wasn't a chiefdom, like Glasnith, or a jarldom, like Iseneld. The Auk Isles were a true kingdom, and their king was a man who had seen too many years and not nearly enough battles. I saw it in his milky eyes when he rode out to meet me. There were fifty Dragonmen behind me, a fraction of the force the king had brought. Six guards flanked him, where I had only two. Like their king, every soldier was decked from neck to ankle in shiny metal armor. Fancy.

Foolish.

I was dressed in the costume Draki had designed for me—light armor painted to look like black scales, and a mask that covered the top half of my face that was etched with the same swirling patterns of knots and dragon heads as Draki's tattoos. To hide my true identity while demonstrating to everyone what I was. Not Lira, not even Draki's consort.

Here, on this field, I was the Dragon's death-bringer.

"What sort of coward sends a child to negotiate on his behalf?" the king of the Auk Isles asked as he looked me over. "The Dragon calls himself an emperor, yet he lets a little girl lead his men onto the battlefield."

Up close, the form-fitting armor made my gender unmistakable even to a half-blind king. There were already legends about the death-bringer, speculation about who Draki's masked enforcer—or enforcers—truly were. *A demon from the Mist? A coven of* volvur? *Draki's battle-mad brother?* But none mentioned a lone mortal woman. Everyone who knew what I could do, how I'd brought storms and stampedes and an avalanche down upon Dragon's Lair, was dead. Or had forgotten me.

To the king I said, "You will bow to the Dragon." My voice came out hollow, like it wasn't my own. Because it wasn't, really—it hadn't been for some time. "You will renounce your false religion and worship the almighty Ice Gods, or you will feel their wrath. You and your men will surrender to the sovereignty of Iseneld and willingly become part of its empire, or you and your countrymen will all die here today."

The king stared at me as if I'd spoken a language foreign to him, but Aukian was similar to Glasnithian, and I'd been studying it for weeks in preparation for this moment.

"You dare think I would hand my country over to that yellow-eyed bastard? A barbarian too stupid and lazy to come meet with me, man to monster?" The king was in a tizzy, spittle spraying from his mouth as he ranted. He leaned in close. "Listen to me, you traitorous little bitch—"

I grabbed the king by the throat.

When his guards tried to aid him, I kept their horses still, kept their armor frozen so they couldn't dismount or reach for their weapons. All they could do was watch.

I curled my fingers, the motion peeling off the king's armor, flinging plates of metal into the air. Reaching out with my senses, I felt the king's fragile flesh, the branching veins beneath, the blood pumping life through his body. I sought my gift of flames—Draki had given it to me through drops of his own blood, Ildja's blood, convincing the fire-goddess to allow me to access it after I passed her ritual by walking through fire.

I could still feel it: hot flames licking at my tender flesh. Now that heat was mine, and I let it travel out of me, into the king, twisting along his limbs. Boiling his blood. Craters formed in his skin as it burned away, steam wafting from the holes. His eyes melted in his skull, white ichor trickling down his cheeks. His blood became lava, erupting, pouring out of him—a living volcano.

No. A dying one.

His screams filled my ears but I kept my gaze steady, my face impassive. Deep inside, a hidden part of me shuddered.

I took his royal sword, passed down through generations, from one king to the next. "This was your choice," I told the king as he died. "You were warned."

With his own blade, I sliced off his head.

I could have killed him sword-to-sword, in a manner more befitting his station. I could have killed him cleanly, ripping his soul from his body. But Draki had been specific, and his command rasped through my head. *When the king refuses, make a statement of his death. Something dramatic, a tale that will strike fear into the hearts of all Aukians. Let them know what is coming for them. Show them who you are.*

As their king's head landed in the dirt and bubbling blood sprayed across the field, as his horse reared in terror and his body slipped sideways in the saddle, the Aukian army raised their weapons, shouting in disbelief. This was not how wars were fought among civilized nations. They were not used to such treachery.

But this was the way of the Dragon. Because I was his instrument, his finely honed weapon, it was my way as well.

Show them who you are.

Who was I? I used to know, used to care, but when the answer came screaming from my lips, it was not Lira who spoke. It was the legend Draki had created.

"I am the gods' wrath! I am your undoing! I am the death-bringer!"

The Aukian soldiers charged. Behind me, the Dragonmen surged forward, howling their animal songs. Two waves crashed around me, slamming into each other in a flash of silver weapons.

I lifted my palm, jerked my arm backward. Swords and daggers ripped from the Aukian soldiers' grasps, flying out of reach, hovering above the heads of Dragonmen who plucked the steel from the air.

I raised my voice and sang. *"Aukian soldiers, kneel and surrender."*

The soldiers hit their knees.

This gift had come from Reyker's mother, passed down to me through the blood he'd once given me, when he carved me with his *skoldar.* This, too, was a gift Draki had shown me how to claim, from Frigmer, goddess of music and poetry. For that ritual, I'd strung a lute with strands of my hair for strings, strumming and singing without ceasing for a full day and night, until my throat was raw, my fingers blistered.

The Dragonmen swarmed the kneeling soldiers, cutting them down with their own weapons.

There was no need for me to ask the Aukian gods for permission to use my power; the scar behind my ear was carved with a dagger forged by gods, and the mark linked my strength to Draki's. I was nearly as powerful as a demigod, my abilities eclipsed only by the Dragon's.

Red stains crept across the meadow. I did not raise the king's sword or touch the blade sheathed at my hip. I let the Dragonmen do their work, just as I'd done in the nations of Skerrey and Sanddune over the last months. My role was showmanship, to quell uprisings before they began. To be a harbinger of the Dragon.

When every last Aukian soldier was dead, we headed farther inland, following the map I carried to the place Draki had specified. Nesting Forest was airy, soaked in sunlight, teeming with birdsong that felt grotesquely cheery after the field of corpses we'd left behind. At what must have been the center of the forest, I stopped.

"Here." My finger rested on a crease in the map, atop a drawing of a gnarled old tree that didn't fit with its taller, greener cousins. The same tree that hunched before me, looking like something that belonged on Glasnith instead of in this bright, chirping thicket.

The Dragonmen passed around shovels from our supply bags and began to dig. I helped when I could, using my earth-shifter gift to draw out chunks of soil, and my wind-wafting to send the piles of dirt away. When they'd gone as deep as they could, hitting solid stone, I climbed down into the pit.

From a sheath on my thigh, I drew the ice dagger given to me by the Fallen Ones, taken and used against me by Draki and his serpent-goddess mother. I stabbed the blade into the stone, and it bubbled like the Aukian king's melting flesh. When I pulled the dagger out, it left a dark slash in the earth. The narrow hole deepened, widened, sucking in dirt and liquefied rock, opening up to the size of my fist, then the size of my head, then big enough to swallow my body whole. Far below, red light glowed. A rasp of wings echoed up, growing louder.

A thick black cloud shot from the hole, screeching into the treetops of the forest. It was hard to make out any individual Destroyer—their bodies were shifting shapes made of skeletons and leathery wings draped in shadow, and they moved together like each one was just a piece of a whole, an entity greater than its parts.

The Destroyers dwelled in the Mist, the infernal afterworld Ildja reigned over, where they tortured the souls of the dead who'd been deemed unworthy. But Ildja had called a host of them from her realm and set them loose in Iseneld to help Draki defeat anyone who dared to resist him. Part of my task as the Dragon's death-bringer was to find other places where the realm between the world of the living and the world of the damned was weak enough to be torn open. Once a rift was created, the Destroyers were able to slide between the realms, to drag men into the underworld alive—worthy and unworthy alike—and rip them apart slowly, letting Ildja devour their souls. This was how Draki meant to conquer every nation, to assert himself as emperor over all the known world. And I was helping him do it, one country at a time.

That deep, hidden part of me wept. *You let him turn you into a demon,* she cried.

I tilted my head, considering. *Yes. This is not me, at least not the me I once was. But this is who I am now, and I must do as my master bids.*

Lira of Stone was no more than a broken whisper lost in the depths of my soul. In her absence, Jarl Lira of Drakin reigned.

My job was done. The Aukian king was dead, the bulk of his army defeated, the Destroyers unleashed to sow fear and chaos among his people. Add to that the legions of Dragonmen divided across the isles to sack and burn villages, and it wouldn't be long before the whole of the Auk Isles surrendered completely. Draki's emissaries were waiting to take over, as soon as that happened.

Return to me, Draki said into my mind from three hundred leagues away. *Come home.*

Home. Back to Iseneld.

My feet carried me forward. I was pulled to the sea, to the pier where our ships awaited. I had no desire to resist Draki's call, but I wondered what would happen if I did.

Our two longships tumbled over the waves as a light storm blew in. We sailed northwest, and the wind pushed us close enough to see Glasnith as we passed it. I kept my eyes on the sea, until a voice made me turn toward the bluffs I'd jumped from all those months ago.

LIRA.

The Dragonmen appeared unalarmed; they hadn't heard someone call my name. Because it had come from inside my mind.

YOU FAILED US, LIRA. YOU FAILED *ME*. AND SOON YOU WILL PAY FOR IT.

This was why Draki had not yet sent me to release the Destroyers on Glasnith. We didn't know how much of Veronis's power remained, what he might do if I stepped foot on his island. *You are not my god anymore, Veronis*, I told the disembodied voice. *I worship Ildja and the Ice Gods now. Glasnith's fate has nothing to do with me.*

A figure danced across the bluffs, and I squinted until my eyes focused like a spyglass, taking advantage of the acute vision that came from having gods' blood in my veins.

Standing on the ledge, right where I'd leaped, was the mystic.

Once, she'd been my friend Ishleen, before she gave herself up to the power of the Fallen Ones. She was hardly recognizable since her transformation—black holes where her eyes should have been, her mortal vision replaced with immortal sight, bestowed upon her by inhuman eyes growing like tumors along her flesh. Just like the dead mystic she'd replaced. One of her arms was extended, her finger pointing at me. Her body was a vessel for Veronis's ire.

GLASNITH WILL ALWAYS BE PART OF YOU. YOU ARE MY DESCENDANT, A DAUGHTER OF AILLIRA. ILDJA AND HER WRETCHED SPAWN WILL TURN AGAINST YOU, AND IT WILL BE YOUR END. EVERYTHING COMES FULL CIRCLE.

"Get out of my head."

The Dragonmen glanced at me with raised brows, but their attention was torn away from me, to the water, as a dark shape rose from below the waves and slammed into our longship.

"Sea beast!" the Dragonmen shouted, reaching for their spears.

Another shape surfaced, and another, until we were surrounded by thick, cylindrical bodies longer than our ships. Brine Beasts. The giant eels lifted their heads from the water, peering at us with bulbous black eyes. Their jaws snapped open, gums crowded with razor teeth.

My heightened senses picked up the mystic's quiet command: "Destroy," she said in the old tongue.

As one, the Beasts darted below the surface and smashed into the longship, cracking the planks, ripping the vessel into pieces right beneath our feet. "Stop," I told the Beasts.

They did not listen.

I looked back at the mystic. She smiled.

Veronis was the god of these creatures, and his blood flowed in my veins. Though I'd renounced the Green Gods, Draki's mark had released the chains on my power. I no longer needed Veronis's permission to use the gifts he'd given me.

But my order was contrary to that of their master. Powerful as I was, I was still only a mortal.

The ship sank, and waves closed around me. From Sjaf and Seffra, I possessed the gifts of sea and tide, and I used them to buoy myself up.

The Brine Beasts circled.

I'd seen something like this before, in one of Reyker's memories. I knew what came next.

The Dragonmen in the surf screamed as the Beasts' teeth ripped into the warriors and towed them under. I felt as if I should care but told myself I didn't. They were Draki's soldiers, expendable, their lives pledged in his service. What did it matter if they died at the end of a sword or in the mouths of monsters?

Something slapped down in the water next to me—a length of rope. The second longship edged closer, and one of the Dragonmen had thrown me a lifeline. As soon I grabbed it, he reeled me in, his hands gripping mine, hauling me from the water. The dark-scaled Beasts reared, readying to attack again.

"My jarl," the Dragonman said. A plea for me to act.

With one hand, I harnessed a gust of wind and tossed it into our sail. With the other, I grasped the water around the Beasts and created a current strong enough to hold them back while our ship rushed away. The Beasts shrieked and wrestled against the current, but I held it steady until we were far enough out of reach.

Blood trickled from my ear, down my neck. I wiped it away with my sleeve.

For the second time in my life, I watched Glasnith—the land where I was born, where I'd read stories to my brothers, talked of my hopes with my mother, learned honor from my father, fallen in love and found a greater purpose for my gifts, the place I'd fought and nearly died to save—disappear into the distance.

I remembered all of this, but now they were distant, trivial recollections. None of it seemed to matter. Draki had cured me of my loyalties, my guilt. Veronis was wrong; I was no longer tied to Glasnith. As the gray-green silhouette of my homeland vanished behind me, I felt nothing but an insignificant twitch deep in my soul.

CHAPTER 2

REYKER

The longship full of Dragonmen sailed closer, closer. Not close enough. The Dragonmen were superstitious about the Haunted Isles, as most people of Iseneld were. Sailors gave the archipelago a wide berth.

Reyker waited in the hidden cove, standing on the deck of the caravel. He was sweating beneath his metal helm. The curling ram horns on either side were an annoyance, and a hindrance to his peripheral vision. Solvei insisted he wear it in battle, so everyone knew whose army he fought for—hers, not his own, lest he get any ideas—but Solvei wasn't here, and he hated the helm. With a growl, he threw it down and slicked his hair back from his face. His crew glanced at him. They would tattle to the jarl, but he would deal with Solvei later.

"Now," Reyker said to the girl next to him. He couldn't remember her name. She was a storm-spinner, a Daughter of Aillira from the Green Isle. That was all he needed to know.

The girl extended her hands, and the mist coming off the sea rose higher, thickening into a dense veil. At the *magiska's* whim, it surrounded the longship, blinding the Dragonmen.

Reyker signaled the other magiskas. The wind-wafter pushed gusts into the caravel's sails so it shot forward like an arrow, and the sea-farer steered it through the fog, straight for their target. As soon as the longship appeared, Reyker leaped across the gap of sea and landed in its bow, sword and axe at the ready.

The Dragonmen shouted, aiming their weapons at him.

Reyker smiled.

There was a time when he'd felt as if he were possessed by his battle-madness, as if the power was a parasite living inside him that demanded to be fed. But since the Dragon's vile fortress had fallen, Reyker had merged with his gift. It wasn't just a thing inside him—it was the flesh on his bones, the heart in his chest. It was him, and he was it. The black river. The Sword of the Ice Gods. Finally, he embraced what he was, as he was always meant to.

He took the lives of the Dragonmen, feeling the river inside him grow stronger with every strike. Beneath the fall of his blades, the strength of each man's pulse faded, and shifted, and was absorbed into Reyker. He licked sweat and blood from his lips, wiped them from his eyes.

Finally, the shouts were silenced. Reyker grabbed one lifeless body after another, dumping each one into the sea. Drawn by the blood in the water, a dozen ice sharks swarmed, feasting on the dead. As Reyker tossed the last corpse overboard, he spotted a Dragonman cowering beneath a bench.

"Are you going to come out, or shall I drag you?" Reyker asked.

"Please." The Dragonman whimpered, and Reyker realized he was not much more than a boy. "You are the Wolf Lord, aren't you? Let me join you. I never wanted to serve the Dragon, but he threatened everyone in our village. I only became a Dragonman to keep my parents and siblings safe. I had no choice."

A choice that was not a choice.

It was a story Reyker knew all too well. Hadn't he used the same excuses when he'd served his brother, to justify the atrocities he committed in the Dragon's name?

Reyker extended his hand and the young Dragonman took it, letting Reyker pull him to his feet. The boy's eyes widened, hopeful. It reminded Reyker of another boy, from another life. A boy he'd spared. A boy who'd later tried to kill him, and almost succeeded. He would not make that mistake again.

"There is always a choice," Reyker told the boy, "and you must be prepared to live with the consequences. Or die with them."

He stabbed his sword into the boy's chest.

Reyker watched the boy's expression transform, his cheeks paling and his mouth dropping open. He couldn't bear to look at what he'd done. Before the boy took his last breath, Reyker threw him from the boat.

In the water, ice sharks fought over the fresh meat.

Turning to the caravel, Reyker helped three of the Daughters of Aillira climb down its ladder into the longship. "You didn't have to kill him," the sea-farer said. "Jarl Solvei keeps saying we need more allies, more of the Dragon's men to join our side."

The Dragon's men would never join their side. Solvei was a fool. But Reyker didn't need to justify himself to these magiskas. He turned to the storm-spinner. "Clear the fog."

The storm-spinner glared, but she moved to the bow and waved her arms.

Nothing happened.

She shook herself, tried again. Still nothing.

"Is there a problem?" he called to her.

The storm-spinner rounded on him. "The problem is this is the fifth attack in three days. Our gifts aren't bottomless wells. We're tired and overworked. We came here to help you fight this war and stop the bastard who's trying to steal our country, but you ask too much of us."

The sea-farer and the wind-wafter nodded, all three magiskas glaring at him. He wanted to roll his eyes, but he lifted his hands in surrender. "All right. I will talk to the jarl. It may be time for her to take another trip to Glasnith."

The cell on the islet was constructed of heavily warded stones, carved with runes. Made for containing someone with extraordinary gifts, where the witches who once inhabited the Haunted Isles could lock up one of their own. "It won't hold him," Reyker said.

Solvei was as tall and broad as Reyker, and the cell felt cramped with the two of them occupying it. She ran her fingers over the dust-coated runes of one wall. "Draki is no *volva*, but we can use this cell as a model, build a stronger version. Eathalin believes she can improve the binding spells embedded in the stones."

"You misunderstand. *Nothing* will hold him."

"Give me another option, Lagorsson. Shall I wait for you to miraculously remember how to kill the Dragon?"

"It was prophesized by gods and seers that I will kill him—that I'm the only one who can. All I need is a magiska to dig the memory out. There must be a soul-reader somewhere in Glasnith."

The jarl turned to him. "Then go. Meet with the Ghost Prince and the Daughters of Aillira. Find a soul-reader. Bring back as many magiskas to aid the Renegades as you can. Gods know their abilities are wasted sitting around on the Green Isle, twiddling their thumbs."

"Me?" The thought of going to Glasnith turned his stomach, though he wasn't sure why. "I assumed you would—"

"I went last time, and I have business to attend to here. It is your turn. Or is this assignment beyond your capabilities, high commander?"

He'd accepted the position as head of Solvei's army shortly after the Mountain Renegades had moved their camp from Fjullthorp to the Haunted Isles. At the time, he'd believed the title was a mark of her trust in him, but it had quickly become a burden, a rudder she could use to force him in whatever direction she wished. "No, my jarl."

"Good." She scrubbed a hand through her short blond hair. "Take Alane and Bronagh with you. And Brokk as well."

A growl of protest rose in his throat.

"That was a request, high commander. Must I rephrase it as an order?"

He swallowed. "No, my jarl."

⸺◈⸺

Icebergs gave way to empty ocean, the caravel skimming across the water under the sea-farer's behest. Reyker stayed in the stern, as if keeping himself a boat-length closer to home—and a boat-length farther from Glasnith—made any difference.

Brokk, Bronagh, and Alane chattered with one another throughout the journey. Reyker did his best to avoid the two magiskas and his former friend, despite being trapped on a vessel the size of a small cottage with no walls to hide behind. When he wasn't helping to navigate, he passed the hours tying knots in a length of rope. Or trying to. They were knots every sailor knew, the sort he'd been using most of his life and should have been able to tie in his sleep, but every time he began to loop the rope, his mind went blank.

He couldn't tie a single gods-damned knot.

Reyker stared at the rope. In a fit, he hurled it overboard. As it fell, it seemed to change before his eyes, the rope shrinking into a necklace with a silver medallion on the end, plunging below the surface with a splash that felt like an ending.

Blinking at the sea, he wondered if he was going mad.

Madness was a condition he could not afford. He moved on to what mattered: cataloging the gifts the Daughters of Aillira wielded, ranking how useful their skills would be. Selecting the magiskas he refused to leave Glasnith without, whether they agreed or not. If he found one who possessed the skill he needed most, a soul-reader powerful enough to pull the right memory from his soul, he would drag her back to Iseneld kicking and screaming. He would kill anyone who tried to stop him.

"You're plotting something foul," Brokk said, coming up beside him. An apple dangled from his fingers—a peace offering, already abandoned. "I can see it all over your face."

"I get barely a word out of you for months, and that's the first real thing you say to me? An accusation?" Reyker scowled.

"I haven't spoken to you because you aren't worth the effort. Your head's been on crooked since we attacked Dragon's Lair. Whatever I tell you won't make it through the layers of stupid you've got stuffed into your ears as of late."

Once, Reyker would have reflected on Brokk's criticism, allowing his friend's observations to keep him grounded. Not anymore. "My crooked head has gotten more soldiers to join the Renegades and earned us more victories—"

"At what cost, Wolf Lord?" Brokk stepped closer, invading his space. "You've always been good at shedding blood, but you used to hate it. You used to regret every life you took. Now you revel in it. What happened to you? What did the Dragon do to you at the Season's Eve ceremony?"

There was a twinge behind Reyker's eyes, like the beginnings of a headache. A memory flashed through his mind. He saw hair the color of wine. He felt a part of himself unraveling, slipping away.

Reyker shook his head, pushing back against the memory. "Nothing. I've become what I have to be to win this war."

"You're a shadow of the lordling you once were. Your father would be ashamed."

"Watch your tongue, Brokk." Reyker's fingers curled into fists. The apple dropped from Brokk's hand and rolled across the deck. They'd almost come to blows on many occasions when they were boys, but it was different now that they were men, strong enough to kill each other.

"Or what?" Brokk asked. "You'll try and strangle me again?" He took another step, and their chests were almost touching. "You get more like your bastard brother every day."

Reyker swung. His punch threw Brokk sideways, but Brokk recovered and landed a punch of his own that jarred Reyker's skull. They were both poised to pounce when an oar came swinging down between them, smacking Reyker in the stomach and Brokk in his ribs.

"Stop it, you fools!" Alane pushed between them, shoving them apart. "We're nearly to Glasnith. We have a job to do, countries to save. There's no time to waste on your petty feuds."

Brokk rubbed the back of his neck. "Sorry, Alane. Won't happen again." His eyes narrowed on Reyker before he turned away.

"You're wrong," Reyker called after him. "I may be a bastard, but I'm not soulless. I'm not Draki."

Alane poked the oar into Reyker's chest, her lips pursed in warning. Behind her, Brokk kicked the apple and mumbled, "Not yet."

At midday, Glasnith's northern coast came into view. The sea-farer guided the caravel toward it, sailing between two long jetties that protected the shore. They disembarked, walked up a pier to the beach, and Reyker glanced around, feeling as if he'd been here before. His pulse beat between his temples like a warning, and he crouched down, digging his fingers into the sand. Images and sensations flashed through his mind—his body shivering, his lungs half-full of salt water. Someone bending over him, dragging him from the edge of death.

A girl. He could almost see her.

"What's this village called?" Reyker asked.

The two magiskas answered at the same time: "Stony Harbor."

CHAPTER 3

LIRA

With my gifts of wind and tide to aid us, the journey back to the Frozen Sun went swiftly. I did my best to hide it when I grew weary, wiping away any blood that leaked from my nose or the corner of my mouth. We spotted Iseneld after a handful of days and slipped through the waves toward the eastern coast. Eyvor, the island serpent, sensed me from below the waves—as I sensed her, like cool scales coiling along the inside of my mind—and did not bother rising to the surface. Iseneld loomed ahead of us, dark and dusted with snow.

Our longship eased into the narrow fjord bordering the village that used to be known as Fjullthorp, before Draki seized it and renamed it Dragon's Domain. The Dragonmen lowered the sail and used the oars to ferry us to the pier, where Draki was already waiting. Whether it was due to the mark he gave me or some other intuition, he always seemed to know where I was.

"Lira," the Dragon said with a smile, reaching out his hand as I stepped off the ship. "My faithful death-bringer. You look well."

"I am, my emperor." I handed him the ice dagger. The god-forged blade was also a key to the nether-realm prison Veronis and the rest of the Fallen Ones were locked in, and Ildja only parted with the key when it was necessary. Draki was careful to keep track of the one weapon that posed a threat to his mother.

"Come," he said, tucking the dagger away. "Your rooms await. Bathe, rest, and then you will dine with me and tell me of your conquest."

The hand constricting mine felt more serpent-like than Eyvor, but I did not cringe or pull away. I couldn't, even if I wanted to.

Did I want to?

Yes, a fragile voice insisted.

I ignored my other. She'd been a nuisance ever since Draki freed me.

After being away from him for more than a week, the emperor's uncanny appearance struck me anew. How could beauty be so disturbing? His golden-green eyes were sharp, calculating. Silken silver hair fell over his broad shoulders. Draki was clad in a sleeveless fur vest that he'd left unbuttoned, revealing taut muscles and inked skin. The pier and everything around it wore a wispy gown of white, but the cold never affected Draki.

"There was an incident," I told him as he escorted me up the pier. "We lost a ship and its crew."

"Ships can be rebuilt. Crews can be replaced." Callous, but practical. That was who the Dragon was, and it was hard not to admire.

I knew what he'd done to me. When Draki's mother burned away my *skoldar*, the protective scar Reyker had used to tie me to his power and help me resist the Dragon, it left me vulnerable. Draki took the opportunity to strengthen our connection, cutting his own scar behind my ear, the Star of the Dragon. Slicing deeper, with a dagger made by gods. Not stealing my will, as he'd done to other magiskas, but reshaping it, offering me a peace I had never known, releasing me from indecision and guilt. I was grateful for it, and for how he'd trained me, molding me into a weapon. I owed him. To repay him, I served as his death-bringer.

It was only that small piece of Lira of Stone, crippled and hidden far below, that caused me to question him, to wonder if my gratitude was a delusion of his making. To wonder if what seemed like freedom was, as my other suggested, a different sort of cage.

We walked from the pier up the dirt path to the Fjordland village that had belonged to Draki's enemies only a few months ago. By the time he went after Jarl Solvei and the rest of the Mountain Renegades, they had abandoned their camp. Draki had claimed it for his own, tearing down every structure and building his own sprawling, impenetrable castle on top of them. Dragon's Domain wasn't finished yet, but it was well on its way to being ten times the size of Dragon's Lair, the fortress Solvei and her Renegades destroyed the night of Season's Eve. The night Draki had officially declared me his consort.

The night I'd poisoned the mind of the man I'd thought I loved.

You do love him, my other cried.

Love? I remembered loving Reyker, but there was a wall between memory and emotion. Knowing and experiencing were different things, one resonating in the mind, the other in the heart. My heart was just an organ, pumping blood, giving life. Functional. Numb.

"Stop thinking about my brother," Draki said.

When I thought of Reyker Lagorsson, something happened to me— my lips trembled, my skin flushed, an involuntary response that took hold of every part of me except my deadened heart. It was the ghost of his touch, lingering, though the man was long gone, run off to help the Renegades in their battle against the Dragon.

"Yes, my emperor." I pushed away the memories of blue-gray eyes and gold hair, a soft mouth that had fit so well with mine. Nothing stoked Draki's anger more than when I became distracted by thoughts of Reyker.

I walked arm in arm with Draki beneath the grand archway, into the palace. Despite the size of Dragon's Domain, it was sparsely populated, with only a fraction of the Dragonmen and servants he'd had at his previous fortress. Part of that was my fault—I'd killed his most faithful servants and soldiers in the avalanche I caused, a foolish attempt to assassinate the Dragon. I'd been wracked with guilt over all those deaths until Draki liberated me.

The other reason there were so few people here was that they simply weren't needed. Guards were unnecessary when you had a host of Destroyers at your disposal. A dark mass of the demons hung above the castle, and another cluster of them flew in circles around the perimeter of the village, ready to tear apart anyone who came close without the emperor's permission.

The sight of them still sent prickles up my spine.

Draki left me at the door to my quarters. As he'd done in Dragon's Lair, he'd settled me into rooms beside his own, in a wing secluded from the rest of the castle. My bedchamber was much larger than I needed, the decorations more opulent than anything I'd have picked out for myself—a crystal chandelier, a canopy bed frame carved from pure marble, candlesticks of glittering gold. Nothing but the finest would do for the Dragon's consort.

The tub was marble, too, and I sank into it with a sigh once the servants finished filling it with hot water. It was a relief to scrub salt and dirt and dried bits of king's blood from my skin. Afterward, I crawled into bed and buried myself in the blankets, falling into a dreamless sleep, only waking when a knock sounded on my door hours later. Another nameless servant, a timid girl no older than I was, brought me a clean dress to wear. Once I was buttoned into it, I made my way toward the feasting hall with two of Draki's guards in tow.

Inside the hall, I was met by the vacant stares of ten skrikflaks. The giant heads hung from the walls, curled horns lowered, each lupine snout set in a permanent grimace. Their stone-breaking howls had brought down Draki's fortress, so he'd hunted them in revenge and to ensure Dragon's Domain could not fall to the same fate.

Beneath the largest of the dead skrikflaks, Draki sat upon his throne. It was a hideous construction of stacked skulls and spines scavenged from the ruins of Dragon's Lair, frozen together with ice that didn't melt, even in the warmth of the hall, because of Ildja's magic. It had been the goddess's idea. *An emperor needs a throne*, she'd said, so he'd built it, but I'd only ever seen him sit in it to brood, as he was doing now, one fist tucked under his chin. Draki watched me enter, something unreadable churning in his gaze.

This was the same throne I'd seen him sitting upon in a dying seeress's vision. All that was missing were giant reptile wings bursting through his back.

Draki rose and stretched with catlike grace, padding down the dais to join me at the long marble table in the center of the room. Servants appeared carrying silver trays of food.

"I trust you slept well?" Draki asked.

"Yes, my emperor."

"My emissaries sent word that the Auk Isles surrendered. Between the Destroyers' havoc and the tale of what the death-bringer did to their king, they lost all hope." He raised a goblet to toast me. "Tell me of your exploits. I want to hear it from your lips." Draki smiled like we were an ordinary man and woman, speaking of ordinary things, instead of death and war and demons. His smile grew brighter—doting, almost kind—as I recounted my time in the Auk Isles. But I wasn't fooled.

I knew what he was. Empty. Apathetic.

Just as I was now, thanks to him.

"Do not worry yourself with Veronis," he said when I'd finished my story. "The traitor is barely a god anymore. He is nothing compared to Ildja. He is nothing compared to me. I will keep you safe from him."

"Of course, my emperor." *But who will keep me safe from you?*

I shook off that thought. Veronis must have been lying. I was Draki's death-bringer, too valuable for him to harm.

We sat in silence broken only by the sounds of Draki's teeth sinking into a bruise-green apple. He didn't eat out of necessity—I doubted he felt hunger as mortals did, and he certainly couldn't starve. But he savored the taste of food, the experience of consumption, as he savored riding a horse, slaying a foe, seducing someone into his bed. Anything that made his blood pump faster, that made his mortal half flare with want. With life.

He bit deep into the apple's sweet flesh, but his gaze was on me. Intense and hungry—always hungry.

I looked back at him, examining the hard lines of his collarbones, the curve of his neck, his full lips wet with juice. He was strong. Beautiful. I stared at him, waiting to feel a hunger to match his own. Waiting . . .

Feeling . . . nothing.

"The attacks have escalated over the past week," Draki finally said, tossing the apple core aside and sawing at the slab of reindeer meat in front of him.

Every few days, the Mountain Renegades ambushed a Dragonman stronghold and burned it to the ground or stole one of their longships and the cargo they carried. They moved quickly, striking different places on and around the island, sometimes attacking in two places at the same time, vanishing before they could be caught. The Renegades were stronger than they'd ever been, and far more vicious.

I'd seen the condition of the bodies the Renegades left behind, when Draki took me with him to the sites of the attacks. There were often charred remains of men who'd been locked inside the strongholds, left to burn alive. Dragonmen were tossed off purloined longships to freeze to death in the chill waters or become meals for the ice sharks. The Renegades used to pride themselves on honor and mercy, qualities they claimed the Dragon lacked and one of the reasons they wanted to dethrone him. Now, the Renegades lacked them too.

I took a bite of my steak, but it was flavorless. Since my transformation, everything tasted like ash in my mouth. "Do you want me to hunt the Renegades down?"

"Soon," he said. "I have a plan to draw them into an ambush. Anything less, and they will see us coming and scatter to the wind. They've become slippery as eels, conniving as foxes. Difficult to pinpoint during their strikes." Difficult for *him*, he meant. And here I'd thought him incapable of being foiled. The admission of failure cost Draki, his fists clenching and unclenching. "Someone is helping them. Someone god-gifted."

Ah. It was a spell that hid the Renegades from Draki, like those that once concealed Aillira's Temple, or Eathalin's veil over Ghost Village. Someone was mimicking Draki's strategies, using magiskas to aid the Renegades in their fight.

Pride and fury battled for dominance across Draki's features. It was clear who he thought was behind the Renegades' newfound triumphs.

"I'll never understand your obsession with him," I muttered, speaking as much to my other as I was to Draki. Reyker was only a man, after all. He was not as beautiful or as powerful as Draki. He was not a god.

No, my other seethed from the dark crevice I kept her in. *Gods are monsters. Reyker's humanity makes him powerful. It makes him beautiful. Unlike that monstrous thing sitting across from us.*

"Did you not still love your father, even after he hurt you?" Draki asked, his voice surprisingly soft. "I have reason to obsess. My brother is my only mortal kin. Regardless of his failings, he is an extension of me. You, on the other hand—what is it you saw in him that was so transfixing?"

"I don't remember." I rarely lied to Draki, but when it came to Reyker, it was better to pretend. If I listed all the reasons why my other believed she'd loved him, it would only rile the Dragon. "Why don't you send the Destroyers after the Renegades?"

"The Destroyers don't know how to be delicate. They might slaughter Reyker along with the rest of the Renegades. That's why I need you. Once everything is in place, you will kill Solvei and her followers. You will bring my brother to me, alive."

At that, my other peeled herself from the shadows, rising up, stealing control over my voice. "We had a deal. You promised to leave him alone."

Draki's brows rose, and I fought to shove my other back down into her hole.

"Our deal," the Dragon said, leaning forward, "was that I would not touch him as long as he stayed off Iseneld. You did a poor job planting that order in his mind because he has been leading attacks on my island for weeks. This is his home, and he cannot resist returning. So he will meet my death-bringer. And you will do your duty. Won't you?"

"Yes, my emperor."

Draki pushed away his plate, nothing left of his meal but gristle clinging to bones. "I reward those who are loyal to me. There is a way to make you even stronger, so that Veronis cannot touch you. So that no one but I can touch you. One of the rituals that made me immortal. When you bring me my brother, I will share it with you. Would you like that, Lira? To be my immortal empress?"

"Yes." I tried not to flinch as my other screamed and cursed inside my mind.

Draki stood, beckoning me to follow. Leading me to his chambers.

I was not the only one he brought here—he took many lovers to satisfy his appetites. When the Dragon hungered, he would feed. But I was the meat he craved most, the flesh he longed to taste. The elusive creature he hunted that always remained just out of reach.

The door creaked shut behind me, and Draki shed his vest like sloughing old skin, leaving his tattooed chest and arms bare. He circled me once, twice, before edging closer, trailing his fingers up my arm, along my shoulder. "Do you desire me, Lira?"

This dance was familiar. We'd gone through the motions before, every time I returned from completing one of his tasks. In Draki's chambers, he was no longer my emperor. I knew what he wanted me to say.

"Yes, master." I meant it to sound lustful, but the words drifted from my mouth like the petals of a dead flower, their sweetness tinged with rot.

He placed my palms on his torso, over the patterns of black knots and dragon heads tattooed across his flesh. They rippled under my fingertips, as if they were alive.

Draki's lips traveled along the curve of my neck. His hands fisted in my hair, and I pretended to tremble. I faked a sigh. Poorly.

He tugged my hair, arching my neck backward. "I command you to want me, Lira."

The scar behind my ear throbbed, a sting that made nerves crackle all the way down my arms, but it did not ignite my passion. "I want you, Draki."

"You don't!" Draki spun and punched the wall, cracking the stone, his whole arm disappearing inside it. When he pulled his arm out, there was a hole straight through to the hallway, and not a trace of injury on Draki's knuckles. "I am your god. You're supposed to worship me in all ways. What is wrong with you? Is it my brother? Are you still in love with him?"

Always, my other cried.

I glanced at the marred skin of my wrist where Ildja had burned away my *skoldar.* "No."

"Then what is it?" He gripped my face, peering into my eyes as if the answer were there for him to read. "Why don't you love me?"

"I do." But I didn't, and we both knew it. This was how it had gone every time he touched me, every time he kissed me.

I'd felt nothing.

Draki let me go with a hiss of disgust. "We will return to the Mountain of Fire, and we will remedy this. Ildja will burn every bit of flesh from your wrist. I will cut my mark into you again with her key. And then you will give yourself to me, freely."

"Yes, master." It was barely a whisper.

"Go." He waved at the door without looking at me. "Get out."

This was a command I could obey.

I went to my room, sitting on the edge of the bed, digging my fingernails into my palms. The night crawled along, stretching into dawn, but I did not sleep. I did not bother to relight the candles that guttered to embers and smoke. With my eyes squeezed shut, I searched my thoughts, my memories, plied the depths of my soul. Seeking the tiniest hint of passion, desire, love.

But there was nothing. Jarl Lira, the death-bringer, was a cave, a shell. A tomb for a girl who'd been buried alive.

CHAPTER 4

REYKER

Garreth of Stone, the nomads' Ghost Prince, was a man with a shrewd gaze and a jaw covered in careless stubble. He looked the part of a disputed leader with the fate of his country weighing on his shoulders. Beside him was a fierce-looking bronze-skinned woman. His commander, Zabelle. She seemed familiar, but Reyker couldn't place how he knew her. His memories of the time he'd spent in Glasnith were scattered and murky.

The Renegades were received in one of the large tents made of animal skin. There were no formal meeting halls since Stony Harbor was nothing but ruins, burnt to the ground by Draki and his Dragonmen. Garreth's army of nomads and refugees were in the process of rebuilding the village, as Reyker had tried to rebuild Vaknavangur, and Reyker was tempted to tell them not to bother, that it would only encourage the Dragon to return and reclaim it.

Alane and the sea-farer—Bronagh, the prince called her, and Reyker tried to hold on to the name, but it was already slipping away—bowed to the prince, a gesture that made Garreth shift uncomfortably, before they took their seats around the table and made their case for why more magiskas were needed to fight the war raging on Iseneld's shores. Garreth listened respectfully until they finished, but Reyker noted the prince's stiff posture and knew he would refuse.

"Forgive me," Garreth began. "I know you traveled a long way, and that your cause is just. But when you came months ago with this same plea, I allowed any Daughters of Aillira who'd found sanctuary with us to join your cause if they so desired. What makes you believe any who refused then will go with you this time?"

"Because you are going to order them to, as their prince," Reyker said, ignoring the warning looks Brokk and the magiskas aimed at him. "Unless you enjoy bowing to the Dragon."

Garreth's mouth tightened. "The Daughters of Aillira aren't soldiers. I won't force them to leave their homeland and risk themselves to save a bunch of . . ." He waved a hand at Reyker and Brokk.

"What?" Reyker asked. "Barbarians? Beasts? Iseneld is full of innocents who will die if this war continues. If you were a true leader, you would fight beside us. You would send every warrior and Daughter of Aillira to Iseneld so we could crush the Dragon together, as allies."

"Dragonmen still hold half the villages in Glasnith, roaming the island, raping and murdering and destroying everything in their path. We need the god-gifted to aid us. I have my own country to protect."

"You won't if we fail. I assume you've heard how Ildja's Destroyers torment and kill the people of Iseneld. And Sanddune. And Skerrey. And now, the Auk Isles. How long do you think it will be before the Dragon sends his death-bringers here to set those demons loose on Glasnith?"

"Rumor has it that *you* are one of the Dragon's death-bringers."

Reyker laughed. He hated those rumors, proof that none of his efforts to undermine Draki would ever erase the stain of the blood they shared, the sins he'd committed as the Dragon's Sword. "If I were, you would already be dead and your island would be mine."

"Where is my sister, Lagorsson?" All traces of Garreth's nobility seeped away as he addressed Reyker directly. "Why haven't you rescued her?"

"Who?"

"Does she mean so little to you that you cannot even remember her name? Lira pined for you when she thought you dead, but you didn't come for her then. Now she's the Dragon's prisoner, and you still haven't gone to her. She painted such a heroic picture of you, yet what I see before me is a coward."

"Lira." Reyker drew out each syllable like it was the first time he'd ever said it. The twinge in Reyker's temples returned, and he rubbed at them absently as the blur of memories shifted into focus: violet hair, green-fire eyes. The girl he'd met when he came to Glasnith before. The one who betrayed him. "Your sister doesn't need rescuing. She made her choice. She's a faithful servant of the Dragon."

Garreth started to rise, but Zabelle gripped his arm, keeping him in his chair, silencing him with a look. "Lira would never serve the Dragon," she said. "Which means you are either lying or you are a fool. And I did not take you for a liar, *yeetozurri*."

The memories were piercing and tangled, wrapping around his skull like a crown made of nettles. When he thought of the girl, there was an ache deep in his mind, a hollow space where something was missing. He'd cared for Lira, hadn't he? And she'd used his feelings against him. "No. Lira was the one who took me for a fool."

Garreth's fist slammed against the table. "Speak ill of my sister again and I will hang your head from a rope as I did your brethren!"

Silence fell. The others glanced between Reyker and Garreth with furrowed brows and pursed lips, searching for a salvageable shred of goodwill to bridge what the two men had sundered.

Alane spoke up. "We've heard nothing of Lira's whereabouts, my lord. I've been unable to locate her with my tract-seeking gift since the warlord took her from the battlefield at Dragon's Lair."

Brokk knew little Glasnithian, so he whispered something to Alane, who did her best to translate. "Reyker was injured in that battle, trying to rescue Lira from the Dragon. He's been . . . different since then. Confused. We think something was done to him—"

A voice rang through Reyker's ears, mournful: *I only wanted to save you.*

Reyker shouted to drown out that voice. "I don't need excuses for my behavior! If your sister means so much to you, Garreth, why don't *you* go and get her?"

Color leeched from the prince's cheeks. "I told you, I have a country to protect. As soon as Glasnith is safe, I will go to Iseneld and free Lira."

"As long as the Dragon lives, Glasnith will never be safe."

"What of Quinlan of Fion?" Zabelle asked. "Your jarl could not tell us what became of him. She said only you knew."

The anger burning in Reyker's veins cooled as another image flashed through his mind: a Glasnithian warrior, lying at the bottom of a crevasse, broken and bleeding, beyond repair. Reyker's hands gripping the man's head. The *snap* of his neck breaking.

Once more, Brokk spoke to Alane, and Alane served as his interpreter. "Quinlan of Fion died a hero's death, aiding your sister. He was given his proper funerary rites. He rests with your gods."

Garreth went still. It was only a moment before he recovered, but something had drained from him, his chin dipping lower, his shoulders limp. "If you'll excuse me, I have duties to attend to. We'll provide you with food and shelter for a night or two, and then you will go. Should you return requesting more Daughters of Aillira in the future, you will no longer be welcome. You," he said, pointing at Reyker, "will not return here again without my sister, or I'll make good on my threats."

Reyker was about to tell the prince what he could do with his threats, but Brokk shoved him outside.

Zabelle led them through the rows of tents, past nomads and refugees, and Reyker spotted a brown-haired young woman patrolling the tree line with a sword. Unlike most of his memories of Glasnith, this one was as sharp as the blades the woman had sliced along his skin, as unforgiving as the iron collar that she'd used to strangle him. Pain-wielder, they'd called her.

The magiska's gray eyes scraped over Reyker and Brokk, then on to Zabelle, her mouth twisted in a snarl. Oh, this woman liked the nomads no more than the Iseneldish. Which meant she must hate the Glasnithian prince who treated with foreign invaders and elevated nomads to a position of power equal to the Daughters of Aillira.

Finally, something he could use, someone he could bend to his advantage.

Zabelle stopped at two spare tents on the outskirts of the village, quarters worthy of their station as uninvited guests. Before Reyker could enter his tent, the nomad commander pulled him aside. "You are not the man you once were, *yeetozurri*, and that is a great shame. I will say this only once, out of respect for that lost man. Do not cause trouble for the prince unless you wish to gain more enemies than you already have."

Reyker had grown tired of threats. This was not how allies were meant to act. "If I snuck into your prince's tent in the middle of the night to slit his throat, I bet I would find you tucked beneath his blankets. Yet he hasn't claimed you as his consort because you're a foreigner with no title. How long before Garreth weds a Glasnithian noblewoman fit to rule at his side, leaving you guarding his bed while another woman warms it?"

The commander's intake of breath turned Reyker's stomach. Gods, why had he said such a thing?

The sort of thing Draki might say.

"I pity you," Zabelle said, "because the next time death stalks you, I doubt a single soul will care to stop it." An apology stalled on his tongue as Zabelle turned away. He thought she was done, but she called over her shoulder. "Not all women want to be claimed, little lordling."

Dinner was a communal event, served out in the open around a cookfire, beneath the flickering stars. There were no tables or chairs, only the ground to sit upon. The nomads and refugees ate together in groups, talking and laughing. Brokk and the magiskas sat with them.

There was much on Reyker's mind, and he had no wish to socialize. He was carrying his plate to his empty tent when he saw the gray-eyed pain-wielder again, sitting alone. Her gaze wandered, her mouth turned down, as if everything bored her and everyone was beneath her. Not unlike the expression Draki often wore.

He could work with that.

She noticed him watching her and drew her knife. His thoughts churned with possibilities, and he kept his steps confident as he sat down just out of knife-strike range. "Nice to see you again, under more favorable circumstances." He tore off a chunk of meat and chewed it loudly.

"Come near me," the pain-wielder said, "and I'll make our last meeting seem like a blissful reprieve." She had tortured him skillfully, her ministrations so agonizing that any other man would have cracked and spilled whatever information she asked for. It was only Draki's rigorous training, the hardened shell he'd forced Reyker to build around his mind and body, that enabled him to resist such torment. "Though it seems," the magiska added with a smirk, gesturing at his face with her knife, "that someone else has had a go at you since then."

Reyker touched the scar that sliced through his right brow and continued down his cheek. "A present from the Dragon."

The magiska's lips pinched. It was not sympathy, but it was something.

"You're quite talented," Reyker said. "I've experienced it firsthand, and I don't fault you for it. On the contrary, the Renegades of Iseneld could use someone like you in our army."

"If you think I would ever fight with filth like you, you're stupider than I thought."

"Your gift is a treasure. The Green Gods chose you to carry it, to use it to serve and honor them. But I'm betting others on Glasnith treat it like a curse, yes?" The magiska did not correct him, so he kept going. "They fear you because of its dark nature. Garreth of Stone rarely lets you use it because he is too self-righteous, and a gift such as yours needs to be expressed. If you stay here, it will wither. In Iseneld, you would have many opportunities to bring pain to those who invaded and destroyed your island. My jarl would welcome you. When we win this war, she will make you an overlord, a position worthy of a Daughter of Aillira."

Promises he could not guarantee, but what did it matter?

"Your jarl," the pain-wielder said. "The woman warrior. I saw her fight in Stalwart Bay. Do men in your country truly follow the orders of an unwed woman with no royal blood?"

"They do. You remind me of her." This, at least, was not a lie. "Jarl Solvei will be pleased to have a strong, like-minded warrior by her side."

She considered. "I will think on it, Westlander."

"Reyker. And you are?"

Her hesitation came and went. "Sursha," she replied.

And just like that, Reyker knew he had won.

CHAPTER 5

REYKER

Sometime in the night, he woke to the howls of a coywolf. Brokk was snoring on the pallet next to him, mouth hanging open. Reyker pulled on his boots and crept from the tent. He meant to walk along the rocky shore, but as he headed down to it, he paused at the edge of the Tangled Forest. The quiet woods called to him, beckoning him to enter. He slipped past Garreth's sentries and made his way through the trees, not certain of his path but knowing he was headed somewhere.

He began to gag—the forest smelled wrong, musty and diseased. It felt wrong, too, like he'd stumbled into a hole in the earth and wound up leagues belowground. He couldn't see much, only what the moonlight illuminated, but it looked as if the trees were rotting. Even so, he kept going, compelled.

When he got to the hovel, he stopped and stared. The pressure in his head was back. Whatever was inside that shack would only make it worse.

"You sense it, don't you?" a lilting voice said.

He spun and saw a girl. At least, that was the best label he could put on her, though it was far from accurate. She had a girlish shape, but her body was rotten, like she'd been dug up from a grave. Eyes winked at him—not from her face, which had only empty sockets, but from all across her blackened skin, hundreds of them, in every color and shape. Another magiska, one who could communicate directly with the gods.

"Something was taken from you," the seeress said, skulking closer. "A truth. A light. Pieces of you broken and bent, stained to seem like what they aren't."

Reyker suddenly found it hard to swallow, hard to breathe.

The seeress placed her putrefied hands on either side of Reyker's head. "There is foul magic afoot, eating away at you. It will spread, until you no longer remember who you are beyond your gifts."

Though the reek of her filled his nostrils, he didn't dare move. "How do I stop it?"

"You can't. It must run its course. But you can hasten it, if you confront the cause of your disease." She backed away, gesturing to the hovel.

He made himself approach it, made his fingers grip the handle. The hinges groaned when he opened the door and ducked inside.

—LiraLiraLiradeerwolftrustgorunDrakisafesavesouldeathlightloveLira—

Memories slammed against the inside of his skull, but only fragments slipped through, the rest held back by bars he didn't know how to tear down. He clutched at his head. He thought he might be screaming, but he wasn't certain if the sound was real or only in his mind.

Blackness dripped over his consciousness, filling him up like ink pooling in a jar.

—LiraLiraLira—

Ildja, the serpent-goddess with eyes of embers and hair that fell down her back in bright streaks of lava, did not like me. That much was clear by her moue when she gripped my wrist and examined it, and by the way she looked at me only if there was no way of avoiding it. "There are no traces of the *skoldar* left," Ildja declared, dropping my arm. "She is free from the boy's influence."

"So why isn't my mark working?" Draki asked.

"I told you this might happen, my son. The girl is stubborn, willful. Some part of her still fights you, even after all your attempts to fix her. Heed me this time and lock her away until Solmangler. She's of no use to you until the holy night is upon us and the massacre can be orchestrated."

Draki stared into the crater. The Mountain of Fire, the heart of the Frozen Sun, churned below, with nothing but an ice shelf separating us from that loch of liquid fire. "Give me the dagger. I will mark her again."

"It will do no good."

"Then I will fill her flesh with marks until it does!"

I sat silently, cold seeping through my fur-lined clothes, Veronis's words playing through my head: *ILDJA AND HER WRETCHED SPAWN WILL TURN AGAINST YOU, AND IT WILL BE YOUR END.*

Draki took Ildja's place, the ice dagger gleaming in his hands, bending my head to the side. He sliced his mark behind my left ear, to match the one behind my right. A trail of blood tickled my neck, my shoulder.

It wasn't like last time, when it felt as if two frayed bits of rope had been cinched together. This mark was just a tug on that knot, ensuring it was still in place. I let my eyes close, let my forehead rest on Draki's knee.

The journey to the glacier through the underground tunnels had been long, and I was too tired to care what happened next.

I seldom dreamt now, so it had been some time since my dreams brought me to the ruins. The strange dream realm hadn't changed—it was all broken stone and old graves littering the land, the echo of a love song Aillira and Veronis once shared that had turned to a funeral dirge.

I wandered the valley, dipping my fingers in the pond that pooled below the waterfall, circling the giant thorntree that still existed here in the past, even though it had been felled, its roots ripped clean out of the earth, in the present.

I thought I was alone until I heard footsteps behind me. When I turned he was there, like he used to be back when we each thought the other dead.

Something was wrong with him. His body blurred at the edges. His lips parted, trying to talk, but he disappeared, reappearing a few moments later, closer than he'd been before. Another flash and he was standing right in front of me, and I could finally hear him.

"What did you do to me?" he asked so sharply I took a step back. "Lira, what did you do?" Then he was gone again. When he returned, he gripped my shoulders, shaking me. "You must undo it!"

I shoved him away and he stumbled to his knees.

My other was stronger in the dream realm, half of me instead of a sliver, and the instinct to go to him was powerful. We fought each other, Lira of Stone lunging forward. She kneeled beside Reyker and took his face in her hands. She wanted to ask him what was wrong, but I won the battle of words, moving our mouth so it said, "I fixed you. I helped you."

As the Dragon had done to me.

"You broke me," he said. His body wavered like sunlight through water, fading, vanishing.

This time, he did not return. My other dragged me through the ruins, searching, calling his name. All for nothing. Once more, Reyker was beyond our reach.

CHAPTER 6

LIRA

My body was covered in scars.

On my ankle, where one of the Brine Beasts pulled me under when I was nine. On my back, from when my father beat me with a knout months ago. Under my collarbones, where the mystic had poured the Fallen Ones' blood into me.

Behind both ears, where Draki had carved his dragon stars, though I couldn't see them. I could, however, see the matching marks he'd carved on my calf. My hip. My wrist, where Reyker's *skoldar* once was. And another, between my breasts, over my heart—as if the mark might sink through my skin into the pulsing muscle and persuade it to pound faster at the sight of him, to beat for no one but Draki.

Draki had announced that we would be touring the local villages tomorrow as emperor and consort, and then he'd ridden away from the castle, leaving me to recover from our trip to the Mountain of Fire while he bedded peasants and nobles across the Fjordlands. Alone in my chambers, dressed in my nightclothes, I touched a tentative finger to the mark on my chest. The scar began to move, a slow dance, rippling like jellyfish tentacles in a current.

I stood up fast off the bed, knocking into the table beside it. The table tipped, and one of the dragon figurines on top of it fell, crashing to the floor.

When I took my hand away from the mark, it had stilled.

The door to my chambers flew open and a Dragonman stepped in, searching for the source of the noise, ensuring I was unharmed. When Draki wasn't sending me headlong into danger, he treated me like a fragile possession, stationing guards outside my rooms, or having them escort me places. Keeping his weapon safe from harm.

"I'm fine," I told the Dragonman standing over me. "Go."

He hesitated. "My jarl? Are you all right?"

"Did you not hear what I just said? Leave."

I looked up at him. He was one of my usual guards. Draki swapped them out often, to keep his men from forming any misguided attachments to their charge, but this one's face was the most familiar to me. He'd been a guard in Dragon's Lair, too—he was one of the few lucky Dragonmen who'd been on scout duty the night of Season's Eve, stationed outside the fortress when it fell. And he'd been with me in the Auk Isles. This was the man who'd thrown me a rope after my longship sank and the Brine Beasts were circling.

The Dragonmen were not supposed to speak to me. They were not supposed to look at me beyond what their duties required. And unless it was essential to my safety, they were never, ever allowed to touch me.

"Lira," he said, so softly I might have misheard.

His face. It reminded me of someone else. "Who are you?"

"My name is Joren. I am—I was—cousin to Andrithur."

Though he lacked the smug tilt to his mouth, in every other way, he resembled the Dragonman I'd saved on Glasnith, who'd later helped me escape from Dragon's Lair. "Unless you want to die at the end of a noose as Andrithur did, I suggest you get out of my bedroom."

Joren glanced around, as if just realizing where he was. He blushed as he took in my sheer sleeping gown. "I meant no offense. I only wanted you to know . . . Andrithur told me what you did for him on Glasnith. He told many of us."

Us. Dragonmen. *Draki's* men.

I knew from my conversations with Hilde—the priestess of Dragon's Lair, before she, too, was slain—that not every Dragonman was as devoted to Draki as they pretended to be.

"Enough." I needed him to stop talking before he condemned himself, before he let something slip that my loyalties to Draki would force me to repeat. I didn't care about this man, but Andrithur had died for me—for my other—and despite my apathy, that sacrifice was my debt to bear. I could repay it by keeping his cousin from destroying himself.

"You aren't alone," Joren said. "You have allies here."

Using Sjaf's gift, I took hold of the steel buckles on his leather armor, dragging him backward and pinning him to the wall. "You've seen what I am. What I do. I am the death-bringer."

Joren flinched. "Draki made you this. I saw what you were in Dragon's Lair. A scared foreign girl standing up to a god."

"Now I'm a god, and that girl is dead. Speak to me again and you can join her." I trailed a finger over the pulse in his neck, pushing heat into his veins—not enough to kill, but enough to hurt, to leave him sweating and gasping. "Tell your comrades. Make sure they understand. I don't need allies because I have the Dragon. He is my master. I am his creature. *Go now, and do not return.*"

This last command, I sang, so Joren could not resist. With a breath of wind drawn from the drafty castle walls, I slammed the door shut behind him.

REYKER

He woke in the hovel, head aching, and managed to stumble back to his tent. The more space he put between himself and the shack, the less he remembered about why he'd gone inside in the first place and what had happened after. Brokk and Alane were up, waiting for him, when he returned. Taking in his sorry state, Alane fetched him tea with a bit of a magiska healer's soporific potion to calm him and help him sleep. He pretended to drink it, pretended to sleep, and they left him alone.

The next day, Alane and Brokk toured Stony Harbor and spoke more with the prince and magiskas, playing at diplomacy. In their absence, Reyker carried out his plan.

First, he sought the pain-wielder. With little more than a nudge, she fed him everything he needed to know about the other Daughters of Aillira: names, gifts, likelihood they would join the Westlanders' fight. Not that this last bit mattered. "What about soul-readers?" Reyker asked. "Are there none of them among you?"

"It's a rare gift. I only ever met one."

"Where is she?"

Sursha gave him a strange look. "You would know better than I."

There was more he wanted to ask, but he was having a hard time translating his thoughts into Glasnithian—the words he needed eluded him, like a tool just out of his reach. He left Sursha and snuck into the healer's tent, seeking the potion she'd used in his tea the night before.

Reyker waited until midnight, when Brokk was snoring along with most of the village, to creep from the tent and past the guards. This time he knew where the forest was leading him, and he was ready. When the hovel came into view, he hesitated only a moment before striking sparks with the flint and stone he'd brought. The shack went up in flames. He turned to one of the tangled trees and set it ablaze too.

The screams began a few minutes later.

He emerged just in time to see nomads rushing to grab buckets, filling them from the wells before running to the bright burning spot within the forest. There were shouts, people calling for their prince and his commander. Cries that went unanswered. Inside his own tent, Brokk hardly stirred. Reyker swallowed the knot in his throat.

The sea-farer called from the tent across from theirs, and Reyker ducked inside. She was blinking in confusion. "Alane won't wake up."

"She'll be fine," Reyker said, scooping Alane into his arms. "Come along now."

The sea-farer looked at him as if struggling to pull her thoughts together, but she obeyed. They found Sursha and the other magiskas standing outside their tents, staring at the flames crawling along the forest canopy. "We need to get you all to the ship before the fire spreads," Reyker told them. "The prince's orders. He tasked me with keeping the magiskas safe."

The Daughters of Aillira looked at him the same way the sea-farer had, knowing something wasn't quite right but unable to understand what it was. All except Sursha, whose clear-eyed gaze pierced him. "He did not," she said, though she followed him down the path to the beach with the other magiskas. "Garreth doesn't trust you."

"Which is why he's in his current predicament," Reyker said.

"What did you do?"

"What I had to." *To protect Iseneld. To save my home.*

Reyker led the magiskas to the caravel. He laid Alane down in the bow and helped the other girls settle in around her. Besides Alane and the sea-farer, there were nine Daughters of Aillira, all with various abilities. If he could convince Sursha to come, it would be an even ten that he could take back to Iseneld.

"You drugged them," the pain-wielder said, waving at the heavy-lidded girls leaning against one another in the boat. "You're taking them to fight in your war, without their consent."

"Yes." And there was no going back—he had come too far. "I dropped a mild potion into their tea to keep them calm and gave stronger doses to those who might have stopped me. But I left yours untouched because you know what must be done to keep the Dragon away from Glasnith's shores, and you know Garreth of Stone refuses to do it."

Sursha pursed her lips, looking over her shoulder at the smoke curling above the village. "The fire will trap them. You would leave the nomads to burn?"

"Of course not." He'd left two of the magiskas standing on the beach.

Now that his escape with the other magiskas was imminent, he could send them back to help. "You," he said to the red-headed fire-sweeper. "Go. Help them subdue the fire. And you." He pointed at the wind-wafter. "Make certain the flames never touch the village."

They nodded, holding on to each other as they stumbled back the way they'd come. Sursha watched the magiskas go, then turned back to him with her arms crossed. Reyker had learned enough about Sursha to know how to prod her in the right direction. He kneeled before her, as if she were a queen. She stepped back, but he saw the twitch of a grin she fought to hide.

"I cannot do this without you, Jarl Sursha. Your country needs you and your sisters, and so does mine. Use your gifts as the gods intended, for people who will celebrate them and revere all the Daughters of Aillira in a way Glasnith's prince does not. Come with me, and we will save the world."

Her grin won out. It wasn't sweet or pleasant, but sharp and self-serving, like the woman herself.

Reyker didn't care. He would use her. He would use them all, burn as many villages as he had to, lie and steal and kill until Draki was defeated.

He would be the weapon Iseneld needed him to be.

CHAPTER 7

LIRA

Draki returned from his jaunt to the local villages with a smile on his face and a lightness in his step. The servants were already whispering about his exploits, how he'd bedded a pretty young priestess who'd taken a lifetime vow of celibacy, and then killed anyone—both in the temple and at the inn he took her to—who spoke ill of the holy woman's choice. There was no way to know how much of the story was true, if Draki had coerced the priestess, if the corpses left in his wake had simply displeased him in some way. Lies and legends trailed him like footprints left in sand.

With his homecoming came a well of expectations.

The Dragon showed up at my door, dressed oddly—in that he *was* dressed. Rather than his usual bare torso or open vest, he wore a white tunic tucked into his trousers and a laced leather jerkin. Even his silver hair, which he often left loose and wild, was tied at the nape of his neck with a leather thong.

He took my arm and escorted me to the stables. Victory—or Vengeance, as Reyker had renamed my brother's mare—was saddled and waiting for us, watching with her uncanny gaze. Draki had found the horse hidden with a family in the Fjordlands and taken her, burning a dragon star onto her flank. Claiming her for his own.

Draki buckled a fur-lined cloak around my shoulders. "I cannot wait to show you off, Lira. My lovely, loyal consort." He lifted me into Victory's saddle before leaping onto her back and taking the reins, his arms settling around my waist.

Since I'd become his death-bringer, we hadn't left the castle together as anything but master and creation. Now, without my mask and armor, we traveled across the snow-blanketed fields of the Fjordlands as emperor and consort. Villagers waved, or bowed, or watched us fearfully. We stopped at farms and cottages and stores, speaking with herdsmen and weavers, tasting bakers' *skyr* and custard pastries, sharing drinks with vintners and brewers. I smiled and made small talk and gazed at the emperor beneath lowered lashes. A loyal consort.

"We have one last stop," Draki said as we mounted Victory once more.

"The sun is already setting." When I'd first arrived in Iseneld it had been the Sun Season, when the sun did not set until midnight, but now, in the Ice Season, it rose and vanished quickly below the horizon.

"True winter has begun." Draki nodded at the snow drifts. "The days will get shorter, tapering away, until one midwinter day, when the sun will not show her face at all. This is Solmangler, the holiest of holidays, when everyone in Iseneld ceases working and warring and comes together to praise the Ice Gods. That darkest of nights is when we will complete the ritual to make you immortal. That is the night all my enemies will get what is coming to them."

"I look forward to serving you for eternity and celebrating your victories, my emperor," I replied. But I was thinking, *Do I want to be immortal?* And then, *Does what I want even matter?*

"*Our* victories," Draki said.

We left the villages for the countryside, and Draki steered Victory along the trail at the bottom of the fjord. Above us was a series of narrow mountains jutting into the sea like fingers, sapphire water cupped between them, sparkling even in the pale afternoon sun.

"It's beautiful," I said.

"It's yours. All of it."

Because it belonged to him. So did everything on this island, and a growing number of countries far across the sea.

So did I.

He stopped at a cottage that sat alone at the tip of a peninsula, far from any village. Draki helped me down from the horse and gestured for me to go inside while he led Victory to a small stable behind the house.

The door opened onto a single room, its walls and roof made of wood and stone, with a hearth at the center. The cottage was a modest size and sparsely decorated—none of the luxury of Draki's usual haunts. One large window faced the fjord's mouth, another faced the open sea. Despite the rustic quality, it appeared to be newly built. "Who lives here?" I asked as Draki entered, kicking snow off his boots.

"I had it made for us." He crossed the room to light a fire in the hearth. "I thought you might enjoy getting away from the castle on occasion, having privacy. Do you like it?"

"It's perfect," I said to placate him.

He sat in front of the hearth, motioning for me to sit next to him. The food he took from his satchel was as ordinary as the cottage: salted fish, fresh bread, a tin of thawing ice berries. No cream or syrup, no exotic spices to tantalize the tongue. While we ate, Draki told me about how he planned to improve Iseneld, starting with the Fjordlands.

"We need more inns and taverns for long-distance travel, more fresh food across the island for the winter months. Now that Sanddune and the Auk Isles are under my control, there will be no need for Iseneld to go without. I'll have my emissaries oversee the shipments of fruits, vegetables, and grains year-round. Iseneld cannot be strong unless her people are strong, and so I will strengthen them."

"Aren't the Aukians and Dunians your people too?" I asked. "You conquered them. You are their emperor. Are they not your subjects?"

"They are." Draki tossed a handful of berries into his mouth. "But Iseneld is my home. This island and its people will always come first. As will you." He looked away when he said it, smoothing back an escaped strand of hair that glistened against his skin like spun silver.

We finished eating and Draki pulled a book from the satchel, placing it in my hands. It was old, the cover worn, the title faded, but if I squinted, I could just make out the embossed letters: *THE FORBIDDEN SCRIPTURES*.

"Is this real?" I asked. "I thought every copy was destroyed."

"I took it from Aillira's Temple." Before he razed the sanctuary to the ground. "The head priestess kept it hidden, and I was curious. Read me something."

"You can't read Glasnithian?"

"Why would I learn to read an inferior language?"

I opened the cover and turned the pages gently. They were whisper-thin, so delicate I expected them to crumble beneath my touch. "What do you want to hear?"

"Answers. About Veronis and Aillira. What was wrong with them? Why were they so foolish, taking on the god of death and the soul-eater?"

My fingers floated over the parchment, through verses and lyrics and poetry. The book's spine groaned, and I pulled back. As if the Fallen Ones had heard us and reached out across our realms, the pages fell open on a story.

I read.

⸺✦⸺

The girl was beauteous, but myriad mortals Gwylor sculpted were equally fair; astute, but neither was this rare amongst her kind. What was it that lured Veronis, that lured his cousins, for Veronis was not the only one who spied upon her in wonder?

In pursuit of the secret to her enchantments, he sought her out, donning the skin of the creatures he had fashioned. In each form—fish and fowl, wolf and deer, insect and reptile—he crept nigh enough to scent her. She delighted in every creature's devotion, caressing his feathers or fur, tender and doting. By some means, she perceived him, no matter the coat he used to conceal himself.

Gwylor's gift to her—a splinter of the god himself, bestowed upon his favorite creation—enabled the mortal to discern thoughts, to distinguish affection from deception, loyalty from duplicity. She could even perceive the motives of gods, an unintended enhancement, and the immortal blessings proved volatile, refusing to bend to the wishes of their architects.

"There you are again," the girl would say when she saw Veronis, her full lips wrought into a smile.

Veronis hailed her by name, but the utterance emerged as no more than a chirp, a growl, a rustle. Always, she would place a kiss upon his brow.

It was Ildja, goddess of demons, who proposed he reciprocate the kiss.

"You must taste her, cousin," the goddess advised. "Crawl to her on your belly wearing a serpent's skin. If she can love you as the lowliest of creatures, it will prove her ardor sincere."

Credulous, he heeded his cousin's instructions.

The girl perched beside the serpent without fear, fondling his scales, bending to kiss his brow. "I see you, my love," she declared.

Veronis returned her kiss, oblivious to mortal fragility, ignorant of the lethal defenses possessed by his own composition: the teeth that tasted her, tipped in venom.

She trembled as the toxin ravaged flesh and nerve and sinew. Her heart toiled beneath her breast, yet she proclaimed, "I know you did not mean it. I forgive you."

Veronis could not bear her demise. He sloughed his guise, morphing from serpent to god, and embraced her. With a spate of power, he dissolved the venom in her veins. "Never leave me," he begged.

The girl closed her eyes against his splendor, and he sheathed his deific frame with mortal skin. She gazed upon him in awe. "Please, tell me your true name."

"Veronis."

"Veronis." She traced his visage with her fingers. "I have longed for you to speak my name with this mouth, so that I might hear it."

"Aillira," he breathed, shaking from the force of that single, exquisite word, a word that sang in all the desolate recesses inside him and made an invulnerable god yearn for such weakness, even if it bore him to ruin. "Aillira."

<hr>

When I looked back at Draki, I expected him to sneer, to mock, but his brow was wrinkled. His eyes slid over me.

I shut the book.

"Tell me something about yourself, Lira," he murmured, moving closer, until our thighs and shoulders brushed. "Something forbidden, like those scriptures. A secret no one knows."

I kept my gaze on the flames. "You've seen inside my mind. You know all my secrets." All but the one I could not reveal, that a piece of my soul still belonged to Lira of Stone. A piece I'd been unable to tear out, a lingering thread that tied me to his brother—thin and strained, yet unbroken.

Draki's chest rose and fell, the force of his annoyance jostling me.

"Wait." I searched for something safe to tell that might sate him. "My friend Ishleen. When we were children, we made up a secret language so we could pass messages during our lessons, right under the tutor's nose. I swore I'd never teach it to another soul."

That was before she turned into a mystic, before I became the death-bringer. Any promises between us, between me and anyone but the Dragon, no longer held weight.

I rummaged through a desk in the corner, coming back with a sheet of parchment and a quill. "A circle means no. A circle inside a circle means yes. An arrow—well, those are obvious." I drew more shapes and lines and symbols, explaining what they represented and how to combine them to make phrases.

Draki leaned in, watching. "How would you tell her about a boy you fancied?"

I showed him: a square inside a square for *boy*, three linking stars for *handsome*.

"And if I wanted to tell a girl she was beautiful?" he asked.

The compliment struck a raw place inside me, a time when another boy who looked a little like Draki had murmured, *Thu aer vakk. You are beautiful.* I shook the memory away, sketching the message—three stars, two interlocking triangles. Beautiful. Girl.

The Dragon would have laughed at such childish games. The emperor, the jarl, the warlord, would have scorned this sentimental display. But the man with me now was not them, not entirely. He was offering me a glimpse of the person he'd been before those titles were attached to him—someone fierce but not yet vicious, angry but not yet evil.

This was Aldrik. The boy Draki used to be, before he discovered he was the son of a goddess and shed his mortal name.

He caught me staring and said, "Come here."

I obeyed, kneeling in front of him.

"Turn around."

I did. A moment later, his chest settled against my back, his arms circling me. He rested his chin on my head.

Draki had held me like this before, but always with need vibrating through his skin into mine, always with his hands wandering across my body—seeking, wanting. But there was no demand to his touch now, no restlessness.

As if instead of claiming me, he was trying to court me.

"Since you revealed one of your secrets, I will tell you one of mine. Part of the price I paid for immortality." He took a deep breath, like he was steeling himself.

Was this all an elaborate act? Was the Dragon betting that vulnerability would win me over where seduction had not?

"It did not happen all at once," he began. "It was a series of trials and tasks, each more challenging than the one before. Each sacrificing some piece of my mortal self. I regret none, save one. A consequence of my invincibility. It left my mortal body inf—" He bit down on the word. "I cannot sire children. I will never have an heir."

Silence saturated the room, as if this truth consumed every other sound. I thought of the boast he'd made at the Season's Eve ceremony. *She will bear me magiska daughters and sons, jarls and queens and future emperors.*

And suddenly, one of the most confounding enigmas surrounding the Dragon unraveled. Draki wanted someone of his blood to stand beside him and share the grand empire he'd created, but he could not bear sons. Which meant Reyker, his younger half brother, was the closest Draki would ever get. This was why Draki could never bring himself to kill Reyker, why he tried so relentlessly to convince Reyker to join him.

Draki was awaiting my response, and I deliberated. What did he want? Not sympathy or apologies, nor reassuring platitudes.

"What use are heirs to the Dragon? You are immortal. You are forever."

His arms tightened around me. Turned me. Draki's fingers found my face, lifting my chin, tracing my lips. His words were a breath against my mouth. "Do what you will, Lira. I am yours." Then he let his arms drop, holding them at his sides.

He was giving me control. This man who was half god, an emperor of five nations, a commander of armies and demons who wanted to conquer everything, everyone. Had he ever let another woman take the lead?

With shaking hands, I unlaced, unbuckled, unbuttoned his clothing. His skin shimmered like gold in the firelight, the planes of his muscles so strong and sharp he appeared to be more statue than man. I pressed my palms to the inked half of his face, following the tattoos down his neck and shoulder, chest and stomach, hip and thigh. The knots and dragons danced under my touch. It was clearer than ever to me that he was a melding of mortal and god. How could anyone not desire him?

How could *I* not?

When I slipped my hands into his hair, his restraint dissolved. My dress was gone, torn from my body before I could blink, followed by the knives sheathed to my thigh and ankle. There was nothing but a sliver of cold air separating my flesh from his. Lying beside the fire, Draki pulled me on top of him and kissed me as he never had before, softly and sweetly, his lips offering rather than demanding.

He'd saved me. He'd made me what I was. I pressed my lips into his, my body into his. I made my hands tug at his shoulders, made my tongue slip between his teeth to taste his mouth, wanting to want him, to please him. Praying those desires would be enough.

Draki took his time, exploring with skillful hands and lips and tongue, giving pleasure without taking any in return. My moans and gasps were not feigned. Draki knew his way around a woman's body, and his touch was indulgent. But . . .

But. Something was missing.

This all felt familiar, yet wrong.

Draki's fingertips were feathers traveling across my skin. He rolled me onto my side so he could kiss every one of my scars. The ones he'd cut into me himself shivered under his lips, undulating like his tattoos. "Light of my soul," he said. "Blood of my heart." Words Aillira and Veronis had once spoken to each other. Words Reyker and I had said, when we'd been portraying the doomed couple at the Birth of Summer festival months ago.

He bowed to kiss the Star of the Dragon carved between my breasts. "I belong to you, and you to me," he said, his mouth hovering over my heart, "my deer."

The name made my stomach clench. It made everything odd about this night stand out in stark relief. The clothes Draki had worn, his hair tied back. Sharing secrets, confessions. Reading from the scriptures. This cottage, the hearth, the fire. Draki letting me touch him freely, letting me learn him before touching me back. Giving before taking. Kissing my scars.

This was all some sort of grand reenactment, the stories of two tragic loves laced together. Veronis and Aillira. Reyker and me.

My other, who I'd managed to keep locked away all this time, broke free with a fury.

She slapped Draki, scrambling out from underneath him. "I am not Aillira," she growled. "You are not Veronis. You are not Reyker, not even close. You're a pathetic brute and I will *never* love you."

I wrestled for control, pushing her back down into her cage, but it was too late.

Any trace of gentleness in Draki seeped out. His features were blank, but the cottage walls creaked and dust rained down from the ceiling, as if his rage had spread so wide there wasn't enough room to hold it. I knew, then, that Veronis's prediction had been correct. I was going to die. Draki was going to kill me.

"I didn't mean it," I said. "That wasn't me, it was—"

Draki's hands wrapped around my neck, lifting me off my feet. I could breathe, but just barely. His fingers twitched, like he was debating whether to crush my throat or tear off my head.

Instinct kicked in, and I reached for my gifts. Wind whirled through the cottage, knocking over furniture. Not a single strand of Draki's hair moved. The knives that lay among my discarded clothes jerked from their sheaths and flew at him, bursting into dust on impact. Fire leaped from the hearth, straight for him, fizzling to smoke the second it touched him.

Blood collected in the cleft below my nose, spilled from the canals of my ears.

When all else failed, I resorted to clawing at the fingers digging into my skin. "Master," I said, or tried to. It came out a strangled croak. "I love you. I love you."

At least, I wanted to.

Draki let loose a roar that shook the roof above us and the floor below. He dragged me to the cottage's door. Opened it. Flung me, naked, into the snow. Slammed it shut.

I lay there, shivering, wheezing. Waiting for him to come back and finish what he'd started, to steal my body and then my life.

When the door remained closed, I slunk to the stables and wrapped a horse blanket around myself, huddling against Victory for warmth. The mare peered at me like she knew what had happened, like she knew how all of this would end, and if only we shared a common language, she could warn me of what was to come.

"You've ruined everything," I hissed at my other. "Are you happy now?"

But for once, Lira of Stone remained stubbornly silent.

CHAPTER 8

REYKER

Reyker stood in the bow of the Renegades' longship, watching the rowboat approach. Solvei stood beside him, and Eathalin, the young spell-caster, was in the stern, with hands raised and apricot hair billowing in the wind as she conjured a veil that hid their presence. The magiska opened a small gap in the veil to allow the rowboat through, and Reyker saw there were two men in it—one rowing, the other bound and gagged.

"Who are they?" Reyker asked. To get here, they had sailed perilously close to their old camp, where Draki now resided, relying on the spell-caster to conceal them. The jarl had brought Reyker on this mission but told him no details.

Solvei had been less than pleased when he'd arrived in New Fjullthorp with a boatful of cagey magiskas and no Brokk—though not as furious as Alane, who had tried to shove him overboard once she'd woken from the sleeping draught he'd given her. He'd been lucky to have Sursha on his side, to calm the magiskas he'd abducted and convince them to fight for the greater good. But now the Renegades were shorthanded, since Solvei had sent a ship and crew to retrieve Brokk.

"They are Dragonmen," Solvei answered.

Reyker gripped his sword. The jarl shot him a look that stayed his hand.

Solvei reached out to help secure the rowboat to the longship, grasping the Dragonman's hand in greeting after he climbed aboard. "I appreciate you meeting us, Joren. This information is too important to risk being shared through messengers."

The man nodded. He wasn't dressed like a Dragonman, but he held himself like one: spine straight, shoulders back, knees slightly bent. Always ready for a fight.

Reyker's stance matched the Dragonman's. Much of Draki's training had been beneficial, loath as Reyker was to admit.

"It's difficult to leave," Joren said, "but Draki is away from the castle at the moment." The man looked at Reyker. "Strange to see you here, Lagorsson. Strange to be on the same side, once again."

Reyker didn't remember this man, nor did he care. He turned to Solvei. "You have a Dragonman spy inside Draki's castle, and you didn't inform your high commander?"

"Before Andrithur's untimely death," the jarl said, "he made a few connections for me in Dragon's Lair among his fellow soldiers. Joren has passed us information at great risk to himself. The fewer people who know of his involvement, the better."

"Does Brokk know?"

Ignoring him, Solvei held her hand out to Joren. The spy drew a sealed bit of parchment from his coat. "The response from the head priestess at the Temple of the Mountain," Joren said.

Solvei opened the message, then smiled as she read. "The priestess believes it possible to build a cage to imprison Draki, but she's advised us to seek the aid of the goddess Seffra and her devoted monks on the isle of Heligur. I'll send an emissary to Heligur as soon as we return to New Fjullthorp."

Reyker grunted. There was no cage that could hold the Dragon; he'd told Solvei as much, but she would not listen.

Joren gestured at the man tied up in the rowboat. "I brought a gift—a Dragonman who bears information I've not been given about an upcoming attack Draki is planning . . . if you can wring it from him."

Solvei nodded. "Our pain-wielder will welcome a subject to interrogate. Thank you for your aid, Joren. I will see to it you and all the

Dragonmen who pledge loyalty to the Renegades have a place in Iseneld once I am high jarl."

A lofty promise, one that required them all surviving this war. An outcome Reyker doubted more and more by the day.

"We appreciate your pledge," Joren replied, "and the protection you and your spell-caster have granted us." Joren rolled up his sleeve, revealing a strap of leather embossed with symbols. "The runes have kept Draki from sensing our movements and our true intentions."

Eathalin was the youngest of the magiskas, only fourteen or so, but she had already proved herself stronger than the rest—she did not tire as quickly from using her gifts, and her spells were the only thing that had, thus far, been able to foil the Dragon.

Joren rolled his sleeve back down. "I hope you will consider showing leniency to the Dragon's consort as well, Jarl Solvei. I'm convinced her loyalty to him has been coerced."

Reyker's mind flooded with images of a girl: scorning him when he tried to rescue her, declaring her love for the Dragon. He started to draw his sword. "You dare defend the consort, after all her lies and schemes? My jarl, are you certain you can trust this traitor?"

Solvei put her hand on top of Reyker's and shoved his sword back in its sheath. "As certain as I am that I can trust you, Wolf Lord."

Draki's sword arced through the air, and I ducked beneath it. "Is this really necessary?"

We'd been practicing in the training pit for nearly an hour, the same drills we'd done when Draki first began teaching me months ago.

"Before you go up against my brother, you must be ready," he said. "Your gifts have weakened as of late. They burn out faster, drain you more thoroughly. You must train harder." His sword sliced toward the ground, and I jumped over the blade.

The seeress Draki had kept imprisoned, the one I'd killed out of mercy, told me I was the wrong vessel, that there was someone stronger I needed to pass my gifts to. The Fallen Ones hadn't intended on me living this long—I was meant to die freeing them months ago—and Veronis had warned I would pay for that failure.

After everything Draki had done to strengthen me, I was still not powerful enough. Despite my pledges and pretending, I was still not truly his consort, because he would not consummate our union until I wanted him.

I would never want him.

Something sinister stirred in Draki's eyes. When he came at me again, his efforts were fueled by the wrath he'd been holding back since we'd returned from the cottage a week ago. He unleashed it in a flurry of strikes and stabs that left me panting as I struggled to block them. He herded me, bringing his sword down every time I strayed too far from him, until he had me pinned against the wall, the tip of his blade resting beneath my chin.

"Is this where it ends?" I asked.

"That is up to you, little warrior."

Draki threw his sword down, beckoning me to attack. All it took was a thought and every sharp bit of steel affixed to the wall of weapons behind us ripped free, sailing toward Draki. In the past, he'd swatted the blades away or let them crash into him and disintegrate, to remind me of his power. This time, he spun the blades so they pointed at me, pushing them in my direction. I lifted my hands and pressed back. He pushed harder.

I wasn't used to using two gifts at once, but I tried, calling up the wind to knock the weapons away. Draki tilted his head and the falling steel shuddered back into place.

The blades edged closer toward me. Sweat dampened my temples. My heels hit the wall, and still the hovering blades crept closer.

"Draki," I said in warning.

His face was a block of stone. "You made a vow to me, Lira, and you failed. You did not give yourself to me wholly. Do you know what I do to oath breakers?"

Spears, swords, daggers, axes—dozens of razor-sharp edges jabbed at my flesh, just shy of breaking skin. Bloody tears streaked down my cheeks as I trembled from the effort of holding them at bay. "Draki," I said again.

He drew the weapons back before burying them in the stone beside and above me, so close the hilts indented my skin. "You have one task left, death-bringer. You will bring me my brother." Draki jerked me away from the wall, so I could see the steel outline of my body drawn in blades. "Do as I command, and I will make you immortal. Fail me again . . ."

He slid his stiletto from his boot and threw it. The knife slammed into the silhouette—right where my heart had been.

My hair was falling out. Strands stuck to my pillow every morning when I rose, clumps floated in the water each time I finished a bath. My gums bled, and some of my teeth had grown loose. I carried the same essence inside me that caused the Grove of the Fallen Ones and the mystics who guarded it to rot, but I lacked the grove's magic to sustain myself, to suspend indefinitely that final step. I'd come to accept that if the Dragon didn't kill me, my gifts would.

I needed the ritual Draki had promised me, so I could keep my gifts and my life. I had to bring Draki's brother back to him.

I'd not seen Draki for days. He was not in the feasting hall when I took my meals. He did not come to my chambers. He did not train me, or join me on rides, or invite me to attend his council meetings. I'd not realized how monotonous life in a castle could be. How lonely.

When a knock finally sounded on my door at dawn one morning, it was Joren, my guard, with a message from the emperor. Draki had summoned me to dress for battle, so I slipped on my scaled armor and mask.

Joren escorted me to the stables, shooting me worried glances. He would not be with me today on whatever mission Draki was assigning me. "My jarl," he whispered, "I must tell you—"

"Silence, fool." The stables were in sight. Anything we said could be overheard.

Victory was saddled and waiting for me, along with a small army of Dragonmen. Draki paced through the stables, avoiding my gaze. "Is it your brother?" I asked, even though I knew. Nothing riled the Dragon like Reyker Lagorsson.

"I sent a garrison of Dragonmen to ambush Gyldenhring, a village in the midlands that's shown support for the Renegades. My brother and his pitiful soldiers took the bait. It's his mother's home village, and he would never stand aside and let it fall. They're using a spell to cloak themselves. The Renegades should arrive in Gyldenhring shortly before you do, with no inkling that a second wave of warriors is marching on them."

I nodded. When I moved to climb into the saddle, Draki grabbed my arm. He pushed a silver ring, engraved with a floral design, onto my finger. A wedding ring.

"What is this?"

"So my brother has no doubts about who you belong to. I would go with you, if I thought I could stand against him on a battlefield without killing him." He met my eyes briefly. It was as close as Draki would ever get to an apology.

"I will bring Lagorsson to you, alive and in chains."

Quiet enough that only I could hear, he murmured, "Will you, Lira?"

Ah. So this wasn't simply about retrieving his wayward brother. I hadn't seen Reyker since Draki changed me, and this was a test to see if I could face my former lover and still do my duty. Could I forsake him to the mercy of the warlord who murdered his parents, torched his home, and ruined his life?

"Yes, my emperor."

The ride to Gyldenhring took half a day. Before the early dark set in, I saw smoke stretching along the horizon—there was clean white smoke, billowing up from the hot springs and fumaroles that pocked the area of bald stone around the village and from the scorching waters of the geysers that leaped toward the sky in rhythmic intervals, and also the dense gray smoke that came on the heels of a plague of fire.

Our horses crested a hill, and there below us was the village in flames. But the fire . . . there was something wrong with it. Some of the flames were orange, but some were solid blue—fey fire, birthed from magic. "Be ready," I called to the Dragonmen. "The Renegades brought Daughters of—"

A ball of blue flame soared into our ranks, slamming into several Dragonmen, setting them ablaze.

I urged Victory forward. At the bottom of the hill, torches sparked to life, illuminating a waiting line of infantry and mounted Renegade warriors, and a fire-sweeper whose face was vaguely familiar—a girl I'd fought beside in Stalwart Bay—standing between the Dragonmen and the village.

A volley of Renegade arrows arced into the air, and I stretched out a hand, spinning the arrows and pointing them at the archers who'd fired on us. Screams rang out as the arrows found their marks. Too late, I remembered I was supposed to be careful—Draki would execute me if I accidentally killed his brother.

"Death-bringers!" someone cried.

I sent a gust of wind at the Renegades, knocking warriors down as they tried to flee. When the wind died, I called to their horses to buck and bolt. The line of warriors dispersed. Even the fire-sweeper ran, leaving a clear path across the barren lands to the village.

We stormed down the hill, Dragonmen fanning out, our horses' hooves pounding against the uneven rock that served as a natural barrier around the village. More arrows soared. I reached my gift toward them, grappling at them with my mind . . . failing to find purchase. My abilities slipped over the arrows like they were coated in oil.

Arrows slammed into Dragonmen. I ducked just in time to avoid being skewered. A warrior near me ripped the arrow from his shoulder, and beneath the blood, I saw no metal. The Renegades had switched to firing wooden stakes, sharpened at the ends.

They'd been expecting me.

Only one person was this clever. What other tricks did Lagorsson have in store? I closed my eyes, focusing my senses, filtering out other sounds, listening for his voice . . .

There.

"On your feet, with wooden weapons only," he was saying. "No horses. No metal. Your wooden shields are warded with runes against the death-bringers' powers, so use them if they target you. Take out the Dragonmen, but listen for the magiskas' warning signals. I will handle the death-bringers."

I scoffed. Not even the Wolf Lord suspected a lone death-bringer, unwilling to believe such brutal strength could come from a single magiska.

The Renegades surged forth from the protection of the village with wooden spears and arrows, hurling them at the Dragonmen, taking some of them down. They crouched, holding on to one another as a cry went up. An earth-shifter made the ground shake, sending Dragonmen toppling from their saddles. Another quake cracked the stone, spilling mud and water from the boiling springs and geysers. Dragonmen tripped and landed in the water, and the night filled with more screams as the flesh melted off their bones.

My other had remained dormant thus far, but now she fought me as I called to the scalding waters, drawing up streams, hurling them over the heads of the Renegades. Aiming a stream right at the earth-shifter—another girl I'd stood with in Stalwart Bay a lifetime ago.

Some of the Renegades fell, writhing as their skin burned, but most were able to lift their shields in time, and they moved in front of the earth-shifter. As boiling water sprayed their shields, something strange happened: the droplets were repelled, bouncing off in different directions, leaving the warriors and the magiska unscathed.

A ball of blue fire crashed toward me. The fire-sweeper was at the edge of the battle, guarded by warriors with shields just as the earth-shifter was. I batted her fire back with my own, adding a handful of wind that scattered flames over the Renegades. Some of the warriors burned outright, while others dropped their guards to smother their smoldering clothes and were stabbed by Dragonmen. But, as before, those able to raise their shields were unharmed, the fire fizzling and ricocheting off the warded wood. When I sent tremors through the ground beneath the shield-bearing Renegades, the earth cracked around them, but remained solid beneath their feet.

Reaching out to the horses, my mind brushed against the animals', commanding them to trample every warrior holding a shield. The horses galloped into the fray, circling the Renegades, rearing and stomping. A few warriors lost their grips, dropped their shields, and fell beneath the flurry of hooves, but every horse that was touched by a shield turned and bolted.

I raised my voice, singing a command for the Renegades to drop their shields, but it did no good. *How are they resisting my song?* Passing one of the dead Renegades splayed on the ground, I saw the man had runes painted around his ears.

Lagorsson.

He and the Renegades were more formidable than I'd anticipated. To get past those shields, I needed to tap into my least-used gift.

Sjaf's gift of war manifested differently from one person to another. For me, it was not its own entity; it was an enhancement of all my other gifts, akin to sharpening a blade, but accessing it was like dipping a toe into madness. The gift drove most mortals out of their minds. Draki had trained me how to give in to the war gift and come back from it in one piece, as he'd trained Reyker—better, because I actually listened. Even so, Sjaf's gift depleted my power and left me exhausted, and I only ever used it as a last resort.

With a growl, I called the war gift to me now, and it answered, pounding through me, tinting the edges of my vision in shades of scarlet. Where Reyker's war gift took the form of a river, mine was a steel thread that I wrapped my other gifts around, weaving its strength into theirs, an unyielding chain. I let the chain go, unleashing everything: battering winds, screeching fire, crumbling earth, boiling water, a command to the horses and any other creatures nearby to attack. Every shard of metal in range—jewelry, belt buckles, pieces of saddles and reins—ripped free, flying at the Renegades like tiny knives.

The waves of power burst from me, out of my control, and the exertion left me dizzy, my gifts waning. Chaos unfolded as a twisting vortex of wind and water, fire and steel churned toward Renegades and Dragonmen alike, while the stone they stood on broke open. A pack of sheepdogs ran from the village and leaped on several warriors, tearing with teeth and claws.

I was mopping the blood from my face when a noise came from behind me, the careening *whoosh* of a weapon.

I kicked Victory with my heel, but the mare ignored me. Something jammed between my shoulder blades with the force of a battering ram and knocked me from the saddle. I hit the ground and rolled, punching at the boulder of a body that landed on top of me, waiting for my strength to return so I could blast the warrior with my gifts. My arms were pinned at my sides, and my squirming was fruitless. My mask had shifted, covering my eyes.

"No more hiding, death-bringer," the warrior said. "Let's see who you really are." My mask was torn off. Gilded hair framed the prominent angles of the face bent over mine.

My other surged forward, crying his name.

His eyes were the color of a churning sea, the black of his pupils threatening to swallow the blue of his irises—the war gift, crashing through his veins as it had through mine. "*You?*" he whispered.

I shoved the Dragon's brother, climbing to my feet and unsheathing my sword. The battle raged on around the village, but the only fight that mattered was in front of me. I slashed at Reyker's calf, thinking to cripple him.

He leaped out of the way, raising a wooden spear. He had one of the warded shields, too, but he left it lying on the ground. "Did you drain your gifts already?" he asked. "So much for the legends of the mighty death-bringers. Where are the others?"

"There are no others. *I* am the legend." I swung my blade at his hip and he spun to the outside of my guard, whisking his staff up so it cracked against my wrist and made my hand spasm, the sword slipping through my fingers. Before it even landed, I was drawing my dagger, jabbing at his ribs, catching him with a glancing blow as he shuffled sideways.

"I see the Dragon taught you something besides betrayal and deception," he said.

Another slash, and a spot of red wet the sleeve of his tunic. "The Dragon taught me everything," I said. "Everything I am, I owe to him."

The staff smashed into the backs of my knees, sweeping my legs out from under me, and I found myself on the ground again, the warrior leaning over me. "What you are is a gods-damned fool. You think Draki sent you here to capture me? He knows what I'm capable of. The Dragon ordered you to walk into a trap, and you obeyed, like a besotted sycophant."

"Liar!" I scrabbled backward, throwing my dagger, but Reyker swatted it aside with his spear. As I reached out for my sword only a few feet away on the stony ground, his hand clamped around mine, grinding my fingers together. He glanced down and froze. My whole body jerked forward as he pulled my hand toward his face.

Staring at the ring Draki gave me.

His irises vanished, pupils spilling over, blacker and blacker. Succumbing to the madness of the war gift. "This," he said, tearing the ring from my finger, his voice so guttural it was barely human, "was my mother's. Why do you have it?" The wooden spear pressed against my neck. "Did you marry the Dragon? Did you make vows to each other *on my dead mother's wedding ring?*"

Oh, gods. What if Draki hadn't sent me here to take Reyker prisoner? What if he'd sent me here—attacking Reyker's mother's village, wearing her ring—to die?

Maybe this was Reyker's test, not mine, one he was meant to fail. To give in to his battle-madness completely. To kill the woman he'd once loved.

He pressed the spear deeper into my flesh.

I drove my fist into Reyker's throat and he dropped the spear. While he struggled to catch his breath, I lunged, crashing into him, locking my legs around his waist. Slipping my hands beneath his tunic, palms against his chest, I dredged up a tendril of power from my first and strongest gift. Entering his soul.

The landscape had changed. It was darker than it had been before. Emptier.

I envisioned claws, digging and shredding at him from within. A bloodless, crippling pain, a sundering of mind from body. I heard Reyker scream, sensed his agony.

I knew this soul, better than any other. But it knew me too. It fought back.

Sensations enveloped me—the crash of waves and wind, the scent of cinders and thyme, the tang of salt and steel. The wall that separated me from my emotions thinned as Reyker's essence slipped over my skin, as fragments of what he felt for me stabbed into the core of my being. Hate, fabricated by my own hand. Love, as pure as water, as deep as a chasm. So many things in between, raw impressions I could not name or understand, pouring into me until I lost track of where my soul ended and his began.

Then I was falling, expelled from Reyker's soul as he shoved me off him.

I had to capture him *now*. Immortality or death—that was Draki's promise. His threat.

Reyker held his spear between us, stumbling back. "Try that again, and I will kill you." He was shaking, his steps unsteady with echoes of the damage I'd caused. A soul was like any other body part—if harmed, it could heal, but it took time.

He didn't have time. The earth rumbled, and we both looked to the crater behind him. The geyser.

It exploded, a fountain of searing hot water and steam spewing forth, shooting into the air. As gravity caught the torrent and pulled it back, the winter winds tore it into rivulets and blew it outward to splash down on a wide swath of stone circling the steaming pit. Right where Reyker stood.

He tried to run, moving too fast, his heel slipping on slick rock. When the water hit him, it would scald every bit of skin it touched, burn through his clothing to eat away the flesh beneath. If it didn't kill him, it would mangle him beyond recognition.

My other screamed so loud my skull seemed to shake from the force, and suddenly I was crouching with my hands up, palms out, trembling as I pressed the last shreds of my gifts into the boiling stream about to shower the warrior. Something ripped inside me and colors swam across my vision, but I caught most of the water, forcing it back into the crater.

The few drops I couldn't hold splashed Reyker, and he hissed at the burns, shrugging off his coat. He turned to me, slack-jawed. "Why did you do that, death-bringer?"

I couldn't answer.

Too much—I had used up too much of myself to fight him, and then to protect him. Blood streaked down my nose, filling my mouth. My muscles gave out and I collapsed in a heap as the world faded. Just before consciousness abandoned me, I was aware of my arms being pinned, my wrists bound with rope.

A voice rasping in my ear. "This changes nothing."

CHAPTER 9

REYKER

Reyker couldn't stop looking at the girl. He'd put the mask back on her, not ready to reveal her identity to anyone who knew what she'd once been to him, but even with her face covered, every time he looked at her, memories spilled out: arguments and smiles, wounds and laughter. Her hands all over his body, making him weaker, making him stronger. Whispers. Confessions.

Lies.

He had trusted her. Loved her. And she'd turned on him. She'd chosen Draki.

The girl was tied up in front of him, slung on her belly across Vengeance's saddle, and the horse—*his* horse, stolen from the family he'd left the mare with—fretted like a nursemaid, craning her neck to sniff the girl's hair and nuzzle her hand.

"Traitor," Reyker said, and Vengeance whickered indignantly.

The girl hadn't done more than twitch in the hours since she'd passed out. He suspected that was due to the sleeping draught he'd poured down her throat, though it might have also been from the draining of her gifts. Which she'd done to save him.

He squeezed his mother's ring in his fist.

No, there must be some other explanation. And he had to stop thinking of her as just a girl. She was Lira of Drakin, the Dragon's consort, the gods-damned death-bringer. Ravager of Reyker's homeland, saboteur of nations. She had helped Draki build his empire. Because of her, the Dragon stood on the threshold of conquering the world.

Why, then, had Draki not come with her to Gyldenhring?

It had to be a trap, rigged to lead Draki right to Reyker and the Renegades. He should leave the girl. He should kill her.

He'd almost killed her during their battle. When he'd noticed his mother's ring, his tenuous grip on the black river snapped, and he saw the warlord's face spliced with Lira's, indistinguishable. His control had slipped. For a second, he'd wanted nothing more than to take Draki's debts out of her flesh, to make her bleed because the invincible Dragon could not.

What would it feel like to kill the girl he'd once loved? Imagining her final breath, the last stutter of her heart, made the black river surge in anticipation, but it also made his chest seize. Once the battle-madness faded, would her death seem like a victory or would it haunt him as so many other lives he'd taken did?

Solvei's longship waited just offshore from where they'd landed. The jarl had staged her own attack on one of Draki's strongholds while Reyker led the defense of Gyldenhring, and judging by her grin, it had gone well. Reyker boarded, with Vengeance in tow. He laid the girl on the deck in her black-scaled armor, lifting her mask briefly and glancing at his jarl.

"Tie a stone to her and toss her overboard," Solvei said in Glasnithian, for Sursha's benefit. The pain-wielder had been a constant presence at the jarl's side recently. He'd been right about their parallel personalities. Solvei was an axe, strong and blunt, aimed between your eyes; Sursha was a knife thrown at your back in the dark.

The jarl's expression was even, unimpressed by the death-bringer's identity. Unsurprised.

"You knew?" Reyker said. "Your spy. He told you the Dragon's death-bringer was his consort. Why do you keep withholding vital information from me?"

"I don't trust you when it comes to her." Solvei nudged the death-bringer with the toe of her boot. "I take it she's to blame that so few of my warriors returned from this venture, yet you want to bring her with us.

What if Draki can sense her? He could follow us to the Haunted Isles. He could send his gods-forsaken Destroyers to kill us all."

"Draki can sense me, but he hasn't come for us. The spell-caster has kept us hidden so far." Reyker nodded at where Eathalin stood in the bow, hands raised, veiling the ship so anyone who looked their way would see nothing but ripples on water.

"Why would the Dragon let his consort, the woman he fought so hard to keep away from you, fall into our hands?" Solvei asked. "It must be a ruse. Kill her and be done with it."

"At least let me put my blades in her first," the pain-wielder said.

Gods aflame, he was surrounded by murderous women.

"I need the girl," Reyker said. Solvei cocked a brow at him, and he rolled his eyes. "Her *gift*. She's the only soul-reader we have. The secret to killing the Dragon is buried inside one of my memories. She can find it. I can kill Draki and end the war."

"That's the only reason you want to keep her? You loved her—"

"A long time ago, before I knew better. She is nothing to me now."

Solvei regarded him doubtfully. "Fine. Put her in the cell on Volva Isle. She'll be a worthy test subject to see if it holds."

"What cell?" A prison flashed through his memory, a cage of metal bars stealing his will to live, a girl on the other side holding him together.

The jarl threw her hands up. "Are you even listening, or has the Dragon's consort rendered you witless already? Lock her in the cell I have modeled Draki's prison after, the one on the isle of dead witches. But the death-bringer is your responsibility. If she does any damage, takes any lives, the fallout will be yours to bear. And, Lagorsson?"

"Yes, my jarl?"

"If you want to remain high commander, keep your brain in your skull instead of between your legs."

The ship plowed through the mist curling around the Haunted Isles, and the spell-caster waved her hands. Where there had been a patch of fog and empty sea, an opening emerged like the parting of curtains. They sailed into it, dropping anchor at the biggest island in the chain, the one Solvei had named New Fjullthorp—the Renegades' home since they'd left the Fjordlands, though there were so many of them now that they were spread across the archipelago.

Reyker slung the girl over Vengeance's back and led the mare down the gangplank, past the camp, to the eastern shore of New Fjullthorp. He put her in a rowboat and rowed the short distance to the next islet over, Vengeance swimming after them.

To Volva Isle. The one island with no Renegades on it—for good reason.

This was the most cursed place in Iseneld, where covens had performed rituals and sacrifices inside a circle of god-touched stones. It was where many volvur died when Draki came to capture them, running straight into the blades of the Dragonmen, taking their own lives to keep their powerful spells out of the Dragon's grasp. The Magiska Massacre many called it, whispering how the spirits of the volvur remained where they had fallen. Witches' blood had soaked the soil and turned it fallow. The air here smelled sour, and the birds in the trees did not chirp—they chanted in humanlike voices. With Vengeance carrying the girl, Reyker made his way through the woods, ignoring the prickles on his skin that urged him to turn and run.

The islet's cell was etched with the same runes as the Renegades' shields, built to trap volvur. If it could hold a witch, it should hold a death-bringer.

He kicked the cell door open. The floor was already splashed with blood from the pain-wielder's sessions with the Dragonman Solvei's spy gave her; in less than an hour, the tight-lipped soldier told Sursha everything he knew.

Reyker peeled off the girl's armor and boots, dropping them in a pile outside. His hands skimmed her tunic and trousers, searching for hidden knives—carefully, like she was a snare that would cinch shut around him if he touched her the wrong way. Once she was unarmed, he bound her wrists again and shut the door, telling Vengeance to wait. Locking himself inside. He had his wooden shield, his staff, and more of the sleeping draught, just in case. The cell should null her gifts, but he wasn't taking any chances.

He left her mask on, so he wouldn't have to look at her face.

The girl was slow to wake. As her eyes opened, she smiled and whispered his name, and for a moment he would have sworn it was sincere.

Then it was gone. She snapped to attention, her eyes cold, struggling against the rope that pinned her arms together. He could see the panic, almost feel the charge in the air as she reached out with her mind, seeking metal, wind, fire, beasts. None of it would come. She sang a command for him to release her—Frigmer's gift, the same one his mother had been blessed with—to no avail. In this cell, the Dragon's death-bringer was powerless.

"What have you done to me?" She took in the walls surrounding her. "Where am I?"

"Tell me how you gained the gift of fire," Reyker said. "You didn't have it before. Draki must have given it to you. With his blood? Did you see him bleed?"

"The Dragon does not bleed."

Of course Draki wouldn't have let her see; he would never be that careless. "Do you want to live, magiska?"

Her hollow laughter slapped against the stones. "Your brother asked me that same question, once. It wasn't until later that I realized the question he was really asking was not if I wanted to live, but what I was willing to do to stay alive. So what is it you want from me in exchange for my life, Wolf Lord?"

Before he could stop himself, he asked, "What did the Dragon want?"

"My mind. My body. My soul." Her face was impassive.

He should end this conversation. He should let it go. "Since you're sitting here, still alive, I suppose you gave him what he desired."

"I could not offer what already belonged to another." She narrowed her eyes at him. "What more do you want from me?"

Being here, just the two of them in a prison, was stirring up their past, fraying his resolve. It would be too easy to pretend she had never betrayed him. Too easy to trust her and wind up with her fingers wrapped around his throat. "To retrieve a lost memory."

At that, her lips quirked. "You would willingly let the death-bringer into your soul?"

"With a wooden pike against your chest, should you decide to try any of your tricks."

"I know what memory you seek. I won't help you destroy Draki. He is my master. You, of all people, understand how devoted I am to my allies."

Reyker's fist tightened on the staff. "Your devotion to me was never real."

"The scars on my back are very real, I assure you."

The twinge in his head sharpened, an image slicing through: the girl tied to a post, blood cascading down her back from a whip lined with thorns. It was followed by another image: the girl's bare back pocked with scars, Reyker's lips touching each one with reverence, telling her her scars were beautiful.

When his vision cleared, the girl was watching him, features scrunched beneath her mask. He looked away. "If you refuse to help me, death-bringer, you will regret it."

"What are you going to do," she asked, "beat me into compliance? You don't have it in you, Wolf Lord, no matter how much you hate me."

"You're right," he said, eyeing the blood-spattered floor, his guts squirming inside him like a belly full of snakes. "I don't."

CHAPTER 10

LIRA

My mouth was dry—that was the first sensation I noticed as I woke. The next was warmth, a blanket resting on top of me. Then light, creeping through the cracks in my eyelids. I opened them and found a woman staring back at me. Brown hair, gray eyes, a grin like a feral cat's.

"Good morning, soul-reader." She pulled off my mask, tossing it aside. "Or afternoon, since the wretched sun does not behave as it should in this part of the world."

"Sursha." The last time I saw her, we were fighting side by side at the battle of Stalwart Bay, and I had just killed four Daughters of Aillira. "Funny to find you here, working with a man you once tortured. Let me guess. The Wolf Lord lacks the bollocks to harm me, so he's sent you, one of my god-gifted sisters, to abuse me in his stead."

I sought my gifts, but where there was usually a spark in my blood, a humming in my bones, there was only ash and silence. The cell was warded with the same smothering antimagic as the Renegades' shields.

I started to stretch, the cold throb in my arms reminding me I was still tied up—my wrists no longer bound in front of me, as they'd been yesterday, but cinched behind my back. Rope was knotted around my ankles as well, so tight it was cutting off the flow of blood, and I jerked my head toward it. "Was this your doing or his?"

"Him?" She snorted. "A hardened barbarian who's seen dozens of battles, killed hundreds of men, and he turns green at the idea of hurting one vicious girl. He's out there now, pacing around the cell. Listening for your screams. But is it to torment himself with guilt, or so he can rush in and save you? What do you think, death-bringer? Will he go through with it, or am I wasting my time?"

I eased myself up, leaning against the wall. My face felt bare without my mask. Far from Draki and stripped of my costume, I felt less like the death-bringer and more like a woman split in two: Lira of Drakin, Lira of Stone. I was both, and I was neither.

Reyker saw it too. He must have, otherwise he wouldn't be here, lurking outside, debating whether or not to let the pain-wielder harm me.

"How can you access your gift if this cell is warded?"

Sursha tapped the collar around her neck, a strip of leather covered in runes. "I'm warded against the wards. Eathalin's spells are clever things." She twirled something small and pointy between her fingers. Not steel. Even with my gifts nulled and my hands tied, she wasn't stupid enough to wave a knife in front of me. "Are you ready to begin, death-bringer?"

My bound hands fumbled along the floor, as if sheer desire could conjure up a weapon to slice Sursha to ribbons for the way she was looking at me—like a fly she couldn't wait to tear the wings off of. "Does it consume you if you go too long without hurting someone?" I asked. "Do you crave other people's suffering the way a starving woman craves food? Or is it subtler, like an unreachable itch begging to be scratched?"

She flicked the object she held at me. It was long and slender and white. A needle.

No. A thorn, from a Glasnithian thorntree. The same sort that my father whipped me with. The scars across my back seemed to strain, as if my fear could tear the flesh anew.

Sursha glanced at the space above my right eyelid, where Draki had tattooed a curling thorntree branch as my warrior-mark, and her grin widened. "At first, I was disappointed not to be able to put my blades to use, but the thorns will bleed you slower. I can take my time. Before I'm done, you will tell me anything I want to know, agree to whatever I ask of you."

"If I don't, will you kill me? A fellow Daughter of Aillira?"

"As you killed our sisters, knocking them off a tower to fall to their deaths."

My other blanched, sending a flicker of shame through me. "I had to. The Dragon was using them against us."

"The same way he's using you."

"He isn't. You don't understand." I looked down at my sweat-stale tunic, missing my armor. "I was weak, broken. Draki helped me. He freed me."

"No, death-bringer." Sursha's eyes were twin moons in the faint light. "You have no idea what it is to be broken. But you will. For what you did to our sisters, to Glasnith. For allying with the Dragon against your own people, I will teach you."

She dug into the satchel at her side and dropped handfuls of white thorns in my lap. Half of them rolled off, hitting the floor with a *clink-clink-clink* that sounded like rain falling, like blood dripping, like everything I'd run from, circling around to catch me once more.

Sursha pinned me down and tore open the back of my tunic. "Be sure to scream loud, so the Wolf Lord can hear you."

⚔

"What if I'm captured?" I ask Draki as I stand in the feasting hall in my scaled armor, preparing to sail to the rocky isles of Skerrey. My first time acting as his death-bringer in another nation.

"It would be quite a feat to build a prison that could hold you," he says with a touch of pride. "But if it happened, you would be ransomed or tortured for information. Likely both."

"Have you ever been tortured?"

He looks at me like I'm daft. "Of course not. I've never been caught, and I cannot be harmed. But I will tell you the secret to resisting: It is all in your mind. Leave your body behind. Tell yourself what's happening isn't real, that what's in your head is all there is, and transport your consciousness somewhere else."

"It's that simple?"

"It isn't simple at all. Most men fail. It took my brother a great deal of time and practice to master this skill, and he hated me for what I forced him to endure, even though it kept him alive. But you—you're a powerful soul-reader. When the pain begins, turn your consciousness inward. Hide within your own soul. Live there as long as you must. And wait."

"For what?"

He tips my chin up, running a finger down my neck. "For me to rescue you."

"Will you?"

He leans close to my ear and whispers, "Only if you deserve it."

Memories swirled around me, and I used them to block out everything Sursha did, every question or demand she made. My body existed on another plane, and I was separate from it, safe inside my soul. Waiting for Draki, even though I knew he wasn't coming.

What finally drew me back to reality was Reyker, damn him. The touch of his hands, the cadence of his voice, so familiar my other could not stand it. She forced us to wake.

To pain.

I lay on my stomach on the stone floor, shivering, spasming, with thorns buried in my back. The pain-wielder had reopened the healed skin of my scars. Rivulets of blood ran down my sides, pooling around me. Enough to make my head fuzzy, but not enough to be dangerous.

"This is my gift," Sursha was saying. "Don't ask for my help if you aren't going to let me use it."

Reyker held me down, keeping my twitching muscles from rolling me over and making everything worse. "I never asked for *this,*" he said. "I told you to use restraint, to scare her rather than hurt her."

"She looks scared to me."

"Go! Go back to New Fjullthorp and fetch the healer."

If not for the wards, I could have used the goddess Leggi's gift to heal myself, but even bleeding and woozy, I doubted Reyker would let me out of the cell. He began removing the thorns, one by one, and though his fingers were gentle, I cried out.

Then I was drifting again.

The branches of the thorntree sway above us. The ruins are so quiet. My head lies on Reyker's chest, his heart thumping beneath my ear.

A dream. This memory is from a dream.

"I want to kill them," I say. "Draki. Madoc. Sursha. Everyone who ever hurt you."

His arm tightens around me. "I felt the same when your father took the knout to you. I couldn't breathe, couldn't think straight. Being at the mercy of the pain-wielder was nothing compared to that. The only pain I can't survive is yours."

"Lira? Can you hear me?"

This time it was a different voice, different hands, that woke me. Sursha was gone, and in her place was another Daughter of Aillira.

"Mabyn." The blood-healer who'd helped me free our sisters in Stalwart Bay. Her neck was adorned with the same sort of collar Sursha had worn. "You're here too? What, did the Renegades raid Glasnith and steal Draki's leftovers?"

"Just one Renegade, actually." Her eyes slanted to Reyker, who watched from the corner of the cell with his arms crossed. "I healed the damage Sursha did. How do you feel?"

"Fine." It wasn't until after I'd sat up that I noticed I was half naked, bare to the waist. I suppressed the urge to cover myself—what did it matter, when the Wolf Lord had seen it all before?—and was rewarded when Reyker spun to face the wall like a blushing maiden.

Mabyn had a wet rag in her hand, and she helped me scrub the drying blood away before passing me a clean tunic.

"What is this?" She pointed at the Star of the Dragon carved on my chest, but I pulled my tunic over it. The healer grabbed my arm, lifting my skin into the sparse sunlight leaking through the roof to examine my wrist—the Star of the Dragon, carved over pink swirls of healed burns. "Where is your *skoldar?*"

I snatched my arm out of Mabyn's grip. "The serpent-goddess removed it."

"Removed?" Reyker turned back, pushing off the wall. "That's not possible. You would have died."

"The blood of the Fallen Ones protected me."

Reyker dropped to his knees and tilted my head to the side, fingers tracing the scars behind my ears. I pushed him, but he was already up, wide-eyed, his lips moving soundlessly. Mabyn drew my hair aside and leaned in to see what had left the Wolf Lord speechless.

She touched the scars. "Dear gods," she breathed. "The marks. They're writhing like spiders. How are they moving if they're cut into her skin?"

"They were made with Ildja's ice dagger," I said.

Mabyn searched the rest of my body, locating the other marks. I felt the scars recoil every time she prodded one. "I'm going to help you, Lira," Mabyn said, pressing her palm against my chest. "I'm going to rid you of them."

"Wait!" Reyker lunged to stop her. "This is god magic. If you meddle, we have no idea what will happen. It could kill her. It could kill you."

"We have to do something. Lira is being compelled. Draki is controlling her."

"He is not," I said.

My other was bolstered. *You see? Draki shaped us into his own creation. This is not who we are, it's who he forced us to be.*

Reyker shook his head. "I've never seen anything like this. I don't know what the Dragon did to her. We cannot risk attempting to fix her until we understand more about these marks."

"I don't need to be fixed." Draki's proclamations, the praise he'd given me over and over, spilled from my mouth: "I am perfection. I am the Dragon's death-bringer. I am as close as a mortal can be to a god."

"What you are," Reyker said, "is a liar, a traitor, a killer. And now, my prisoner. My responsibility. So if there's a way to heal you, I will do it." His gaze, like his voice, was a contradiction—soft and hard, all at once. "Whether you want it or not."

CHAPTER 11

All the magiskas crowded around the death-bringer, observing her, consulting on her condition. They kept calling her by name: *Lira* this, *Lira* that. Reyker didn't use her name. It sounded wrong, and it turned his mind into a tangled mess just hearing it.

It was the young spell-caster who solved the riddle. Eathalin touched the death-bringer's marks—those squirming ridges of scar tissue stamped across her body—and felt the strength of the spell, traces of power not of the mortal world. "This is not compulsion," she said. "It's a fracturing of Lira's true self, allowing the darkest parts of her consciousness, parts Draki has cultivated in his own image, to take control."

What Reyker heard was what he'd already believed—that the girl had fallen victim to Draki's ploys. She was a fool if she'd expected more from the Dragon.

The death-bringer cursed and shoved at them, swearing she was fine, she was perfect, she was a mortal goddess.

Outside, with the door shut on the death-bringer's shouts, Eathalin said, "These marks cannot be healed. They can only be contained, through blood magic." Her gaze went to Reyker. "She needs your *skoldar*."

"What? You think the power in my blood can compete with that?" He waved a hand at the cell. "She's covered in dragon stars cut into her flesh by a half god with a divine weapon."

"You are a divine weapon." The spell-caster was young and small in stature, but she had the presence of a sage priestess. "Your mark, your blood, will loosen the Dragon's hold on her. It will give her a chance to fight. She can do the rest."

"Find someone else."

"There is no one else," Alane said.

Eathalin nodded at the other women. "They are all bound to one another, every god-gifted sister having marked a fellow Daughter of Aillira. As I marked you." She touched the scar on Reyker's wrist where she'd cut a spiral above a crescent moon, the Glasnithian symbol of spellcasting. A precaution Eathalin had offered him, one he'd accepted since Draki had nearly cut a dragon star into his face. "You were bound to Lira. Though her *skoldar* was removed, you can mark her again."

He shook off Eathalin's hand. "I don't want to be bound to her."

"You owe us this much, Wolf Lord," the soft-spoken healer said. "You stole us from our island and convinced us to fight for you. Now save our sister from the Dragon's sorcery, as she saved all of us."

Her words cut at his conscience, shaming him, but he would not give in. "If there is another way to help, I will find it, but I won't . . . I can't . . ."

He hadn't understood the first time he'd marked her, not until he washed ashore in her home village and she found him, touched him—the *skoldar* was a tether, linking their senses, drawing them together no matter where they went.

"You must do this, or she will be trapped this way until death," Eathalin said.

"I will not bind myself to the death-bringer. Not again."

Before the magiskas could argue and beg and sink him deeper in guilt, he walked off into the trees, over the ashes of long-dead witches, women who had died to protect the world they loved. People more honorable than he would ever be.

The caravel sent to retrieve Brokk returned that night. A scout spotted its sails and Reyker decided to make himself scarce, too distracted to deal with the fallout of stealing magiskas from their allies, too ashamed to face the friend he'd stranded there. He left New Fjullthorp, rowing across the slim stretch of sea to Volva Isle, where he passed the hours walking from one shore to the other, while Vengeance plodded after him, keeping him company. Back and forth, planning out the Renegades' next strike, trying to predict Draki's next move.

Pondering how to make the death-bringer recover the memory he needed. If it would be easier to give her his damned *skoldar* and ask nicely.

He didn't notice his feet carrying him through a stone archway into a circle of megaliths. Not until Vengeance whickered in warning, and he was struck by the sensation that he was not alone. In front of him was a woman, standing at a stone altar.

This was where the volvur had performed their rituals.

"Who are you?" he called. Leaves were tangled in her hair. She was covered in layers of dirt, so he couldn't tell how old she was. Her eyes were glassy, unseeing. A hole gaped in her chest, a mortal wound that did not bleed.

Desiccated. Dead, yet not.

There were rumors about this stone circle. That it had once been a doorway to the gods' realms, like the loch in the Grove of the Fallen Ones, and this had left an imprint of power upon the space. A curse. That anyone unlucky enough to die here would be damned, their body stuck in permanent stasis in the mortal realms, unable to be burned or remain buried, and their soul would be dragged down to the shadows of Ildja's Mist, regardless of guilt or innocence.

More undead women stood around the rim of the circle, their bodies in the same shape as the one before him. Despite their sightless eyes, they all seemed to be focused on him.

His hand rose, even though he hadn't told it to. It touched the woman's arm. She did not move, but he felt a shift in the air. A shift inside himself, like something inching closer. His palm, where it rested on the woman's tattered sleeve, grew cold. That coldness wended its way up his shoulder, along his neck, piercing his mind.

All at once, he was swept backward in time, dropped into a body that was not his own.

There are corpses everywhere, piled around the stone circle. Women. Dead volvur. The kin of the woman whose memory I inhabit. I look up at the sky, where the sun should be, but it has not risen. This is the day of night. Solmangler.

Draki's face appears before me, drenched in blood, none of it his own. He pins me—the woman—down on the altar. "Come here, Reyker," he says, holding out his sword. "You must be the one to kill her."

Behind him is a blond boy of fourteen.

Me. The boy I used to be.

"I won't do it," the boy says, trying to pull away, but two Dragonmen hold him in place.

The boy stares at me—at the volva. Then, abruptly, the sword is in the boy's hands. He raises it, trembling. Draki roars in his ear.

The boy brings the blade down.

Reyker jerked back, his arm falling away from the volva's body.

The Magiska Massacre was not just a story he'd heard. He had been here. A witness. A participant in the slaughter, though he didn't remember it.

"I didn't hurt you," he told the undead volva, willing it to be true. "I was a boy in that memory. A child. I wouldn't have done such a thing then, not even if Draki threatened me."

But he didn't know that, did he? He wouldn't unless he let himself see the rest of the memory. Unless he made himself confront one of the nightmares he had suppressed.

"It won't change anything. It won't help you."

The volva didn't move. She didn't blink.

Reyker couldn't unmake the mistakes of his past. "I'm sorry," he told her, because there was nothing else he could do. He left the volva to go back to the rowboat, to get off this slab of land tainted by his sins. Though the islet was no bigger than a village and he'd traversed it many times, he couldn't find the path. Maybe Solvei was right, and the death-bringer's presence had scrambled his wits.

"You know the way, don't you?" he asked Vengeance. When the horse snorted and turned, he followed. It was several minutes before he realized Vengeance was leading him to the girl. "Oh, you traitor," he said as the cell came into view, but Vengeance pushed her muzzle into his back, urging him forward.

He heard a *thump*, something pounding on the cell from within. It spurred him into a run.

Reyker unlocked the door and cracked it open. There was the death-bringer, standing on the other side. He slipped in and slammed the door, but the girl calmly continued to ram herself against it as if he weren't there.

"Stop, magiska," he said, blocking her.

"I've been away from the Dragon too long. I must go to him." She spoke like someone trapped in a dream, her eyes fixed on the door as if it was the only thing she could see. She charged at it again and ran straight into Reyker.

He pinned her against his chest. "Why must you go to him?"

"Because he is my savior. My master. My god."

Reyker closed his eyes. This was not the girl he had known. Even at her most deceitful, she would never give up her sense of self, never bow like a beggar at anyone's feet.

"Lira?" Her name on his lips made him shudder. "Are you in there somewhere, or did he vanquish you?"

She blinked, and her gaze cleared. Her voice was no more than a wisp. "Help me." Another blink, and she was gone.

But Reyker had seen her—not the death-bringer, not Jarl Lira of Drakin. Lira of Stone, who'd dragged him out of the harbor, who'd kept him from giving up hope after her people enslaved him. The girl who'd healed his soul. Despite what she'd done since, that girl was worth saving.

"All right," he said—to her, to the volva, to the gods. "You win."

It wasn't instant. It was the slow seeping of sand through fingers, of water through a sieve. It was the careful peeling away of so many layers that had been tied around my eyes and heart and mind.

Draki was still there. He always would be, his claim on me fortified by the blood and weapons of gods, too powerful to be severed. But the hooks he'd dug into me had loosened, the noise passing through the cord between us muted.

Left in its place was me. Whoever that was.

I didn't trust it at first, this new perception. It felt like a trick, a rug that could be jerked out from beneath me. But as the hours passed, and my awareness remained, I sank into it and released a sigh that had been building inside my lungs for months. I could sense Reyker through the *skoldar*. It had forged a bond between us, and he pulled against it like a sparkfly trapped in a spider's web.

My fingers traced the curves of the cuts scabbing along my wrist, shaped like a flame—like the Dragonman tattoo above Reyker's right eyelid. The wound throbbed, and I relished it, this mark that had opened the lock on my cage, binding me to the man I loved so madly I'd been willing to destroy us both just to keep him alive. For the first time in many moons, I prayed for something other than power. To the Green Gods. To the Ice Gods. Thanking the fates that I'd found my way back to myself.

Then, on the heels of this buoyant gratitude, came the tightening grip of guilt, the slow sink of despair. The things I had done for Draki. The violence I'd enacted, the deaths I'd dealt, all at his behest. Though I'd been under his spell, it was my hands wielding the ice dagger that tore open a hole between worlds and loosed Ildja's demons on entire nations. It was my gifts that scorched and ravaged and broke apart kingdoms.

I pressed my hands against my ears, but the screams I heard were in my mind. Cries for mercy that I disregarded. Cries of pain that I ignored. I screamed back, begging forgiveness, offering apologies that were far too late. I saw the horrified faces of Skerrians, Dunians, and Aukians as they fell, looking back at me, realizing what I was. The death-bringer.

"No!" I slammed my palms into the wall. "I am not the death-bringer."

My guilt could not mend what I'd torn. Regret meant nothing to the dead. Draki had crushed me beneath his will, and if I surrendered to shame, I was still giving him control. The Dragon made me a weapon. He made me his monster. I could use that. I could avenge those I'd hurt.

I could avenge myself for all the ways he'd violated me in body, mind, and soul.

"Draki!" I stood and beat my fists against the stones in a fit of fury that drowned out every other emotion. "I am coming for you. Do you hear me! I will be the end of you."

Though it was distant, muffled by the space between us and the rampart of my *skoldar*, I heard the Dragon laugh.

CHAPTER 12

REYKER

Gods aflame. He couldn't find his shelter.

In the hours since he'd cut his *skoldar* into Lira's wrist, he'd been remembering more about their time together, but other things had grown foggier. He'd been wandering around New Fjullthorp in the dark, circling one wooden shack after another. It didn't make sense—he'd been staying here for months. How could he suddenly forget which one was his?

Perhaps this was the gods' payback for helping the death-bringer.

Footsteps made him turn. It was late, and the only people awake were the scouts and sentries. "Couldn't sleep," he said to the sentry walking up to him. "Thought I'd stretch my legs." The sentry was tall and broad, practically a giant. He must be new, one of Solvei's recruits.

The man swung a meaty fist at Reyker.

Reyker ducked beneath the giant's arm and slammed a palm into his nose, then kicked the backs of his knees. The giant went down, and Reyker braced his arm against the man's throat. Another sentry heard the scuffle and shouted for the jarl.

Solvei was there in seconds, clothed and armed as if she slept in her leathers, dreaming of battles.

"Lagorsson!" The jarl put her sword to his neck. "Let him go or I'll send you to Sjaf before your time."

"He attacked me," Reyker said, but he loosened his hold enough to let the giant breathe. "He could be a Dragonman sent to infiltrate our forces."

Solvei's laughter was brittle at the edges. "Is this some ridiculous game between the two of you? Pretending you are enemies and playing at killing each other?"

The giant coughed. "Doesn't feel like playing. He broke my gods-damned nose. Get off me, Wolf Lord."

Reyker released the man and stepped away. "Why did you attack me? Who are you?"

Solvei and the giant shared a look. They spoke at once, asking if this was a joke, if he'd taken a hit to his skull, if he was drunk. Reyker glared at them. "No to all three."

"I came to punch your teeth in," the giant said, "because you drugged me and left me to rot on Glasnith, at the mercy of our supposed allies, who you betrayed! You stole their magiskas like your bastard brother does. You took Alane away from me." The giant's cheeks reddened.

Reyker shook his head. He had done these things, yet his recollections of them were faded and faint, as if they'd happened long ago. "Who is Alane?"

The giant lunged at Reyker. Solvei pulled him back. "Do you truly not remember this man, Lagorsson?" she asked.

Reyker studied the giant's features. "I do not."

The giant huffed and Solvei smacked his chest. "Something is wrong with him, Brokk. Something has been wrong with him since the day we destroyed Dragon's Lair." She turned to Reyker. "Where are you from, Lagorsson?"

"What?"

"The village you were raised in. What was it called? Answer me."

"Vaknavangur. You know this. Why are you—"

"And your parents?" Solvei pressed. "What were their names?"

"Lagor and Katrin." Saying their names aloud was a thing he rarely did, and it sounded wrong, profaning what should be sacred, like cursing in a temple.

"How old are you, Wolf Lord?"

He opened his mouth, but nothing came out. He knew. *Of course* he knew. And yet, somehow, he didn't.

"Who lived in your village with you and your parents?" the jarl asked. "Can you name anyone else?"

Reyker could see them, the men's heads falling beneath the executioner's axe the day Draki invaded Vaknavangur. He could see the women and children rounded up, screaming, weeping, forced to watch their fathers and husbands and brothers die. Every face was there. He had memorized them, spoken their names each night for years—a prayer for their souls, a promise to avenge them. But he couldn't name a single one of them now.

Her questions kept coming, demanding details about his childhood, his time as a Dragonman, his time as a Renegade. Some things he remembered clearly, but others were hazy or blank, yawning black holes in his mind. Each gap felt like a small death he held within himself, a vast field pocked with graves.

"What were your parents' names?" the jarl asked again.

"I already told you. Lagor and . . . and . . ."

Oh. Gods. The hole caved inward until it was a crater, devouring everything around it. His mother. His beautiful, beloved, dead mother. Her name, lost to that crumbling pit.

Reyker wrapped his hand around her wedding ring, tucked in the pocket of his coat. His knees buckled.

"Get some sleep, Lagorsson," Solvei said. "I'll have the healer and the spell-caster take a look at you in the morning." She put a hand on his shoulder, but it did little to lessen the blow of her words. "Until we sort this out, I'm removing you from your duties. You are no longer commander."

The lock clicked open, and I sat up.

The man who entered my cell was so big he barely fit through the doorway. He stood in the middle of the cell, a wooden spear in one hand and a warded shield in the other, looking down at me. "You're the one causing all this trouble? Awfully small to be such a savage gods-damned killer."

"Appearances can be deceiving." I studied him, too, the nagging familiarity of him: his skin a shade browner than even the most tanned Iseneldish natives, the ginger streaks in his thick black hair, the glint of compassion in his eyes. The foul mouth. "How many people assume you're a brute because of your size, Brokk?"

Brokk nearly dropped his weapon. "My best friend doesn't know me, but you do. Through his eyes, I suppose. His soul. Lagorsson is my lord, but he is also like a brother to me. I'll do whatever I must to get him back."

"Back from where?" I tried and failed to keep my voice steady.

"You aren't the death-bringer."

"I was." I lifted my wrist so he could see the fresh cuts of my *skoldar*. "Until Reyker released me. Now tell me what's happened to him."

Brokk paused, regarding me. A few beats of silence passed before he sat, taking up a quarter of the cell with his bulk. "No one knows. Mabyn couldn't heal him, couldn't even figure out what's ailing him. Eathalin believes it's a spell, twisting his soul, rotting it from within. Eating it like the gods-damned serpent-goddess, only he's not dead yet. He's been a different man since he went after the Dragon on Season's Eve. You were there. Did Draki do this to him? Or was it you, soul-reader?"

Bile rose in the back of my throat. I wanted to deny Brokk's accusation, but I couldn't. "Reyker's sickness is my fault."

Brokk listened as I explained what took place on Season's Eve. The vision I saw, in the seeress's soul, of Reyker dying. The deal I'd struck with Draki to keep Reyker safe. How I'd used the gift I'd been born with—enhanced by the Fallen Ones' blood in my veins and altered in ways I didn't understand by Eyvor, formerly the keeper of souls—to implant false memories so Reyker would think I'd betrayed him. And then, to ensure he would stay away, I'd woven a spell to make him forget me. "I've never created a spell before. Something must have gone wrong."

"Can you undo it?" Brokk asked, running a hand through the scruff of his beard.

"I can try, if he'll let me."

"Oh, he'll let you, if I have to sit on him and beat him senseless first."

A small laugh escaped me, the first one in a long while, and Brokk grinned.

There was a peculiar bond stretching between me and this man I'd only just met, written across our hearts rather than carved into flesh, one that burned as brightly as the affection we shared for Reyker. "He's lucky to have you looking out for him," I said.

Brokk grunted. "He's a lucky bastard, all right. Here's hoping that luck doesn't run out."

CHAPTER 13

LIRA

Brokk didn't have to sit on Reyker, but he had threatened and practically dragged his friend toward the cell. I hadn't been outside in days, and despite the ropes binding my wrists and ankles, despite the snow on the ground and the sickly sun overhead, it was a relief. Renegades surrounded me on all sides, wooden weapons trained on me. Jarl Solvei was there, with Sursha at her side. They all watched me like I might turn rabid and attack them.

Reyker stood several paces away, refusing to look in my direction.

"You told him?" I asked. Brokk nodded. As if Reyker didn't have enough fabricated reasons to hate me, now he had real ones. Not that he could tell the lies from the truth, thanks to what I'd done. "I'm sorry—"

"I don't want to hear it." Reyker's tone held the force of a slap. "Just repair what you broke and find the memory that tells me how to kill Draki, so I can get back to fighting this war."

He had every right to be angry, and I had no right to hold it against him. I did anyway.

"What I did saved your life. It was awful, but I don't regret it."

"Of course you don't. Just as you don't regret making me your clan's slave or throwing me into a cursed loch so your gods could pick me apart. As long as I live, it doesn't matter what happens to me or how I feel about it. My choices mean nothing to you."

"Do you actually remember those things, or did someone else tell you about them?" I glared at Brokk.

Brokk cleared his throat. "This is an argument best saved for another time."

Tension fueled the silence between Reyker and me, the awkwardness worsened by the audience of Renegades, until I could no longer stand it. "I can't do anything with you over there. To enter your soul, I have to touch you."

Reyker sat sideways in front of me, his head and body angled away. "Get on with it."

This was the first time I'd seen him since he gave me his *skoldar* and lifted the veil Draki had thrown over my senses. Everything I felt for him had snapped back into place—I wanted to pull him to me, to kiss the scowl from his mouth, but I'd lost that right.

My fingers grazed the warm skin below his collarbones, and we both shivered. My palm slid under his tunic to settle on his chest, over his heart, the powerful muscle kicking against my hand. When I closed my eyes and tried to transfer my consciousness into his soul, I hit a barricade. "You have to let me in."

Reyker gritted his teeth. "Fine."

The barrier dissolved, and I detached from my body. The sky in his soul was red, streaked with blue lightning. I fell through it, into the steep, sheer-walled canyon, landing atop the black river that split the canyon in half, the fused elements of water and fire roiling under me.

After I'd woven the spell to make him forget, the canyon had cracked and half the jewels sticking from the rock—the bits of Reyker's soul that contained his memories—broke free, sinking to the bottom of the river. I could sense them there, below the surface.

I reached for one, slipping my hand beneath the curling black waves. My fingers closed around a jewel's rough edges, and Reyker's memory surrounded me.

The ice sheet covering the pond crunches beneath my boots. Father kneels beside me, nodding as I dig down with the chisel until it punches through to the water below. He hands me my spear. I wait quietly until a trout swims by. The fish is fast, but not as fast as me.

Father smiles as I pull the trout free from the hole in the ice.

"Did you teach Aldrik to ice fish too?" I ask.

Father's smile fades. "He never had the patience for such things."

I sit back on my knees, gutting the fish with my knife. "I miss him. I wish he hadn't left to join Gudmund's army. I wish he'd come home."

"Reyker." Father's tone makes me go still. When I look at him, his brows are furrowed, his mouth pinched into a grim line. "I brought you out here to tell you this. You must stop waiting for him. Aldrik isn't coming home. Your brother is dead."

A flash of lightning streaked around me. A quake shook the canyon. More fissures formed in the walls, and several jewels fell from the crumbling rock, splashing into the river. Disappearing into its dark depths.

Bloody fates.

He was forgetting everything.

I had done this to him, and that meant I could undo it. I would fix what I'd broken. Seeking the threads of the gift Eyvor granted me, I pressed my hands to the cliff wall. "Heal," I whispered, pushing the energy effervescing inside me out through my palms. It flowed from my fingertips like a stream of tiny violet stars.

"Restore."

The stars drifted along the canyon, coating its walls and the river in glowing constellations.

"Remember."

The light brightened.

The canyon groaned, the cracks in it widening. A rockslide cascaded down the walls, carrying more jewels in a cloud of dust. The jewels hit the black water and sank.

"I said *heal*." A wave of stars burst out of me, dancing across the holes in Reyker's soul. Not healing. Not fixing. "You have to trust me, Reyker. You have to give me control or I can't help you."

His voice thundered from the sky. *How am I supposed to trust you after everything you've done? My memories tell me you're a liar, a manipulator. You tell me that's a spell you planted. Neither truth inspires trust.*

"Please, Reyker. You must."

I cannot conjure trust where none exists, no more than I can conjure anger, or fear, or love. Can you?

Panicked laughter bubbled up my throat. The only way to undo the spell was to convince Reyker he could trust me, but the spell was designed to keep him from ever trusting me.

His words from that fateful day when I'd poisoned his soul floated back to me like a vengeful ghost: *You cannot do this to me. I will never forgive you!*

"No," I said, leaning my head against the crumbling canyon wall. "You never will."

Everything.

That's what he was going to lose. Every last memory. Every fragment of who he was. Because of her. He could still see her face, when she'd told him. Pale and pitying. Why hadn't he forgotten *that* yet?

If you'd just trust me, she'd said. *If you'd just let me in . . .*

Like this was his fault.

Yes—yes, it *was* his fault for ever trusting her. Draki had tried to teach him this lesson, to rely on no one but himself. For once, he should have listened to his brother.

He swore he could sense it, an emptying inside him, a hole carved straight through his center. He needed to fill it, to feel something. Anything.

He ran to the shore, where mist swirled in a gauzy gown over the smooth skin of the sea. Heedless of ice sharks, he stripped off his clothing, his weapons, and waded into the freezing water, diving beneath the surface. He swam underwater until his lungs burned, and then he drifted up, turning to float on his back.

Above him, the sky-well came to life, green and violet ribbons dancing through the dark. He stared into them, waiting to see a flash of his future painted across the stars, as he had before. But this time they were only colors and light, telling him nothing.

Because that was his future. Nothing.

Who was he without his past? Why did anything matter if he wouldn't remember it once it was over?

The cold seeped into him, a bone-deep ache, but it wasn't enough. He needed to feel more.

He still couldn't remember where his gods-damned shelter was. When he opened the one he thought was his, he found a young woman. She was crouched on the floor, sharpening a knife. There was a pile of sharp instruments scattered around her that made his skin prickle with a lost memory. He knew the girl, but he couldn't remember from where. Her name, their history, had been eaten by the void.

"Sorry," he said, backing out of the door as she looked up. "I didn't mean to intrude."

"Didn't you?" She glanced at him—his damp trousers, his bare feet and chest, his hair dripping seawater. "You must have come here for something."

She beckoned him in. When he didn't move, she grabbed his arm and pulled him inside, shutting the door behind him.

"I got lost," he said. The words sounded stupid. He felt stupid. He should leave, but the woman was blocking the door, the knife still in her hand.

"You know what I think, Westlander?" She had a smile like a fox, seductive and sly and dangerous. "I think you're in love with pain, just as I am. You crave your own destruction. That's why you came here tonight. That's why you brought me here, isn't it? Not for the Renegades or the war. For you. Because no one else can hurt you the way you want to be hurt."

She drew the knife lightly over his shoulder, across his collarbones, his chest, his stomach. Scratches formed, tiny droplets of blood blooming. The sting was almost pleasant. The woman traced the scrapes with a fingertip, her sly smile tinged with desire.

Reyker had tried to take women to his bed over the last months, but he'd never made it through the door of his shack. Something had always stopped him. A ghost. A dream.

Lira. Even when he couldn't remember her, she'd been there, haunting him.

Not anymore. He would forget her soon enough. He would forget everything. And if he couldn't remember, there was no longer such a thing as consequences. No regret. Nothing but this moment. What he felt. What he wanted to feel.

Something. Pleasure, pain—it was all the same to him, as long as it filled the emptiness left by everything he'd lost.

He put his hand on the woman's waist, drawing her closer.

"Hurt me," he whispered, bringing his lips close to hers. "Destroy me."

His boots crunched over the icy ledge. Below him, the heart of the Mountain of Fire churned. Smoke billowed up, filling the crater, curling around him in spirals. Displays of the depths of Ildja's fury. "Careful, Mother," he said. "You'll melt your home's lovely décor."

Ildja's face was as red as lava, and Draki wondered if steam was about to shoot from her nostrils. "You let the death-bringer go."

"Yes."

Magma spurted up from the hole, splatting against the glacier's floor. Ice sizzled and liquefied around his boots.

"Why?" Ildja demanded.

Why, why, why? He had asked himself that question many times. There were too many possible answers.

Though her mind submitted to my will, her heart would not.

I could not bear to look at her anymore, knowing she would never truly belong to me.

After everything I did for her, everything I offered . . . She. Still. Chose. Him.

"The experiment failed," he said. "I found another use for her."

Or so Draki had thought. He'd offered her to Reyker, thinking his brother would slip, that Reyker would see Katrin's ring on her finger while his mother's home village burned around him, and he would kill her in a fit of battle-madness. Murdering the woman he loved. The final blow that would tip Reyker so far into his own darkness he would never claw his way back out.

But instead of killing her, Reyker had given her another *skoldar*.

"Her only use," Ildja said, "is that she carries the blood of the Fallen Ones. This is what we have waited for. We have the key to the prison-realm. We have the vessel. All we need is to wait for the cosmos to align at midnight on Solmangler, when our powers will be at their strongest, and Gwylor can open a rift in the sky-realm that will obscure the sun indefinitely. You must find the girl so you can be ready to take her gifts for yourself, along with the rest of Aillira's cursed daughters."

"I know exactly where my death-bringer is. She's with him."

The goddess hissed. "Why must you make everything about your half brother? He's not even immortal! He'll die soon enough. Or I can end him—"

"No." His tone was too sharp. Ildja's eyes narrowed, and Draki dipped his head in contrition. "We've discussed this. With a bit more persuasion,

I can turn Lagor's son to my side. I will use him and the death-bringer to destroy the Renegades and each other."

Ildja cupped Draki's cheek, her fingers like icicles, her ember eyes burning into him. "You grew quite fond of your little pet. Promise me you can do what must be done. Promise me that when the time comes, when the sun does not rise and the power of the stone circle is at its strongest, you will kill her."

His mind flitted back to that day in the Blood Ring, that brief moment when Lira's rage had eclipsed her morality and she'd allowed herself to kiss him. It had been such a pure thing, exquisite in its desperation, all-encompassing in its hunger. He had thought it was the first true spark of passion between them, and he'd been right. But it was also the last.

Did he want her so badly because she was the one thing he could not have? Or because the one thing she truly wanted was his brother?

"I will." He met Ildja's gaze. When he first came here in search of his mother, he was barely a man. He'd tromped across the glacier and climbed into the crater, screaming the goddess's name. Though he'd been half-frozen, half-starved, half-mad, Ildja had looked him over, giving a stiff nod. *Yes*, she'd said. *You are mine.*

She did not deny him or turn him away. Ildja saw promise where Draki's father had only ever seen an evil to keep shackled. Ildja did not love him—Reyker was the only one who ever had—but she took care of him. She trained him herself, and Ildja had taught him well, not just how to wield his powers over others, but how to calm his own mind, control his own will. Wanting was weakness. Desire could ruin a man, even one who was part god.

Draki would not be free until he was rid of the girl.

"When all is ready," he said, "we will strike. Reyker will suffer." His brother's agony would not end until Reyker shattered. Draki would put the pieces back together, shaping his brother into an invulnerable conqueror, a commander of kings. A god to stand beside him.

Then Draki's family would be whole.

"Lira." Draki rolled her name on his tongue, as if he could taste her blood, feel her life draining away. "Lira's fate will come full circle. On Solmangler, we will reignite the immortal war and she will die as she was always meant to. As a god's sacrifice."

PART TWO
DARKNESS DESCENDING

CHAPTER 14

LIRA

The leather bands circling my wrists, ankles, and neck chafed, but at least I wasn't tied up. Eathalin gave me an apologetic look, even though it wasn't her fault. All she did was design the runic wards on the bands—the same ones that were carved in my cell—on Solvei's orders. It was the only way the jarl would agree to let me out of my prison.

We climbed into the rowboat. Alane took one of the oars and Mabyn took the other. They had come with Eathalin to escort me to New Fjull-thorp, for support. Or perhaps those were Solvei's orders, too, that my gifted sisters be ready to take me down at the first sign that Draki still possessed my mind. Only a wisp of him lingered, spinning lazily through my head, dropping whispers into my thoughts that I finally had the strength to ignore.

"If the runes can cut off Lira's power," Alane said, "maybe Solvei can trap the Dragon after all."

"Trap him?" I asked. "How?"

"You'll see."

The rowboat touched ground on the island and I stepped ashore. As we made our way inland, we passed a large, cage-like contraption. I stepped closer to inspect it. The cage was unfinished, still open at the top.

It was covered in runes like the ones on the straps I wore, constructed of metal bars and—"Are those bones?" I asked. They were tied to every bar with lengths of rope. The cage was reminiscent of Draki's throne, and I backed away on instinct.

"Consecrated bones," Eathalin said. "From priests and magiskas Draki and his mother killed. And the iron is supposedly from the first mine in Iseneld, made by sons of Sjaf and blessed by the god of metal himself."

"Solvei means to try and imprison Draki inside this?" I shook my head. Shoving him in a box made of bones and praying it would hold was beyond foolish—it bordered on madness.

"Once she gets enough bones to finish it," Mabyn said. "It's a last resort."

Because what else was there to do? Without Reyker's memory, we were just guessing at ways to stop the Dragon, shooting arrows at an invisible target and hoping for a hit.

The four of us continued up the path to the village. New Fjullthorp was ten times bigger than Volva Isle, most of it taken up by wooden shacks. According to Alane, the Renegades numbered into the thousands, with more joining every day as the reputation of the jarl and the Wolf Lord spread across Iseneld. New Fjullthorp was their main base, and there were a few hundred Renegades milling about, talking, eating, drinking. It reminded me of the nomads and made me miss Garreth and Zabelle fiercely.

Every conversation stopped as Eathalin led me to the hovels the Daughters of Aillira shared. I spotted Sursha and Solvei, the two of them standing a little too close, their postures a bit too relaxed, to be merely a jarl and her favorite new magiska. If I'd had to put a name to it, I'd say they looked downright smitten with each other.

When they noticed me, Sursha smiled. Mabyn held my arm, like she could tell I was considering rushing over to punch the smirk off the pain-wielder's face.

There were others here I recognized from the battle at Gyldenhring. Their expressions were an assortment of rage, suspicion, and fear. How could I blame them? They knew me as Draki's death-bringer, hurling fire and water and steel at them. I'd killed their fellow warriors, their friends and families.

Unarmed, with the runes blocking my gifts, I was defenseless. A deer in a den of wolves.

I searched the crowd for Reyker, but he was nowhere to be seen.

The other Daughters of Aillira were waiting for us at the hovel. Keeva, the bone-healer, handed me a bowl of stew. "Welcome, soul-reader."

Not death-bringer, not Lira of Drakin.

Not ever again.

"Apparently everyone in Iseneld knows how to catch their dinner from the ocean," Alane said, settling beside me with her bowl. "Since no one else comes to the Haunted Isles, sea life is plentiful here. Between that and food the Renegades steal from the Dragonmen's ships and carriages, there's usually enough to go around."

The stew was rich and spicy, with chunks of crab, shark, and eel. In the cell, they'd only fed me hard bread and unseasoned fish. It was an effort not to tip my head back and slurp straight from the bowl.

A shout came from a young woman somewhere in the crowd behind us. "Dragon whore!"

I went still, the spoon stopping halfway to my mouth.

Eathalin and Mabyn blanched. Keeva gasped. Alane glared, looking for the source of the slur. Some of the Renegades laughed, others nodded. It started as a murmur, growing louder, until it was a full-blown chant echoing through my eardrums, beating against my bones. "Dragon whore. Dragon whore. Dragon whore!"

The stew in my belly threatened to come back up. I'd been through this before with the nomads, and with my own clan. Hated for my power. Hated for the men I gave my loyalty to.

Other cries followed.

"Kill the traitor!"

"Torture her until she tells us what she knows!"

Solvei watched her people, arms crossed, head cocked—the jarl wouldn't intervene on my behalf. There was no point trying to explain that Draki had stolen my loyalty, or to justify any of the things I'd done in his name. People calling for blood rarely listened to reason. There was nothing to do but be ready for whatever punishment the Renegades chose to dole out. If they attacked, the other Daughters of Aillira would defend me. But I preferred to defend myself. My fingers slipped beneath the thick leather on my wrists. Could I tear them off in time?

Alane started forward, like she was ready to take on all the Renegades herself. "Stuff it, the lot of you!"

"Enough." Brokk appeared behind her. His command carried across the wind, ringing out over the whole village until silence fell. "The soul-reader is no traitor. She was bewitched by the Dragon. Give her a chance to prove herself."

Among the Renegades there were whispers, shaking heads.

Brokk bounced the flat of his axe against his palm. "Anyone who seeks to harm the soul-reader must go through me."

"And me." Alane.

"And me." Eathalin.

Keeva, Mabyn, Bronagh. All the Daughters of Aillira, save Sursha, lifted their heads high and stood with me. I didn't have to ask why—they'd all felt the Dragon's spell. And most of them had fought at my side. We were sisters by gods and gifts, and sisters in battle. Though I wasn't certain I deserved their loyalty, I was grateful all the same.

A hundred sets of wary eyes turned away from me as the Renegades went back to their business. I sighed, unclenching my fingers from the leather bands.

"Thank you." My throat was so tight, it came out strained. "All of you."

Brokk nodded and sat down. Keeva handed him a bowl of stew, and he ate as if nothing was wrong, keeping his axe close at hand. The other Daughters of Aillira spread out, eating and chatting, but I noticed how they positioned themselves around me, facing the Renegades. Ensuring no one could sneak up on us.

I leaned toward Brokk. "The magiskas behave like soldiers. Did you train them?"

"Those who were here before I left," he said around a mouthful of food. "But mostly it was . . . well, you know."

"You can say his name."

"I'd rather not." His shoulders bunched, tension coiling beneath the muscles.

Something was very wrong between Brokk and Reyker, but it wasn't my place to ask. "Where did you come back from?"

"Stony Harbor. I believe you've heard of it." Brokk grinned at my expression. "I was your brother's hostage for a few weeks. Dear gods, I could hardly stand it. Glasnith's food is bland and the ale is weak—no offense—but at least the nomads know how to throw a grand party, and the Prince of Ghosts was quite cordial, under the circumstances."

Over the next hour, I made Brokk and the Daughters of Aillira tell me everything about their time in Stony Harbor, every detail about what happened after the battle of Stalwart Bay. Garreth was doing his best to rebuild our home village and keep the nomads and refugees safe, but between the Dragonmen and the lack of leadership, Glasnith was still in shambles. Even with Madoc dead, the chieftains of the stronger clans refused to recognize Garreth as Torin's heir, since he'd been exiled, and few were willing to ally with nomads. On top of his other concerns, Garreth had been ready to declare war with the Mountain Renegades after Reyker abducted the magiskas, but Brokk talked him down, with Zabelle's help.

Later that night, as the Renegades began to retire, Brokk walked me back to New Fjullthorp's beach, where the rowboats were. I hadn't bothered asking if I could stay in one of the hovels with the Daughters of Aillira. I didn't want to put them at risk, and I'd never feel safe there, surrounded by warriors who wanted to tear me into tiny pieces and send them to Draki with a bow on top. Better to sleep alone in a cold cell.

"There's something else you should know," Brokk said. "In the days before I left Stony Harbor, the nomads received word the Dragon was spotted in Glasnith, near the Boglands. He opened a rift into the Mist and let out a host of Destroyers."

I pressed a hand to my mouth. It was fitting that the horror I'd unleashed on other countries would be released on my own. "I should be there. Garreth needs me." Except I couldn't go back, not without risking

Veronis's wrath. My island, my brother, were in danger, and there was nothing I could do.

"Solvei won't let you leave. Besides, some of us want you here. And some need you, even those who won't admit it."

I kicked at the sand. "How is he?"

"Confused. Furious. Scared. He's always struggled with the beast inside him, but he used to be honest, honorable. Now . . . he's forgetting how to be those things. He's forgetting why he ever wanted to be those things in the first place."

By trying to save him, I'd been Reyker's undoing. And Draki had known it, hadn't he? This was what the Dragon had wanted all along. "If I don't stop it, we're going to lose him, Brokk. I could fix him, if he'd only let me. How do I get him to trust me again?"

He scratched at his beard. "If I figure that out, you'll be the first one I tell. Good night, magiska."

The Renegades wanted nothing to do with cursed Volva Isle. There was something wrong with the islet—I sensed it as I rowed across the strip of sea between it and New Fjullthorp, growing stronger as I walked up Volva Isle's shore. It was in the soil beneath my feet, in the wind whistling through the trees. An unholy presence, an imprint of tragedy. But the spirits of dead witches didn't frighten me. It was the living I had to worry about.

"I know you're here," I called as I entered the woods. "You gave me your *skoldar*, remember?"

Did he remember, or had he forgotten already?

"Is it true what they're calling you?" Reyker stepped out from the shadows and leaned against a tree, his eyes bright pools shimmering with moonlight. "Were you the Dragon's whore?"

Coming from him, the question startled me. It stumped me. I never lay with Draki, but he'd done intimate things to my body—in his bedchambers, and at the cottage by the fjords. I'd let him into my mind, into my soul. I gave myself to him in every other way. "If I say yes, you'll hate me more. If I say no, you'll call me a liar. Am I wrong?"

"No." He worked something between his fingers, the way some

people did with talismans or effigies of a god. As it spun from one finger to the next, I caught a gleam of silver, cut to look like petals. His mother's ring.

"I'm not his wife," I said. "I didn't marry the Dragon."

His pause was brief. "I don't care."

Now who was the liar? "Why are you on my island, Wolf Lord?"

"Your island." He laughed, tucking the ring into his coat. "The same reason you are. No one else comes here. No one bothers me. No one treats me with pity like I'm some lost child, or with fear like I'm going to turn into a mindless animal and try to eat them. *Will* I try to eat them, do you think?"

I snorted. "If you do, go for Brokk first. You'll be so stuffed the rest of us will have time to get away."

"Brokk? Who . . ." He shook his head. "It doesn't matter."

That's right—he'd already forgotten Brokk, his childhood companion, his closest friend. He'd forgotten most of the Renegades and Daughters of Aillira. He'd forgotten his parents' names, their faces. How long before he forgot me too? "I won't say I'm sorry for the hundredth time, because it only seems to infuriate you."

"Good. Then I won't have to ignore your feigned apologies for breaking my mind."

"Reyker."

"Don't." His voice dropped an octave. "Don't speak my name with that tone, like I was the sun shining on your world and you're in the dark without me. I'm not your sun, I'm not anyone's sun. I'm the dark. I'm the gods-damned storm that swallows up the light."

"That's what Draki made you. It's not who you are anymore."

"It's all I remember. Doesn't that make it true?"

Gods, we were back to this—back where we were when he washed up in Stony Harbor and I spent weeks, at the mystic's behest, attempting to redeem him. I'd only been able to lead Reyker to the light in his soul because he'd put his faith in me. He'd trusted me, loved me, as I'd loved him—deep down, where it took us both a while to recognize we were bonded by more than a shared purpose. By erasing his memories,

I'd erased his faith, his trust, his love. Without it, everything else fell to ruin.

"If you won't let me heal you," I said, "at least let me look for your memory of how to kill Draki." Shared purpose—perhaps we could start with that, build on it, as we had before. I held out my palm, a useless tool since the leather bands were blocking my gifts.

"Keep your meddlesome hands away from my soul, death-bringer."

He spun and stomped off through the woods, and I followed him. "Stop being childish."

"Me? You're the one—" Reyker halted, and I stumbled into him. In front of us was a gateway to a circle made of tall, pillar-like stones. It was strange. Familiar. A finger of dread ran up my spine and back down again.

There were people inside—twenty or so women, coated in grime, gathered around something in the circle's center. "Who are they?" I started toward the stones.

Reyker put his arm up to stop me. "Leave them be. These are the undead of Volva Isle."

The witches who'd died when Draki came here. Some of them never left.

"I recognize this place." I pointed at the pillars, at the bloodstained stone in the center that the undead had crowded around. "Before I killed Draki's seeress, I saw her visions. I saw myself inside this circle, floating above the altar."

"*That* altar? You're certain?"

I nodded, watching the witches. They were standing upright, yet they were still as statues, their eyes as empty and gray as slate. Made of flesh without blood, their bodies present but their souls gone. Damned. "Maybe I can help them. Maybe some of the power Eyvor gave me from her time as a soul-keeper could free them."

Reyker grabbed my wrist and tugged me away from the stones. "You will not enter that cursed circle. Not ever. You kill anyone who tries to take you inside it, understand?"

"Why?" I dug my heels into the dirt. "What happened there?"

"I don't . . . I can't . . ." He let go of me, taking a deep breath. Closing his eyes. "I have to. Stay here."

"Reyker?"

"Stay. Here." He walked cautiously through the archway, right up to the witches. "I'm ready," he said, as if they could hear him. "Show me."

He put his hand on one of the undead witches' arms.

CHAPTER 15

REYKER

He had to remember. It was his idea to bring the Renegades to the Haunted Isles, and there must have been a reason. If whatever happened to the volvur could happen to Lira, he had to know what it was. Whether she deserved it or not, he didn't want her death on his conscience.

What had Draki done on Volva Isle? What had Reyker done?

He put his hand out and touched the volva. This time, he did not slip inside the volva's memory. Instead, whatever power was left inside her, inside this cursed space, reached into him and ripped open his own memory of that day, unearthing the long-buried bones of his sins.

The sun did not rise today. By the time Draki's longships reach the Haunted Isles, the long night of Solmangler is nearing its peak—midnight, the darkest the world ever gets.

I've grown up hearing hearthside tales of the volvur who inhabit this place. How they geld their newborn sons, sacrifice their male lovers, eat their elders. As our ship draws closer to Volva Isle, I see the volvur, gathered along the shore where they've lit bonfires, holding hands as they watch us.

As one, they raise their linked hands toward the sky.

Though there is no sun, shadows rise from the bonfires, stretching taller and wider than our ships, twitching like living creatures. They break apart into tendrils that dart out and wrap around Dragonmen, crushing them, strangling them, dragging them over the railing. Some of the tendrils sprout jagged shadow teeth that close around the warriors, tearing them open just as easily as a wolf or an ice shark could.

One of the tendrils wraps around my calf, ripping my legs out from under me. I fall, and the shadow drags me along the deck. It's going to pull me into the sea and drown me. My fingers scrabble at the wood. I kick at the shadow, but it has no substance.

Then Draki is there, stomping on the shadow. It shrivels and breaks apart like puffs of smoke.

"Stay next to me, unless you wish to die today," he says. Draki pulls me up by the collar of my uniform. He doesn't let go as he moves back toward the bow. Shadow creatures attack the rest of the ships, but anytime one appears near ours, Draki grabs it and the shadow disappears.

Draki smiles at something on the island.

Behind the volvur, a giant column of fire rises. It splits into a hundred cords of flame that seek out the shadows, coiling around them. Smothering them.

The shadows clear. The volvur turn.

There stands a woman, her features illuminated by her fountain of fire. Her hair is redder than sunset, her complexion paler than ice. Her eyes are crimson and they gleam in a way that's eerie and beautiful and makes my teeth chatter. She wears silver-mottled serpents around both her wrists like bracelets, another on her neck like a torque.

Ildja. The serpent-goddess. Eater of souls.

Draki's mother.

The volvur raise their hands to attack Ildja with more shadows, but she calls up her flames and burns the shadows away as soon as they form.

Draki orders his men ashore. Those still living leap out of the longships, into the water. Draki pulls me along with him.

I step upon the shore, hating my brother, hating his soldiers, hating the leather armor strapped to my body. I look just like the rest of them, another one of the Dragon's lackeys.

The volvur have ceased fighting. They've backed up from the beach, clustering together between Draki's army and his mother. They have no weapons that I can see.

Draki moves out in front. "Surrender," he says, "and you will come to no harm."

One of the women walks away from the others to stand before Draki. She slaps him, raking her nails along his cheek. "Even if that were not a lie, volvur do not surrender, my son," she says.

The scratches on Draki's face heal in an instant, leaving behind dried streaks of blood. He grabs the woman by the neck. "I am not your son."

The cry from the volvur begins small, growing quickly, until it rings across the island from a hundred voices. "No surrender! No surrender!"

As one, the volvur rush at us, an unarmed army screaming out their rage.

The Dragonmen bring their swords up. Draki shouts at them to stand down, but before they can lower their blades, over half the women have run themselves through. My sword isn't even out, but a woman comes up beside me and pulls it free, falling upon it even as I try to stop her. I look at her, lying on the ground in a puddle of her own blood. She smiles up at me. This is her victory.

The Dragonmen manage to grab some of the women who haven't made it onto a blade yet. "Take them to the stone circle!" Draki orders, towing the volva who called him her son. "Bring my brother as well."

Two Dragonmen take hold of my arms, dragging me alongside the volvur.

When I reach the stone circle, Draki is there with his mother. "The volvur's gifts reside in their flesh," the goddess is telling him, "passed down on their deathbeds from one generation to the next. Consume the source of their strength and that strength becomes yours." She touches Draki's bloodstained cheek. "You will not need your healing powers because you will never bleed again."

"Do not do this, Aldrik," the woman who slapped Draki says. "When your mother left you here, we named you and took you in, even though you were a boy. We could have sacrificed you, but we raised you as one of us."

Draki's gaze trails over her and the rest of the volvur. "You raised Aldrik, and he was appreciative. But Aldrik is dead. You are not my kin. You are nothing to the Dragon."

There's no malice in his eyes, only hunger—killing the volvur is a means to an end.

"It must be done on the altar," Ildja says. "The stones were brought here from Gwylor's palace of death. They increase the power of the blood magic tenfold at midnight on Solmangler."

"And damn their souls," I whisper. That's how the story goes: those the volvur sacrifice upon this cursed altar on Solmangler, when the veil between worlds is at its thinnest, go straight to the Mist.

Ildja opens her hands in a gesture of indifference. "Yes. That too."

Draki pushes the volva down onto the altar. With his bare hands, he cracks her chest open so fast I almost miss it, shoving his fist into the gaping wound. Ripping out her heart.

It's still beating. The volva is dead, but her eyes are open, her mouth forming a prayer. She watches Draki take a bite of her heart.

Behind me, the volvur's screams are deafening. Draki shoves the heart in his mouth, and Ildja looks on in approval, her flame-red lips smiling. A strangled sound escapes me. When he's done with his meal, Draki takes the next volva, and the next. He eats the hearts of twenty women who were once like mothers and sisters to him.

A monster. My brother is a monster.

I knew it when he stabbed our father, when he executed everyone in Vaknavangur, when he cut his dragon star into my mother and made her his thrall. But after all that, some part of me still refused to believe every trace of Aldrik was gone.

Draki stands there with the blood of a coven dripping down his chin, remorseless. Invigorated. He's grown taller, broader, his muscles expanding as the volvur's life force flows into him. His eyes glow with power.

There's only one volva left, a young woman no older than Draki. He pins her to the altar, unsheathes his sword. Holding it out to me.

"No." I pull against the Dragonmen. "I won't do it!"

Ildja clucks her tongue. "Why waste it on him?"

"It's not a waste," Draki says. "Reyker. Do not make me punish your mother for your disobedience. Come here."

"I won't. I can't."

"The volvur sacrifice people. She's not innocent. She's a killer."

"So am I."

A priest. I murdered a priest to protect Aldrik. I damned myself for my brother, and this is how he repays me.

Draki pulls me from the Dragonmen, wrapping my hands around the sword hilt. "You want to be strong, don't you? You want to trample your enemies. You want death to submit to you, rather than you to it. This will make you heal faster, keep you alive through things no ordinary mortal can survive."

He shoves me forward until I'm standing over the volva. Her lips are drawn back from her teeth like a predator.

"Take her power, Reyker. Or I will."

The volva's eyes narrow on me. And she nods. Not him, *her expression says.* Anyone but him.

"Do it, Reyker!"

Everything collides: Draki's threats, the volva's choice, my own desire— yes, I want to be strong, strong enough to stop Draki, to make him pay for what he's done.

The sword rises. I barely feel it. It falls.

I take out her heart. Lift it to my lips. Sink my teeth in.

Gods forgive me, I pray, even though I know they won't.

⸺✦⸺

Reyker wasn't certain if the volva let him go or if his knees finally gave out, but somehow the connection broke and he opened his eyes. There was a moment of panic: *What happened? Where am I? Who . . .* who am I?

He was sitting on the ground inside a stone circle, surrounded by women with slack faces and gray skin, their eyes flat and cold like rime-coated basalt. Someone was calling his name. He could still taste the heart in his mouth, the way the muscle gave beneath his teeth, the salty tang of blood coating his tongue. He bent over and retched until his stomach was empty and he was spitting bile.

"Reyker?" A girl stood in the stone archway, her features pinched. She was about to step into the circle.

The girl. He had to keep her away from here, though he wasn't sure why. "Don't come in!" he shouted.

She froze, and he waved her back.

Her name. What was her name? There was a twitch between his temples as he remembered. Lira, her name was Lira, and he cared for her, but he couldn't trust her. Why?

A flood of images, memories of his time with Lira, the way she'd seemed to love him only to turn around and betray him. As soon as the memories settled, he forgot what he'd wanted to know in the first place, or why. He felt an absence. Something was missing. Another piece of himself, slipping from his grasp.

"A trade," he whispered.

Whenever he tried to remember something, to dig up buried fragments from his past, it left him disoriented. Because every time he reclaimed one memory, he lost a dozen others. That's what Lira had seen when she entered his soul and tried to heal it—when she'd pulled out a buried memory, the cracks inside him spread, his past thoughts and feelings and impressions crumbling and sinking below his consciousness to a place where he couldn't reach them.

He started to laugh.

"Come out here," Lira said, "or I'm coming in after you."

He wiped his mouth and got to his feet. The volvur stood around the altar, motionless. The sight of them, and those pits where their hearts used to be, almost made him sick again.

"What happened when you touched the witch, Reyker?"

It was hard to face Lira when his limbs were weak and his thoughts were clouded and all he wanted was to hold her and confess everything, even if her kindness was a ruse. To hear her tell him he wasn't a monster like his brother, even though it was a lie.

"We have to leave the isles," he said, passing under the archway, keeping his distance from her. "All of us."

She grabbed his sleeve, her hand warm over the thin cloth that kept their skin from touching. "Why?"

"Because the Dragon knows the Renegades are here. That's why he sent you to fight me in . . . in . . ." His mother's home village. The name was gone.

"Gyldenhring," Lira said. "I thought he sent me to attack your mother's village to provoke you into killing me."

"But he knew if I let you live, I'd bring you right where he wants us. The site of his Magiska Massacre. He's planning to do it again." Reyker's stomach cramped. The volva's heart—her heart was still inside him, pumping through his veins, surging through his lungs, strengthening him. A debt he could never repay. A sin he could never erase. "He'll sacrifice you to steal your power, Lira."

"The Solmangler ritual," she murmured, her fingers digging into his arm. "He said he could make me immortal."

Reyker shook his head. "This is how he's going to make himself a god. The Dragon means to slaughter every Daughter of Aillira."

The Renegades made quick work of packing up camp and carrying what they could into the belly of the ships, as if they'd been expecting this day to arrive. Reyker stood at the edge of the settlement, watching Lira help the other magiskas gather their borrowed clothing and roll up their pallets, listening to the jarl bark orders—Solvei insisted on bringing what she referred to as her Dragon Catcher, though it took a score of men to deconstruct the cage and carry all the metal poles aboard her longship.

The laces on one of his boots had come untied, and Reyker bent over. His fingers fumbled.

Gods aflame. He'd forgotten how to tie his shoes.

Behind him, someone coughed. He turned to see the giant warrior. The man pretended to drop the knife in his hand and knelt down, his body mostly blocking Reyker from the rest of thc camp's view. Without a word, he knotted Reyker's laces.

"We were friends," Reyker said. It wasn't a question. The jarl told him. Lira told him. He felt it, the empty spot in his soul where the warrior used to be.

"As close as brothers," the man replied. "Closer, in your case."

"Then I must ask you a favor, brother to brother."

"Something more than tying up your boots like you're a bed-wetting bairn?" The insult was delivered with a grin, and Reyker suspected there was a great deal of banter in his missing memories. "It's Brokk, by the way."

"Brokk." Reyker stood up straight, and the warrior rose with him. He took a deep breath and said, "When the time comes, I need you to kill me."

CHAPTER 16

LIRA

The ships were packed with the remnants of the camp, Renegades and magiskas spread across the fleet. I was on Solvei's longship with Mabyn, Alane, and Victory—whom Solvei had grudgingly allowed on board. And, of course, Sursha, who never strayed far from the jarl's side and rarely took her eyes off me. Solvei had allowed me to remove the warded straps, freeing me to help in case any Dragonmen followed us, but I was still the death-bringer to the jarl. Sursha had a blade ready, and she wouldn't hesitate to bury it in me if I so much as blinked in a way the jarl didn't like.

The longship's bow cut through the gray water. Fog swirled around us, kept in place by the storm-spinners on the other vessels. No one spoke. The Haunted Isles were a few leagues behind us, but if Reyker was right and Draki knew where we'd been all along, he must have some way of monitoring us.

Alane closed her eyes every few minutes and used her seeker gift to search the sea for ships. So far, there was no sign of Dragonmen.

This should have been comforting, but it wasn't.

I was the Fallen Ones' vessel, and that made me Draki's crown jewel. If he could not control me as his death-bringer or trick Reyker into killing me, he would steal the power the gods gave me. But I'd given some of my blood to the Daughters of Aillira I fought with in Stalwart Bay, most of whom were here, fighting alongside the Renegades. Draki would kill us all to get every last drop.

"How much farther?" Mabyn whispered, watching the sunlight fade, the sky overhead turning as hazy and gray as the sea. It was the third time she'd asked since we'd left.

The jarl ignored her. Sursha glared.

"A while yet," I said.

Our ships were headed for one of the Holy Isles—Heligur, a hermitage where the most devout worshipers of Seffra, the mother-goddess of Iseneld, dwelled. It was a full day's sail, southeast of Iseneld. Solvei meant to ask the monks for asylum. The Holy Isles were Seffra's home in the mortal realm and, like the Mountain of Fire, they were considered hallowed ground, a place Draki could not attack without bringing Seffra's ire down upon him.

Heligur's monks had saved Reyker after Madoc's mercenaries sank his ship. Though they weren't magiskas, the monks were renowned for their knowledge of healing both body and mind. Maybe they could help Reyker again, since I had failed. If he was a weapon of the Ice Gods, they had to care what happened to him. They had to try.

"Brokk and Reyker want the magiskas to go home to Glasnith," Alane said, coming up beside me. "They think it's too dangerous for us to stay, knowing what Draki plans to do."

Home. Garreth. Part of me still wanted to return to Glasnith, to find a way around Veronis's threats so I could help my brother and the nomads defend our island against the Destroyers. The rest of me knew the crux of the war was here, where Draki was. Iseneld needed me more than Glasnith.

I shook my head. "Not until it's over. I'm not leaving this fight."

"I told Brokk the same thing." Alane's gaze traveled to the caravel crammed full of warriors, bringing up the fleet's rear. Brokk and Reyker stood together in the stern, watching the mist. Waiting for what might come for us.

"But you could," I said to Mabyn. "Any of the Daughters of Aillira who want to. Reyker shouldn't have forced you into this war. You can go back—"

"No." Mabyn's jaw was set. "I won't pretend I'm glad to be here, or that

I'm not frightened, but the Renegades' purpose is just. This war isn't only about Iseneld. What the Dragon has done to Glasnith and the countries beyond, what he'll continue to do if we don't stop him . . . The Daughters of Aillira must fight. It's what the Green Gods made us for."

Alane and I nodded. We were all in this together, until the end.

"Iceberg!" one of the Renegade scouts shouted from his spot perched at the top of a mast. Everyone turned to the giant white wall that seemed to rise up out of nowhere, blocking our path.

Maybe the fog had kept us from noticing the floating mountain. Or maybe Draki had hidden it.

The wind-wafters and tide-tellers sprang into action, and so did I, all of us pushing wind backward into the sails to slow the ships and dragging up currents as a buffer between us and the ice. Most of the ships were spared, but two in the front were moving too fast to avoid the iceberg. The bows of both longships crashed into it and crumpled like dried leaves. The air was stained with the sounds of wood splintering and people shouting, the ships already sinking into the freezing water.

"Get us closer," Solvei said. "We have to get them out."

Feeling the waves beneath us, I called to the current, using it to carry the longship forward. We'd just pulled abreast of the sinking boats when another cry rang out. "Ship coming!"

A dark silhouette glided through the haze.

"It can't be," Alane said. "There was nothing a minute ago."

"Never underestimate the Dragon's tricks," Solvei mumbled. She went to the mast, climbing halfway up and holding a spyglass to her eye. Whatever she saw made her snarl. "Battle formations! Magiskas, push them back. We don't want to fight unless we have to."

Her message was relayed from one ship to the next, Renegades scrambling. Sursha and the warriors on our vessel were pulling people out of the water, Mabyn checking them for injuries that needed healing. Solvei went to Alane, who'd already shut her eyes tight, spying on the ship from afar.

I squinted at the silhouette, my vision adjusting until I saw the ship clearly. It was three times the size of the caravel, with twice as many sails, and every inch of it was painted to look like scales. A massive dragon figurehead loomed from its bow. I couldn't see beyond the fog blanketing its railing.

"It's the Dragon," Alane said. "He's blocking me from seeing the deck. I can't tell how many soldiers are aboard."

The iceberg was too wide to sail around before Draki's ship pinned us against it. If the magiskas tried to move it with wind and tides, it would drain us enough that we'd have no power left to fight. We were trapped.

My gaze was drawn to Reyker's, his expression calm as he regarded me across the distance. The caravel was the first ship Draki would reach. I wanted to scream at him to run, but there was nowhere to go, and he wouldn't listen.

Reyker's lips moved, and my ears sought the sound beneath the whistling wind. "Prove me wrong. Show us you are not his death-bringer." Then he turned away, unsheathing his weapons. Ready to face the threat bearing down on him.

At least he wouldn't have to face it alone. Brokk and the rest of the warriors raised their axes and swords. I held up my hands, along with the other Daughters of Aillira on the ships around me. Victory came to stand with us.

The ship broke through the mist. We unleashed everything we had.

Wind beat at Draki's ship, tearing its sails. Waves swamped the deck, rocking it to and fro. Currents spun it in a wild circle. Fire bloomed from stem to stern, blackening the sails. Fog and hail drifted from the sky.

I reached out with my gift of metal, wrapping my power around the nails that held the planks together, tugging. They shuddered. I took a deep breath and sent out a torrent of power, prying the nails out all at once, ripping the deck out from under the crew's feet. The ship fell apart, and everyone on it dropped into the water.

Everyone.

No one.

There were no bodies. No humans.

Where the boat had just been, hundreds of skeletal shadows hovered in the air.

CHAPTER 17

LIRA

"Destroyers!" Brokk roared as the shadows spread out over the fleet, blocking what was left of the sun, hanging over us like a dark chandelier. The Destroyers broke into flocks and swarmed the ships, until I could no longer see beyond the vessel I was on.

In a flurry of teeth and claws and flapping wings, the Destroyers tore into the Renegades. Men and women fell around me, dead before their bodies hit the deck. The creatures went after the ship, too, cracking the mast, smashing the planks. Wrecking everything in their path.

Positioning myself in front of Alane and Mabyn, I pushed a gust of wind at the Destroyers aiming for us. It didn't hurt them, but it held them at bay, so I did it again. At my side, Victory shrieked, rearing as a Destroyer dove from behind and clawed at her, the flurry of her hooves batting it back.

Solvei, Sursha, and the other warriors sliced at the Destroyers that attacked them, hacking off wings and tails with their weapons. The demons screeched, black blood pooling across the deck. "The Destroyers can be maimed!" the jarl screamed. "Stab them!"

I kept pushing Destroyers away, giving the warriors a chance to take them down. My concentration faltered as a voice echoed inside my head.

You cannot hold them forever, little warrior. The feel of him brushing against my mind was silky and sharp, like ribbons lined with razors.

"Where are you, Draki? Why don't you come after us yourself instead of hiding behind your mother's pets?"

Tempting, but I expect this way will be quite entertaining. I will make you a deal. If you can beat them, I'll let you escape. For now.

I would show him. The Daughters of Aillira were stronger than the last time we faced Draki, and we wouldn't let him take us without a fight.

The cage Solvei was constructing for Draki lay in pieces in the stern. I called to the metal, dragging the chunks across the deck, lifting them overhead to create a barricade between the ship and the second wave of Destroyers about to fall upon us.

The Destroyers crashed against the bars. Their bodies jerked at the contact, as if they'd been struck by lightning. More Destroyers came up behind them, line after line knocking into one another, hitting the cage. Every demon that touched the bars convulsed.

I heard Solvei whoop with glee.

The Renegades cut down the stunned Destroyers, swords and axes tearing through hollow bones and leathery membranes, pieces of the demons flying in every direction until all those that had attacked our ship were dead. I released the sections of cage, breathing hard and sticky with sweat.

With the Destroyers dead, we had a clear view of the fleet—what was left of it.

Half the ships were lost, sinking into the sea or already underwater. Some were torn apart by Destroyers, others were in flames. I saw why as I watched a fire-sweeper send balls of flame at the Destroyers, setting them alight. The creatures were from Ildja's realm beneath the Mountain of Fire—flames couldn't harm them. But when the burning Destroyers landed on our ships, the fire spewing off them ate through every bit of wood and rope and sail the demons touched.

"Stop trying to burn them!" I shouted, even though there was no way the fire-sweeper would hear me. If I tried to push the Destroyers back with wind, it would spread the flames on the ships. A tide-teller pulled a wave over the deck, putting out the fire, but several warriors toppled overboard.

The only ships still afloat were the ones with wind-wafters, using their gifts to keep the vessel from being overrun as I had, or storm-spinners, who formed shields against the Destroyers using rain and snow, lightning and hail.

Alane gripped my arm, pointing. "They're alive."

The tightness inside me loosened as I followed her finger to where Brokk and Reyker stood back-to-back on the caravel, cutting down one Destroyer after another with sword and axe. They were protected by a thick blizzard raging above them, allowing only a few demons to slip through at a time, but the storms and winds were weakening as the Daughters of Aillira drained their gifts.

"The cage?" Solvei called, running up to me. "Can you use it to help the others?"

I shook my head. "There are too many Destroyers. Using the cage could trap the Renegades and magiskas beneath it." And deplete what was left of my gifts, saving a few lives at best.

Our ship drifted closer to the one next to it. Solvei told the warriors to get the gangplank ready, so they could board and help those still fighting. To me, she said, "Do something, death-bringer. Save my people, and I will be forever in your debt."

"*Our* people." The words came without thought. It was the truth, and not only for the magiskas. The Renegades had no gifts to aid them, no gods commanding them—they had everything to lose, yet they risked their lives to free their country from Draki's tyranny. They needed my protection as much as my own countrymen did, and they were just as worthy of it. "I'll do everything I can."

The jarl nodded before clambering across the plank to the other ship, jumping into the fray. The rest of the warriors on our ship were right behind her.

Alane stayed beside me, bow in hand, nocking arrows and shooting them into the throng of Destroyers. Victory was on my other side, ready to stomp on any demons that got close. Mabyn hurried from one bleeding Renegade to the next, healing their wounds as quickly as she could. More injured warriors from the other ship were being hauled across the gangplank by their comrades. I threw a gust of wind over them, shoving away the Destroyers seeking to attack, and Alane filled the demons with arrows.

If only you had come back with my brother as your prisoner, Draki purred inside my head, *I would have shared the magiskas' hearts with you. It might have kept your gifts from unraveling your body like a worn-out rug. You could have been my immortal empress.*

"You can go straight to the Mist, you lying bastard." But I wasn't certain he was lying. Worse, I wasn't certain what would have happened had Draki commanded me to eat the hearts of my sisters when I was still his devoted death-bringer.

I like you better this way, little warrior. Your conscious hate is far sweeter than your blind reverence.

There wasn't enough metal for me to wield, not without taking the Renegades' weapons and leaving them unarmed. Wind, water, fire, earth—none of it harmed the Destroyers. I sang at them, but it did no good. Did Destroyers even have ears?

"They're taking her away!" Alane stopped shooting and pointed at two Destroyers clutching a girl—Neev, a fire-sweeper—in their talons, flying back the way we'd come. Back toward Volva Isle. The Destroyers were already too far away to reach with our gifts.

"No," I said. "No, no, no. Come back."

Another pair of Destroyers swooped down and snatched up Darah, an earth-shifter. How could we stop them without risking harm to the magiska?

I reached out with Veronis's gift, but it was as I'd suspected—the Destroyers weren't beasts, they were demons. Their minds, if they had them, were blank and guarded by barriers I couldn't cross. But there was a sliver of sentience there, an essence—not a soul exactly, but something like it. They were such simple creatures I didn't even need to touch them to feel it—a pith, slick and dark, with an odor of sulfur and a taste like clotted blood. I prodded it with Eyvor's gift.

Nightmares flooded through me.

My body is stretched and torn apart, every bone broken, every organ ripped out, every bit of skin flayed with slow precision. I drown in my own blood. I burn and freeze and suffocate, crushed beneath an unbearable weight. The pain is endless. I die, and die, and die—

"Lira!"

Someone was shaking me. My throat was raw. I coughed and gasped like I hadn't taken a breath in hours.

All those souls the Destroyers had tortured. All that pain.

When I managed to open my eyes, I was on my knees, Alane and Mabyn holding me up between them. "You were screaming," Mabyn said.

"Lira." Alane stared ahead, her voice shaking. "What did you do?"

The Destroyers hovering over the ships had turned their skeletal heads toward me. "I saw them," I whispered. "What they do to the souls in the Mist."

"I don't think they appreciated it."

A shudder went through the demons. Another signal. Those left alive flapped their wings, abandoning their battles. They came for us.

For me.

The wind-wafters and storm-spinners shifted their efforts, trying to hold the horde of Destroyers back, but only slowed them down. Solvei dove across the gangplank, sword out, throwing herself in front of me. Alane, Mabyn, and others followed. Reyker leaped the distance between the caravel and the ship next to it, where Solvei had just been. As soon as he landed, he was running to the gangplank, with Brokk on his heels.

All of them, rushing to save us, three foreign girls.

To save me, the Dragon's death-bringer.

I called up my war gift. It was the first time I'd used it since having my conscience restored, but I wasn't wielding it against mortals, so I let it take hold of me, let it turn me as savage as the monsters I was facing. I wrapped my battle-madness around Eyvor's gift, fortifying it, then hurled it like a noose around the monsters her sister had made.

—rip tear shred bleed fang claw die die pain cold flesh deep rend slash die die—

Beneath it all, I hear a scream. I recognize the sound, the voice—because I am of her lineage and carry her lover's blood in my veins, because I've heard her scream in a vision, a hopeless wail torn from her throat as Gwylor struck down Veronis.

These Destroyers tortured Aillira in the Mist. Her pain is splashed across them like old bloodstains.

The images, the agony, assaulted me, threatening to drag me under, but I held on, tightening my grip. With every ounce of strength the Ice Gods and the Fallen Ones had granted me, I *pulled*. I wanted to wrench their piths away, smothering the kernel of life Ildja gave them. The Destroyers thrashed. It was like I'd caught a giant shark with a fishing line and I was trying to reel it in. Blood oozed from my mouth. My eyes.

I pulled again, harder, and felt something give.

The demons were paralyzed, and they ceased their clawing and biting. When their wings stopped swishing, many of them fell into the sea and sank. The rest crashed onto the ships, and the warriors jumped on them, stabbing with their swords, hacking with their axes.

It was over.

My vision flickered between too bright and too dim; my ears wavered between roars and silence. Light and sound spun around me, and I struggled to regain my bearings.

My senses returned to me slowly, revealing a deck littered with bodies—both Destroyers and Renegades. So many dead. Solvei and Brokk wove through the carnage, searching for survivors. Reyker was bent over a bleeding warrior, tying a tourniquet where the man's arm had been ripped off. Other warriors moved the bodies of their fallen comrades to the sides of the ship, throwing the severed pieces of Destroyers overboard.

I was lying flat on my back. I drew in a rasping breath that became a cough. There was fluid in my lungs, and I couldn't seem to get enough air.

Mabyn lay beside me. Her eyes met mine, bright and unfocused. Alane leaned down, pressing a cloth to Mabyn's neck, but it was soaked through. I could make out claw marks peeking from beneath the cloth.

My hand found Mabyn's, squeezing her fingers as she bled out, and I gasped and wheezed. Mabyn pulled her hand free and pressed it to my side. Warmth pulsed from her palm into my lungs, and the pressure eased until I could expand them fully.

Mabyn closed her eyes.

Alane wept, dropping the cloth and pulling the healer's head into her lap.

Wait . . . what just happened?

I sat up and touched Mabyn's cheek. Her skin was already cool. "I don't understand. She healed me. I was hurt, but I wasn't dying. Why did she heal me instead of herself?"

"She didn't have the strength left to heal her own wounds." Alane set Mabyn on the deck, covering her with a cloak. "Neither did you."

Dead. Another one of our sisters had fallen, another casualty of the Dragon's war. What village was Mabyn from? Who were her parents, her siblings? Did she have a lover, a betrothed—anyone else who would care that she was gone? "We have to get a message to her family."

"We will," Brokk said, coming to sit beside Alane. "As soon as we can." He rested his arm against hers, and she leaned into him slightly. They were both covered in cuts and bruises and looked as exhausted as I felt.

Victory pressed her muzzle into my shoulder. The mare had claw marks across her hindquarters and clumps of her mane had been ripped out, but she was still standing. "Rhys would be so proud of you," I murmured, pressing my cheek against her forehead.

Solvei stomped over to us. "Is the Dragon here?"

Draki. Gods, I'd forgotten about him in all the chaos. Now I lurched to my feet, scanning the water, the ice, the sky.

Alane closed her eyes and did the same, using her gifts. "I don't see him, but he's fooled me once already."

"Where are you?" I growled, certain he would hear me wherever he was.

It was several seconds before he answered. *I have what I need, and a deal is a deal. I'll return for the rest of you soon, little warrior.*

What he needed. The magiskas he'd taken.

"Who? Who do you have?" Besides Neev. Besides Darah. Because there was no way he'd be satisfied with just them.

This time, there was only silence. Draki was gone. I bent over the bow, looking for the other Daughters of Aillira. There had been eighteen of us when we left, but I counted only eight—including myself, and Mabyn— among the ships still afloat. They could have been on the ships that went down. Or they could have been carried off by Destroyers while I was too busy fighting to notice.

Eathalin. She was among the missing. Dead? Or taken?

I wasn't sure which fate was worse. My *skoldar* told me nothing— there was no jolt of panic or pain, no fraying to indicate the spell-caster's life being torn away. The mark had never connected me to Eathalin the way it had to Reyker.

The deck rocked beneath me. We were moving. I hurried to where Solvei stood at the helm, shouting to the crew. Sursha was with the jarl, but even the pain-wielder seemed shaken, her cheeks wan, her lips pressed together instead of curled into their usual snarl.

"We have to find the other magiskas," I said.

Solvei shook her head. "First, we get to the closest piece of land and repair the damage to the ships. Everything else is secondary."

"Draki took them!" Maybe some were dead in the sea, but not all. "He staged this entire ambush to get to them! We have to—"

"Lira." It was the first time the jarl had ever called me by name. It was enough to shut me up. "Thank you for what you did. You saved us from the Destroyers. Now let me get us all to safety so we don't lose anyone else."

She was right. Just because Draki was gone didn't mean we were safe. There might be more Destroyers on the way, or any number of other horrors Draki dreamed up to throw at us.

I walked toward the bow, stopping when I noticed Brokk and Alane. Her shoulders shook with sobs, and he'd wrapped his arms around her, tucked her head against his chest. I was glad they had each other to hold on to as the world fell apart. And I was keenly aware that I'd had that myself, once. That it was no longer mine because of my own choices.

My gaze slipped to the dead Renegade closest to me. Then the one next to him. The one next to her. I went down the row, looking at all of them, stretching out my gift to brush along the vacant spaces inside them where their souls had been. So many dead. Should I go back to Glasnith, and convince the other Daughters of Aillira to do the same? If we did, would it protect the rest of the Renegades, or would Draki hunt them down regardless?

I leaned against the hull, closing my eyes. Breathing in the salt air, swaying with the pitch and yaw of the ship. Letting it sink in that against all odds, some of us—Daughters of Aillira and Renegades alike—were still alive. Still free. Our fight was not over. In the midst of so much death, it was an anchor to cling to.

"Are you all right?" Reyker's voice was rough, but when I opened my eyes there was no suspicion in his expression.

"Are you?" I asked. His clothes were as bloody as mine and he was covered in dozens of small wounds.

He shrugged off my question. "You did well today." His tone was that of a commander to a warrior, the same way my father had spoken to his men. Instead of feeling proud, I felt hollow. There was too much between us to pretend like I was just another one of his warriors. "Your friend, the healer who died. She was one of the magiskas I brought here by force, wasn't she?"

"I let Mabyn stand beside me while I took down the Destroyers. I didn't push her away when she healed me instead of herself. There's plenty of blame to go around."

"Even so, I would take it back, if I could."

So would I. This, and so many other things. "Ten magiskas are missing. I don't know if they died in the attack or if . . ."

"If the Dragon took them." He stepped closer. "If they're alive, we'll find them."

"I'm so tired of losing people."

Reyker looked at the dead Renegades and bowed his head. "I fought with these men and women for months. I want to honor them, but I can't. Because I don't remember any of them. Their names. Their faces. Nothing."

"I'm sorry, Reyker." I brushed my fingertips against his.

"I believe you." His fingers twined with mine. For an instant, it felt like nothing had changed, like we were the same Glasnithian girl and Iseneldish boy who'd stumbled into each other's lives, defying our clans and countries and gods to be together. "I wish it was enough."

Reyker squeezed my hand once before letting go. He turned and walked away.

I didn't call after him, even though I wanted to.

CHAPTER 18

REYKER

What remained of the Renegades' fleet sheltered beside a pile of ice-crusted rocks that barely counted as an island. At least it was a buffer from the wind and waves that had grown rough over the hours since they'd fled the place where the Destroyers attacked, dangerous conditions with so much damage to the ships.

The dead still surrounded them. The fallen deserved to be burned on a pyre, but there was no time to move the bodies, no time for a proper funerary ritual. There weren't enough blankets or cloaks either, so many of the dead looked on, eyes still open, as if watching to see what they were missing. Occasionally a seabird landed, and someone would shoo it away before it pecked at the corpses.

Reyker and the least injured Renegades helped the shipwrights patch up the vessels. When the ships set sail again, there was no more avoiding what he had to do. His forgetfulness was accelerating; he couldn't wait until reaching . . . their destination, whatever it was called. By then, the plan he'd clung to at the expense of all his other thoughts might slip away too.

It had to be now.

A horse stepped in front of him. Why was there a horse on the ship? "Move," he said, swerving around it. Its liquid-brown eyes were more human than horse, and it stared at him with an expression that was almost mournful. He patted its neck, and the horse nipped at him gently before letting him pass.

He went to where the girl lay beside the other magiskas. They slept side by side on the deck beneath the fading starlight. The giant brown-skinned warrior—*gods aflame, what was the man's name?*—kept watch over them.

"You're really going through with this?" the giant asked.

Of course he didn't remember telling the warrior his plan. "If you know what I aim to do," Reyker said, "then you know there's no other way."

The giant nodded.

Reyker crouched down in front of the girl. She'd wiped most of the blood away, though her skin still had a faint scarlet tint, and beneath it she was sickly pale. He'd forgotten her name, and most of their history, but the imprint of his feelings for her was intact, a twisted knot he had no idea how to untangle. He wanted to let the girl dream, to curl up beside her and dream too.

What he wanted and what the Renegades needed to win the war were different things.

Reyker touched the girl's shoulder. She woke with a start, throwing her hands up. A gust of wind caught him off guard, knocking him flat on his back and shoving him across the deck.

"Oh." The girl blinked away confusion and hurried toward him. "Did I hurt you?"

"Just my pride," he said, getting to his feet. She smiled, and it made his breath catch. "I'm sorry I woke you. I wouldn't have if it wasn't important."

She tilted her head. "What is it?"

Reyker led her to the hatch, down into the small cabin Solvei used for storage. Between the barrels of fresh water and crates of salted meat, it was cramped, the air thick with the scent of cod and turnips. He lit the lantern hanging from the ceiling and turned to her.

Here was what he knew: She'd lied to him, turned his own mind against him. He hated her for it, but when he was fighting Destroyers and saw them turn to attack her, he had not stopped to think. He had jumped between ships, rushing headlong toward her, every pulse of his heart demanding he reach her in time. Maybe her love was a lie, but his—his was not.

"Do you trust me?" He looked away as he spoke. "I have no right to ask of you what I cannot give in return, but I need it. I need you to do what no one else can. To go into my soul and find the buried memory that shows us how to kill Draki. And I need you to keep going until it's done, otherwise the magiskas will die. The Renegades will die. And whatever my brother does to me will surely make me wish I was dead too. Can you do it?"

She was quiet for a moment. "I can," she said. "If you promise me something in return. When we get to Heligur, you have to let the monks try and heal what I did to you."

Reyker doubted there would be much left of him by then, but he gave his word. He pushed aside the spare anchor and a few crates, sitting down in the far corner of the cabin. The girl sat across from him. "Are you ready?" he asked.

"Are you?"

He sensed she did this often, turning his questions back on him, and he was unsure how to respond. No, he was not ready. To lose himself, to lose everything that made him who he was, with no idea what he would be on the other side. He was terrified.

"Reyker?"

She was so close he could have touched her. He could have kissed her, one last time. He knew he had kissed her before, but he didn't remember. He wanted something beautiful and real to hold on to as his life was sucked away. But if he kissed her, she would know something was wrong. He couldn't give her any reason to suspect, to refuse to proceed. "I'm ready. Begin."

Her hand settled over his chest, and he focused on where their skin met, the warmth there. He clung to it as his head pulsed, as she plunged into the black river of his soul and dredged up a memory.

Then another.

And another.

Pieces of his past, his essence, the things that made up who he'd once been, who he was, who he could have become—it all poured down from the walls of his soul. He held fast to the feel of her hand, even after he forgot who she was, and why she was touching him. Even after he forgot his own name. Her hand was a light in the deepening darkness, and he tied himself to it as she tore him asunder.

Reyker was hiding something. The careful way he spoke, the longing in his gaze—like he was telling me goodbye. It made me wary about what I'd find in his memories, if there were things in his past he thought would turn me against him.

My hand sank below the black waves, closing around the first memory I found, and I plucked it from the riverbed. When I drew it from the water, images unspooled around me. I slipped inside Reyker's skin, wore it as my own.

I almost fell out of his soul.

Sursha. She had her arms around him. Her lips on him. She straddled him, running her blades across his skin, and he didn't resist. His hands roamed over her, his body burning for her as he used to burn for me.

I was going to be sick.

He wasn't mine. Reyker stopped being mine the moment I went against his wishes and tainted his soul. I'd wondered if he'd taken lovers, sworn that I wouldn't blame him if he had, but to bear witness to it, to know he chose *her* . . .

I shoved the memory away.

The river rippled at my feet, beckoning me to see more. I didn't want to, but this wasn't about us, it was about killing Draki, winning the war. I was a soul-reader. I would do my duty.

In the next memory I unearthed, Reyker was on Volva Isle. He raised his sword, killing a witch upon the stone altar, carving her heart from her chest. Lifting it to his lips. He was only a boy, and I felt his shame, his revulsion, as his teeth tore through pink muscle, as thick strings of blood slithered down his throat. But his hands and mouth were coated in the magiska's blood, just as Draki's were. He kept chewing, swallowing, until he'd consumed the volva's whole heart.

Reyker had never told me about this. Why didn't he tell me?

I shucked off the images and took a breath.

Memories kept breaking free from the canyon walls, dropping into the water. Reyker had said not to stop, so I kept going, grabbing one memory after another.

Some I'd seen before in Reyker's soul. For the second time, I wept when I stared out through Reyker's eyes at Quinlan's broken body, lying at the bottom of the crevasse he'd fallen into. Reyker's hands—my hands—gripped Quinlan's head and snapped his neck. A mercy. Even so . . . It felt different this time because I was angry, confused. Because I'd begun to doubt if Reyker was the person I believed him to be. Quinlan had loved me, and Reyker knew it. Though he'd never seemed jealous, was it possible he enjoyed ending Quinlan's life, that he was glad Quinlan was dead?

No. Doubting Reyker's fidelity was one thing, but doubting his empathy, his humanity? I owed him the benefit of that doubt.

Most of the memories were new to me. More horrors Reyker had experienced or committed himself on Draki's orders. His first kill, when he stabbed a priest in the chest at his brother's insistence; the rival warriors he'd slaughtered and skinned because Draki threatened to kill the warriors' families, too, if Reyker refused.

But some of it, Reyker had done on his own. I watched him drug Garreth and Zabelle and the Daughters of Aillira, watched him herd my sister magiskas into a boat and steal away in the dead of night. I watched Dragonmen who were barely more than boys beg Reyker for leniency, and Reyker put his blade through them anyway.

It was as the mystic once warned me—his soul was a battleground. Reyker was everything I feared, and worse. He was also everything I hoped, and more.

I saw how he went to great lengths to protect his people—as he'd done for Hilde, and the children of Vaknavangur—accepting Draki's cruelty so he could stand as a shield between the Dragon and the innocents of Iseneld. How he'd stayed on Glasnith after he thought I was dead, doing what he could to keep my clan and the Daughters of Aillira safe.

When we first met, he had lost his hope, but as soon as I helped him reclaim it, he became what he was meant to be: a sword of his gods, a weapon of light to beat back the darkness. By twisting his mind, I'd taken that away from him. I bore some responsibility for every brutal act he'd committed since.

I didn't know how long I'd been in his soul. Hours. Days. Sorting through hundreds of memories, searching for any detail that might reveal Draki's weakness. I was drained to the point of exhaustion, and I imagined Reyker was too.

My hand reached into the water—it was almost a reflex now, to grab a memory, live through it, grab the next. Weariness made me stumble, my knuckles pressing through the silt of the riverbed, sinking in it up to my wrist. My fingers brushed a hard shape, and I groped for it, digging deeper. Not a smooth gem. A sharp-edged stone that sliced my palm. I drew it from the water, an ugly bit of rock, slippery and cold. Everything about it was different from Reyker's other memories.

I squeezed the rock and it shuddered, smothering me in sights that blurred at the corners, in sounds that were somehow too loud and too quiet. I was in Dragon's Lair, before it was destroyed, before I ever stepped foot on Iseneld. And I was no longer me—I was a boy on the cusp of manhood. As I'd done countless times, I shed the skin of my own essence, donning Reyker's in its place.

Mother's eyes are bright blue, and now they are clear for the first time in months. She broke through the haze of Draki's hold on her, the power of the scar he cut behind her ear that leashed her to him. She's only been able to do this a handful of times since he marked her. It never lasts more than a few minutes.

She presses the handle of a knife into my hand. "You must cut it out of me, Reyker."

Mother turns, pulling her hair aside; it's paler than my own, spun white-gold where mine is burnished honey. She has always been the light that shines through me, the sun to my moon. She is the only person I have left to live for. I cannot refuse her.

"Quickly," she urges, "before he realizes something is amiss."

The knife is dull, stolen from the kitchens. I press the tip to the edge of her scar. "I don't want to hurt you."

"He will hurt me more than you ever could. He will hurt us both if we cannot escape."

I push the knife in, slicing just below the skin, peeling away the scar. Her blood trickles around my fingers, down her neck, but she doesn't make a sound. When the circle of flesh is carved away, I hand it to her and press a cloth to her wound.

Mother stares at the mark that stole her will. The Star of the Dragon. She holds it over the flame of a candle, watching it burn, filling the room with the stench of smoked flesh. "Pack your things," she says. "Your warmest outfit and blanket."

I do as she tells me, shoving my heavy coat into a satchel. I'm rolling up my blanket when she cries out. I drop the bag and run to her. "What's wrong?"

Red soaks the cloth on her neck. I remove it and blood spurts from it like a fountain. "I must have cut a vein." I rip the blanket I was about to pack and wrap the strip around her neck.

"No." Mother's smile is bitter, her teeth bared against the pain. "It's a spell. He warned me, but I didn't believe him."

"Warned you about what?" My voice swells with panic.

She cups my face in her hands, the bitterness fading to sorrow. "This isn't your fault, Reyker. It's his. Don't let him use it against you."

"Use what? I don't understand!" But I do. Blood keeps gushing from her neck, too much for such a shallow wound. Too much to staunch.

Mother screams, folding in on herself, tremors wracking her.

"Hold on," I tell her. "I'll get help."

I run from the room, down the hall to Draki's quarters, throwing the door open without knocking. An offense I'll pay for later, but I don't care. I don't care if he beats me, if he flays me, if he takes my head as he took the other men's in Vaknavangur, as long as he saves her.

Draki sits in a chair in front of a mirror, his tunic slung over the back of it, his torso bare. There's a needle in his hands, a pot of ink on the table beside him that tips over as he rises in a fury, my name a roar in his mouth. "Reyker—"

I toss every shred of pride aside, hitting my knees. "Please. My mother needs help."

He sets down the needle and follows me to Mother's room. She's curled in a ball on her side, moaning, clawing at the wound. I collapse beside her, taking her hands, looking up at the man who is my brother, or used to be. "Save her. Please, Draki. I'll do anything you ask."

His eyes narrow. "Come here."

I go to him.

"You cut the mark from her skin?"

"Yes."

"You planned to run away. To leave me."

"Yes." I don't dare lie to him, not when my mother's life hangs in the balance.

Draki spins me around, grabbing my shoulders. "Then you must both be punished. For your defiance, you will watch the thing you love most in this world die."

The words are a gut punch, a drop into freezing water. It takes a moment for the shock to dissolve. "No, please. She was like a mother to you!"

"Aldrik's mother. Alas, Aldrik is dead."

Why had I expected any different, after what he did—what we did—to the volvur? I struggle in his grip, trying to run to Mother even though there's nothing I can do for her. "Don't do this, Draki!"

"You did this. Katrin was mine, yet you tried to take her from me. You are mine, but you were going to run from me."

I scream and weep and fight, but he holds me in place, forcing me to watch, keeping me from reaching her. I can only watch her shudder, her life bleeding out across the floor.

"This is your lesson, Reyker. You can never take what belongs to the Dragon."

Mother calls for me, and a black burning wave washes over my body. It is pure rage, undiluted hate. I give in to it with a howl, finally tearing free from Draki. I go to my mother, pulling her into my arms, but it's too late. Her eyes are still open, still blue, but the light has gone out of them. My sun is gone, leaving nothing but cold darkness that seeps into my bones, swathing my heart. I look at Draki. The warlord. The Dragon.

I become the cold.

I become the darkness.

The memory began to dissolve, dumping me back into my own head, but I held it tighter. This was the one. It had to be. Draki wouldn't have let Reyker live with the secret to destroying him, not unless he knew it would be buried, unreachable. Reyker would never have missed a detail so vital unless it was overshadowed by something else, a memory too unbearable to relive.

But he had to. *We* had to.

"It's here," I whispered into his soul. "I'm sorry, Reyker. I need to see it again."

The canyon walls shook, shedding gems, more of Reyker's past lost to the river. I couldn't afford to wait. I clenched the rock in my fist, letting it cut deeper into my hand. The memory opened like a wound, and while part of me was Reyker, mired in the pain of what was happening, another part of me was detached, observing.

There. In Draki's quarters. The needle. What was he doing with it?

I tried to linger, but the memory kept moving. When it ended, I didn't let go.

"Again," I said. "Slower."

I concentrated on every feature, every element.

The knife. Mother's blood. Running down the hall, throwing open the door. Draki, in front of the mirror. The needle. The ink.

The images were distorted by Reyker's panic—the reflection thrown by the mirror didn't matter to him in that moment. But it was there all the same. A red teardrop on Draki's arm. A second droplet on the tip of the needle, a fusion of black and red. Blood and ink.

A tattoo that Draki was giving to himself, one of many trailing along his forearm.

A needle puncturing skin. Drawing blood.

Weapons were useless against him. Blades crumbled to dust as soon as they touched him. Not because of the weapons, I realized. Because of who held the weapons.

Draki was half god, but he was also half mortal, and every mortal could bleed.

The Dragon could bleed.

But only by his own hand.

CHAPTER 19

LIRA

I released Reyker's soul and hit the floor. The cabin swayed around me, but I wasn't certain if it was from waves or my own exhaustion.

"I found it, Reyker."

He was slumped against a barrel, eyes closed. Searching his soul, experiencing his past, had been miserable for me, but it had been worse for him. I'd watched my brother die, watched my father die, once. I couldn't imagine living through it again and again.

"Reyker?"

He didn't answer. Didn't move.

"Reyker." I sat up, taking his head in my hands. His pulse beat steadily beneath my fingertips. "Open your eyes."

Nothing.

I shook him. "Open your eyes!" His lashes fluttered, blue irises peeking out through the cracks in his eyelids, and I sighed. "Bloody fates, you scared me. I thought . . ."

His eyes widened, the black of his pupils swelling. He looked at me, but there was no familiarity in his gaze. Like I was a stranger.

Like he'd forgotten me.

"What's wrong, Reyker?" I wanted him to open his mouth and call me by my name. Or magiska. I'd even have settled for death-bringer. Anything—anything to erase that vacant stare he was giving me.

"Say something." I brushed my fingers along his cheek. "Talk to me, please."

His lips parted, jaw working. A noise leaked from his mouth—a groan, a whimper. A roar. He pulled back, breathing hard, features twisted.

Then he lunged for my throat.

- - - - - -

The throbbing in his head changed, replaced by . . . nothing. He was not himself, whoever that had been. He was a creature. A *thing*.

There was another creature in front of him, touching him.

He could hardly think, didn't understand what thinking was, what understanding was. His blood pumped because his heart told it to, his lungs breathed because the reptilian part of his brain commanded it, but beyond that were sensations he couldn't name, experiences he had no way to process.

The other creature's lips moved, but the sounds made no sense. He could tell this creature wanted his lips to move, too, to make those same sounds. The idea felt familiar. So did the motion, as his lips opened and curled. But those sounds, the ones he was certain he should be able to make, wouldn't come. The noise gushing out of him wasn't right.

The creature's reaction proved it: shaking its head, back and forth, back and forth, while its lips kept forming shapes he couldn't decipher, conveying to him that he was not what he was meant to be. The creature touched him and he reared back, retching a wall of sound until the creature let go. All the words he'd once had, all the ways he'd used to put meaning on the world around him, were gone. He couldn't say what color the creature's hair was, or what sort of structure they were inside of, or what the liquid leaking down his cheeks—and the other creature's—was called. The information was all in his mind somewhere, but there was a barrier between it and him, a bridge he didn't have a way of crossing.

He was lost, broken, cut off—from this creature, from any others like it. Alone, drifting in a place he didn't recognize, his skin so tight it didn't feel like his own.

No. Not alone. Something whispered inside him, flowed through him. Instinct—but stronger. Immense. Unfettered.

It turned its gaze on the creature in front of him. *Prey,* it declared. Though he couldn't understand the words, he knew what they meant, knew what to do as the entity surged within him, as it became him, giving commands, taking control.

Hunt.

Feed.

Kill.

CHAPTER 20

I slammed a gust of wind into Reyker, pinning him to the wall as he snarled and raged.

"*Be still*," I sang at him, and his body slackened. It wouldn't last. My sung commands wore off within minutes, so I called to the length of chain attached to the spare anchor, winding it around his arms and legs, looping a length around the heaviest barrels for good measure.

Reyker struggled awhile before going quiet. "*Sleep*," I sang, and he gave in to weariness, passing out with his body twisted in uncomfortable angles. I wanted to move him, to rearrange his limbs so he wouldn't wake up sore, but if I touched him, he would startle. He would roar.

He would try to kill me again.

Because he didn't know me anymore, just as he didn't know himself. Reyker hadn't just forgotten his past. He'd forgotten how to be human.

Footsteps crept down the stairs, someone heavy trying to walk noiselessly, and failing.

I was leaning beside the door, keeping an eye on Reyker as he slept. I closed my eyes, not wanting to talk to anyone. Maybe if whoever it was saw we were asleep, they would leave.

They didn't. As the person passed me, I peeked from beneath my lashes and saw Brokk, staring at Reyker. I was about to call out to him when he pulled a dagger from the sheath at his hip, its blade glimmering in the light of the lantern.

My palms were up without a second thought, calling the steel to me, and the dagger flew from Brokk's hand to mine.

He turned to me and sighed. "You should go. You don't want to see this."

I stood slowly, pointing the dagger at him. "What were you going to do?"

"What Reyker asked me to."

"What he asked . . ." The secret in Reyker's eyes, the way he told me goodbye without actually saying it. "He knew! He knew the damage it would cause to have me riffling through his soul, that he wouldn't come back from it. So did you. You should have told me! *He* should have told me!"

"You would never have done it, and it had to be done." Brokk reached out to put a hand on my shoulder, but I swiped at it with the dagger. "He did it to end the war, to keep the rest of us safe. To keep *you* safe."

"He hates me."

"He loves you too."

Our exchange had woken Reyker, and he edged backward as far as he could, growling. Brokk called his name, kneeling just out of reach. Reyker's expression was feral, his body hunched, his teeth bared—a cornered wolf. He lunged for Brokk, straining against the chain.

"I'm sorry, brother." Brokk's voice broke on the last word. "At least tell me it worked, Lira. Tell me you found what we need."

"I found it, for all the good it does us." I explained what I'd seen in Reyker's memory, the means by which Draki could be harmed. "I ripped Reyker's mind apart for nothing."

"It's not for nothing. We'll find a way to use it against the Dragon. I won't let Reyker's sacrifice be in vain. At least now, we can give him peace." Brokk moved toward Reyker. He didn't require a weapon—with a twist of his hands, he could snap Reyker's neck.

I sucked wind through the cracks in the walls and ceiling, knocking

Brokk across the cabin into a stack of barrels. "Go near him and I will kill you."

The warrior climbed to his feet. "This was Reyker's decision! Will you take it from him, this last wish, as you took so many other choices out of his hands? Look at him. He's suffering. Don't force him to live like this."

I looked. I saw Reyker's blue-gray eyes, his gold hair. The lips I'd kissed, the arms that had held me. It was Reyker's flesh, but there was no trace of the man Brokk and I loved inside it.

"I can fix him." Reyker could curse my name, bed whomever he wanted; he could find a thousand ways to torment me, but this? No, he could not leave me this way. I would not allow it. "If there's any way to bring him back, I will. And if not . . ." I couldn't finish that thought. "He deserves a chance. I'm going to give him that, and if you or any of the Renegades try to stop me, I'll make you regret it."

Brokk's glare softened a fraction. "Now I see it. The death-bringer in you."

I was glad there were no mirrors in the cabin, nothing that would force me to see what Brokk saw.

The fleet arrived in Heligur a few hours later. The longship rocked and feet clambered on the deck overhead as everyone disembarked. Reyker watched me warily, sometimes with a growl, other times with a whimper. He didn't want me here, but I was afraid to take my eyes off him, afraid he would escape the chains. If he'd forgotten how to swim, he might leap from the ship and drown. He might kill someone. At the very least, he would run away, and it might be impossible to hunt him down without harming him.

At Solvei's request, some of the monks came aboard. There were four of them, a mix of old and young, draped in homespun robes tied with rope. They wore expressions that were kind but dispassionate. I supposed they had to be, to tolerate living in seclusion and denying themselves earthly pleasures. On closer inspection, I realized they were all impaired in some way—one had a sunken skull and milky eyes, another limped on a peg leg. A third had no arms. And their skin was covered in scabs and scars, boils and pockmarks.

They looked down at Reyker. He was hunched on all fours, snarling.

"The Sword of the Ice Gods." This from the fourth monk, the oldest of them, a man I knew from Reyker's memories of his time here. Gothi, he was called. With his mouth open, I saw the monk had no teeth. "The Dragon's brother is much changed since last we saw him."

"Can you heal him?" I asked.

The monks bent their heads close but did not speak—or perhaps they had lived together so long, they did not need words to communicate.

"This may be the will of the gods," Gothi said. "He is a more efficient weapon now."

"If this is what your gods want, they do not deserve your devotion."

Gothi smiled, exposing empty pink gums. "Your anger is understandable, but it will do him no good. This is beyond our ken. If you wish to heal him, you must seek the goddess of the water for her blessing."

"Seffra?" Wife of Sjaf, mother of Iseneld. "She's here?"

"It is Seffra's gifts that strengthen our abilities. We can do nothing unless she wills it. Follow the healing stream to its source, and if she deems you worthy, she will reveal herself. But there are risks. Many who seek her wisdom do not return, and she will not grant you an audience unless you pass her test and provide an offering that pleases her."

I was sick of gods and goddesses, suffering their trials, paying their tolls in blood. "Is that what happened to all of you? You mutilated yourselves for Seffra? Why must there always be a sacrifice when gods are involved?"

If the monks were offended by my tone, they didn't show it. "Why is childbirth painful for the mother?" Gothi asked. "Why must life always end, eventually, in death? Creation has a cost, and that cost is destruction. One must always balance out the other. For us to heal a body or mind that cannot be treated by mortal means, we must place their illness somewhere else. Sometimes into the land, the water, the darkest places we can find. Sometimes the only place it can go is into ourselves. Would you take his ailment into yourself, if you could?"

"Of course I would."

"So would I." He pulled down his robe, revealing a jagged scar on his chest that matched the one on Reyker's. Had this man saved Reyker before by siphoning the damage the wound had caused him? "Monks do not last long here. We give ourselves for our patients because it is our duty. It is our privilege to suffer and die so that others might live."

"A privilege?" I took in the ailments and injuries the monks bore with new understanding. "It seems a torment."

"It is both, as most wondrous things are. Love, for example. Your intentions are pure and your love for this man is obvious. I do believe Seffra will see you, but whether she will agree to your request and what she will ask for in return, I do not know. Take something with you, a trinket you can hold. A memento to keep you grounded. The goddess's tests are trying, and it's easy to lose yourself."

I was already gathering up a sack of grain, dumping out its contents, filling it with supplies from the storage room. I would make the goddess agree, or I would wring her immortal neck. "I've faced Gwylor and Ildja. I'm well aware how dangerous gods can be."

"Yes. I see that you are." Gothi looked at my hands. One of my fingernails had peeled off, and the rest were tinged blue, barely clinging to the cuticles. He looked at my thinning hair, and the fallen clump of it lying on the floor. "Yours is a disease we cannot heal, unfortunately. As the Fallen Ones' vessel, their blood is bonded to your own. The only way to be rid of its corrosion is to bleed yourself dry."

I'd known I was dying, but hearing the monk say it made it all too real. "Don't tell anyone. Please."

Gothi placed his hand over his scarred chest. "I am a monk, not a gossip. But you should not carry such a burden alone, nor should you let those who care for you be caught unaware. Good luck, child. You will need it."

The monks left me to prepare. Once I was ready, I sat as close to Reyker as I dared. He thrashed against the anchor's chain, growling, slaver dripping down his chin.

"I'm going to save you, stupid boy. That's what you and I do. We save each other."

He snapped his teeth at me.

"I love you too."

I'd meant to seek out Alane, but when I emerged from the cabin, she was waiting on deck alongside Bronagh the sea-farer and Keeva the bone-healer. Victory was there as well, scraping her front hoof nervously over the planks.

"Brokk told us what happened to Reyker," Alane said, "and the monks told us what you aim to do about it. You might be gone for a while."

With a goddess involved, there were many uncertainties, including time. I'd learned that from the day I'd spent in Aillira and Veronis's ruins that had passed as a week outside the fey realm. "Reyker can't be left alone."

"He won't be," Keeva and Bronagh replied at once.

"Did Brokk also tell you what he wishes to do to Reyker?"

"Oh, yes," Alane said. "And if he thinks I will allow such a thing, he is sorely mistaken. I can see him coming before he gets near the ship. Bronagh can cut us loose and sail to the other side of the island."

"And I can break his knees if I must," Keeva added, waggling her fingers.

"We won't let anyone hurt him," Bronagh said.

I pulled Bronagh into a hug first, then did the same to Alane and Keeva, at a loss for how to express my gratitude. "Thank you. All of you."

"Just fix him," Alane said over the sound of Reyker howling below. The three of them had been with Reyker when he first returned to Iseneld. They had fought with him, protected one another, and they had their own bonds with him beyond what he meant to me. Reyker had touched the lives of many. I owed it to them, as much as I did him, to make this right.

Victory too. The mare lipped at my hair, blowing her hot breath on my cheek, and I scratched between her ears.

"I won't return without a cure," I promised. "No matter how long it takes. No matter the price."

CHAPTER 21

LIRA

Heligur was a spit of land dropped in the middle of the sea, not much bigger than Volva Isle, dotted with buildings of wood and stone. The infirmary was the largest, taking up most of the space, and to either side of it were the monks' dormitory, library, and temple. The islet was connected by a strip of coastline to another, larger island. Gudyafass—named for Seffra's waterfall—was ten times bigger than Heligur, with a narrow mountain range that broke through the earth at the island's center shooting straight up to the sky, its peaks vanishing into the bellies of clouds.

If Seffra was anything like Ildja, I would have to be ready for a fight. Heeding Gothi's warning, I took my memento and tied it to my wrist.

The path started where stream met ocean, and I followed the water backward toward its source. The trail was worn and easy to see from the pilgrimages of monks and visitors who'd sought Seffra's guidance. In some places the stream was slender and flowed gently, while in others it was wide enough to seem more like a river, rough enough to drown anyone who stumbled into it. The stream overlapped the path often, and I picked my way across, walking on stones or wading through cold water. I cupped my hands and drank, the water clear and crisp, the tang of something fresh yet ancient, like tasting life itself.

My leg muscles burned on the steep slopes as the path wound higher and higher, along deadly drop-offs. Despite the need for caution, my thoughts wandered elsewhere. To the longship with Reyker. And to the highlands of Iseneld, with Quinlan.

Gods, how I missed him. I wished he was with me on this journey. I wished I could go back to that moment on the glacier and convince him not to cut the rope, rally the strength to pull us both out of the crevasse.

Wishes are like a lame horse, Quinlan would say if he were here, smiling crookedly at his own wit. *Worth keeping as long as you don't expect it to get you anywhere.*

I climbed a hill lined with moss-slicked boulders that was as tall as five cottages stacked atop one another, water spurting out between the rocks. At the top was a ledge, and I stopped to rest, chewing on a piece of dried cod and looking out over the landscape. The weather was milder than on Iseneld, thanks to warm air scraping along the sea. Far below, there were still patches of waning-green grass and trees with a few brown leaves clinging to their branches, but this high up, the fatal kiss of winter was unmistakable, the ground bleached yellow, the trees bare.

The path turned to mud and slush as the stream misted the air and sent rivulets off in every direction, like long fingers seeking to touch as much as they could. The sun faded, so I lit a torch and kept going, up through the first layer of clouds. Then I heard the waterfall.

I'd heard many on my trek across Iseneld, but none like this. The water didn't crash and pound, it *sang*—not a human voice, but the voice of nature, chanting a song of existence in an unknowable language. It was the most beautiful sound I'd ever experienced. I paused to listen without meaning to, and tears ran down my cheeks.

Moving became harder the closer I got to the falls. Without warning, I was on my knees. My body wanted to stay and bask in the music, the weightlessness it bestowed, the overwhelming joy of being. Worries were trifles. All those silly mortal activities—drinking and eating and sleeping— were inconsequential. There was no need to leave this spot.

Time was inconsequential, too, stretching and bending around me. It was dark, then light, then dark again. The sun, perhaps—setting, rising, setting, barely registering beyond the mire of music. There was nothing but the song, filling me, transporting me. My head felt stuffed with feathers. Soothing. Addling.

Something scratched my wrist.

I shouldn't care—I *didn't* care—yet I glanced down and saw . . . a gleaming black mask, its surface ridged like scales. A token of my sins.

Once, I had been the woman behind that mask. The death-bringer, a tool of ruin. The sight pricked my mind, loosening the music's hold.

Up. I must get up.

With effort, I stood, but only made it a few steps before the song leeched my purpose and buckled my knees. If I kept listening, it would enthrall me again. I tore bits of cloth from the edge of my tunic, balled them up, and stuffed them deep into my ears. I could still hear the water, but it was muffled enough that I could think around the sound. As the bliss I'd felt dwindled, I was tempted to pluck the cloth out and be swept up in the song once more. Instead, I squeezed the mask in my fist to keep me focused. There were many wrongs I had to right.

With my head clear, I finally noticed the state I was in—every muscle cramped, every joint aching. I was desperately thirsty, weak with hunger. My trousers were wet from pissing myself. Beneath the dense clouds, it was impossible to tell the hour. How long had I been kneeling in the same spot, spellbound?

At least a day, I decided. Maybe two.

As I made my way to the stream for a drink, something crunched under my boots.

Bones. I kicked at the wilted grass and my toes hit a rib cage, a skull. They were everywhere—skeletons of people who'd come here to worship Seffra and been bewitched by the waterfall's song. They'd sat down and never gotten up.

"What is wrong with you?" I shouted at Seffra before slapping a palm over my mouth. Not the best idea to insult a goddess and then beg her for a favor.

I chewed on a hunk of bread from my satchel as I tread closer to the falls, adjusting my makeshift earplugs to keep out as much sound as possible. The trail ended at the bottom of a staircase-shaped cliff enclosed by clouds so thick they vanished everything beyond. The stream rushed over the top of the cliff, but most of it ran down its center. I kept to the side of the cliff as I climbed it, using a branch I'd found to steady myself. The climb was slow going, straining my sore muscles.

Cresting the cliff, I got my first look at Gudyafass.

Like the mountain range, the waterfall's narrow width only served to enhance its grand height. It was a towering curtain of water crashing down from the summit of the tallest mountain into a pool that fanned out before me. A spray of mist soaked me in seconds. The waterfall's song had become a thundering weapon, and no amount of cloth kept it out. I staggered and stumbled my way through the pool, humming as loudly as I could to drown the music that threatened to turn me into another skeleton. When I was near where the falls hit the pool, I craned my neck and peered upward. It was like a pearl-hued pillar of marble, except it flowed and frothed, a mystical dance that had no steps.

"Goddess Seffra! I must speak with you. Please grant me an audience."

I waited, but there was no answer.

I called her name, offered promises and prayers, begged and beseeched. There was no sign of the goddess. Either she wasn't here, or she didn't care to listen to my plea. I came all this way, suffered through her song, for nothing.

I tore my death-bringer mask from my wrist and threw it into the falls. "Damn you! I'm trying to save the Sword of the Ice Gods, the weapon you and your kin created!"

The water falling just above the pool began to shift, becoming something else. The shape resembled a giant hand; then, as if it were made of flesh rather than water, the hand reached out and grabbed my mask.

IS THIS MY GIFT?

I yelped and jumped backward. The voice had spoken inside my mind, a sound like water rushing from someplace dark—a song from an ocean trench, a hymn from rain pouring through a hole in the sky. The waterfall shuddered again, and within the watery pillar two legs took shape, then a torso, arms, a face. The form of a woman, somehow both natural and ethereal, stretched above me, as big as a mountain.

TELL ME WHY YOU BROUGHT ME THIS.

I didn't know if I was supposed to bow, but my knees were already buckling, so I kneeled in the pool and lowered my head. "To remind myself of my choices, and those who've paid dearly because of them. That's why I'm here."

The face in the waterfall rippled. NO, NOT ONLY FOR HIM. YOU ARE HERE TO UNBURDEN YOURSELF. SO SPEAK.

It was a command, one I could not refuse. My lips parted, and out spilled everything—everything that had happened since Reyker washed ashore in Stony Harbor. Every death I'd caused, directly or accidentally. Every decision I'd made that had led me here. Confessions of my part in furthering the war that threatened the lands and the people she and the other Ice Gods had created and fostered. It was a relief to say it aloud, and because she was a goddess it felt like a prayer of atonement.

While I purged my sins, Seffra swayed and danced as if she could not remain still. When my words ran dry, she erupted into sounds that resembled laughter.

WHAT A DISASTER ILDJA HAS UNLEASHED UPON THE WORLD WITH HER WOMB. HER SPAWN MUST BE CONTAINED, AND THIS IS WHY THE SWORD OF THE ICE GODS WAS FORGED. IF HE IS BROKEN, HE MUST BE HEALED.

A sob escaped me. "Thank you."

BUT.

I stiffened. She was a goddess. Of course there was a *but*.

AS YOU HAVE LEARNED, EVERY CHOICE COMES AT A PRICE. MY BLESSING OF HEALING IS NO DIFFERENT. IF I AM TO HEAL THE RIFT IN THE SWORD'S MIND, HIS PLAGUE MUST BE TRANSFERRED TO ANOTHER. THE COST OF HIS HEALING IS THAT YOU WILL CHOOSE WHO TO TRANSFER HIS AILMENT TO.

Gothi had warned me of this, but I'd not expected to be charged with making the selection myself. It struck me like a blow.

There was only one right choice. Maybe it was a fitting punishment, but bloody fates, I did not want it.

"Me." I smiled at the irony. I'd get Reyker back only to lose him, to lose everything. To forget everything, including myself. But what did it matter, since I was dying? "Give me his ailment."

YOU? NO, MAGISKA. YOU ARE NEEDED IN THE BATTLES TO COME, AND YOU ARE MISSING THE POINT OF THIS CHOICE. OFFERING YOURSELF IS THE EASY WAY OUT. OFFERING ANOTHER, AND LIVING WITH THE CHOICE, IS THE COST OF HEALING THE MAN YOU LOVE.

"What? No, please. I cannot damn someone else for a mistake I caused."

YOU CAN, OR THE SWORD'S MIND WILL REMAIN BROKEN.

I shook my head, thinking. I couldn't leave Reyker as he was—for selfish reasons, but also because the Renegades needed him to win this war. If I could not offer myself, then who?

"Draki," I said.

THE DRAGON IS IMMUNE TO SUCH MAGIC. YOU CANNOT CHOOSE HIM.

"Then one of his Dragonmen."

The waterfall churned. YOU STILL DON'T UNDERSTAND. THE PRICE OF HEALING IS PAIN. YOUR CHOICE MUST BE A SACRIFICE. IT MUST BE A LOSS THAT HURTS YOU.

Pain. Loss. With gods, there was always a sacrifice.

Gothi had already taken on one of Reyker's wounds to save him. This was his calling. To heal others, to his own detriment. I opened my mouth to say it—

LAST CHANCE, MAGISKA. IF YOU DO NOT OFFER A SUITABLE NAME, YOU WILL HAVE FAILED THIS TEST, AND I WILL HEAR NO MORE.

My mouth snapped shut. I didn't know the monk. To condemn him would cause me guilt, but not the kind Seffra wanted, not a deep wound that I'd have to live with for the rest of my days. Then who?

To make the right decision, I had to think like a goddess.

I had to think like the death-bringer.

Besides Reyker, Garreth was the person I loved most in the world, but as the fledgling leader of Glasnith, he had a role to play in the war as much as I did, didn't he? Even if I could bring myself to offer him, Seffra might refuse. The same problem arose with Solvei, and though I respected her, I didn't truly care about her. I didn't know how important Brokk was to the war, didn't know if I cared about him enough for Seffra to deem him a fitting sacrifice, but I did know he would gladly give his life for Reyker's—for that, I had to assume Seffra would reject him. Eathalin was bound to me through her *skoldar,* but she could already be dead, and even if she wasn't, she was Draki's sacrifice now.

The shape in the waterfall shifted impatiently and began to fade. A NAME, GIRL. GIVE ME A NAME NOW, OR I WILL REVOKE THIS TRADE.

Who? Who was close to me, but not vital to the war, someone innocent who did not want to be sacrificed? Who would it hurt me to lose? Who was worth Reyker's life?

The name came to me and I didn't stop to think, didn't give myself time to second-guess or agonize or reason out my choice.

"Alane."

CHAPTER 22

- - - - - -

The creature that used to be a man, used to have a name and a home and a purpose, now had nothing but a single-minded goal: escape. The thing pinning him hurt. He did not like it, and somehow he knew if he could slip out of it, everything would be better.

He'd been pulling and squirming for some time, listening to the clanks and rattles as another section slid away and the tightness around his limbs loosened—a little more, then a little more. A sharp pull, and he could move his arms. It made it easier to worm his legs out, until the last sections clinked to the floor, no longer trapping him.

Free.

The creature ran, up, toward the light. Four other creatures were there—three shaped like him, a larger one coated in fur—and they cried out. Something stirred in his gut, pressure building behind his chest, pushing out through his limbs. *Prey*, it whispered.

He lunged for them.

One of the creatures threw her hands up. There was a sonorous *crack*. Pain flared up and down his leg.

Not prey. Not that one.

Instinct told him to fly. He would not be trapped again. He hurried in the opposite direction, as far as he could on his hobbled leg, until he reached a barrier. He scaled it and found there was nothing under him.

He fell. When he landed, it was cold and the cold seeped into his mouth when he tried to breathe. He flailed until his head was out of the cold and he could see. Arms and legs thrashing, he inched forward and felt something slippery but solid under him. He crawled his way higher, shaking wetness from his eyes, blinking against the sting.

His leg hurt, but he crouched, scanning for threats, for obstacles.

More shouts rang out around him. More creatures, inching closer. Herding him toward something—a thing made of metal and bone. Some distant part of his mind recognized the contraption for what it was, and panic flooded his veins. They would trap him. He could not stand it. Beyond the creatures, past the cage, he saw land covered in shapes he could hide in, a place for him to hunt and be away from all the things seeking to hurt and confine him. He wanted that place. He would do whatever he must to get to it.

The creatures stood between him and freedom. Slowly, their appearances changed. To shining hair and eyes, black shapes scrawling down face and body. *Brother.* Another word he did not understand beyond the bile on his tongue, the clawing in his guts.

That thing under his skin came out again, rising, filling him. He let it. Oh, it felt like the world was his. It tasted like blood in his mouth and under his nails. It spoke to him, gave commands he understood on a visceral level.

Hunt.

Feed.

Kill.

He growled, loping toward the creatures. They stepped forward, surrounding him, corralling him. Looking at him with those loathsome faces.

KILL.

The command flooded through him, became him, stripping everything else away. He arched his neck and howled with the pleasure of it.

He launched himself at the creatures and tore out their throats.

CHAPTER 23

The walk down the mountain was a blur. A haze settled over me, stifling my thoughts, numbing my senses. What I had done was so unspeakably awful that I could not accept it. It was not me who made that choice. It was not Lira who spoke Alane's name and damned her—my friend, my sister magiska, a Daughter of Aillira. It was the death-bringer, possessing me one final time.

At least, that's what I told myself.

I neared the bottom of the mountain as the sun was setting. Someone was there, limping up the trail toward me.

"Reyker?" I held my breath, my gifts flowing to my fingertips.

He looked at me, releasing a long-held sigh that collapsed time and distance. "Lira."

I ran, skidding over pebbles, kicking up dirt. We crashed into each other and I threw my arms around him. He buried his face in my hair but kept his arms stiff at his sides, his hands squeezed into fists.

I drew back. I'd been blinded by relief, but now I saw the blood splattered on his boots, matted in his hair, painted across his skin. I searched him for injuries, finding his right knee bent awkwardly. Nothing to explain all this blood. "What happened?"

He held up his bloody hands. "I didn't mean to hurt them." Reyker sank to the ground. His breath hitched, and then he was weeping. "I didn't mean to."

I pulled his head to my chest, thinking of Alane. "No. Of course you didn't."

There was a watchtower on Seffra's isle, at the top of a high hill, overlooking the bay between the sprawling coastlines of Heligur and Gudyafass. We walked to where the stream flowed past the tower. Reyker stripped and waded into the water, scrubbing dried blood from his skin, washing it as best he could from his clothes and hair. My trousers smelled of piss, so I shed my clothing as well, joining him in the icy water to rinse them. When we were clean, we wrapped ourselves in musty blankets he'd brought from inside. The tower's spiral stairs led us to a dust-coated room with a pallet on the floor. Reyker threw open the doors to a deck facing the sea, letting in fresh air and light.

"I need to heal your knee, Reyker."

"Later." It was the first thing he'd said in nearly an hour. He'd listened, silent, as I told him about my journey to the falls. My sacrifice to Seffra.

Neither of us had offered apologies or granted forgiveness. There was no need to say what we both already knew. We were beyond words, beyond pain, like a burned limb whose nerves have been charred until there's nothing left to feel. Reyker went out on the deck and leaned against the railing. I followed, standing a few paces away, staring out at the ocean slapping the shore and the fog clinging to the coast.

"Marry me," Reyker said, his gaze fixed on the sea.

I choked on a laugh. "Your romantic timing is for shite."

"I just butchered a dozen of my own people. Not Dragonmen who chose to do the bidding of a tyrant, but noble soldiers willing to give their lives to free their country." He paused, swallowing. He hadn't told me whose blood had been on his hands, and I hadn't asked. "I can't undo it, and I can't keep going unless I know there's an end to all of this, something good waiting for us on the other side. Hope. A future. I need to know that if I become a monster again, you'll be there to bring me back."

"I will."

Finally, he turned to me. "Then I don't care what you do, who you betray, how many you kill. As long as you'll have me, I will be your wolf."

I took a step toward him. "And I will be your deer."

"You are no deer." He took a step to match mine, until he was standing before me. "You are as much a wolf as I am."

I reached up, taking hold of his face. "Marry me here. Now."

"Without a priest? Without a temple or witnesses? It doesn't count."

"We are the priests. This is our temple. The sky and sea are our witnesses." I let my blanket fall at my feet, then tugged his free.

His hands gripped my waist, drawing me against him. He bent his mouth to my ear. "Lira of Stone, of Glasnith, of Iseneld—whoever you are, whoever you become, I will belong to you. All that I have, all that I am, is yours, until the end of my days and forever after. This I vow to you eternally, before the sky and the sea and the gods."

It was a moment before I could speak. "Been practicing that awhile, have you?"

His lips touched my neck, and I felt him smile against my skin. "Only since that first night beneath the thorntree."

I sank my fingers into his hair, thinking. As best I could, I gave voice to the fullness of all the things I felt for him. "Reyker Lagorsson. I will stand beside you, fight with you, until every star falls from the sky and the ocean swallows the land and our bodies turn to dust. I will love you in this world, and any world that comes after. This I vow to you eternally."

Our mouths came together, and so did our flesh. We didn't make it back inside the tower. We consummated our vows on the deck, letting the sky and the sea and the gods bear witness.

Fragile light drifted through the watchtower's windows, illuminating the pallet he lay on, the blanket draped over him. And Lira, her arm thrown across him, her legs tangled with his. "I don't want to leave this tower," she said. "Let's stay here forever."

He took her hand and their rings pressed together—his mother's wedding band on Lira's finger, and a band of steel she'd forged from the blade of a knife on his own. "I would," he said, "if you asked it of me."

"No, you wouldn't. I can already see you planning and plotting."

Reyker sighed. He was the Sword of the Ice Gods, created as a weapon to end his brother—it was his duty. His fate. But with his mind restored and Lira beside him, he couldn't help being bitter over this burden. "We should head to Heligur soon, so I can check what day it is. I've lost track, and Solmangler is nearly upon us. Draki won't harm any of the captured magiskas before midnight on Solmangler. I'm going to make him an offer. A trade. Me, in exchange for a guarantee of safe passage for all the Daughters of Aillira to return to Glasnith."

"He'll never agree to that," Lira said.

"He doesn't have to. He only has to show up, so I can kill him."

Reyker started to rise, but she straddled him, shoving his shoulders down. "How? Are you planning to sweet-talk Draki into falling on his own sword?"

"I'll figure something out."

"There's nothing to figure out. Draki isn't going to kill himself, and he'll kill you if he realizes you know his secret."

"He won't." But Reyker wasn't certain anymore. The destruction of Dragon's Lair had changed things. Draki's obsession with Lira had changed things. He didn't think Draki would kill him on purpose, but if he pushed the Dragon far enough, angered him past his breaking point— then, maybe. "Not if I'm careful."

"Even if he doesn't, he'll hold you captive. Between Draki and his army of Destroyers, we'd never get you back."

"That is a risk we must take. This is my choice. I'm asking you to respect it. If I don't go, Draki will kill all the magiskas, and the Renegades, and your brother. Everything we've been through will be for nothing. Alane's sacrifice will be for nothing."

The words hurt her, but they were necessary. She hung her head, hair falling across her face. Reyker brushed the wild strands back and held her gaze. "I know what I'm fighting for," he said. "Not just our people, our countries. For you. A home. A future."

Lira had described the three visions she'd witnessed inside the seeress's soul: Herself, floating above the altar in the stone circle on Volva Isle. Draki, sitting on a throne, with wings sprouting from his back. And Reyker, his face bloody, some invisible force tearing his soul from his body. She assumed the vision of Reyker had been what was meant to happen at Dragon's Lair, had she not intervened.

Though it made him a liar and a coward, Reyker did not tell her that every seeress was a conduit for the Ice Gods, and that her visions always came true, in one form or another.

"I am a weapon of the Ice Gods. You are the vessel of the Fallen Ones. If anyone can stop a mad demigod, it is us. Together."

How he wanted to believe his own bluster. But in his head, the whispers that taunted him when he'd lost his mind, the refrain he thought he'd escaped when Seffra healed him, began anew. Growing louder. Crowding out all other thoughts.

Hunt.

Feed.

Kill.

CHAPTER 24

LIRA

I managed to hide the tufts of my hair that fell out before Reyker saw them. Luckily my loose molar waited until I was alone at the stream to drop from my gums. I wasn't certain how long I could keep from him that my gifts were killing me, but I was determined to wait until all the Daughters of Aillira were safe.

We made our way across the strip of coastline connecting Gudyafass to Heligur, not knowing what awaited us. "They'll want to kill me for what I did," Reyker said.

"You weren't yourself. They'll forgive you . . . in time."

Me, they would never forgive. No one had forced me to bargain with Seffra. No one made me choose Alane.

A Renegade scout spotted us and ran inland, sounding the alarm. Warriors rushed out from the dormitory and the infirmary, from tents erected around the other buildings. They formed lines, drawing their weapons. The remaining Daughters of Aillira were there, Keeva and Bronagh among them. I couldn't bear to look their way. Instead, I looked at the cage Solvei had made for Draki, reassembled beside the monks' temple. The top was enclosed—the structure was finally complete, likely with the monks' aid.

Reyker lifted his hands to show the Renegades he was unarmed. "My mind is healed. I'm no threat."

"I'll be the judge of that." Solvei stood on the stairs of the infirmary, brandishing her sword. "Do you remember what happened the last time you were here, Lagorsson?"

"I do, and it sickens me. I'm sorry. More than you'll ever know."

"Well, I guess that fixes everything. We can just forget that you ripped apart fourteen of your comrades. That you would have done the same to me, if Sursha hadn't put herself between us."

The pain-wielder. Dead.

I'd hated Sursha for torturing Reyker and me, for sharing Reyker's bed when his mind was fractured, but she was a Daughter of Aillira, and that loss grieved me. Another one of my sisters, gone. It grieved Solvei far more, judging by the lines etched across her features.

"My jarl—"

"I am not your jarl. Not anymore." Solvei turned her fury on me. "I suppose we have you to thank for Alane's madness."

"Yes." Her eyes glinted with fire, but I didn't let myself wilt. I'd made my choice, and I would face its consequences. "It was Seffra's price."

The Daughters of Aillira gasped.

Brokk stepped from the doorway behind Solvei. "You?" he said softly, as if he hadn't believed it until this moment.

He leaped over the railing and ran at me.

Reyker intercepted him—for Brokk's protection, not mine. My hands were already up, ready to subdue him by any means. "You did this, death-bringer!" Brokk shouted from over Reyker's shoulder. "Fix her. Fix her, or I swear I'll kill you."

"I can't. Seffra made a trade. The goddess's bargain was final."

Brokk shoved Reyker away, looking between the two of us. "I curse the day I met either of you. You destroy everything you touch, bring suffering upon everyone around you. Alane defended you both. She is kind and brave, and she doesn't deserve—" A sob shook him.

"Brokk." Reyker reached for his friend. "I'm sorr—"

Brokk's punch knocked Reyker off balance, and he stumbled. Power bubbled in my blood, simmered through my fingers, but Reyker waved me off.

"What if it was her?" Brokk asked Reyker, jerking his chin at me. "If someone had hurt her as she did Alane, what would you do to them?"

"You know what I'd do," Reyker replied. "But you're a better man than me. You've always been better."

Brokk swung at him once more, and this time Reyker caught his fist and pulled him close, whispering something that made Brokk sob harder. The warrior kneed Reyker in the stomach and pointed at me. "If you can't undo it, then go. Both of you. No one wants you here, and gods help me, if I ever see you again . . ." Brokk shook his head, casting a final glare at Reyker before storming off toward the other side of the island.

From the corner of my vision, I saw Keeva edging closer.

With Brokk gone, all eyes returned to Solvei. "I agree with my high commander. The two of you are no longer welcome. You are no longer Renegades."

"We're at war," Reyker said. "Lira and I are your strongest soldiers. You put everyone's life at risk by sending us away."

"I put everyone's life at risk by allowing you to stay."

I felt the sudden pulse of power Keeva sent out, meant to crack my bones, and dodged just before it hit me, sucking the earth from beneath her feet and knocking her flat. "*Stay down*," I sang at her, and she lay there in the dirt, cursing me, unable to move.

The other four Daughters of Aillira came to Keeva's aid, attacking me, and I met wind with wind, fire with fire. I was about to sing at them as well, when several monks rushed from the temple, gesturing frantically— the ones who had arms, at least. Gothi was among them.

"These are holy islands," Gothi said. "Seffra's domain. Such violence is not allowed here. Too much blood has already been spilled." He looked at Reyker. "If the Sword of the Ice Gods had not been stricken by forces beyond his control, Seffra might have struck him dead for profaning this sacred ground, and the rest of you with him."

The command I'd sung wore off, and Keeva stood, spitting like she'd tasted something foul. "You aren't worth it, death-bringer. The gods will see that you get what's coming to you."

With that, the surviving Daughters of Aillira turned their backs on me.

It was no less than I'd expected. Even so, it felt like an amputation, some crucial piece of me torn away.

But they weren't who I'd come here for.

I moved to the infirmary stairs, ignoring the two Renegades who barred my path, appealing to Solvei. "Let me see Alane. I can't fix her, but I can ease her pain." We both knew I could have commanded the jarl with a song, forced her warriors out of my way; that I refrained from using my gifts was a show of good faith.

"It is Brokk's decision," Solvei said.

"Brokk isn't thinking clearly. Don't let Alane suffer just to spite me." I lowered my voice. "Do you think I want to see her? Do you think I want to confront what I've done and what it cost? If you want to punish me, let me do this."

She considered, then nodded for the Renegades blocking me to step aside. Reyker moved to come with me, but Solvei said, "Not him." The Renegades who'd let me pass brought their weapons up again.

"It's all right," I told Reyker.

"Are you sure?" He'd described to me, as best he could, what it was like to lose his memories, to be trapped inside himself with no way to communicate, little understanding of the world. He'd only spent three days in that condition, but it had seemed like an eternity to him. It would be the same for Alane.

He knew what I meant to do.

Reyker could read my expressions as well as I could read his—*I need to do this alone*, I said silently.

The infirmary's main room was large and open, with pallets lining either side of the walls. Monks flitted between them, checking on patients, or praying over them.

"This is Lagorsson's handiwork," Solvei said, coming up behind me. There were eight patients lying on the pallets, men and women with varying injuries. "These are the lucky ones who survived his attack."

"It's unfair to blame Reyker for something he couldn't control."

"I don't. I blame you for it. But I blame him for refusing to see that some part of you was tainted by the Dragon and trouble hounds at your heels."

I had no response. I thought I'd left that part of me behind when Reyker gave me his *skoldar* again, but if that was true, why was there a trail of bodies from Volva Isle to Heligur? Most was Draki's doing, but whether I caused the havoc or it followed me, I was still a death-bringer.

Solvei led the way down a winding hall and opened a door at the end of it. The room was small, empty except for the bed where Alane sat with her back to the door.

"Alane?" I called. She was quiet, still. I touched her, but she didn't move.

When Reyker lost himself, he became a storm, and at the cyclone's center was wrath—the black river of violence that cut through his soul. Alane was different. Not a tempest, but a grave. No one had restrained her because she wasn't a danger to anyone. She didn't acknowledge me as I kneeled and took her hands. "Has she been like this since she . . . changed?" I asked.

"She has. The monks did several tests. Alane doesn't react to light or noise or pain. It's as if she's not even in there."

With a steadying breath, I put my palm to Alane's chest and slipped into her soul.

What I saw were flashes of green cliffs and gray seas, stark mountains and snowy plains. Glasnith. Iseneld. The most beautiful places Alane had been. She returned to them, over and over, through her tract-seeker gift. It made sense that if Reyker had been reduced to his war gift, Alane would be stripped of everything but her god-given abilities. I spoke to her, called her name, but she didn't answer. Whatever else she had been, all the things that had made her Alane were gone.

I pulled free from her soul and sat back.

"Is she in pain?" Solvei asked.

"No. But she's stuck, unable to move on." I let the walls around me fall, let Solvei see my trembling hands and hear the quake in my voice. "What should I do? I can leave her like this, or I can end it. Tell me what you want me to do."

The jarl's expression hardened. "The most important thing I've learned as a leader is that when you make life and death choices for others, you must own those choices. No one else can share your burden. No one else can grant you forgiveness. You traded Alane's life for your lover's. Kill her, or leave her be. The choice is yours. But she is dead, no matter what you do."

Solvei moved to the door.

"Did you love her?" I asked. "Sursha?"

The jarl paused. "Make your choice, magiska. Then you and the Wolf Lord go your own way." She left, her footsteps fading down the hall.

I took Alane's hand, squeezing it, though it lay limp in my own. "Should I wait for Brokk? Would you want him here, to hold you at the end? Is it worse to deny him that, or for him to bear witness?"

Alane stared at nothing, said nothing.

What would I want in my final moments?

Reyker. I would want him there, even though it was selfish, even knowing how it would hurt him. But I doubted he would sit still and let me go. He would rage. He would fight.

So would Brokk. However different he was from Reyker, they both possessed fierce loyalty to those they loved. I couldn't do what needed to be done if Brokk was trying to kill me.

I entered Alane's soul once more.

"I'm sorry, Alane. For so many things."

Images spun around me: the fjords of Fjullthorp, the beaches of Stony Harbor. Glaciers and bluffs. Meadows and lava fields. One place appeared more often than any other—stone buildings circling a giant thorntree. Aillira's Temple, before it fell.

"I'll protect the rest of the Daughters of Aillira. I won't let Draki have them." It was the only thing I had to offer, a feeble attempt to make up for all I'd stolen from her.

As gently as I could, I pulled at her soul until it separated from her body.

The images went black. Her soul slipped through my fingers, a dense sparkling mist that brushed over my skin and evanesced into the ether.

That night, I stood on the deck of the watchtower on Gudyafass as plumes of smoke from Alane's funeral pyre ascended, higher, higher, until they broke apart and merged with the stars.

CHAPTER 25

Gray eyes burrow into me. Nails and knives scrape along my shoulders, down my stomach. Her crimson lips part to reveal a flash of white teeth as she says, Destroy me.

My hands circle her neck. Crack.

When I pull back, the pain-wielder has become the volva. Her beating heart sits in my palm. She blinks and her face shifts.

Green eyes. A tattoo of a thorntree branch beneath her brow. She takes a breath, pushes it from lungs to lips, whispering, In this world, and any world that comes after.

All that I have, all that I am, is yours, *I try to say, but a black river gushes from my mouth, rising around us. The river seems to speak, and the sound of it is*

Hunt.

Feed.

Kill.

Reyker woke, sucking down a lungful of air, rubbing the heels of his hands over his eyes hard enough to hurt. It was still dark, but he felt as if he'd slept a long time. He was lying on the pallet in the watchtower, alone. He pulled on his trousers and boots and went down the stairs.

Lira sat beside the stream with Vengeance, who had followed them when they returned from Heligur. She was pale and hunched beneath the blanket she'd wrapped around her shoulders. Her hair was thinning, the roots coming in white as the moon. The strain of these last weeks had taken a toll on her health. "The sun didn't rise," she said.

He peered at the stars' positions, calculating the time to be two hours past dawn. Usually there was some hint of light by this time of morning, a touch of blue in the black. Today, there was none. "Solmangler."

Once every year, the sun did not show its face. Legends said this was the Ice Gods, testing their people to see if they truly loved the gods who created them, if they were still worthy of the blessings and bounties the gods bestowed. The people humbled themselves with fasting and prayer, begging the gods to bring back the sun. A holy celebration of life, and how life always lived alongside death, the distance between the two no thicker than a razor's edge, a testament to how they all survived by—or at—the gods' mercy.

"Did you sleep at all?" he asked.

She shook her head. Last night, she'd refused to talk. She'd let him hold her, but had kept her back to him, shutting him out. The monks had granted them permission to stay in the vacant watchtower, but the bliss that swathed them that first night as husband and wife had dissolved in the wake of Alane's death, Solvei's rage, Brokk's misery. They had come so far, yet found themselves back where they'd begun—lost, alone, with nothing but each other to hold on to. So he'd held her, while he still could.

Yesterday, while Lira was with Alane, Reyker had stood upon a hill on Gudyafass and lowered the shields he'd built around his mind to protect it from Draki. They had been leveled when he'd lost his memory, and he had no doubt Draki had sensed it, sensed *him*, and knew exactly where he was. *Meet me on the open sea*, he'd said, *three leagues northwest of Heligur, at four hours past midday on Solmangler. In exchange for the magiskas, I will give you what you've always wanted. Harm a single one of them, and there will be no deal.*

There had been no reply, but Reyker knew his brother. Draki would meet him. And when he did, Reyker would attempt to slay the Dragon.

There was nothing left to do but wait.

"You should rest," he told Lira, rubbing Vengeance's neck as the mare pushed her muzzle into his chest.

"Why? We'll all be dead soon." There was no bitterness in her tone, only resignation. "We'll either die because we lost this war, or we'll die winning it. That's why we have to fight. All of us. We lure Draki here, make our final stand."

He sat down next to her. "We cannot fight on Heligur. Seffra might kill us if we bring battle to her shores."

"Then we take our fleet and meet him on the water."

"What fleet? Half our ships are gone, the other half damaged. If we try to fight Draki on the sea, our ships won't last."

"Fine. We repair the ships and sail to Dragon's Domain. Take the battle to his doorstep."

"Even if the Renegades agreed to fight with us, even if Draki wouldn't see an attack coming from a thousand leagues away, you cannot be there, Lira. You would be delivering yourself into his hands, giving the Dragon exactly what he needs to become strong enough to destroy the world. If Draki takes your heart, you will doom us all."

"So I should do nothing?" She threw off the blanket. "My sisters are dying, Reyker, and I've helped kill them. There are so few Daughters of Aillira left, and you think I should just hide here while Draki picks them off? Wait until he comes for me, after absorbing their powers, so he's ten times harder to fight?"

Reyker tasted blood in his mouth. He felt the soft muscle of the volva's heart tearing between his teeth. "I will go to Draki. I will find a way to save the magiskas."

"Oh, so I should hide while you take all the risk, forsaking those pretty vows you just made to me."

"I will not let you be sacrificed on that altar!" He was shouting without meaning to, standing though he didn't realize he'd gotten to his feet. The thought of what the Dragon meant to do had loosened his hold on his war gift—no, that was a lie. His hold had loosened when he'd killed his comrades. He'd overfed it, and now it starved, calling to him constantly, begging him to find someone to hurt. "I will be damned before I let that happen. Gods forgive me, I would sooner let Iseneld and Glasnith burn than let him take your heart."

Feed.

Kill.

Lira watched him, and though it was ridiculous, he worried she'd heard the voice talking to him. "I need to tell you something," she said, taking his hand, placing it over her chest. Her heart beat too quickly, a skittish animal under his palm.

Prey.

He jerked back, battling the river as it writhed inside him.

"I didn't fix you, did I?" Her hand fell limp at her side. "Not completely."

The river was Sjaf's war gift, if what Draki had told Lira was true. All this time, he'd had no name to put to it, labeling it madness. Knowing it came from the sea god, knowing it was meant as a gift rather than a curse, made it no easier to bear.

"You cannot fix fate," he said. "This is how the Ice Gods made me." Maybe it wasn't just losing his memories that had strengthened his cursed gift. Maybe it was because they were getting closer to this war's finale, to the purpose he'd been created to serve. He tried to smile, to keep his voice light as he said, "It doesn't matter. We're all going to die, remember?"

Reyker coaxed Lira into the watchtower, onto the pallet. With his arms around her, she fell into a fitful sleep.

He didn't think he would ever harm her, so long as his mind remained unbroken, but the desire was there, to hurt, to kill—anyone, everyone. When Brokk had punched him, it had been a struggle not to rip off his friend's head. When Solvei had berated him, his instincts had screamed to tear her apart. The river didn't care whether he fed it Dragonmen or Renegades, monks or magiskas.

There was only one person who deserved the full force of the darkness inside him. He just needed to hold on to himself a little longer before he could set it free.

CHAPTER 26

The temple on Heligur was made of staves and built around the largest tree on the island. Inside, it was quiet, filled with flickering candles and burning incense. The monks took turns kneeling before stone effigies of the Ice Gods.

Reyker stood in the back of the temple, wondering what he was doing. In a few hours he would sail to meet Draki. Restless, he'd left Lira asleep in the watchtower with Vengeance standing guard outside. He'd come to the temple, lining up alongside monks who had given pieces of themselves, sacrificed their sight or hearing, their limbs or flesh, to save others in Seffra's name.

The line moved, the monks shifted, and Reyker found himself in front of a statue of Ildja. The artist had gotten her wrong. The figure wasn't nearly beautiful enough, and the features were serene rather than vicious.

"Bitch." He spit at Ildja's likeness.

Around him, the monks protested at his blasphemy.

Prey, the river hissed. Reyker slapped at his ear, as if the voice wasn't coming from inside his mind.

"Come now," Gothi said, stepping out from beside the statue of Sjaf. "We've been graced by the presence of a warrior touched by the Ice Gods themselves. Allow him to worship as he sees fit." The monk nodded at Reyker. "Will you walk with me, Wolf Lord?"

The two of them left the temple, and Reyker followed as the monk strolled inland, past naked trees and brush, their leaves newly fallen, swathing their roots like shed robes. "Did you help Jarl Solvei complete the cage she's been constructing?" Reyker asked.

"I did," the monk replied.

"And do you think it will work?"

"If the gods desire it."

"Ildja is a god."

"Yes." Gothi smiled. "One of many."

They arrived at the ruins of a temple. The tree in the center still stood, cut off by a moat of rubble. The statues here had been knocked over, their stone faces shattered beyond recognition, as if someone had taken a hammer to them. Gothi bowed to the statues.

"Did someone desecrate one of your temples?" Reyker asked.

"Misguided monks inspired by jealous gods, long before my time. Purists who refused to acknowledge the Ice Gods' kin, the extended pantheon of our world's creators. A broken family, but a family nonetheless."

"The Green Gods." Reyker's gaze scraped over the smashed statues. Could one of them be Gwylor? Or Veronis?

"And the Sand Gods of Sanddune. The Bush Gods of Savanna. The Salt Gods of the Auk Isles. Though my deepest devotion lies with the gods of my homeland, with Seffra in particular, I've sought to learn about and show reverence to them all."

So many gods, all of them related. It shouldn't have been surprising, yet Reyker had not thought beyond the stories he'd been told since boyhood and those he had discovered of late.

"Many of the gods had spouses," Gothi continued. "A few even begot children. Though only one, to my knowledge, was able to have a half-mortal child without surrendering her immortality. What Ildja and her spawn have done to this world does not sit well with Seffra. I doubt it pleases any of their kin. The Ice Gods made you to be a foil to your brother, as Gwylor and Veronis were to each other. The gods await your response."

"My response?" His laughter split the quiet. It did not belong in this holy place, just as Reyker did not belong. "I need a command. A message. A sign."

"Are you certain they have not given you one?"

Hunt.

Feed.

"An order to kill everyone around me?" Reyker asked.

"Perhaps you are not truly listening." The monk shook his head. "Now, if you'll indulge me, there is something I must ask, Lord Lagorsson. A story I want to tell you. Years ago, before I came to Heligur, I had a wife. A son."

Reyker said nothing, curious about this turn of conversation.

"My wife died of heartbreak after our son was killed. My son . . . well, Knut was not content to simply be a holy man like his father. He studied the art of war along with the gods' scriptures and became a warrior-priest. He obsessed over the prophecy about the god-man who would conquer the world in the name of the Ice Gods. While serving under Overlord Eldjarn, he was sent on a mission from which he never returned: to execute the sons of Lord Lagor Ivarsson."

Reyker's sword was out before Gothi finished speaking, the tip pointed at the man's neck. "If you brought me out here to exact your revenge, you are a fool."

Feed.

Kill.

"So it was you who killed Knut, not your brother? I suspected, but I did not know for certain. If I wanted you dead, I'd have left you in the sea where I found you. I'd have let you bleed out instead of sharing the burden of your injury." Gothi pulled his robe open, revealing the scar on his chest that matched Reyker's. "The last time you were here, you were too ill, and then you were in too much of a hurry to return to Glasnith. I had no chance to speak with you. All I want is to know of Knut's last moments. What he said. If he suffered. Had Knut succeeded, your father would have wished for the same."

Slowly, Reyker lowered his sword, even as the black river pleaded with him to use it. Gothi was old, his body bent and worn from drawing others' wounds into himself. The holy man was no threat. "I supposed it's the least I can offer."

They stood side by side, under a sky of endless night, next to the faceless gods of the world outside Iseneld. The monk and his son's murderer.

Reyker relived that day, that moment, as if it had just happened. How the warrior-priest, Knut, had attacked him and Aldrik while they were out hunting. How Knut was the one to reveal what Aldrik was: the son of Ildja, a half god destined to leave a trail of destruction as he claimed an empire. How Aldrik had goaded nine-year-old Reyker into stabbing the priest to silence him. Reyker's first kill, the first hint of his battle-madness.

Had he not killed the warrior-priest, might he never have awoken his curse?

Had he not killed Knut, might the priest have done what Aldrik feared—spread the word about who Aldrik was, perhaps resulting in Aldrik being hunted down before he had a chance to sell his soul to Ildja, eat the hearts of a coven, and render himself invulnerable?

Had the act of Reyker murdering Knut been the catalyst for everything that came after?

Gothi's gaze was faraway, his eyes damp. Reyker should have apologized. Gods knew he was sorry for taking this man's son, for *every* son he'd ever taken, rightly or unjustly, but he couldn't form the words. All he could say was, "Would you still have saved me, if you'd known?"

"Of course. You were gravely wounded and this is my purpose. I've devoted my life to healing those who need it. Pride, wrath, retribution— these things have no bearing on a monk, no place on Heligur. That is why you cannot hear the gods' message. It is why Sjaf's war gift drives so many to madness. The mortal mind is congested. Your guilt, your thirst for revenge, your fury at how you and those you care for have been wronged, takes your gift to a dark place, bends it to your will instead of the gods'. Even when you lost your memories, your soul clung to its rage. Let it go, and you will finally hear the gods clearly. You will understand your true purpose."

Every insult, every wound, every kill. The cruel things that had been done to him, or that he had done to others on Draki's orders. "How am I supposed to simply let go of those things?"

"By holding on to something else."

It was the lesson Lira had taught him in Stony Harbor. She had helped him let go of his hate, enough to learn how to love. Enough to allow himself to be loved in return. By chance or by fate, they had found each other. She had healed him, then broken him, then healed him again, and he was that much stronger for it.

He closed his eyes and looked inward, at the boiling black river of his soul. The warlord's face swam along its surface, as it always did. *Be still*, he told the river, and the boiling faded to a simmer. *You don't own me anymore*, he said to the image, washing away the unearthly eyes, the cruel smile. In its place, the water was a blank canvas. He envisioned his parents, painting his childhood memories of them across the river. He pictured Vaknavangur and its people, Brokk among them. And Lira, the way she'd looked at him as they spoke their vows.

The river fought him. It whispered violence into his thoughts, but he felt its hold loosen. He did not hear the gods, not yet, but their absence was keen, almost tangible. Like an empty stage, a lonely instrument—a promise that if he waited and listened long enough, someone would come play him a song.

He opened his eyes.

Gothi put one hand on Reyker's shoulder. The other wove around Reyker's head, tracing a symbol of blessing along the air. "May the gods light your path and shield you from your enemies, Wolf Lord."

"I don't deserve your forgiveness," Reyker said, "but I will do my best to earn it."

"Yes," the monk agreed. "I believe you will."

His talk with the monk had inspired him to try once more to make amends. The jarl had banished him, but if he could find the right words, maybe she would reconsider. If nothing else, he wanted another chance to apologize and explain before it was too late. Reyker walked in circles, chewing over what to say to Brokk and Solvei. When he could no longer postpone, he headed back toward where the Renegades were camped.

The blare of a ship's horn made him jump.

Reyker ran for the cove. By the position of the stars, he knew it was barely midday, but there, just beyond the edge of Heligur's shore, was the warlord, standing in the bow of a longship under the pallid moonlight. A fleet floated behind him, every sail bearing the Star of the Dragon.

Brother, Draki said. *Your message was so intriguing, I could wait no longer. Is my death-bringer around, or did that beast inside you lose its temper and tear her to pieces?*

"Get out of my head, Draki."

Then come here so we can speak like men. Like family. Or must an example be made of the rest of your pitiful army?

Renegades were spread along the beach. He saw Brokk and Solvei, wearing their war faces, their axes and swords ready. The Renegades' heads swung back and forth between their jarl and Draki's forces, awaiting orders. There were so few of his comrades left. Another battle might spell the end of Solvei and her resistance.

The black river twisted and burned inside him.

How was he supposed to remain calm, to temper his rage so he could hear the gods' command, while Draki threatened everything that mattered to him?

"Neither you nor your men can come ashore," Reyker said. "The monks have pledged their protection to us. These are Seffra's isles and she won't abide you waging war on them."

Not me. But alas, I cannot control all those Destroyers who escaped from the Mist.

In the distance, hovering over the dark waves, were hundreds of winged, skeletal shadows. Reyker wasn't certain what Seffra would do if they attacked—perhaps she would retaliate, or possibly Ildja had found a sacred-ground loophole for Draki to exploit. Either way, he wasn't willing to risk the lives of the Renegades and monks.

"All right. I'll come to you."

He looked over his shoulder toward Gudyafass. Toward Lira. He'd hoped they would have a few more moments together, yet what would it have mattered? A day, a year, a thousand lifetimes—it would never be enough. She must have heard the horn, was likely riding Vengeance here now, but Draki was not patient, and there was no time to wait to say goodbye.

As Reyker hurried to the pier, Brokk caught up to him. "I see you're trying to get yourself killed again, you stupid bastard."

Reyker spun and threw his arms around Brokk, pulling him close. "You are my one true brother," he said. "Once I'm gone, tell the Renegades to flee. Take the magiskas as far from here as you can, to the ends of the earth if you must. Protect them with your life, Brokk. *All* of them. Swear it."

"I swear." Brokk hugged him hard. "We will meet again, brother."

They released each other, and Reyker spotted Solvei standing on the beach with the other Renegades. Reyker saluted his jarl, knocking a fist against his chest and raising it into the air. She stared at him for a beat, and then she returned the gesture.

The black river shifted, its murderous call silenced, if only briefly.

Reyker unmoored one of the monks' rowboats and jumped in, rowing across the bay to meet Draki's ship. Once he reached the longship, he climbed over the railing and tied the rowboat to it. The gesture felt foolish, based on the expectation that he would leave the ship as he'd arrived—of his own volition, with his body mostly intact.

Hovering above the ship, the Destroyers hissed, the rasp of their wings sending shivers along Reyker's nerves. At least if they attacked, Lira could keep the Renegades safe. He didn't dare look at the shore, afraid he would see her there and lose his resolve.

Draki leaned against the mast. "Why have you called me here?"

There were ten stone-faced Dragonmen on board, standing stiffly at their posts. None had drawn a weapon yet. The ship itself did not move, anchored against gusts and waves by the Dragon's power. His brother was shirtless as usual, tattooed skin glowing, sword strapped to his back. How was he supposed to get Draki to draw that sword and stab himself?

If what Gothi said was true, all the pieces were lined up. Reyker knew the secret to killing Draki. His gift was awake. He needed time to study his brother, regain his trust. To wait for the gods to show him his path.

"It's over." Reyker took off his belt, tossing his sword at Draki's feet. "You've won. Most of the Renegades are dead, their army weakened beyond repair. Let them live out their days on Heligur as exiles, never to return home. Let the magiskas go back to Glasnith. You don't need them. You're already the most powerful sovereign in history. No one will stand against you, and even if they did, they would be swiftly defeated."

Draki circled his hand impatiently through the air. "What exactly is it you are offering?"

It was a deal Draki would never uphold, but Reyker didn't need him to. He only needed to distract Draki for a few hours, long enough for the others to escape.

"Me," Reyker said. "That's what this is about, isn't it? Not the Renegades or the magiskas, not even Lira. This has always been about you wanting me to stand at your side, not as an unwilling tool, but as a peer who shares in your victories instead of undermining them. I've fought you for so long, and I'm tired of fighting."

They weren't lies—gods aflame, how he wished they were.

He kneeled, bowing his head. "I give in, Draki. I give up. Let the others go, and I'll come with you. I'll be your dutiful Sword."

For as long as it took to form a plan and carry it out, to find a way to get the Dragon to put a blade through his own heart, Reyker could do this. He could pretend to be the Dragon's Sword one last time. And if he lost himself in the process, if he failed to kill Draki . . . well, at least Brokk would have gotten the magiskas away by then.

He lifted his head and found Draki's eyes fixed on him, unblinking. The river wanted to control him, to break his fist on Draki's face, shatter his sword against Draki's neck. To repeat the same mistakes of his past. With a deep breath, he loosened his clenched fingers. When the river screamed at him to *Hunt-Feed-Kill*, he spoke over it calmly. *Preserve. Defend. Shield.*

"You're a traitor," Draki said. "I cannot trust you."

There was such hunger in those quiet words. They were not a refusal, but an invitation to be proven wrong. One last push, and Reyker would have him.

"If I betray you, you can kill me. You can sail to Heligur and kill every last Renegade. You can sail to Glasnith, round up the magiskas and bring them back. What do you have to lose?" Reyker dropped his voice to a whisper. "Turn down this trade, and you can imprison me, torture me, but it will be as it was before. I'll fight you. I'll deny you. This is the only way we both get what we want . . ."

Say it. You must say it.

". . . my jarl. My emperor. My brother."

CHAPTER 27

LIRA

I woke to the blast of a horn, with heavy lids and a head full of cobwebs. Outside, someone screamed. Victory brayed in alarm.

"Reyker." I rolled over, but he was gone. Victory shrieked again, louder this time. I strapped on my weapons and pulled on my boots, clambering down the stairs.

A figure stood by the stream wearing a black velvet dress that accentuated her liquid-fire hair, her glowing ember eyes. She gripped Victory's mane in one hand. In the other, she held Keeva by the neck.

"Let them go, Ildja."

Fire bloomed from the goddess's hands. Victory's mane burned and a ring of charred flesh circled Keeva's throat. "I have to spill a bit of blood. Which one should it be? You love the mare, but she is only an animal. The girl is your sister magiska, yet she came here to kill you." Ildja kicked something at me, and it landed at my feet—a wooden spike, carved with runes. "Shall I let you decide, soul-reader? You are quite practiced with such choices."

I noticed the ice dagger tucked into the satin ribbon at Ildja's waist. "You cannot harm us," I said. "This is holy ground. Seffra forbids it."

"Yes. My sweet, peace-loving cousin. Seffra will not tolerate spilled blood on her scraggly island." She dragged a fingernail along Keeva's throat, breaking the skin. "My son wants you alive, soul-reader, but I've no use for a horse, and all I need from the healer is her heart."

Ildja flicked a red droplet from her fingertip, letting it fall to the ground.

She was a goddess—there was no way for me to defeat her unless I could wrestle the dagger from her and stab her with it, a near-impossible feat. But that didn't mean I wouldn't try. "Don't threaten us, you fire-eyed bitch."

Ildja clenched her teeth. "I am the eater of souls, mortal scum. For that insult, I will take a bite of yours."

Behind us, the stream bubbled and churned. A pillar of water rose up, higher and higher, forming the shape of a woman.

"You will do no such thing, cousin," Seffra said in her liquid voice. Though she spoke the language of gods, the Fallen Ones' blood enabled me to understand. "These three creatures are guests on my island, therefore their fates belong to me." There was no kindness in Seffra's defense of us. It was clear, by her dismissive glance, that we meant no more to her than a spider, a boulder, a speck of dirt that happened to find itself sitting on land the goddess claimed dominion over. "Long have I hoped you would break our accords, Ildja, so that I might censure you for the barbarous acts you committed against so many of our kin. If any god deserves to be locked away in a prison, it is you."

"Seffra," Ildja replied with a smile. "Mother goddess, adored by mortals. They have forgotten what we are, just as you have. Just as my poor, pitiful sister did, before I taught her a lesson. We are not simply blessings and praise. We are terror and awe, the shadows they fear and the deaths they run from. The time has come to remind them. To remind *you*."

Ildja's human guise shifted, black dress swirling into ebony smoke, alabaster skin blurring into white fire, so bright I couldn't look directly at it. Her body stretched and grew until she was taller than Seffra, floating above the ground.

Seffra's human shape shifted into a waterspout that sliced through the air.

Keeva seemed to regain her senses, enough that she was able to leap onto Victory's back. I thought she'd try and leave without me—a thing

Victory would never allow—but she waited, throwing me an impatient glare.

I crept toward them, trying not to attract the goddesses' attention.

"It is Solmangler," Ildja said to Seffra. "The sun will not rise again until everyone in this realm, mortal and deity, submits to the rule of the Dragon and the will of the death gods."

The water that made up Seffra's body pulsed, spinning faster. "You and Gwylor mean to place yourselves above the rest of us?"

"We have always been above you. If you will not bow to me, Seffra, you can join our cousins in the prison-realm."

I made it to Victory, pulling myself up behind Keeva, and the mare took off.

Over my shoulder, I watched as the two goddesses crashed together. The force of it shook the mountain. Ildja and Seffra thrashed and hurled each other about, moving so fast their forms were streaking phantoms.

The ice dagger appeared in what must have been Ildja's hand. Ildja's arm was a blur, the blade a flash of white piercing the gyrating streams of Seffra's body. The mother-goddess's soul drained into the ice. Her essence was made of water, and it danced frantically inside the blade as the stream that gave her form evaporated. The entire stream—winding from the mountain summits, traveling down to merge with the sea—dried up in an instant, every drop, every fragment of Seffra, dissolving.

Far out on the sea, my heightened hearing sensed a rumble. An inhuman cry.

Ildja's voice echoed from the depths of the flame. "Come, sea god, I await you."

The goddess morphed again, stretching and rising, becoming a giant cloud of fire and ash, floating higher, until she covered the island and blotted out the black sky.

Just as we reached Heligur's shore, rain began to fall in bright-red smears—liquid fire, dripping down like burning oil. Embers, showering the island in trails of gold.

A wind-wafter used her gift to protect as many of the monks and Renegades as she could, and a tide-teller stood at the edge of the sea pushing up a shield of water, but there was too much fire and too many people. The infirmary, the temple, the dormitory, the woods beyond—they were all burning. Those who couldn't fit beneath the magiskas' shields ran for the water, trying to escape the fiery rain by diving beneath the waves.

The only thing not burning or melting was Solvei's cage. The bars were covered in lava, but it dribbled off the metal and bones like water off a duck's back. This meant something—I knew it did—but there was no time to think on it.

The monks rushed to help those who'd been injured by the fire. Brokk and Solvei did the same, helping those the monks hadn't gotten to, and Keeva dismounted to join them.

"To the ships!" Solvei called. "Help your kinsmen. No one gets left behind."

But the ships and the pier they were tied to were on fire like everything else. A tide-teller crouched at the dock's edge, trying to put the fires out, and I hurried to add my gift to hers. We doused the pier and the ships until the fires were out, then forged shields over the area to keep the flames from rekindling. The ships were blackened, but still afloat. Better to chance them sinking than burn to death.

Solvei was right behind us, helping one Renegade while carrying a second over her shoulder. Victory had two injured monks slung across her back. Every Renegade who could walk aided those who couldn't, and a crowd formed at the pier. Some of the planks had collapsed, and Brokk straddled the gap to help people get across without falling. I stood aside, letting Renegades, magiskas, and monks pass.

"Where's Reyker?" I asked once everyone else had boarded.

"Gone," Brokk said. "With Draki."

It was Reyker's plan. He wanted me to respect his choice, allow him a chance at killing the Dragon. But it was wrong for him to do this alone.

"We have to go after him," I said.

Brokk started to reply, but a scream cut him off. People on the ships were pointing at a wave as tall as the mountain on Gudyafass moving along the sea's surface, towing icebergs in its wake. It stopped in the middle of Heligur's cove, and an outline appeared on the wave's face, formed of salt water and ice crystals. Two thick, leg-like columns pushed free of the foam, followed by a torso with fins instead of arms, and finally a giant head that was half-man, half-fish, with shark teeth jutting from his mouth. The creature's voice was guttural, his words slurred by those fangs. "Serpent-goddess, eater of souls!"

"All-God Sjaf," Brokk whispered. "Gods a-fucking-flame."

Sjaf. Seffra's husband. Strongest of the Ice Gods, save Ildja.

The firestorm that was Ildja sizzled with lightning, crackled with a sound akin to laughter. Sjaf roared and grabbed at one of the icebergs floating on his back.

"Brokk! Lira!" Solvei shouted.

We ran, leaping over the broken pieces of the pier.

Sjaf's fin closed around the massive chunk of ice and hurled it at Ildja. Lightning and sparks split the iceberg apart. The fragments crashed down across the island and the sea, and a lump of ice as big as one of the ships came hurtling at us. It slammed into my shield and I fumbled, pushing my fire gift out, melting it.

My head spun. Blood poured from my eyes.

Brokk and I made it to the ship just as Sjaf scooped up another iceberg. The magiskas were spread out across the ships, lifting shields of wind and water and fire. The sky shattered with lightning, but one of the icebergs slipped through and hit the center of the churning cloud. Ice and fire rained down.

The ships rocked as Renegades raised the sails and took the helms. Blocks of ice plummeted into the sea outside the magiskas' shields. The storm shrank and shrank, into the figure of a woman, a goddess, falling from the stars. A translucent blade glinted in her hand.

Sjaf snapped his shark teeth at her, but she landed between his thrashing fins. Ildja shoved the dagger in. The wall of water went white with foam and froth, bubbling, eddying. It lost its form as Sjaf's soul was sucked into the dagger. With a roar, the mountain of water came thundering down, rushing for the fleet.

Standing in the bow, I struggled to catch the flood, pouring every bit of strength I had into holding it back. My heart knocked against my sternum, my lungs strove to draw air. The wave's crest hung suspended above the ships, casting them in its shadow. The tide-teller and wind-wafter steered the flect past the wave as fast as they could.

As soon as we were beyond its path, I let the wave go. Swells shook the ships, but the bulk of the water's fury was behind us. My muscles shook and I collapsed. An arm hooked around my waist, settling me onto the deck. I looked up at Solvei. "I suppose we can't toss you overboard after that," she said.

Blackness gnawed at the edge of my vision. Through the blood clogging my ears, I heard the muffled *scritch-scratch* coming from above us. I didn't want to see, but I had to.

I glanced up as a dark mass of Destroyers dove at our ship.

CHAPTER 28

DRAKI

His longship cut through the sea, splitting the waves like flesh yielding to steel. This was his gift. It rendered the strength of mortals and the forces of nature impotent.

Heligur was far behind them, a distance too great to be perceived by mortal eyes or ears, but Draki could see the smoke and fire rising from the isle and hear the roars of Seffra and Sjaf as his mother sent them to the prison-realm. She might as well have killed them—to an infinite being, eternal captivity was worse than death.

He smiled at his brother, who was still on his knees. Draki had not given Reyker leave to rise, and like an obedient vassal, he had remained where he was.

Reyker had never bowed, never called him by his titles, not in all the times Draki had threatened and punished him. It did something to Draki. A strange flutter was building behind his sternum. He'd tasted victory many times, sacking villages, executing enemies, but breaking a person, breaking his *brother*, who had battled him endlessly—it was sweeter than breaching an impregnable tower, felling an unconquer-able foe.

He spoke into Reyker's mind. *If you go back on your word, I will do to the Renegades what I did to the men of Vaknavangur. I will flay every magiska from scalp to toes. And you will watch.*

Reyker gritted his teeth. His pupils swelled, blacker than night, then receded. "Understood, emperor."

"I have something for you." From the sheath on his back, Draki drew his sword—their father's sword, which had been lost to the sea after the attack on Dragon's Lair. He had spent hours diving through the wreck of his fortress, searching for the weapon. It was worth it for this moment, as he presented the sword to his brother.

"This is new." Reyker's hand trembled as he ran his finger along the etchings in the blade—black flames, like the ones above Reyker's right eye. Draki had carved the design into the steel himself. "Why did you kill him?" Reyker whispered.

He'd never asked before.

Draki had not intended to execute Lagor, only to shame him, to keep him in a cage and parade him around in front of any lords who refused to accept the Dragon's reign. But then Lagor had raised this sword, aimed it at his own son's neck. "What is that excuse you're so fond of? 'A choice that is not a choice.' I gave Lagor a chance to surrender, to live. Instead, he tried to kill me. He defied me in front of my men. He is the one who taught me that such offense cannot go unpunished."

Draki waited for Reyker to argue, to curse him, but he remained silent, staring at the sword. Then at him. It was a single moment, their shared past and shared blood winding around them. Draki knew those bonds felt like a noose to Reyker, but to him, it had always been a tether—allowing his brother a semblance of freedom while keeping him from straying too far, never letting Reyker forget where he'd come from or who he could be.

"You will use this only in my service," Draki said. "Take it."

Reyker gripped the hilt. Above the shine of the blade, something else glinted—a metal band on Reyker's finger. A ring.

The flutter died in Draki's chest. "You wed her?"

Reyker touched the ring. It seemed an unconscious gesture, as if he meant to conceal it despite knowing it was too late.

Draki's laughter was threaded with rage. "You cannot serve me if you hold another above me." He'd learned this lesson with Katrin. It wasn't until after she died that Reyker truly gave in to his war gift. "Cut it off."

Reyker stared at him. "What?"

"Taking the ring off is not enough. Your finger must go, too, so you cannot simply put another on in its place. Consider it your first act of devotion to your emperor. Prove you are fit to stand at my side."

Dragonmen leaned forward to see if Reyker would comply. Draki wondered himself. He had not planned his next steps if Reyker refused— perhaps he would threaten to cut his whole hand off. Perhaps he would follow through.

Reyker looked at the ring. The Dragonmen coughed and fidgeted.

Draki sighed. Yes, he would have to make an example of Reyker. If not the hand, maybe an eye would do.

Before Draki had decided, Reyker spoke. "I broke my vows to her when I stepped onto this ship." Reyker splayed his hand beneath their father's sword, resting his other fingers atop the blade as he angled it diagonally over his ring-finger. He put his weight on the sword hilt in one swift thrust that sank the blade to the bone. His expression almost serene, Reyker sawed through his finger bone. When it was done, he sat back and smiled at his amputated finger sitting in a spreading pool of red.

Maybe Reyker was ready to stand at Draki's side, or maybe the madness of his gift had finally breached beyond the battlefield.

"Someone get my brother a bandage," Draki said. The Dragonmen scrambled to find a suitable length of cloth, and Reyker wrapped his bleeding hand.

Draki pocketed Reyker's finger and picked up the wedding band. It was smooth, unadorned steel. "You gave in easier than I expected," Draki said.

"I told you. I'm tired of this fight. I just want it to be over."

"So you say." Draki tossed the ring in the air. "If you pass your next test as dutifully as you did this one, I might believe you."

Reyker's eyes narrowed. His lip curled. There it was—a trace of fear, of fury. "What test?" He glanced out at the water, at the smattering of stars overhead, and Draki saw the truth register as Reyker's shoulders sagged. "We aren't sailing to Iseneld, are we?"

"I thought you would be happy to return to your home on the Haunted Isles. Several of your companions await your arrival."

"What are you going to do, Draki?"

"It is Solmangler." Draki gestured at the blackness enveloping them. "We must pay tribute to the gods of old. And to the ones about to replace them."

The Destroyers' talons dug into my shoulders and ankles. Far below, the sea reflected the sky, an obsidian mirror, so the darkness seemed endless. All I could hear was the rasp of wings and the howl of wind.

On either side of me, Keeva, Bronagh, and the other three Daughters of Aillira were trapped as I was, each woman gripped by a pair of Destroyers. We were high enough that if we fell, hitting the water might kill us. If my gifts were at full strength, maybe I could have brought the creatures down, buffered us with wind to soften our landing, but I wasn't willing to gamble when the price was our lives. Too many of my sisters were already gone.

Even if I took out every Destroyer, there was nothing but ocean for leagues in all directions. And there was Ildja, flying ahead of us on the back of the largest Destroyer. Leading us to Volva Isle, to the stone circle. To our deaths.

Another spurt of blood cut a path from my nose to my chin as I dredged up a thread of power and called out.

Deep below the surface, on the bottom of the sea, I sensed an answer to my call.

CHAPTER 29

REYKER

Where his finger had once been, there was only a throbbing wound, the bandage already soaked through. Reyker couldn't help but think of Hilde, the harpist-turned-priestess he'd befriended in Dragon's Lair. Hilde had been maimed by a Dragonman, the three middle fingers on both her hands sawed off before Reyker arrived and put his sword through the bastard who'd done it. One finger didn't seem like much in comparison. He pulled the cloth free as the longship anchored just off Volva Isle, and he followed the Dragonmen over the side of the ship, into the water, trudging up to the shore.

He knew what was coming, the choice Draki would force on him. He took deep breaths, struggling to remain calm, to allow the gods to wield his gift rather than the other way around. *Help me,* he cried out to them. *Show me how to stop this.*

Reyker remembered everything now, as he crossed the isle's hills—being here as a boy, witnessing the massacre and its aftermath, the piled bodies of dead witches, their blood caked on the soles of his boots. He sensed their spirits sweeping past him.

His blood joined theirs, dripping from his hand into the earth.

Ten magiskas were lined up outside the stone circle, bound and gagged by thick rope painted with runes—wards, smothering their gifts. They were young, some of them barely women. Some had come to Iseneld voluntarily and others Reyker had brought here, but they had all fought bravely against the Dragon's forces.

They were all about to die for it.

Reyker found Eathalin among the magiskas. He slipped a knife into his bloody bandage and dropped it beside her. When he glanced up, he was facing the Dragonman who'd given the bandage to him on the ship. Joren, Solvei's spy. His features were so similar to Andrithur's, it was like looking at a ghost.

Their eyes met briefly. Joren gave a slight nod.

Draki stood in the stone archway, waiting. His eyes shifted and he brushed at his arms, as if he, too, felt the phantom touch of the women who had raised him, the volvur he'd killed. The Dragon was not as unshakable as he pretended.

"Brother. It is time." Draki beckoned, and the first magiska was dragged into the stone circle, a Dragonman on either side of her.

An earth-shifter. Darah. Her name was Darah.

The undead volvur who died inside the stones stood around the altar, motionless, their eyes clouded. Though their bodies remained, and some echo of their souls could still pass along memories of their deaths, they were no more than shuffling specters. They did nothing as the Daughter of Aillira was pinned to the altar, thrashing and crying through her gag.

Reyker stepped between the girl and Draki. "We had a deal."

"That I would not lay a finger upon the Renegades and magiskas"—Draki waved Reyker's severed finger at him—"*if* you prove you are fit to stand beside me. So the question is, how much do you care for your comrades? How much do you love my death-bringer? One heart, Reyker. Take one magiska's heart for yourself and consume it, and I will spare the rest."

"I don't believe you." Reyker had taken a volva's heart. Even if the Dragon wasn't lying, he could not bear to take another.

Draki shrugged. He darted past Reyker and punched his fist through Darah's chest so fast Reyker would have missed it if he'd blinked. The earth-shifter's cries fell silent. Her heart pulsed in Draki's clenched fingers.

"I can ask you this question"—Draki counted the magiskas left—"nine more times." He shoved the heart into his mouth.

The other Daughters of Aillira were screaming. Blood dripped from the corners of Draki's lips. His skin glowed, his veins shimmering beneath, warmed by the life force he'd stolen. He sighed at the surge of the girl's strength flowing into him.

Reyker was going to be sick. He was losing control, the river tightening around him like wire, pushing out all rational thought.

No, no, he had to stay calm. *Help me*, he pleaded with the Ice Gods. *Wield me. Show me what I must do to destroy him.*

There was no answer.

"There you are, spell-caster," Draki said as Eathalin was led to the altar by two Dragonmen.

Reyker tore the girl away from the Dragonmen, held her behind him. "I won't let you do this."

One second Draki was across the circle from Reyker, and the next, Draki was right in front of him, grabbing him by the collar. "You've never been able to stop me before. What makes you think this time will be any different?" The Dragon kicked him, and Reyker went flying into one of the megaliths. He crashed into it and slid to the ground.

Draki dismissed the Dragonmen and took hold of Eathalin's chin, making the girl flinch.

Inside Reyker, the black river swirled into a vortex.

Please.

Calm. Calm.

Help me.

"You," Draki said to Eathalin, "are the one who continues to challenge me, the one I attacked the ships to find when you fled these isles. You are meant for more than a sacrifice. When Ildja returns, we will remove your *skoldar* and make use of her dagger." He traced a dragon star across the girl's collarbones. "Would you like to be my empress, little warrior?"

Damn the gods for ignoring him. He could not wait.

Reyker staggered to his feet and drew his father's sword. "Get away from her."

"Defy me," Draki said, "and our bargain is void. What is the spell-caster to you? A gifted foreign girl from across the sea, one you barely know. Is she worth the lives of your comrades? Would you truly trade the woman you claim to love for this child?"

Lira had been no more than a gifted foreign girl when Reyker met her, yet he had risked himself to keep her safe from Draki. And it had changed everything. "If I did not try to save this girl, I would not be the man Lira loves. I am the weapon of the Ice Gods. I am my father's son." He pointed his sword at the Dragon.

"I will not suffer your foolishness, brother. Not tonight, when I have waited so long for this. A Solmangler unlike any other. Ildja has used her key to rid Iseneld of Seffra and Sjaf's oppression. Soon, any god who fails to recognize her sovereignty and mine will join the Fallen Ones in their prison."

Was that why no one answered him? If the gods he pleaded with were locked in a cage, he truly was alone. "Sjaf is the father of Iseneld! You used to worship him."

"Once I've consumed the magiskas' powers, I will be stronger than Sjaf. I am Iseneld's father, Iseneld's god. I am everyone's god. I want you at my side, brother. Rule with me, and we will remake the world."

"You have gone completely mad." Outside the circle, a crowd moved across the island—Dragonmen corralling twenty women toward the stones, tied up with wards as the other magiskas were. The Dragon must have stolen them from Glasnith. "Why are they here? Lira did not give the Fallen Ones' blood to them."

"The blood of Veronis runs through every Daughter of Aillira," Draki said. "I will not spare a drop. The rest are on their way. My mother is fetching them from Heligur. I did consider letting Lira live, but it would be a waste when she's already dying."

The sword slipped, and Reyker fumbled to catch it.

"You didn't know? Did you rut your bride without even looking at her? Her body is coming apart. She bleeds like a sliced artery every time she uses her gifts." Draki took out Reyker's ring, closing his fist around it. When he opened his hand, the ring was nothing but dust, trickling through his fingers. "No point in keeping her alive now that I've found a new consort."

Draki moved toward Eathalin and Reyker brought his sword up. "You won't touch another Daughter of Aillira."

"You never learn, Reyker." Draki grabbed the blade with his bare hands and snapped it in half. He shoved Reyker aside.

Eathalin tore off the warded ropes that bound her, the small knife Reyker had left in his bandage clutched in her hand. She vanished. So did the land outside the stone circle, disappearing in a shroud of fog. Draki roared, racing for the archway, and Reyker lunged to stop him.

Eathalin was free. She could blind the Dragonmen. With Joren's help, she could unbind the rest of the Daughters of Aillira and get them to a ship. Reyker needed to buy them time. If the gods could not aid him in slaying the Dragon, he would make do without them.

He raised his father's broken sword.

I will save the last of Lira's sisters. I will defend the descendants of Aillira and Veronis from the seed of Ildja, the kin of Gwylor, to the end.

Volva Isle was within sight when the world vanished. One moment there was black sky above and black sea below, the green humps of the Haunted Isles rising from the waves. The next, everything went bright white. I couldn't see anything but the Destroyers carrying me. Beneath the veil, storm clouds formed, crackling and glowing with lightning.

The onslaught began all at once.

The veil dropped. Wind and rain and ice slammed into the Destroyer Ildja rode, throwing it off balance.

Below were two of the Dragon's longships. Lined up along the bow of each ship were over a dozen young women—Daughters of Aillira, their hands stretched to the sky. Eathalin was in the center of the line on one of the ships, smiling up at me. There were Dragonmen, too—Joren, and the warriors he'd convinced to join him.

My sisters were alive. They were here.

A veil of white surrounded Ildja's Destroyer, but a burst of flame burned it away. The goddess flicked her wrist and the Destroyers not carrying magiskas dove at the ships.

Eathalin clasped hands with another Daughter of Aillira. They held up their arms. A translucent dome shimmered to life around the ships, and the Destroyers slammed into it and bounced off. The dome receded and Dragonmen filled the Destroyers with arrows. Tide-tellers pulled waves up; storm-spinners froze the tips of the waves into icy spikes and drove them into Destroyers. Beast-callers sent a frenzy of ice sharks leaping out of the water, snatching Destroyers from the air.

Ildja screamed in fury. Flames erupted along the longships' masts, engulfed the sails.

The Daughters of Aillira on the ships scrambled to smother the flames, raising another dome of protection. Ildja's ember eyes burned brighter, and lava coated the dome, melting through it, dripping onto the ships' decks, eating away the wood.

My Destroyers weren't far from Ildja's. The goddess's back was to me, her focus on the ships. "Keeva!" I shouted. "Break them!" I jerked my head at the Destroyers holding me.

Keeva nodded. Though her wrists were trapped by a Destroyer's talons, she was able to stretch out her palms and aim them.

My Destroyers' skeletal bodies snapped into pieces, and suddenly I was free, falling. I was above Ildja, and with a gust of wind to guide me, I slammed into her. The impact knocked her Destroyer lower and sent her toppling off it. I grabbed on to the Destroyer's wing to keep from falling after her.

Only Ildja didn't fall. She floated.

Ildja drew the ice dagger as she hovered over the sea, covered in flames.

"Your heart is meant for my son, but you may force me to kill you here. You and all your loathsome sisters."

The beast following us below the water turned the glassy ocean into rolling hills of froth. Just a little lower, and Ildja would be within reach. I funneled all my power into one last gust of wind that I threw at the goddess, pushing her down a fraction.

"You think to hurt me with a breeze? No mortal can defeat me." Ildja raised her palms and her fire-red skin darkened to blue, like the heart of a flame, readying to unleash an inferno that would burn me and the ships to ash.

"No mortal," I agreed.

Now, I told the beast whose mind slinked against my own.

There was a rumble along the seabed. The water foamed and waves churned as a massive head surfaced. White scales, covered in seaweed and barnacles. Blue eyes teeming with rage. A fanged mouth opening wide, but not to devour her own tail, as she had done for a thousand years, since Ildja cursed her; Eyvor had chewed through her tail, the gnawed stump jutting up from the water, swishing back and forth. Now the sea serpent stretched her weary jaws one last time, leaping to snap her sister out of the air. Her mouth slammed shut, closing over Ildja and the ice dagger with a *crunch*.

From inside her sister's mouth, the serpent-goddess screamed.

There was a flare of white light, a swirling cloud of black, and the snake went limp.

Her body crashed down toward the ships. I grappled for wind and water to catch the giant serpent, and the other Daughters of Aillira did the same, pushing out fire and wind, water, and storms. Eathalin threw up her domed shield.

Eyvor's body smashed into the shield, cracking it. It held.

I smiled.

My grip on the Destroyer's wing slipped.

I fumbled to slow my descent, but I couldn't pull enough wind to me fast enough. I hit the water and sank. The fall should have broken my ribs, knocked me unconscious. It should not have felt like landing in a pile of feathers that whisked me up to the surface and held me aloft without my having to swim.

"Your vessel," a voice said, "has fortuitous timing."

Seffra, her liquid body shaped like a woman nearly as large as the island-serpent, held me in her watery hand. She wasn't looking at me, but at the man floating beside me, pale and thin, his eyes tinged with madness. Unmistakably familiar.

He tipped his head in greeting. "Soul-reader."

I could only whisper his name. "Veronis."

CHAPTER 30

REYKER

He had his purpose—chosen by him, not the gods. All at once, the storm inside him faded. The river felt less like a force he had to hold back, more like one awaiting his command.

"You despise weakness, Draki," Reyker said. "You find it, exploit it, cut it out of people to make them stronger. Except when it comes to yourself."

Draki's jaw twitched. "Get out of my way or I will snap your neck."

"Will you? I am your greatest weakness. So why have you not cut me out of you? You have crushed and beaten me, but no matter how much I resist, you will not cross that line. Why have you not killed me yet, Draki?"

"Because I bore easily and torturing you amuses me."

"Lie." Reyker pointed at Draki with the broken sword.

Draki swatted the blade aside. "Because you mean so little your death would be a waste of effort."

"Lie!" Reyker spread his arms, blocking the archway. "Do you know what I think? I think I remind you of what it was like to be mortal. I think you miss that vulnerability, when death could arrive at any moment. There are no thrills in being invincible, no passion for life when it lasts forever. No reason to live when you have no one to share it with."

Draki had gone as still as stone.

Reyker kept pushing. "You have no one, Draki. Your soldiers and subjects follow you only out of fear. You killed the witches who raised you, killed our father and my mother even after they took you in. Your own mother abandoned you at birth because she could not stand the sight of her half-mortal child, and now she uses you as a means to an end. Lira could not love you no matter how much you twisted her mind. You are my brother, my only family left, and I cannot love you. You made yourself into a monster no one could love, and that terrifies you. That is your weakness. You pretend to want to be a god, but secretly wish you were mortal. You wish you were me."

It was true, all of it, and Reyker had somehow known it all along without understanding it until this moment.

Draki grabbed Reyker's shoulders and shook him. "I am the pinnacle of what a mortal can hope to become. You will die and be forgotten, but I am forever."

"And you will spend your eternity alone." Reyker let his grip on the sword loosen. "No matter how much power you gain, part of you will always be the sad, serpent-eyed little boy no one would play with. No one but me."

He shoved the broken sword into Draki's hands, as if refusing the gift.

One more push. "I don't want to play with you anymore, Aldrik."

"That is not my name!" Draki stabbed the sword at him. It was a threat, a warning that would have pierced Reyker only a fraction, had he not thrown himself forward.

The serrated edge sliced through the scar on Reyker's chest, sinking deep enough that he knew he would not survive it. He had cheated death too many times, and now he would pay his due. It should have hurt, but around the wound, he was numb, and everywhere else his nerves hummed with energy, with the vigor of being perched on the cusp of fulfilling his purpose.

"Why did you do that?" Draki's eyes were wild, bewildered. "I only meant to injure you. Not . . . not . . ."

Reyker's shirt stuck to his torso, red instead of white. His legs gave out and Draki caught him.

"Healer!" Draki shouted into the fog that still surrounded them. "I need a healer!"

"Gone." Reyker smiled. The numbness was spreading from his chest to his arms to his stomach.

Draki aimed a hand at the fog and it dissipated. Outside the stone circle were dozens of dead Dragonmen, and no magiskas. Cursing, Draki eased Reyker onto the altar. "I absorbed enough of the Fallen Ones' power through that magiska's heart. I can heal you myself." He grasped the sword hilt and slowly drew it from Reyker's chest.

Reyker folded his hands over Draki's, helping him remove the blade. He felt nothing but the black river, coursing through every vein, pumping through every organ, knowing he was close, so close to the end. This was what he was made for.

The blade's edge emerged and Draki stared at the ugly wound, Reyker's life leaking from it with each pulse of his heart. "You're a gods-damned fool," Draki said.

Draki's voice filled Reyker's mind. *Why must mortals be so fragile? Why did he not listen and obey? I only want what is best for him. How can he not see that?*

With a start, Reyker realized Draki was not speaking to him. He was overhearing his brother's thoughts. His gift had burned his senses into razor focus—every smell and sound and image was sharp, tinged in gold. His soul was unraveling, one stitch at a time, but he held on.

"Are you happy?" Draki asked. "Is this what you wanted?"

One heart. One measly little heart was all I asked of him. If he dies . . . No, he cannot die.

Draki's hands squeezed the sword hilt. He seemed not to notice how Reyker's hands squeezed it too. "I should let you die," Draki said. "It's what you deserve."

The river was a tidal wave, drowning him, but he wanted to drown. He was the river and the river was him and as one they angled the blade, inch by inch, so it pointed at Draki.

As one, they plunged the blade into Draki's chest.

Reyker heard Draki's final thought before the sword met skin: *Don't leave me, brother. You cannot leave me.*

The blade did not shatter. It did not dissolve. Guided by Reyker's hands but held by Draki's, the sword impaled him. The jagged tip burst through his back.

Draki gasped, his mouth falling open at the sight of his own blood spilling out around the blade. "What is this?" His eyes darted from the wound to Reyker. "What have you done?"

"What I had to." There was no anger left in Reyker, no malice in his action, only relief at having completed the task the gods had created him for.

Draki struggled to pull the sword from his chest. If he succeeded, the wound might heal. Reyker held fast to the sword, using every bit of strength his war gift gave him to keep it in place. The river flowed into his arms, keeping them steady, and for the first time, the only time, he was stronger than Draki. He had to hold on long enough for Draki to bleed to death, and pray he did not bleed to death first.

"This is not how it ends." Draki's voice was laced with pain. He hissed, curling into himself.

Dying. Draki was dying, as surely as Reyker was.

The Dragon's blood flowed over both of them, mixing with Reyker's, trickling onto the altar. Reyker's voice was fading, but he managed to whisper. "You were right. I will not leave you. You have damned me to the Mist, but I will take you with me."

Draki looked at his brother with pity. "No, Reyker. The Destroyers will torture you, Ildja will devour you. And you will be there, for eternity, alone."

It took only a second for Reyker to understand.

How had he not expected this? How had he overlooked what he was—a male magiska, the last one living in Iseneld, maybe in all the world. And he was here on Volva Isle, inside the death god Gwylor's cursed stone circle, beneath the dark sky and the pale moon that marked the long night of Solmangler.

"Goodbye, brother." Draki's fist slammed into Reyker's wound. Cracked open his chest. Fingers curled around his heart. A ripping noise like the sundering of life, like the annihilation of worlds, filled his ears, blotting out all other sounds. Followed by an emptiness, an aching cold that whistled between his ribs.

Reyker blinked and saw his heart in Draki's hand.

For those final moments, he wasn't certain if he was alive and witnessing his own destruction or dead and dreaming, the first of the Mist's many torments. He watched Draki clench his heart and bring it to his mouth. Watched him tear his teeth through its walls, shredding its chambers, swallowing the part of Reyker that had kept him alive, the part he thought the warlord had destroyed long ago. But Draki hadn't. Not until now.

Cracks formed along the blade in Draki's chest. The sword broke apart in Reyker's hands, crumbling to dust. Blood stopped flowing from Draki's wound, and a scab grew over the hole. No, not a scab. *Scales.* The scales spread along Draki's arm, down his torso, up his neck. His face.

Reyker's soul pulled free from the wreck of his body. He was above himself, looking down at where Draki bent over him.

Draki roared as something spurted out of the wound on his back, stretching up from his spine. Bones, long and thin, forming arches. Scales grew over them, and thin membranes connected them.

Wings.

Draki's wings flapped, scraping at the wind. He rose above the altar, holding on to Reyker, and Reyker floated. Then Draki let go, and Reyker's body fell.

Beside the place where Reyker's soul hovered, the air stirred. Some part of him had still hoped for one of Eyvor's veil-dwellers, a spirit that would lead him to Fortune's Field, guide him to a place of rest, but no. It was a Destroyer that shifted between planes in a susurrus of wings, a rattle of bones. Reaching for him.

My soul is yours, Lira, it will always be yours.

The Destroyer's talons sank into Reyker, dragging him out of the circle, out of Volva Isle, out of the mortal realm.

Into the Mist.

CHAPTER 31

LIRA

"Faster," I said to the wind-wafters and sea-farers helping me steer the longships toward Volva Isle. Reyker was there, alone, with Draki.

"We're trying," Bronagh snapped. The battle had drained our gifts, and the ship was traveling too slowly. Seffra could not help—at our behest, and Veronis's cajoling, she had gone to Heligur to fetch any Renegades and monks who still lived. I poured what was left of my gifts into billowing the sails and dragging the ship through the current. Every few minutes, I had to bend over the railing to retch up blood.

Veronis stood nearby in his mortal body, savoring the air, the sea, the night sky and its myriad stars. The form he wore was tall, muscular, with brown hair and eyes, a visage that appeared to be thirty or thereabout. Haggard, yet handsome. Ordinary. *This* was the god from my visions, the Great Betrayer of legend, the Fallen One who had bullied and threatened me, infected me with these gifts against my will. Daughters of Aillira crowded together a few paces away, some glaring at the dethroned god they'd been taught to hate, while Eathalin and others gaped at the persecuted hero they'd spent their lives worshipping in secret. Veronis was both, and he was neither.

It was disconcerting that after everything the god had put me through, he could stand there seeming so . . . human.

"How did you get out of the prison-realm?" Eathalin asked.

It took the god a moment to collect himself. I recalled the twisted being I'd glimpsed beneath the loch, the ruin he had become after eons trapped inside a dark cage. It left a stain on him, carving furrows across his features. The smile he attempted was grim. "For me to be freed, the prison's key had to be destroyed and one who shared my blood had to take my place within the realm. Few things can destroy a god's key. I knew Ildja's fire could, but Eyvor's fangs—that, I did not expect."

"So Ildja took your place?" Keeva asked.

Instead of me, as Veronis had tried to trick me into doing when he'd sent me to the Mountain of Fire.

"Or Eyvor," Veronis answered. "They are both my kin. The key's destruction created a rift between this place and the prison-realm. My cousins were sucked through the rift to the other side, opening the door for two souls to exit. I leaped through the rift first. Before anyone else could go, Sjaf pushed Seffra after me, and we were transported here. The sisters bought our freedom, not that they had a choice in the matter."

Relief and pity washed over me. Ildja was trapped, but so was Eyvor, a goddess who had done no wrong, who had already borne a vicious curse and would now bear another. "Will you be able to free her? The soul-keeper?" I asked, without taking my focus off the sail and the tide. We were almost at the isle.

"Not until I find a way to do so without letting Ildja out. With the key destroyed, the prison can only be opened from the otherworlds. As much as I wish to release Eyvor and the rest of the Fallen Ones, I cannot risk the serpent-goddess escaping. Not even Gwylor would open the prison for her, not when it means facing off with a host of enraged gods." Veronis's eyes narrowed. "Why do you care what happens to Eyvor?"

"She helped me, even if it was in the name of revenge. Every other god I've come into contact with has used me, hurt me, threatened people I love."

His whole face twitched, like he couldn't find an expression to match his emotions. "You and your sisters would be dead without the gifts I gave you."

He seemed insulted. Indignant.

Good.

"Damn your gifts," I said. "You tried to steal my will as surely as Draki did."

I wasn't done with Veronis, but the longship's bow ran aground. I wasted no time, vaulting over the railing, wading through the shallows to shore.

My *skoldar* prickled—the prickle became a violent twinge, a stinging cold, then nothing. Even when I wasn't aware of my *skoldar*, it always felt like a part of me, something alive. But this was an absence of sensation, a deadening I'd never experienced inside my own flesh.

A sound carried over the treetops, a scream that was half human, half something else. Beast. Demon.

A reptilian creature rose high above the island, its wingspan larger than any bird. At first, I thought it was a different species of Destroyer, but then I saw bits of tattooed skin beneath the scales. Strands of silver hair. The greenish-gold tint of its irises.

The thing that had been Draki looked back at me with feral eyes, more animal than man or god. His body jerked, as if struggling to gain control of the new form it had taken. I raised my hands, ready to summon whatever power I had left in defense against the creature, and the Daughters of Aillira on the longships did the same. Was Draki still invincible in this form?

White light radiated behind me. When I turned, Veronis's eyes were glowing. "Care to fight someone closer to your own species, spawn of Ildja?" he called.

Draki screamed again, wings beating the air as he raced away from us, in the direction of Iseneld.

"Well," Veronis said, his eyes dimming. "That was interesting."

Once before, Draki had gained godlike powers by siphoning them from magiskas. But Eathalin had said nothing about Draki having wings after killing Darah, and all the other magiskas were here. All, except one.

I ran, my pulse roaring in my ears. Hoping. Praying. The stone circle was ahead of me, and I ran harder, until I was inside, at the altar.

My mind refused to make sense of what my eyes were telling me.

The volvur were there, as was the corpse of the earth-shifter, all with clouded gray eyes and vacant stares. Dead, yet not. And on the altar . . . on the altar . . .

Another corpse. Eyes open yet unseeing. Blood. And his chest—

I stumbled to my knees.

This was not how it happened. This was not what the seeress showed me. I was the one on the altar in her vision. I was the one—

Blood dribbled down my chin. I reached up and touched my face. It was coated in blood. Just as Reyker's had been in the vision.

The images the seeress showed me had moved so quickly. Had they overlapped somehow? Or had our fates been as tangled in the vision as they were in our reality, Reyker's life tied to mine and mine to his, interchangeable, indistinguishable?

His life.

His *life.*

"Reyker?" I crawled onto the altar, easing his head into my lap. Smoothing his hair back from his face. Pressing my palm over the hole in his chest.

I opened my mind to him, seeking his soul. Finding nothing. No trace of the red sky or the black river, the sheer canyon walls studded with the gems of his memories. What I walked through was a shell, so empty there weren't even shadows.

Wait. There, in the center of the hollow—a flash of silver. I crouched down beside it. A shattered piece of a sword. The only thing left behind.

When I touched the broken blade, I slipped into Reyker's skin. Seeing what he saw. Feeling what he felt.

How he had fought. How he had died.

As soon as Reyker's soul passed into the Mist, I was thrown from the memory. I grabbed the sliver of sword again. I experienced Reyker's death as if it were my own, five times, ten times, trying to change it, to push Draki away, to block his fist, to resist the Destroyer who took Reyker's soul. To whisper into his mind that I was here with him, and his sacrifice had not been in vain because he had saved the Daughters of Aillira from the Dragon.

Nothing I did changed the outcome. Reyker died, alone with his murderer, wracked by his failure to take Draki with him. Damned to the Mist, as he'd always feared.

Over. And over. And over.

I might have stayed inside that memory forever, but something shook me, and I tumbled back into my own body, blinking against the light of torches. Victory stood over me, nosing my shoulder. The mare pressed her muzzle against Reyker's cheek, sniffed at his hair. Raised her doleful gaze to mine before lying down beside the altar.

I sensed that hours had passed since I'd come into the stone circle, yet there was no sun. It was still Solmangler, and would continue to be until we undid whatever Draki and Ildja had done to keep the sun from rising.

Beyond the stone archway, Daughters of Aillira and Renegades and monks gathered. Solvei and Brokk were among them, bedraggled but unharmed. Brokk's eyes were red, his jaw clenched. The jarl nodded at me, in sympathy and solidarity. I could not bring myself to nod back.

If I let it in, I would feel pain, exhaustion, my own death closing in. But there was no room left inside me, no space beyond the grief as vast as the stars.

I reached for Reyker's hand and found his ring-finger missing. Severed. His wedding band gone. It was the final chip in a timeworn trinket, the last pebble dropped onto a mountain I was trying to hold up. "Stupid bloody Westlander!" I screamed at Reyker. "Why are you so determined to leave me?" I held his face between my hands. His eyes—once fathomless, alight with fervor, with ardor, with *life*—were shallow, dull.

"You can save him."

I jerked my head up. Veronis strode through the stone circle, and I held my palms up, tempted to unleash a torrent of magic upon him, though I doubted I could hurt him with the powers he'd foisted on me. "I'm done with your tricks and empty promises," I said.

"It's not a trick. He's not dead, not entirely. His body will remain preserved here in the center of Gwylor's stones. His soul is lost to the Mist, but Ildja is no longer there to guard it. You can cross over and bring him back, restore his soul to his body."

Hope ignited beneath my breast, sharp and brief, fizzling as I remembered who I was talking to and as I glanced at the wound that had stolen Reyker's life. "What good will it do to bring his soul back when he has no heart?"

"Seffra can heal him. She can grant him a new heart."

"Seffra does nothing without recompense. Whose heart will she take in return?"

"I have no plans to stay in this wretched mortal realm, and you cannot snatch a soul taken rightfully to the otherworlds without replacing it with another. I will give the boy my heart and exchange my soul for his in the death-realms. All I demand in return is for you to complete your final task as my vessel."

My first task had been to break Veronis out of his prison, and despite my spectacular failure, he'd made it out. There was only one other thing he'd asked of me. "To reunite you with Aillira in the otherworlds. To find and release her soul."

Veronis's stoic features cracked at the edges. "She's imprisoned on the border where Ildja's and Gwylor's realms meet, halfway in the Mist, halfway in the Halls of Suffering, so they could take turns tormenting her."

I thought of what I saw when I touched the Destroyers with Eyvor's gift—how they tore Aillira open, shredded and burned and broke her over and over. If I didn't save her, it would continue for eternity. If I didn't stop it, they would tear Reyker apart too.

"I would go to her myself," Vernois said, "but the realms are warded such that no god may enter without the master of the realm's permission. Only a mortal can."

This was what Veronis had wanted all along. His love for Aillira bordered on madness. A madness that would drive him to any lengths.

I unsheathed one of my knives. He didn't fight back as I leaped from the altar and pressed my blade beneath his chin. "Did you do this, Great Betrayer? Did you use your influence to ensure Reyker ended up here, in this circle, dead and damned, so I would have no choice but to go after him? No choice but to go right where you needed me to?"

"The Sword of the Ice Gods was born for death," the god said. "It lived inside him. It fueled him. It brought him here, not I. Full circle, as I warned you."

The Dragon had become a dragon. The boy born to die was dead. Full circle.

The knife shook in my hand, but I lowered it in resignation. "Ildja may be sealed inside the prison-realm, but Gwylor is not. If I trespass in the Halls of Suffering and release one of Gwylor's prisoners—"

"He will sense it and try to stop you. You must not be caught, or he will lock you up beside Aillira and torture you for eternity. Even if you got away, damage done by a god to a soul can affect your physical body once you return to it in the mortal realm."

"Don't get caught. Understood." My stomach churned, and I put my hand over it. "After I set Aillira free, how do Reyker and I get out of the otherworlds?"

"There are portals hidden throughout Gwylor's prisons. Use your gift to find one. As a soul-reader, you are the perfect soldier to enter a place where souls are boundless."

The perfect soldier. Veronis's vessel. Was this how *my* fate came full circle, pivoting back to the moment I put my blood into the loch to save Reyker from a venomous arrow?

My stomach roiled again, and I retched up another bellyful of blood.

"I can open a rift between realms to let you into the Mist," Veronis said. "You can use your gift to tear your soul free, but if you want to have a body to return to, you must pass my blood on to someone strong enough to carry it without corroding."

I spit, wiping my mouth on my sleeve. "Who?"

"You already know. That's why you chose her."

Outside the stone circle, the Daughters of Aillira drew closer. Keeva, Bronagh, Eathalin. But not Alane. Not Mabyn. I even missed Sursha's scowl.

I called to Eathalin, and the spell-caster hurried to my side. I took her hand, rubbing my thumb across the *skoldar* I'd given her. The connection the mark forged between us wasn't as strong as what I shared with Reyker, but it was a bond just the same. "Since the day I met you, I've known you are the strongest and bravest among us, kind and patient and wise beyond your years. You are the only one whose gifts ever affected Draki. The only one fit to carry the Fallen Ones' blood and use it to protect the Daughters of Aillira."

Eathalin was quiet, her head tilted as if she might have misheard. "Me? No, that can't be. There must be someone more deserving." She looked to Veronis, waiting for him to agree, but the god said nothing.

"I won't force it upon you," I said. "This decision is yours."

She squeezed my hand. "Yes. Of course I will carry the Fallen Ones' gifts. I will wield them in defense of our sisters."

My chest twisted with pride and fear. Would Eathalin regret it once the burden belonged to her? Was Veronis wrong—would the gods' blood harm her, as it was harming me?

"Lira," she said. "It's all right. I'm ready."

I gave her my knife.

Eathalin sliced her palm. When she handed the knife back, I pushed the blade into the thin white scar on my wrist, opening it, and the veins beneath. Blood spilled, and I held my wound above Eathalin's, feeling the Fallen Ones' gifts draining out of me, the sanguine thrumming that once filled me fading to silence. As the gifts I'd carried transferred to Eathalin, her eyes widened, her breaths turning to gasps.

She didn't fight them. She let them in, and it made her stand taller, setting her skin aglow. The gifts belonged to her, in ways they had never belonged to me.

The threads of power that once pulsed out of every inch of me, gathering energy from the world, connecting me to nature, to life, snapped one by one, leaving only the gift I was born with, the one that ran deeper than my blood.

My pulse fluttered, struggling against blood loss. My head spun and my vision blurred, darkness dancing circles around me, pulling tighter with each rotation. As my legs gave out, arms were there to catch me. Keeva, Bronagh. All the Daughters of Aillira had gathered around Eathalin and me—faces I knew, and ones I didn't. My sisters were here, and together they lifted me onto the altar beside Reyker. They kept their hands on me, whispering prayers, offering support.

Veronis knifed his fingers at the air, prying open an invisible window.

Where his hands moved, a void appeared, colder and blacker than the night around us. Despite the cold, sweat beaded along my scalp. I did not want to go into that place. It reeked of rot and viscera.

"Now or never, soul-reader." Veronis's voice was strained, his muscles shaking from the effort of holding open the rift.

I looked at Reyker. But this—this was only his body. The rest of him, the *real* him, was gone.

Veronis was right. Reyker's path had always led toward death. We had fought it, together and apart, on Glasnith and Iseneld and the oceans between. But our fates were still tied, as they had been from the beginning. I would find him and bring him back, or I would stand beside him and share his suffering. I could not leave him alone in the dark.

"Lira!" Veronis called. His grip was slipping. The window was closing.

I shut my eyes and dove into myself, past my failing flesh, my stuttering heart. Into my soul. Funny that I had walked through the souls of so many others, yet never tried to read my own. It was a landscape of emerald moons and violet rain, a storm of sparks and star dust. I reached for its core, wrapped my power around it like a chain, and ripped it up from the roots.

I was dying.

I was free.

The shivering tempest that made up my essence floated out of its cage of bones and flesh. I could see everything—Victory standing vigil beside her fallen masters, the Daughters of Aillira holding me, Gothi and several other monks coming to heal me, to replace the gods' blood I'd given up with ordinary mortal blood. My own soulless body next to Reyker's undead corpse. The stone circle. And beyond it, Volva Isle, the sea, Iseneld, Glasnith, the world. Everything.

It was beautiful. I wanted to stay.

I could not stay. Sounds echoed from the rift, erasing any doubts. They were screams of anguish. Horror. Hopelessness. The screams of the damned. I was nothing but a soul now, and I aimed what was left of me at that hole torn between realms, straight through the chasm that led to eternal torment, to find my namesake and my wolf.

PART THREE

BEYOND THE MIST

CHAPTER 32

I am.

That is all I know.

Who. Where. When. These labels are stripped away. There is only aware-ness. Existence. This feels like an interval, a point between what was and what will be. A place I've been before, many times, if time and place were relevant anymore. They aren't. There is only here, this instant. Only me.

I. Am.

Nothing is around me, but then the nothing becomes something.

An airy wooden structure, antlers dangling from the high rafters, the familiar space filled with long tables and a stone hearth. The feasting hall in Vaknavangur. Men stand on the far side of the hall, watching me. These are the men of my fallen village—the farmers and hunters and fishermen, warriors all, men who taught me so much. Shadows streak across their necks where the executioner's axe severed head from body. One of the men steps forward and opens his arms. Tall and blond, his beard carefully trimmed. His eyes blue and gray, like my own.

"Son," he says.

I forget myself. I run to him, weeping, laughing. I throw my arms around him, realizing I'm as tall as he is. A thing that never happened in life because he died before I reached manhood. But he's here—all those who died that day are here, gathered to welcome me. It can only mean one thing: My soul has been accepted into Fortune's Field. I am home.

"I missed you, Father," I say, my voice unsteady. "Where is Mother?"

His grip on me tightens. "She could not bear the shame of seeing you."

"Shame?"

Before I can pull back, a blade slides between my shoulders.

I stumble, startled by the pain. Being stabbed feels the same in death as it did in life. When I touch the knife sticking out next to my spine, my fingers come away wet with blood. If I am dead, why am I bleeding?

My father's features are cold. He's never looked at me this way. No, this is the expression he saved for Aldrik. His anger and disappointment, always for Aldrik. Strange that I ever wondered why my brother hated me.

"Father?" I say. "Why have you done this?"

"You failed me, Reyker. You failed us all." The men around him draw swords and axes, knives and spears. "You let us die and did not avenge us. You served the one who murdered us."

"Yes." No use denying, protesting. Lying. "I have made peace with my failures. If you must have vengeance, take it. I won't fight you."

The men descend upon me, blades falling, falling.

I. Am.

Pain. Anguish.

Acceptance.

And then I am no more.

⎯⎯◇⎯⎯

Nothingness hems me in, swirls like smoke, creating, becoming. Green grass. Black stone.

A lava field. A sword in my hand.

A man in front of me, wearing the garb of a warrior-priest. A sword wound marring his chest. Gothi's son. My first kill. He is younger than me now.

I drop the sword.

The black river no longer runs through my veins—it emptied on the altar, soaked the heart my brother took from me. Without that rage bubbling beneath my skin, funneling into violence, I can think clearly. I can view my past without the haze of self-loathing.

"I'm sorry," I tell the priest. "I wish I could take it back. Killing you was the first of many mistakes."

"Your apologies will not save me," he says. "They will not save my mother, who died from the sorrow you caused."

"No, they won't. But it's the truth, so it must be spoken."

The lava field vanishes, replaced by walls of ice. A glacier. The priest is still here, but now a second man lies at my feet. His body is broken, his brown eyes locked on mine.

"You killed me," Quinlan of Fion says.

"A mercy kill. I would do it again."

"Mercy?" He glances at the priest, and they laugh together.

"You know nothing of mercy." This voice echoes. The glacier has become a cave, and an older man emerges from its shadows, an axe in one hand. Einar. "I was your friend when you had no one, Reyker. I looked after you like a son when you had no father. And how did you repay me? With an axe to the chest!"

"I begged you not to fight me. You left me no choice."

The cave is gone. Beneath me, one battlefield after another flashes to life. Iseneld. Skerrey. Glasnith. Covered in bodies and blood. At each village, the corpses stand up and turn to me, joining the others. Soon, hundreds of warriors from across three countries crowd together. The people I killed circle me, some with snarls, some with smiles. Some merely stare, their faces void of emotion.

"There is always a choice." It's Sursha who speaks, stepping forward, knives in hand. Her head is bent at an awkward angle—her neck broken, like Quinlan's. Behind her is a line of Renegades, all with their necks broken or their throats torn out.

"There is always a choice," the priest says. Then Quinlan. Einar. Then it spills from the mouth of every warrior, all of them passing judgment, declaring me guilty.

I am.

Guilty.

I kneel before them, bow my head. "I cut you all down, in the heat of battle, in defense of those I sought to protect, or in cold blood on the Dragon's orders. In every instance, the choice was mine. I am sorry for your deaths, though I do not ask your forgiveness. I will accept whatever punishments you see fit."

The warriors look at one another in confusion. Light flickers over some of them and they cease to be human. They are monsters. There is a glimpse of bones, of wings, until I blink and their skin settles, mortals once more.

The priest is the first to move, digging fingers into my arm, tearing out a chunk of my flesh. Quinlan follows, ripping out a fistful of my hair, taking part of my scalp with it. Then Sursha's fingernails slide into my eye socket, plucking out my right eye.

Pain is a second skin, a garment that slips over me as easily as a tailored tunic; we are old friends, and our intimate acquaintance is a buffer of sorts, a rope I cling to as I dangle between the precipice of sanity and madness.

The rest of the men come, one by one, to claim portions of me. Sometimes their shapes waver, and their hands curl into claws, their teeth elongating like fangs.

Piece by piece, they take me apart. Slicing. Shredding.

Destroying.

My left eye is taken, and I can no longer see them. My other senses sharpen. My attackers shriek with glee, sounds no mortal could make.

In these shuddering last increments before I die, time unfurls, and I see this same scene replay itself. This has happened to me before. It will happen again. These are not my victims, enacting well-deserved vengeance. These are Ildja's monsters, creatures of the Mist. I owe them nothing. I will not break for them.

Even in death, I am. Reyker Lagorsson. Wolf Lord of Vaknavangur. Sword of the Ice Gods. Commander. Warrior. Comrade.

Brother. Son. Husband.

Survivor of the Mist.

I am.

Numb. Blind. Bodiless.

Dark words caress what is left of my mind, whispered on a dark wind.

WHAT A SPECIMEN YOU ARE. A WEAPON OF GODS, AN INSTRUMENT OF DEATH, TORN APART AND PUT BACK TOGETHER SO MANY TIMES YOU ARE NIGH IMMUNE TO SUCH TORTURE. THOSE WITLESS DEMONS IN CHARGE OF YOUR SUFFERING DO NOT UNDERSTAND YOU.

I cannot move. I cannot ask questions, demand answers.

YOU DEFY THEIR ATTEMPTS AT SHAME AND GUILT BECAUSE YOU HAVE ACHIEVED ENLIGHTENMENT BEYOND THE WEIGHT OF YOUR SINS. YOU DIED TO SAVE INNOCENTS, AND THAT FINAL ACT OF SELFLESSNESS GRANTED YOU PEACE IN THE FACE OF DAMNATION. HOW MY SISTER WOULD ADORE DEVOURING YOU, IF SHE WERE HERE. YOU SEE, TO THE DESTROYERS, YOU ARE A SOUL THEY LACK THE MEANS TO SHATTER. BUT TO THE GOD OF DEATH, YOU ARE A TOY TO DISMANTLE. A CHALLENGE WORTH SAVORING.

I have no mouth to scream with, no legs to flee upon.

What I am is not enough, and yet it is far too much.

WE WILL DISCOVER WHAT FRIGHTENS YOU MOST, WOLF LORD, I ASSURE YOU. AND I HAVE A FAIR IDEA WHERE TO START.

I'm not dead. Not completely.

If I concentrate, I can follow the fragile tether linking soul to body, sense the mortal casing I called home on the other side of this realm, lying on a bed of stone inside a circle of monoliths. The tingle of a breeze on my skin. Half of me exists in that world.

The other half is here, in this cursed place, where I have no body, no skin or bones—I remain in soul form, a squall of memories, emotions, impressions. The corridors I rush through resemble a swamp, thick with steam, coated in gray slush.

Beneath the haze, embers glow like shining veins in the dark, trickles of lava that burn me whenever I accidentally brush against them. The floor seems to move, every inch slithering with serpents of all colors and sizes. Constant reminders of the fiery serpent-goddess who ruled over this realm.

Sometimes I stumble across a chamber and peer inside, hoping. Dreading.

Every chamber is the same. They have no true walls or ceiling, yet the space feels enclosed. A private dungeon. Inside each one is what used to be a person, flickering between soul and an illusion of flesh, the earthly body they wore, surrounded by Destroyers that peck and claw and shriek, devouring the damned. The bodies scream, the souls bleed—or something like it, ichor oozing from their cores, spilling out of incorporeal wounds.

None of them is Reyker. So I turn away from their screams and continue searching, despite the sickness squirming within me. I can't help them. Though Veronis said I was the perfect soldier to enter the otherworlds, so far my knowledge and instincts have done nothing but enable me to hide, to render my soul translucent. My gift lies dormant, and if the Destroyers catch me, I'll wind up in one of those chambers too.

There must be a hundred thousand chambers, scattered across the endless Mist. How will I ever find Reyker? What will be left of him if I do?

There is no pattern to the passageways. By Ildja's design, it is a sprawling labyrinth. I don't know how long I've been here. Hours. Lifetimes. In a place built on eternity, how do you measure the passage of time?

The maw of another chamber juts up from the fog ahead of me, quieter than the others. No screams, no whimpers, no pleas for mercy. I brace myself and look inside.

Empty. No soul, no Destroyers. It's the only vacant chamber I've seen. It feels . . . wasteful. Out of sync with the rest of this realm.

I slip into the chamber and sensations overwhelm me.

Reyker. I can smell him. Taste him. His essence. His pain.

Drops of ichor are spattered across the chamber. I run a tendril of my soul through the droplets, and images crush me. I see what the Destroyers did to him, the tricks they played on his mind, the methods they used to tear him apart. I realize what the ichor is—not blood. Hope. Pleasure. Love. This is how the Destroyers punish, the goal of their torture. They try to squeeze out every ounce of happiness, drain every last drop of courage, until nothing is left but fear, agony, despair.

The other chambers were drenched, ichor painted as thick as the fog, but Reyker's chamber is merely sprinkled with it, no more than dawn's dew beading on a patch of grass. They could not drain him. He was too strong to succumb.

My relief is smothered by uncertainty. Did Reyker escape? Did the Destroyers take him somewhere worse? *Is* there somewhere worse?

A sparse trail of ichor leads away from the chamber, and I follow it. I race through the twisting corridors of the Mist, to its outer edges, where Reyker must have been taken. Where the Mist overlaps with the realms of Gwylor. The Halls of Suffering.

CHAPTER 33

Lips touch mine.

They are almost familiar, like something from a distant dream. It comes to me in snatches: the Green Desert, a celebration, a ghost seeming to possess me for an instant. Another ghost watching me from behind the eyes of the woman I love.

"Lira?" Her name leaves my mouth as little more than a breath, but already I know it isn't her. She isn't here. Longing and relief weave together in a pattern that tears me in half.

Whoever kissed me releases a disappointed sigh.

"Boy?" The voice is a rasp. A hand slaps my face, and I drag my eyelids open. A woman is bent over me. Her long, tangled hair is the color of snow. Her skin is pale and lined with age, but her eyes—her eyes are young, bright green. Like the lights of the sky-well.

She has a body. I have a body. It doesn't make sense in this place, but nothing does. I press my hand to my chest and it rises with breath, pulses with the movement of my blood. I have a heart—or at least the semblance of one. I have clothes, a simple tunic and trousers. The woman wears a frilly dress that must have been elegant before it became stained and tattered.

"Who are you?" I ask, sitting up. "Where—"

The question dies on my tongue as I see the giant thorntree above us, its deep-red branches curling downward, its slender white needles that I know are sharp enough to pierce flesh. Moonflowers and clovers circle the trunk, and I run my fingers over them.

The roots of the tree are straggly tentacles, and something moves between them—blue scales, a triangular head, jaws unhinging. I scramble out of the way as the bog adder strikes, its fangs snapping at the air where my hand had just been.

"Watch out for that one," the woman says. "He's ill-tempered. That's why I named him Grumpy. Kills me at least once a day, I'd guess. But I don't blame him. The god of beasts created serpents to be benevolent, but then the eater of souls claimed them and put a dash of her demons into them. It's not your fault, is it, Grumpy?" She stares at the adder fondly. It hisses in response.

Gods aflame. The woman is mad.

I search my surroundings and see a forest of thorntrees. When I walk near the next one, another adder launches from the tree's roots. The same thing happens as I approach a third tree. And a fourth. The snake makes the same movement, from the same spot, among the same odd configuration of roots stacked like the limbs of an octopus.

I break into a run, but it does no good. There is no end. Turning in a circle, I squint at the thorntrees stretching in every direction, at the bog adder lounging in the same position in the same patch of moonflowers.

This is no forest. It is one tree, replicated, a mirror image unfolding infinitely. An illusion, like the bodies we seem to wear that cannot be real.

A prison.

The madwoman skips after me, wild hair whipping around her shoulders. "There's nowhere to go. Believe me, I've wandered for years in every direction. He lets me out sometimes, so the serpent-goddess and her Destroyers can have a go at me. The rest of the time I'm here, right where I died the first time."

"What do you know of Ildja?"

The madwoman smiles. "I know she is missing. I've heard the spirits whisper that the Mist has misplaced its master, and that means my Veronis is avenged."

"Your . . ." I blink, looking her over again, thinking on the stories of Glasnith. Taking in those eyes, the way their color makes my chest ache. "Aillira?"

"Beloved and cursed, mother and betrayer. But you are not my Veronis come to save me." Her pout sheds years off her wrinkled face, making her seem childlike. "I could tell by your kiss. I could have reaped your mind, but it's impolite to do so without asking."

If she is Aillira, then she's been trapped here for centuries. No wonder she is mad. "I am Reyker Lagorsson of Iseneld. Do you know how I came to be here with you?"

"You are one of Sjaf and Seffra's children—I tasted them on you, the salt and steel and ice. How does anyone come to be caught between the Mist and the Halls of Suffering, son of Iseneld? Gwylor has plans for you. He brought you."

Gwylor. The death god of Glasnith. "Why?"

"To torment me. Or you. Or both of us, most likely. I spurned his affections and stole his secrets. His favorite cousin turned against him, half his family went to war with him, because of me." The words are a rote narration of her supposed crimes that Gwylor must have drilled into her over ages. "Gwylor shows me things. How your people ravage my country and murder my descendants, led by Ildja's bastard son. What did you do to anger the god of death?"

"I tried to kill Ildja's bastard son."

"Gwylor's nephew? Oh, yes, that would do it."

"And I married the Fallen Ones' vessel."

Aillira leaps at me, hands fisting in my tunic. "The vessel? They found her! Oh, then the girl must have the key. She must have freed Veronis." Aillira lets go of me and spins around the thorntree, singing in a language I don't understand. Grumpy watches, hissing his contempt.

"The key was lost," I tell her gently. To Ildja, who used it to lock up more of her kin.

"Then why is Ildja absent when you, who tried to murder her son, are here? That vindictive shrew should be tearing your soul apart. Nothing would stop her. Nothing but a prison."

Aillira sings louder, and the song itches at me. I've heard it before—not the words, but the melody. Lira sang it to me, an old ballad about a woman whose lover was lost at sea. Here I am, locked in a gods-forsaken death realm with Lira's ancestor, listening to that same song about two souls kept apart by fate.

An absurd laugh escapes me. Aillira laughs, too, holding her arms out as she continues to twirl. "Dance with me, son of Sjaf. Gwylor will come soon to spoil our fun. Let us enjoy these last moments. Let us shout so loud those we love will hear us from this pit!"

She slips on a tree root and falls. Right on top of Grumpy.

The adder sinks its fangs into her arm.

I pick her up as the snake retreats into a hollow between roots. She feels frail in my arms, lighter than a woman of her size should be. Whatever Gwylor and Ildja have done has reduced her to a wraith.

"Veronis will come for me." Aillira tugs at the collar of my tunic, tears spilling from the corners of her eyes. "He will come."

This promise, this plea, is the thread she's used to stitch up the wounds Gwylor left on her soul while her sanity spilled out between the seams. She says it over and over as her skin goes cold and sweat leaks down her neck, as her breaths turn to gasps and her pulse judders. This is why the damned are granted bodies, I realize—so violence can be done to them. Souls don't flay as easily as flesh, don't bruise and blister and bleed as exquisitely. Breath can be lost. A pulse can be silenced. The pain of death can be experienced on an infinite loop.

I hold Aillira as her veins turn violet and her body seizes from the adder's venom—a pain I know. A pain I lived through. With her dying breath—How many last breaths has she had? How many times has she died this way, alone?—she says it again. "Veronis will come."

"Yes," I tell her, hoping it is not a lie. Certain that if Lira was Gwylor's captive, no force in this realm or any other could stop me from getting to her. "He will."

Aillira is dead for some time before she groans and sits up. The color of her veins has returned to normal and her pale skin has pinkened again. I move in front of her, putting myself between her and the beady black gaze of the adder.

"Are you all right?" I ask, peering at her over my shoulder.

She answers with a fit of tinkling laughter. "We are dead, son of Sjaf. There is no 'all right' anymore. There is only suffering or not."

"Are you suffering?"

She rubs the unblemished spot on her arm where the adder bit her. "Always, but not in the way you mean. It doesn't matter. It will happen again. It always does. I don't mind, though. I enjoy being dead. *Truly* dead, blissfully unaware. Why do you think Grumpy only bites me once a day? I've tried to make him bite me the moment I wake and he never does."

I drop my head into my hands. What misery must Aillira feel that the agony of adder venom is worth the brief reprieve of oblivion? How long will I be here before I feel as she does?

"Oh." Aillira picks something out of the clovers beside her. "This is not for me. It must be for you." She hands me a braided length of golden hair, tied with a green satin ribbon.

I run my thumb across the ribbon, my stomach clenching.

"This was my mother's," I whisper. "I went hunting and came back with a white fox. A rare quarry, hard to catch. Its pelt earned me enough to buy her three ribbons. One red. One blue. And this one." She had loved the green ribbon best because it was the color of spring. She died with this ribbon in her hair. I squeeze the braid in my fist. "Gwylor left it. As a threat. Is it real, or another trick?"

"It is real," Aillira says. "Gwylor does not play tricks as the Destroyers do. This is a torment, to make you obsess over what is to come. He'll bring your mother here. He'll hurt her in front of you. He did the same to me with my children, after he and Ildja had broken my body so many times it no longer frightened me. It is a different sort of horror that shatters you in a different way."

"She is in Fortune's Field! How can he get to her? How—"

"He is the death god of Glasnith, brother to the goddesses who ruled the otherworlds of Iseneld, and Fortune's Field has no keeper. Anyone who has crossed over, he can find. If taking you apart doesn't break you, he'll take them apart instead and force you to witness."

I close my eyes and see my mother's face, smiling as she ties the green ribbon into her hair. "How will I bear it? How did you?"

"I didn't." Her voice crackles. "We all have our breaking points. Gwylor brought you here to remind me how it feels to have a companion, so it will hurt all the more when he takes you away and I am alone for the next century. Kindness is another sort of cruelty." She leans her cheek against my shoulder. "Isn't that right, Grumpy?"

Grumpy is coiled around the thorntree's trunk, tongue flicking in our direction. Blissfully unaware.

⚔

I don't know if time exists in this place or if it's another illusion meant to drive us mad, but it seems to trickle by, achingly slow. Despite my efforts, Aillira is bitten by the adder once more. She's still unconscious when I hear the scream.

I know that voice. I race toward it, not pausing to wonder how she could be here, not dwelling on whether Aillira is wrong and the god of death does mean to trick me.

Every thorntree is the same, the same, the same. Except, beside one of them, is another bit of hair. Only a few strands, unbound, but these are not blond.

They are the deep violet of wine.

CHAPTER 34

LIRA

I've traveled past countless variations of wastelands, private prisons created to intimidate their captives. The Halls of Suffering have more substance than the Mist, and its halls more closely resemble an endless, twisting maze that sprawls outward only to turn back in on itself. Reyker is in one of these wastelands. His soul is so close my gift tingles with urgency.

But someone else is here with me too. I have to find the right prison before I'm caught. I've rendered myself lucent, yet whatever tracks me isn't fooled. It follows, relentless.

Ahead of me is a flash of red. A thorntree. And beyond it, a thousand more just like it. He's here. I can sense his soul on the other side.

I push toward the trees and meet a hidden barrier, dense and sticky. The moment I touch it, there's a shift in the air, and suddenly I'm no longer in soul form. I wear a replica of the body I left on Volva Isle. A jolt of energy shoots out of the barrier, searing my nerves. I cry out and jerk back, but the barrier is stuck to me like I'm a moth in a web. Another jolt sings through me. I struggle so hard pieces of my skin and hair tear away as I finally stumble backward out of the barrier's grip.

I'm out in the open, exposed.

Someone materializes next to me.

Before I can scream, a hand clamps over my mouth. "Be quiet," she says. Dazed, I nod, and she lets go of my mouth to grab my arm, dragging me down the corridor.

I keep staring, but I can't bring myself to believe yet.

She turns a few corners, as if she has traveled through this maze before and knows it well, and then stops to face me. "How could you be so foolish, walking right through the door of a prison in the Halls of Suffering? Gwylor can feel it when a soul tries to enter or exit a prison. He knows you're here now. He'll be looking for you. Didn't I raise you to be careful, to be smart?"

I have no response. All I can do is watch my mother pace along the corridor.

She looks just as she did when she died, but she is not the same woman who held me and baked me apple tarts after a nightmare, who read me stories and cheered covertly whenever I bested my brothers at a skill. Death has hardened her. I see it in her stiff posture, the tight lines around her mouth.

"What are you doing here?" I finally ask.

"Waiting for you. I felt you cross over. I knew you had come."

"I don't understand."

"Of course you don't. You were never supposed to know about any of this."

When I open my mouth, she waves at me to shut it. I do.

"We don't have much time, so I'll talk quickly," Mother says. "On the eve of my eighteenth birthday, I pledged myself to Aillira's Temple. I followed the Forbidden Scriptures and worked with the priestesses to retrieve the key that would release the Fallen Ones from their prison. I was their chosen vessel."

The vision I had in the temple ruins comes back to me—Mother, bringing the key to the head priestess. Because *she* was the intended vessel?

My thoughts twist together and my mind trips over them. "You're a Daughter of Aillira?"

"Don't interrupt. After I found the key, I met with the mystic in the Grove of the Fallen Ones. She told me what Veronis wanted. The head priestess revealed the prophecy of the god-man of Iseneld, what would happen to Glasnith if the death gods and their scion remained unopposed. I agreed to take the key to the Mountain of Fire and sacrifice myself to free him. But then, I met your father."

I know this story: Father was visiting the chieftain of Taloorah as an envoy for the Sons of Stone. As he was leaving, a storm rolled in. He turned his horse back and came across a wagon with one of its wheels stuck in the mud. The driver was elderly, so a young woman was trying to dig the wheel out for him. Father ran to help, and the two worked side by side to get the wheel unstuck. By the time they finished, they were laughing, drenched in mud, and completely infatuated with each other. Father stayed in Taloorah for days after the storm passed.

They wed only a few moons later.

"Torin didn't know I was a pledge at the temple. I kept it a secret, pretending I was a servant to the temple priestesses. With him, I saw the life I could have, the life I didn't know I wanted so badly until it was there in front of me. I ran away from the temple. When the mystic came for me, I refused her. I turned my back on the Fallen Ones, on my duties to my country. It was selfish. Stupid, to think there would be no reckoning for defying the gods. To think they would not demand a sacrifice as punishment for my insult." Finally, she ceases her pacing and looks at me.

"The Brine Beast," I whisper.

"I couldn't let it take you or your brother. I never wanted you to pay for my mistake. And yet you have." Her voice catches. Some of the warmth I remember seeps back into her expression. "I found the old mystic's soul wandering through the Halls of Suffering. She told me what happened. After I died, the gods set their sights on you."

"Why us? Why were we chosen?"

"If the vessel lost the key or failed to open the prison-realm with it upon her death, she had to be able to travel freely through the otherworlds to find a way in from where the Halls of Suffering and the Mist intersect. A perilous task, one only a powerful soul-reader could attempt."

The perfect soldier to enter a place where souls are unbound.

"But that means . . . You're a soul-reader, and you never told me?"

"Your powers didn't manifest until after I died, Lira. I didn't know you would inherit my gift. Besides, I couldn't risk anyone finding out. Your grandfather would have exiled me from Stony Harbor for my deception. I would've lost you, your father, your brothers."

"You named me Lira. You gave me your medallion—a symbol of Veronis and Aillira's love."

"Part of me hoped you'd put the pieces together on your own. I refused to give my life for Veronis's cause, but I still believed in it." She pulls me close, holds me tight, and I can't help but hug her back. "When you were born, I knew you would grow up to be strong. You deserved a name befitting of that strength, the legacy of a mortal woman who rallied gods."

These bodies aren't real, none of my perceptions are real, but she smells of apple tarts. She smells of sea salt from the harbor she died in. "I miss you, Mother."

"Oh, my dear girl. You have no idea how much we miss you."

We.

"Rhys? Father?" That's who she must mean, but I dare to add another name to the list. "Quinlan?"

"Yes. All of us were in the Eternal Palace, but then Gwylor took them and locked them away, for a time. He said it was because of you. Don't worry, I sought aid from the veil-dwellers in Fortune's Field. The veil-dwellers helped me free them and sneak them into Eyvor's realm. They're safe, hidden. They send their love. And Quinlan said to do this." She tugs a lock of my hair, and I laugh, blinking away tears. "They wanted to come with me, but only a soul-reader can pass through these halls undetected."

My brother and father, my dearest friend, are at peace. For now. "Gwylor could hunt them down again. I can't leave you all—"

"I took care of it," Mother says. "I broke the lock to the prison-realm. The Fallen Ones will notice soon. They'll have a second chance at Gwylor, and we must be gone before the battle begins. Not even soul-readers can survive the carnage of warring gods."

Veronis's warning flashes through my mind. "Ildja is in that prison! You'll set her free as well. We have to lock it back."

Mother's eyes widen. "Only Gwylor could forge a lock to hold them. It's taken me ages to figure out how to break it. It would take longer to find the right magic to fix it, and by then—"

I don't wait for her to finish. Mother reaches for me, but I'm off and running, back toward the thorntrees, to Reyker. If Ildja finds him, she'll tear him to pieces. If the lock can't be fixed, at least I can complete my mission to save him and Aillira.

I haven't made it far when a terrible rending sound shakes the corridor. Energy crackles around me and fissures spiderweb across the ethereal fabric this realm is made of. The floor under my feet seesaws. Ahead of me, the largest fissure opens wider, into a screaming wound. Shadows and fog spill out like entrails.

One of the shadows is so thick it seems to have substance. It rises, three times my height and twice my width. A tail. From behind the fissure, a triangular head materializes. Deep-set eyes, the glowing red of embers. Black scales rimmed by veins of lava. A long tongue flicks out of the darkness.

The serpent-goddess bares her fangs and rears. Her head smashes against the inside of the prison and pieces of the wall separating us crumble.

I stumble away, crashing into something in my haste.

Fingers sink into my skin. I look up, into a face that is almost like a man's, yet vastly different in ways my mind refuses to process. There's a shift, a flicker, and I can see inside him—I'm looking at him and into him, both at once, and it's like staring down a tunnel into infinity, dotted with windows from the past. I can see all the way from here to the creation of my world, fires and floods, disease and famine. Wars, endless piles of bodies. The disasters blur together into chaos, a maelstrom, and my eyes don't understand what they're seeing, but they register the heat, the pain.

My eyes are burning in their sockets.

LITTLE SACRIFICE. The voice ricochets through my head, vaguely human, yet so much worse. DON'T YOU KNOW THE COST OF LOOKING AT A GOD'S TRUE FORM?

I close my eyes, pulling against Gwylor's grip. He shoves me toward the prison. Toward the goddess.

The serpent hisses at her brother. I dare to open my eyes, but bright spots dance across my vision no matter how much I blink. I listen as Ildja smashes her head against the wall again and rubble falls, as the scrape of scales makes it clear she's torn her way out.

Hot, sour breath mists my cheek. I'm jerked off my feet, out of Gwylor's grasp, and a lash curls around my throat, wet and rough—Ildja's tongue. When I look at her, all I see are glowing streaks of lava dripping from a fountain of fire. It burns my eyes, just as looking at Gwylor did. Her tongue draws me closer, and even though I can't see it, I know her mouth hovers just above me.

The soul-eater is going to eat me.

REYKER

"It's not her," I say. Unconvincing, even to myself. "She can't be here. She's alive."

Aillira twirls around me. "Are you so certain?"

I'm not. Draki wanted Lira's heart. Would she stand a chance against him in his dragon form? For how long, when her own gifts were killing her?

I hold my mother's hair in one hand and Lira's in the other.

"Even in death, there are things left to lose," Aillira says.

A screech of thunder rocks the false forest. In the distance, a single thorntree tilts. I spring to my feet. "What is that?"

"That is the sound of Gwylor's undoing." Aillira claps her hands. "The sound of fate giving the gods their due."

Another *boom* resonates overhead. A chunk of sky tumbles down and smacks into the ground near us. The tilting thorntree falls, and others begin to slope sideways.

The hole in the sky gapes open next to one of the trees that still stands. "Look!" I say, pointing at the hole. "We can get out."

"Do you have wings I can't see?"

"We can climb the tree."

"You think I haven't tried climbing them in the thousand years I've been stuck here? Those needles are as sharp as blades. You'll bleed out and be useless until the prison revives you." She plops down and folds her hands in her lap. "We must wait. The cracks will reach the floor soon enough."

"You've waited a thousand years to escape, and now you want to wait longer? No. I won't stand here doing nothing while this realm collapses. Not when my mother and my wife might be out there." I crouch beside her. "Come with me. I can carry you on my back. You won't have to touch the thorns."

"It isn't supposed to happen this way. Veronis is supposed to find me. What if he comes, and I am already gone? What if he . . . what if he does not come? What if he has forgotten me?"

Once more, she has reverted from madwoman to lost child. It unsettles me more than her wild dancing, her frantic babbling. I think of the stories from Glasnith's scriptures, and the things Veronis did to Lira as his vessel. As much as I would love to beat the fallen god senseless for it, his callousness arose from his desire to save this woman. "Veronis gave up being a god for you. He fought the god of death for you. Since you've been separated, all he's done is scheme up ways to free you both and reunite with you."

Aillira stares at me. She raises her hands, cupping my face, and pressure builds between my temples. The sensation is like a net skimming along my mind, sifting through fodder to catch what it seeks: every detail, every scrap of knowledge I possess about Veronis. When she's done, she lets go.

"I'm sorry. I should've asked first." She gets up, humming the sea ballad. "Yes, gallant lord of Iseneld, you may carry this queen of damnation to safety."

She hops onto my back, her arms looping around my neck, legs around my waist. I place my hands carefully on the first branch and pull myself up. Needles slice me no matter how carefully I move. The ground shakes and more cracks open around us as my fear screams at me to hurry.

By the time I reach the top of the tree, my fingers and feet are slick with blood. If we fall, Aillira and I will be impaled by the thorns. I hold tight to the branch, angling as close to the hole in the prison wall as I can. "Jump," I say.

Aillira braces her feet on my back, pushing off with such force she nearly knocks me from the tree. She's surprisingly agile, keeping her body straight as she clears the gap and disappears through it. I swing off the branch and dive after her.

We land in a hallway of sorts. Fifty paces ahead, a giant serpent drags a girl across the floor with its tongue.

Ildja. Lira.

I scream Lira's name, hurdling down the hall. I've been here before, on a bluff in Glasnith. So close. Too far.

My feet skid in the blood sliding down my legs. I trip and hit the floor.

The serpent-goddess's mouth snaps shut, swallowing Lira whole.

CHAPTER 35

LIRA

Just before Ildja's jaws close around me, I hear voices calling from opposite ends of the corridor. Mother. Reyker. Shouting my name.

But a third voice, a woman's voice I recognize from somewhere, drowns them out, screaming, "Her fire! Steal her fire, Lira!"

Then everything is gone as I'm clamped in a vise, a tunnel, wet and spongy, rancid at the bottom. I can't move. I can't breathe.

The serpent's throat spasms, inching me farther down her gullet, closer to that foul stench and the echo of boiling liquid radiating up out of her stomach. Around me, the gloom gives way to blinding light. A thin membrane separates me from the rivulets of lava, pulsing as they shoot through her veins. The flow emanates from a well that sits just below me. A fountain of magma. Just looking at it feels like hot pokers are stabbing through my eyes.

The core of Ildja's fire.

The serpent's throat squeezes me like a corset. I squirm and shift, working to get one elbow up as I slide deeper. The fire is just above me. I blink past the tears streaming from my eyes, focusing on that spot on the other side of the membrane. The fountain's wellspring. The goddess's essence, the closest thing she has to a soul—her true form.

No mortal can defeat me, Ildja had said. But down here, my mortal flesh is a mirage wrapped around an immortal soul blessed by the soul-keeper.

I have one hand free, cocked at an awkward angle. It will have to be enough. With my nails, I dig through slimy film lining the inside of the serpent's throat. I punch my fist through and curl my fingers around that fire. It sears and blisters, inflaming every nerve in my body. I might have let go, might have submitted, had I not known I could survive it.

This is not the first time I've held a god's fire.

The serpent jerks. I wrap my hand around the molten wellspring and pull with every bit of strength left in me. It burns my eyes and blisters my skin, simmers my blood and turns what little breath is left in my lungs to steam, but I hold fast to that fire. The branching rivers of lava streaming off it run dry.

Ildja screams and bucks, but as the fire in my hands cools, the mushy innards locked around me crumble. There's no goddess, no serpent, nothing left but a drop of her fire that flares against my chest and melts into it, disappearing under my skin. Before I can think too much on this, I realize I'm suffocating. Buried alive, in a pile of Ildja's ashes.

Two sets of hands dig through the ash to find me, pulling me free. Then there are strong arms around me, holding me close. There are gentle fingers brushing soot from my face. I can't see the skin they wear—the damage to my eyes burned away those illusions—but I see the landscapes of their souls, the lights that glow within them. The depths of their love.

I press my forehead to Reyker's and squeeze my mother's hand. "Mother, meet Reyker Lagorsson of Iseneld. My husband."

That's all I can manage before this false body gives out and all awareness seeps away.

REYKER

Lira goes limp in my arms. She's covered in burns and ashes and I'm too stunned by what just happened to ponder the logic of the words coming out of my mouth. "Is she dead?"

She must be dead, if she is here. But can a soul die?

Gods cannot be killed, yet Lira killed a goddess. She killed *the* goddess. The strongest. The worst.

"Is she dead?" I ask again as Aillira kneels between me and Iona, Lira's mother.

Aillira cups Lira's chin. Dipping into her mind, as she did into mine. A smile spreads across her face—not mocking or sad. Joyous. "No deader than you. She came here to retrieve you, son of Sjaf, and to free me. Your body is restored back in the land of the living and all it needs is your soul. Veronis is there, too, waiting for me."

NONE OF YOU WILL EVER LEAVE THIS PLACE.

Gwylor looms over us, surveying the pile of dust that was his sister. When I look at the god, I see a man that is not a man because he is simultaneously a black-feathered bird picking the entrails from a corpse, and the maggots eating the corpse, the earth the corpse is buried in, and the corpse itself. The corpse is me. It is everyone. My eyes are burning, and I have to look away.

HERETICS. BETRAYER-WHORES. YOU'LL PAY FOR WHAT YOU'VE DONE.

I don't know whether we should run or fight. Before I can move, the walls and floor quake. Smoke pours out of the hole Ildja made, and dozens of figures step through it one by one. While some look human, many take the forms of beasts or shadows or shapes the likes of which I've never seen. Others I cannot look upon; like Gwylor, they wear their true forms, and the sight swells my head and burns my eyes. All carry themselves with the same fury. I know what they are. Gods, goddesses. The Fallen Ones, let out of their cage for the first time in over a thousand years. And a man-shaped figure made of water who must be Sjaf. A woman glowing with light who resembles depictions of Eyvor, the soul-keeper.

The gods have us surrounded.

We are nothing to them. They want Gwylor, and they won't hesitate to stomp on us if we're in their way. We need to get out of here, but there's no path for getting past them.

"Stop!" Aillira shouts. "None of you know how to kill him. But I do."

The Fallen Ones glance at one another.

WHO ARE YOU? Several of them ask at once, their voices like untuned instruments, musical yet jarring.

"Do you not recognize me?" Aillira says. "I am Veronis's wife, the mind-reaper who stole the secrets of how to kill the eater of souls and the god of death."

Gwylor lunges for Aillira, but several of the Fallen Ones block him from reaching her.

"Gwylor built the Halls of Suffering with pieces of his divine essence. To render him as fragile as a mortal, you must break the locks and tear down every prison in these halls."

At first, a hush hangs over the host. Then one of the gods howls and smashes his fist through a wall. That's all it takes for the rest of them to scatter, some rushing into adjacent hallways, others tearing at the walls and ceiling and floor around them. Soon, the ground tilts and pieces of the hall rain down on us from every direction, smoke and sprays of dust clouding the air. Gwylor screams, chasing them, fighting them, but there are too many and he already seems to be weakening.

The shimmering material the prisons are made of isn't like anything on earth, but it's solid and heavy. I pull Lira against me and leap backward as a hunk of falling rubble nearly flattens us.

Aillira touches my shoulder. "Go. Save your world from the monster Ildja made. I will free the damned and protect them. When the Halls of Suffering are no more, I will do the same to the Mist. There will be no more torturing of souls. Tell my Veronis I am here, waiting." She turns and skips after the gods, dodging wreckage, barking orders.

She stops at a prison to help the two captives ducking out through the broken wall. I freeze when I see them. My mother. My father.

They appear frightened but unharmed. Father has his arm around Mother's waist, and they scan the mayhem in the hall. Their eyes find mine.

It takes a few moments—I was more child than man the last time they saw me—but as soon as recognition sparks, Mother lurches forward, calling my name. Father holds her back. The space between us is filled with wild gods and flying debris, too dangerous to cross, but the distance melts away when Father beats a fist against his chest and raises it in salute. Mother stretches her arms out toward me, an embrace I can almost feel.

Holding Lira, all I can do is nod at them. "I'm all right. I'm going back to stop Draki. I love you," I say, hoping they'll understand.

"They know," Iona says beside me, watching our exchange. "You will see them again. But you have to leave now." She smooths Lira's hair back from her face and kisses her forehead. "Keep my daughter safe." She pushes me toward the hole the gods came through. Their prison. It's crumbling, but at least there are no deities inside.

"I will." I take one last look at my parents before entering the prison-realm.

It's dusky, thick with mist, but I know where I am by the scent of rot. Beneath the fog, grim silhouettes hang above my head—trees and brush eaten up with mold. This realm is a mirror of the Grove of the Fallen Ones, everything reversed. The sound of lapping tells me I've found the loch, and I stare up at the rust-colored water hanging over me, filled with bones and organs, trinkets used to bargain with the fallen gods. Lira's blood is in this loch.

A fetid droplet splashes on my head, another on my arm. I start to move out from under the loch, but dirt falls from around the trees. Like the rest of this realm, the Fallen Ones' prison is disintegrating.

"Lira. Wake up."

She stirs, just barely. Her eyes remain closed.

"Please, Lira. I need you. I don't know how to get us back. What do I do?"

At that, her lashes flutter, and I stifle a gasp. Her eyes are charred black. She shows no signs of pain, but neither does she show signs of sight. Loch water drips on her brow, leaving a reddish-brown trail as it slides into her hair. She touches the drop and smiles up at the filthy water trickling over us. "We can use the portal in the loch."

"How do we get to it?"

"It will come to us." Her palm presses against my chest. "Don't let go."

The flesh I wear tears free like a discarded garment. As I was when I died, I am nothing but a soul, and the sensation is disorienting. Some part of me clings to Lira as she casts off her own false body and I see her as she truly is—light and color and contours, things I don't have words for, things I couldn't describe with any mortal language. She's frightening and beautiful, a force of nature that could unravel me, and I cannot look away.

The loch's trickles grow to a torrent. The realm collapses around us. We are two souls submerged in the drowning dark, but I hold her and she holds me, and if this is all that's left of our existence, I will not fear it. I will not let go.

CHAPTER 36

LIRA

The first thing I noticed as I woke was the absence of power thrumming under my skin. There were no sparks from the Fallen Ones' blood or the Ice Gods' gifts crackling along my nerves. I thought I would mourn their loss, but without the burden of all those weapons, I was buoyant.

Next came the scent of salt air, the creak of a ship, a gentle rocking that could only be the sea. A hard mattress beneath me, blankets tucked around me. I was in a berth belowdecks, sailing across a calm body of water. The sound of soft breathing came from nearby.

My eyes felt heavy. I opened them, but nothing changed. It was as dark as it was when they were closed. A feeling crept over me—a sinking sickness, in my guts and under my sternum. The sight of Ildja in her true form had burned me, the damage seeping from soul to body, just as Veronis had warned.

It is temporary, I told myself. *It will pass.*

When I turned my head, I yelped. Reyker was there, lying on the berth across from mine. I couldn't see his body or his face, but my vision tunneled until I was looking at the red sky and sheer canyon cliffs of his soul.

My cry woke Reyker, and he leaped across the gap between our berths, yanking me to my feet. "What prison is this?"

"No prison. We made it out of the otherworlds."

"Wait." I heard him step back, felt the heat of his fingertips grazing my cheeks. "Are you alive?"

"I am. So are you." In the center of my empty vision, Reyker's soul burned bright like a fever. I closed my eyes and focused on my other senses. We were both clean—the scent of soap clung to our skin, all the blood washed away, and the garments we wore smelled fresh. Someone had taken good care of us. "We're safe, Reyker."

I spread my palm over his chest. The scar there, a starburst of ridged flesh under my hand, where Draki's fist had broken him open. The drum of his heart vibrated up my arm. A god's heart.

"Safe," he said, as if the concept were foreign. He put his hand on top of mine. "You came for me."

"Did you think I wouldn't?" I leaned against him. He rested his forehead on mine and we stood in silence, listening to each other breathe, waiting for doubt to fade under the weight of truth. We were together. Safe. Alive.

"You're all right?" he finally asked. He tilted my chin up, but I turned my head, averted my eyes so he would not notice any strangeness in them. "What's wrong, Lira? Why won't you look at me?"

"Nothing's wrong." I couldn't set such a burden on him. Not yet, after everything he'd been through. Not when he might blame himself.

"Please don't lie to me."

Footsteps thumped above our heads, snapping the tension between us. It sounded like a stampede. I felt Reyker reach for a sword that wasn't there. "Later, I'll tell you everything," I said. "For now, we should find out what that racket's about."

Reyker's steps moved away, and when he returned, he wrapped a fur-lined coat around me. "Later."

I let him lead me out of the cabin, up the stairs. Beyond Reyker's soul, my vision remained a void. It took effort not to trip. As we emerged from the hatch, bitter-cold air struck my cheeks. I suspected it was night, though I couldn't be certain.

The dark of my vision was broken by the glow of two dozen souls.

They hit me at once—shapes and colors, memories and emotions, so many it was overwhelming, filling my sight, making me dizzy. I shut my eyes.

"Who are they?" I asked Reyker.

There was a pause, full of questions and concern, but I squeezed his arm in a silent plea. "Nomads," he answered. "Practicing battle formations."

I opened my eyes, blinking at the soul lights. One of them stuck out—a lone figure stood in what must have been the bow. His soul was painted with green fields and gray stones, forests and mountains and earth. Glasnith, carved into his very essence. *Family*, his soul called to mine. *Home.*

I ran to him, not caring if I tripped, throwing myself at my brother. Garreth's arms came around me, and I pressed my face into his shoulder. "You're here," I said, not yet believing it. "I didn't know if I'd ever see you again."

"I'm sorry I didn't come sooner." He pulled back, and I felt his eyes on me, scanning me from head to toe. "You were dead, Lira."

"Only a little. How did you find out?"

"Eathalin came to Stony Harbor and told me herself." Garreth sighed. "She told me a great many things that were alarming enough to make me abandon Glasnith and bring the whole of my army here."

"Army?" I'd been so focused on Garreth, I hadn't noticed that the brightness at the edge of my vision wasn't coming from the nomads. There were other souls floating in the dark, clusters of them spread out to either side and far into the distance—a thousand of them at least. Their combined light was like staring at the sun.

Garreth had brought a fleet.

Focusing on one soul at a time, I could make out subtle differences revealing their origins. Some held pieces of Glasnith inside them, as Garreth's did. Others had bits of ice and fire—sons and daughters of Iseneld. They all had streaks of silver running through their cores, iron and steel, the soul-deep mark of a warrior. The Daughters of Aillira were clearest, their souls shining with threads of indigo and ivory, connecting us to one another.

I rubbed the heels of my hands over my aching eyes.

Reyker joined us. "You did it, Garreth. You allied nomads and mercenaries with the Renegades. And . . . gods aflame, those are *Dragonmen.* You allied with the Dragon's defectors?"

"Joren," I said.

Garreth grunted. "The Dragonmen were here when I arrived. Though I'd prefer them all to be prisoners rather than soldiers, Jarl Solvei and her spy vouched for them. There are Aukians among us, too, and warriors from as far as Sanddune and Savanna."

An army of nations.

I shook my head. "Garreth, how did you manage this?"

"I didn't. Not alone. It took a great deal of effort from Zabelle, Eathalin, Solvei. And you two." The air shifted as Garreth waved a hand between Reyker and me. "The former Dragonman who gave up his own heart to save the Daughters of Aillira. The Glasnithian daughter who marched into the otherworlds after him. A tale that inspired men and women of different clans and countries to unite. To fight the enemy who threatens us all."

For such a story to spread, for these warriors to come together and form an army . . . it was not a thing that occurred overnight. "How long were we gone?" I asked. "How much time passed here while Reyker and I were in the otherworlds?"

"Two months," he replied.

My breath whistled through my teeth as I exhaled. In the distance, the soul of an island danced. It was fire and ice, strength and heart. But a dark stain spread across the center of Iseneld's soul. "In those two months, what has the Dragon done?"

"You should rest, Lira. We'll arrive at our destination within a few hours. The leaders of each nation will assemble, and we will speak then."

"We will speak now, Garreth."

His arm tensed beneath my hand. "The sun has not risen. Not once. Crops have failed in every country. The oceans are dying. The Destroyers are gone, but the Dragon has another monster, worse than the others. It flies across our lands, poisoning our wells and forests, tearing down our sanctuaries. Veronis protected us from it until he departed for the otherworlds, but he couldn't kill it. According to Veronis, Gwylor tore a hole between worlds to conceal the sun from our nations. The rift is still tied to Draki's power. He's unlikely to close it willingly, and the only other way to shut it is through his death. If we don't defeat the warlord and his beast, nothing will survive."

"The warlord is the beast," Reyker said, and I knew he was remembering his own death, the creature Draki had turned into after absorbing Reyker's power.

"What are you talking about?" Garreth asked.

"We cannot wait," I said. "Stop at the first place where we can safely anchor. Call the assembly."

CHAPTER 37

The heart beating inside his chest was not his own. It was part of him, keeping him alive, but it was not *his*. A foreign object, squirming, flexing, constantly reminding him that every second of his life from here out was borrowed.

If the heart was truly his, it would have accelerated at the sight of Dragon's Lair—crumbled cliffs, chunks of rock and bone sticking out of the sea, all that remained of Draki's fortress after the screams of the skrikflaks brought it down. The ships skirted the wreckage, six of them anchoring in the shelter of the sea caves while the rest formed a shield, setting up lookouts.

The only thing stranger than his new heart was the absence of the black river twisting in his veins. The quiet inside him was obtrusive. Like his finger, the loss was a presence, an empty space that felt full, itching, burning, as if it had been replaced by something he could not see, something that did not feel like it belonged to him.

The leaders of this patchwork army convened on Solvei's longship. Reyker found it amusing, and unsurprising, that the jarl had asserted her dominance among a union of royals and rulers. As soon as he stepped off the cog's plank onto the longship, he was grabbed, wrapped in a bone-creaking embrace.

"Lazy bastard," Brokk said. "Taking a holiday in the afterworlds, leaving us to clean up your mess."

Reyker forced a laugh. "I suppose the Mist was a holiday compared to Solvei's ire. Good to see you, brother."

Something wet pressed the back of Reyker's neck. He spun, and Vengeance licked his face like an overgrown sheep dog. "Your horse wouldn't leave the stone circle until your soul was restored," Brokk said. "Loyal to the end, that one."

"I missed you, too, you stubborn mare." Reyker wiped horse spit off with his sleeve, scratching Vengeance between the ears.

He had his life back. His horse. His best friend. His wife.

Why, then, did he still feel hollow? What was this soul-deep ache that tainted his surroundings in shades of bleakness?

They made their way to the bow where Solvei stood. At their arrival, introductions were made. Besides the jarl, Garreth, and Zabelle, there was Joren the Dragonman spy, a Dunian princess, a Savannan tribal leader, an Aukian duke, and two mercenary chiefs—a Bog Man, who must have pulled up a bucket of silt to coat himself in, and one of the Ravenous, his shorn head painted with scarlet stripes. The duke and the tribal leader had translators with them, and the princess settled beside Zabelle, who was Dunian-born and shared the princess's mother tongue.

Lira sat with Eathalin, the two of them representing the Daughters of Aillira. If Reyker hadn't known her so well, he might not have noticed the white pinpricks speckling Lira's pupils like tiny stars, the way her eyes didn't quite meet the faces of those she spoke with, or the slight tilt of her head as she used her other senses to take stock of her surroundings.

Could she still love him, even though she'd lost her sight trying to save him? Could he love her the same with a heart that was not his own?

Brokk's elbow dug into his side.

"Lagorsson," Solvei said, her tone indicating this was not the first time she'd called his name. Everyone was looking at him. Lira's eyes shifted toward him, but she wasn't seeing his face, only the scarred depths of his soul.

"What?" he asked.

The jarl's smile could have drawn blood. "Tell us what you know of the Dragon's beast, the monster that stalks our lands."

Reyker's borrowed heart thumped steadily beneath his ribs. He told them everything.

The quiet stretched out. The leaders glanced at one another.

Garreth leaned forward. "So Draki used to be an invincible demigod confined to a human body. But your power transformed him into an invincible demigod who can fly. And spit poison. And tear the roofs off cottages with a swipe of his claws. Well done, Wolf Lord."

"Stop it," Lira said. "This is not Reyker's fault. He came closer to killing Draki than anyone else ever has."

The Dunian princess steepled her fingers and spoke softly to Zabelle, who translated for her. "The Wolf Lord's failure turned a monstrous man into a monstrous . . . monster?"

"Yes," Reyker said. He had handed the madness of his black river over to Draki. He'd thrown a bucket of sulfur on a wildfire. "I accept your blame, but it doesn't change the situation. The Dragon must be killed. My failure taught me that I cannot do it alone."

"Your botched execution attempt lost us the element of surprise," Solvei said. "He'll know better than to let anyone get near his grip on a weapon again."

"Not if the Dragon doesn't remember," Eathalin said. All attention fell on her, and though her cheeks reddened, she continued. "The spell Lira put on Reyker's soul. Something like that could work on Draki. To make him forget what Reyker did, and that we know the secret to harming him. To make him forget why he's fighting us, at least long enough to take him down."

Solvei's jaw clenched. "Magiska powers don't affect the Dragon, and that spell turned Lagorsson into an animal."

Reyker closed his eyes and saw Sursha again, shielding Solvei. Saw his hands snapping her neck. He shuddered.

"My spells hid us from Draki for months," Eathalin said. "I'm the only magiska whose gifts ever confounded the Dragon, and I'm stronger with the blood of the Fallen Ones. I can design the spell to only target specific memories. We don't have the option of experimenting on Draki, but we know this magic worked on his brother. Draki is weaker now that Ildja and Gwylor have been defeated."

Lira put a hand on Eathalin's arm. "No one doubts your abilities, but you would need to touch the Dragon to place the spell inside his soul. How do we get him to stand still long enough for you to bespell him? How do we keep him from killing you?"

"The cage," Solvei said. "We can trap him."

Reyker groaned, and beside him Brokk stifled a snort.

"It didn't burn," Lira said. "I was skeptical, too, but on Heligur, the cage was dripping with Ildja's fire and it didn't burn. It might work. Though there's still the problem of how to lure Draki into it."

"Draki doesn't know I'm alive," Reyker said. "I can serve as bait—"

"*No*," Lira and Brokk snapped at the same time.

"The *how* can be discussed later," Zabelle said. "We have an army full of magic wielders, battle veterans, and the two people closest to the Dragon. Joren and his men have confirmed that the beast has built itself a nest inside the castle grounds at Dragon's Domain, where it spends most of its time. For now, are we in agreement on traveling to the Dragon's castle and attacking him with Eathalin's spell?"

Eathalin and Lira nodded.

"Agreed," Reyker said. "My jarl?"

"For lack of better options," Solvei said, "I agree."

The princess, duke, Dragonman, tribal leader, and mercenaries voiced their approval, and it was down to Garreth. The Ghost Prince shared a loaded glance with Zabelle. "Agreed," he said.

They discussed strategy and argued over details for another hour, and Reyker bit his tongue as Solvei insisted on the inclusion of her cage. After the assembly dispersed, each sovereign carried the plans back to their soldiers. The army would stay here, in and around the caves, long enough for everyone to rest and prepare. Tomorrow they would head to Dragon's Domain for their final confrontation with Draki.

Another final battle. Every time Reyker thought he'd reached the end, a new conflict sprang up. Who would he be when the war was truly over and there was no one left to fight?

Out past the cliffs the sea was choppy, rows of white-tipped waves rolling under their ship. Reyker's body knew the sea well, his legs never faltering, his senses singing in the dampness, the salty gusts, the rock and slap of the water. He wavered at the sight of Lira leaving, crossing the plank with Eathalin, the two of them boarding Garreth's ship.

He belonged at Lira's side, but the nomad ship—its energy, its people, the way they chattered, the songs they sang—felt like Glasnith. Reyker was a Mountain Renegade, and Solvei's ship—its raucous camaraderie, men and women dressed in wolf pelts chewing on dried elk flesh, warriors sharpening axes with lava rocks—was Iseneld. It was home.

There was a small, shameful part of him that briefly wished he was still in the Mist, where he'd felt strong for defying the Destroyers. Where at least he'd felt like himself.

Garreth stepped in front of him, blocking his path. "Do you know what my sister has suffered because of you?"

Reyker was already on edge, and he couldn't stomach backing down. "More than you ever will."

"If not for you, Lira would never have made a deal with the Fallen Ones. She'd never have come to Iseneld. She wouldn't have been impris-oned by Draki and turned into his death-bringer. She wouldn't have gone into the otherworlds and lost her sight. If we didn't need you to kill the Dragon, I'd throw you in a cell for what you've cost her."

"Lira is a warrior," Reyker said. "A protector of innocents. A goddess killer. If you think she was better off before, trapped by a clan that didn't acknowledge her value on an island that cloisters magical women like lepers, you don't deserve to call yourself her brother. Now get out of my way so I can board your ship and be with my wife."

"Your what?"

Reyker pushed past the nomad leader and strode across the plank to the cog.

He heard Brokk's laughter, turned to see his friend slap Garreth on the shoulder. "Looks like you and I are brothers by marriage. Welcome to the family, princeling."

CHAPTER 38

LIRA

A single candle lit the cabin. It was a hazy splotch, a little less black than the darkness around it. I stared at the splotch, focusing so hard my head ached, until my vision flickered with the blue heart of flame. As soon as I relaxed, the image was lost, the fire no more than a dull smear.

Every element had a soul, or at least an essence. I was used to seeing mortal souls, so those were easy. Other things—the sea, the mountains—were harder, but if I concentrated, their light revealed itself briefly. With practice, I might regain a different form of sight. But I would never see as I had before. Were it not for my gift, I'd be completely blind.

The door creaked open. Light filled the space, swirls of color crackling in the storm of Reyker's soul. The wood groaned as he sat down on the berth across from mine.

"Do you want to talk about it?" he asked.

It. My ailment.

"No. And before you ask, yes, I'm all right." I was, because I lingered in denial. If I accepted this, it would lead to thoughts of the future. How I would never again see the snow-covered fields of Iseneld, the green hills of Glasnith. My brother's smile. Reyker's eyes. My own reflection. If I had a child, I would never see my child's face.

Better to dwell in denial for as long as I could.

"You're not all right," Reyker said. "I'm not either. Not yet, not after everything that's happened. I'm grateful you came for me, grateful to be out of the Halls of Suffering and the Mist, but . . . being alive doesn't feel the same as it did before. It doesn't feel the way I expected."

The words startled me. They hurt, though he hadn't meant them to. "How does it feel?"

"Disorienting. Colorless. Too quiet. Too . . ."

"Trivial? Ephemeral?" Bitterness seeped into my voice. "That's what life is. That's what it's always been. At least you'll get a battle soon. Maybe that will be loud and bright enough to make you care about being alive."

"Please don't get angry at me for being honest."

"I'm angry because you married me one day and then ran off and made me a widow the next! I *died* to save you. I searched the otherworlds for you, dragged you out, and now you're offering to be bait so your brother can rip out the heart Veronis just gave you!"

"Ah. That." I pictured him wincing, dropping his chin. How long until I forgot what he looked like? How long until his face was nothing but a dull smear in the dark of my memory? "Everything is tangled up inside me, Lira. I need time to make sense of it all, to clear my head, so I can be the kind of husband you deserve."

"Time is a luxury you and I have never had."

"I wish I could fix it." The berth creaked again as he leaned in closer. "All the things we lost. Your sight. My heart. A part of my soul I didn't want, but it was mine, and now it's gone and I don't know what takes its place. I don't know if I can fight Draki without it."

I sat up straighter, squinting at the shapes and colors swirling in my vision, the elements that formed Reyker's essence. Heat pulsed in my chest, like flames igniting my heart without burning it.

Between one blink and the next, I was inside Reyker's soul.

Without touching him, without anything more than a thought. I did not fall, I merely shifted from one place to another, from the corporeal realm to the spiritual one. I stood between canyon walls, where the black river used to roar, its currents a concoction of water and fire. What flowed beneath my feet looked similar to the river, but this close, I could tell it was something else. Dense blue smoke. Gray ribbons of liquid steel.

I dipped my hands into the river of smoke and steel, letting it glide between my fingers. At my touch, it chimed, a euphonic song that was untamed, unbroken.

Reyker's soul in its natural state, without the will of gods invading it. The way it was meant to be.

I called a memory to me: our first kiss. A polished ruby leaped from the river into my palms. The memory wound around me, and I could smell it, taste it. I could *see* it. The wooden walls of the stables, the straw scattered across the dirt floor. Me—I saw myself through Reyker's eyes, felt what he felt that first time we gave in to desire. The hitch of his breath, the tingle in his skin. The ache in his chest that was love.

With only a thought, I was back in my body—no jolt or dizziness. A seamless transition. The heat below my sternum cooled, and I gasped, pressing my palm against it.

"Lira?" There was a rustle as Reyker kneeled in front of me, arms bracketing my legs. "What is it?"

Confronting Draki and the gods, journeying through the other-worlds—those experiences had taken so much from us that I'd never bothered to wonder what we might have gained. "I know how to defeat the Dragon."

⁕

The fleet had entered the Fjordlands. I could tell by the nomads' silence, the tension ratcheting until it was like the string of an instrument, waiting to be plucked, to unleash a song of falling swords. The same sort of vibrations had run through the Dragonmen before a battle, back when I'd been the death-bringer. The battlefield was a mother, calling her warriors home. I'd tasted it, and though it didn't enthrall me as it did others, neither was I immune.

Joren's Dragonmen spies had gotten close enough to confirm the Dragon was in his nest inside Dragon's Domain, so the storm-spinners wove fog and rain around the perimeter of our ships to hide us from anyone who might warn him. The hiss of raindrops on the sea filled my ears.

I was still getting used to looking upon so many souls at once. I shut my eyes to give them a rest, breathing through the ache behind them that had become my constant companion.

"Is there nothing I can say to convince you not to do this?" Garreth asked, leaning beside me on the bow's rail.

His tone was too soft. Before, he would have raised his voice, ordered and threatened. Already, he'd begun to treat me like I was fragile.

"You can't win this without me. Not even Eathalin can do what I can."

We'd practiced, the two of us reaching for the soul of one unsuspecting nomad after another. Eathalin was more powerful than I'd ever been as the Fallen Ones' vessel. She could weave an intricate spell, the sort that would do exactly what we needed it to, but she still couldn't place it inside someone's soul without touching them. That drop of Ildja's fire I'd absorbed by killing her had enhanced my soul-reading gift. Not unlike the power Draki gained by eating magiska hearts.

"I'm not defenseless, Garreth. I can see every soul that's near me and tell if they mean me harm. In some ways, that makes me safer than the rest of you."

"We'd be having this same conversation if you hadn't lost your sight," he said, "I'd just be slightly less worried about giving you a sword. Promise me, no matter what happens, you'll put yourself in no more harm than necessary. Promise me you'll stay out of—"

"I saw Mother. In the otherworlds."

That shut him up quick.

There had been no time to discuss it earlier, no easy way to bring it up, but now—as the ship sailed nearer to Dragon's Domain, to an unknown fate—I told him about Mother. About Father and Rhys and Quinlan. I couldn't see his expression, but I heard him sniff and swallow, tears pressing on his throat when he said, "Thank you. I needed to hear that. I've needed it for a long time."

I wrapped an arm around him, and he did the same to me. "If we don't survive today," I said, "at least we know they're on the other side, waiting."

"They can wait a bit longer. Let them hear of our brave deeds and be filled with pride."

That was how we entered the outskirts of Dragon's Domain. As brother and sister, the last two Stones, side by side.

Eathalin came to stand with us. Her soul was a collage of stained glass and silk garlands, soft edges buttressed with iron. Her gifts were chunks of marble, sculpting themselves into art as she let a trickle of her power cloak the fleet. It was risky for her to expend even this small amount of energy when she would need every grain for the spell against Draki, but we'd never get close to the Dragon if he saw us coming.

"It's time," Eathalin said.

The cog broke off from the other ships, angling toward the rocky cliffs along the mouth of the fjord. As Eathalin and I waited to disembark, Zabelle came to us. Her soul was full of the sand dunes and baked earth of her homeland, the briny air of the Auk Isles, the knolls of the Green Desert. Eathalin hugged her. I touched Zabelle's shoulder and whispered, "Good luck."

A sun orbited the center of Zabelle's soul. It flared every time she looked at Garreth. It glowed now, as she looked at Eathalin and me. "If either of you die," she said, glancing between us, "I will kill you."

The sound of a plank sliding into place meant our bridge was ready. Garreth helped Eathalin across first, then me. "Take care of each other," he said.

We did not ask the gods to protect us, to watch over our loved ones. The gods had gotten us into this mess in the first place. It was up to all of us to win this fight, to keep one another safe. Mortals would finish the war the gods had started.

Eathalin linked her arm with mine as the cog pulled away.

My eyes strayed to the rest of the fleet, the souls floating against the dark backdrop of my vision, and found Reyker, as they always did. As they always would. His soul glowed from the deck of Solvei's longship, Victory at his side. I sensed him looking back at me, his gaze like finger-tips stroking my spine.

Our goodbye had been rushed. Strained. He'd wanted to come with me, but we needed to be separated. Together, it would be too easy for Draki to kill us both and leave the army defenseless. As long as one of us was alive, there was a chance.

I turned away from Reyker as he and the rest of the fleet were swallowed once more by the cloaking spell. Eathalin wrapped a thin veil around the two of us, and then we began to climb. Up the rocky slope, picking our way along the steep hills. Eathalin was a lodestar, and I followed the lights of her soul, the sounds of her scrabbling. In the most perilous spots, she reached for my hand and guided me. Slowly, we made our way to the top of the cliff.

Eathalin called a gull from the sky, sent it swooping down to signal the fleet that we were in place. Though I couldn't see it, I knew what was happening. Concealed by Eathalin's spell, the fleet sailed into formation, lining the fjord on either side, as well as blocking its mouth. Meanwhile, a single ship drifted toward the shore of Dragon's Domain. No souls were on board. It was propelled to the middle of the fjord by wind-wafters and tide-tellers. A decoy.

"How long do you think we'll have to wait?" Eathalin asked. For all her strength, she was still scarcely past girlhood. Fear shook her voice, and I squeezed her hand.

"Not long."

The stillness filled with the sound of our breaths, our quiet fidgeting. The cold seeped into my bones. Five minutes stretched into ten, twenty. Thirty. Where was the Dragon?

A shriek made every hair on the back of my neck stand stiff. The susurrus of air being displaced reverberated through the fjord—the unmistakable flapping of wings, too large and loud to be a bird. I could just make out the blurred shadow that was Draki's soul, heading for the ship.

Eathalin whispered, "It begins."

CHAPTER 39

The moon was a harsh white orb dangling from the sky, illuminating the throne—skulls and spines, frozen in ice. Joren and the Dragonmen had taken it with them when they left Dragon's Domain for the last time. It had been Joren's idea to use it as bait.

The lone ship floated into the middle of the fjord, the rest of the fleet still veiled by Eathalin's spell. As they waited, the minutes stretching out, Reyker entered that calm space Gothi had helped him tap into, his breaths deep, his body relaxed. To his right, Solvei ground her teeth. To his left, Brokk squeezed his axe, mouthing, *Come on, you bastard.*

When the Dragon finally appeared, Reyker's stomach dropped. It was the size of three horses put together, bigger than Reyker remembered— gods, had it grown? If it kept growing, would it one day be as big as a castle, a village, the whole of Iseneld?

They watched the Dragon circle the decoy ship. The beast landed awkwardly, rocking the vessel, sniffing at the throne.

"Now," Solvei whispered, waving her hand.

The magiskas across the fleet went to work—those with gifts of water and wind and metal combining forces, moving Solvei's Dragon Catcher from the longship to the boat the Dragon was on. From the cliff behind them, Eathalin stretched her veil to conceal the cage as the magiskas steered the cage along the waves, lifted it into the air. As they positioned it over the Dragon's head. Dropping it into place.

It came down with a crash. The Dragon screamed, pressing against the bars.

The cage did not move.

The beast thrashed and howled, chewing at the bars, clawing at them. And the cage—that cage Reyker had scoffed at and mistrusted, the cage Solvei had poured all her efforts and expectations into—*did not move.*

Solvei's hands were up, fists pounding the air. She grinned at Reyker and Brokk.

The archers moved into place, and the sky sang with arrows. For an instant after the arrows launched, Reyker dared to hope they would penetrate, dared to hope that with the Dragon pinned, with Ildja and Gwylor dead, the beast would be rendered vulnerable.

The arrows hit. Crumbled to dust.

Reyker realized his own foolishness. Draki had never been vulnerable—he was born half god, and even when weapons could still break his skin and shed his blood, his body had healed itself too quickly for the damage to overtake him.

But the cage, the cage was something. The Dragon was trapped, the Dragon was—

Spitting black poison onto the bars. The poison boiled and frothed, and beneath it, the bars were eaten away.

"Well, fuck," Solvei and Brokk said.

There was a shimmer, and Eathalin's veil dropped. The Dragon could see them. It roared, retching up more poison, dissolving the cage's bars.

Their longship, along with a score of others from the fleet, wove across the fjord in precise patterns. Some magiskas steered the ships, while others poured their powers at the Dragon. Nothing they threw at the beast landed, and fear tightened Reyker's throat. Would Eathalin's spell work, or was it like the cage, like Reyker guiding the blade in Draki's hands toward his chest—another desperate, doomed attempt at the impossible?

They had an alternate plan, in case the cage and the spell failed. Renegades had taken turns with their axes, whittling the top of the mast on Solvei's longship into a stake, so they might lure the beast onto the mast's sharp tip. But would Draki have to be holding the mast with his claws for it to penetrate?

It had been hard enough getting Draki to stab himself as a man.

The poison had eroded the bars enough for the Dragon to push through. Its scales caught on the bars' edges, shearing off. Leaving a streak of red.

"Blood," Solvei said. "The Dragon is bleeding!"

Not that it mattered. The Dragon bellowed, beating its wings, and took to the air. It barreled toward the eastern side of the fjord, smashing through fifteen ships as if they were made of twigs. Warriors screamed as the vessels sank.

"Get down," Reyker told Bronagh and Keeva. The magiskas had requested to fight alongside him on Solvei's ship, and he needed to keep them alive. Nowhere on the ship was safe, but they ducked behind the supply crates, out of sight.

"Tear the cage apart! Use it as a weapon!" Solvei was shouting at the magiskas who had lifted the cage, but they were spread out across the ships, too far to hear.

Wings shuddering, the Dragon lurched above another line of ships. With a choking sound, the beast retched on the ships below, thick black fluid spilling from its throat, coating the vessels like tar. As it had done to the bars, the poison bubbled and ate through everything it touched, planks and sails and flesh. There were more screams, more warriors falling beneath the steaming vomit.

Behind him, Vengeance whimpered. Brokk made a similar noise. "Your magiska wife best not fail," Brokk said.

"She won't."

Reyker felt the thrum of power graze his skin as Eathalin's spell winked to life, and he knew the Dragon felt it too. The beast's head rotated like a bird's, its black eyes seeking the source of energy. There was Lira, crouched on the cliff, holding a globe of lightning between her hands.

The Dragon snarled, muscles bunching, wings stretching.

"Brother!" He'd stayed low so far, not wanting to endanger the others by giving away his presence, but now he ran forward, sword raised. The Dragon's attention snapped to him. Dread coiled in Reyker's belly. He really didn't want to die again so soon.

Hurry, Lira.

Draki stared at him with eyes that swallowed light, black mirrors that devoured worlds. No trace of recognition for the brother he had spent years tormenting. This was not Draki—not all of him. It was the undiluted beast, stripped of Draki's cunning and cruelty. Reyker didn't know whether that made it less frightening, or more.

The beast bared its fangs and came for him.

I heard the slap of Draki's wings, the roar of his rage.

There was a blue hum of power coming from Eathalin, a corona enveloping her as she poured her energy into the spell. I sensed it, a prickle along my nerves, a weight saturating the space around her. A tangible sphere, growing stronger.

Below us, I watched the shadow of Draki's soul. The way it moved, the sounds that accompanied it, made it clear he had skimmed along the water and slammed into several ships. There were screams, the splintering of wood. The shadow shook and dove, lashing out clumsily. Something was wrong. There was no calculation to Draki's strikes, no finesse. Only the brute strength of a feeble-minded animal.

Dozens of bright souls winked out. I searched frantically for the lights and landscapes that were Reyker's, Garreth's, and Zabelle's souls. When I spotted them, some of my fear abated, but then the Dragon's shadow descended again.

Eathalin pushed more of herself into the spell, and the sphere she held grew, the veil around us dissolving as she used up every bit of magic she had. At the first flicker of her soul, I grabbed her wrist. "Stop," I said. "Any more, and you'll drain yourself to death."

"There's nothing left, anyway," she said, just before she fainted. I caught her, easing her to the ground. Lifting the sphere from her palms.

I'd touched the fire of gods. Eathalin's spell was nearly as powerful, but it didn't hurt. Its heat wasn't born of hate—it was healing, inviting, a taste of the gentle soul that made it. Even so, it had enough energy to destroy a village. It pulsed in my hands, barely contained.

With Eathalin's veil gone, no amount of distraction could hide the vast, vibrating beacon I held. I felt it when Draki saw me, the shadows in him roiling with fury as he prepared to lunge.

"Brother!"

The Dragon froze. A soul of smoke and steel rushed forward, calling Draki to him. Buying me time to do what had to be done.

The Dragon charged at Reyker.

I reached for Draki's soul, the drop of goddess fire in my chest sparking to life.

An abyss yawned around me, blotting out the stars, darker than the darkest spaces of the night-black sky. There was a wrongness to it, a foreboding that permeated everything. It reeked like a field full of corpses, the tang of rot souring my perception. It was colder than the glaciers in the hinterlands of Iseneld. A metallic scraping made my ears ache.

I tread carefully across the jagged terrain.

What remained of the Dragon's soul was tattered, just as I'd remembered, but the landscape had changed since he'd stolen Reyker's power. Something snaked through the core of his essence. Not water. Not fire. A river of jagged ice and shards of bones, grinding rather than flowing. Digging a trench straight down, through the epicenter of his soul.

I bent over the river's surface, staring into its depths. Jerking back at the impression emanating from it. Draki, writhing, screaming, banging against an invisible prison. The river was corrosive. It was hurting him.

No. Worse. If souls could bleed, his would be hemorrhaging. If they could rot, his would be gangrenous. This river, its power, was a form of Sjaf's war gift, given to Reyker by the gods to be a weapon, a means to kill Draki. And that's what it was doing. Ripping his soul apart, from the inside. Harming him, as the Fallen Ones' gifts had come to harm me. The gods-damned unkillable Dragon was finally, *finally* dying.

His mutation into a scaled beast might have just been a repercussion of the river's poison. If only we'd waited, Draki would've eventually dropped dead on his own. But now, people I loved were in his path.

The scraping noise grew more insistent. I followed it and found symbols scratched along the air, like a knife carving messages into a tree. The shapes itched at my mind, familiar. A code. The secret language I'd told him about that fateful night at the cottage on the fjord, the symbols Ishleen and I created as children to speak without words. Draki knew it as well as I did, having trespassed inside my head.

I read the symbols, translating. *Trapped. Free me.*

"Trapped?" I shook my head, puzzling through his message. "Your mind is trapped inside this beast?" The creature's actions must have been driven by instinct. And Draki must be unable to transform back into a man, otherwise he'd have freed himself. He couldn't even speak aloud within his own soul. "At long last, you've gotten exactly what you deserve."

The scrape of metal, and more symbols took shape. *Free me. Reward you.*

"Stuff it up your arse! You trapped me this same way, inside my own mind. You put an axe in my brother's spine, you tore Reyker open and ate his heart!"

Unfortunate. Necessary.

"I wish there was more time to let you suffer, to make you pay for every one of your sins. But before your memories are destroyed, I want you to know this: I killed your mother. I took her fire. That's what gave me the power to ruin you."

I tuned out the wild scratching, the symbols that cursed and threatened.

Opening my hands, I released Eathalin's spell. It streaked like a comet across the expanse of Draki's soul, bursting into thousands of tiny pieces, each one trailing incandescent webs. The fragments shot higher, higher, weaving back and forth, spinning a pearlescent net of silver and gold, rose and cobalt. The webbing stretched as far as I could see, pulling tighter, wriggling like a living thing, ensnaring memories, thoughts, and emotions that had transformed Aldrik into Draki.

His soul trembled in defiance and the river churned harder, cut deeper, but between the loss of the gods who'd bolstered him and the parasite of a river that was bleeding him dry, Draki was too weak to fight Eathalin's spell.

I let go of his soul and returned to my body, opening my eyes.

Below me in the fjord, where there should have been a thousand lights born of a thousand souls, there were only a scattered few hundred left. The rotting shadow of the Dragon thrashed about as Eathalin's spell did its work.

One of the souls I loved was on top of the Dragon, clinging to it precariously.

Another soul I loved was hit by that flailing shadow, knocked sideways by the force. Off the ship. Into the sea.

REYKER

Brokk dragged him to the deck as the Dragon dove at them, its body snapping the mast in half, its tail skidding across Reyker's leather armor. The wind from its wings rocked the longship as violently as a cyclone. He and Brokk held on to each other to keep from rolling.

The Dragon moved on to attack another ship, the screams scraping Reyker's heart raw. The longship stopped bucking and he rose, dazed. He was the only one standing.

Sprawled across the longship's deck were ten Renegades the Dragon had collided with, reduced to sacks of crushed bones. Keeva and Bronagh crawled out from their hiding place behind the barrels and rushed among the bodies, looking for survivors. When it was clear there were none, the magiskas knelt and recited prayers in Glasnithian and Iseneldish.

Reyker staggered to the railing and saw another twenty corpses floating in the water.

His mouth tasted of bile. What had he done?

There was movement in the corner of his eye. He turned toward it and sighed as he saw Vengeance, paddling through the water. The mare had been knocked overboard, but she was a good swimmer, already halfway to the rocky shore.

He looked at the cog carrying Garreth and Zabelle, the ship closest to his own. It was in one piece, but black poison coated the bow, eating through the hull. The surviving nomads were crouched defensively, and Reyker couldn't tell how many of them still lived.

"Jarl?" Brokk shouted, checking the dead. "My jarl?"

Solvei. Gods aflame. Reyker searched for her among the dead in the water.

Brokk dug his hands into his hair. "Solvei, where are you? Gods-damn it, answer me!"

"Speak to me that way again, and I'll have your tongue removed."

Solvei hung from the railing opposite Reyker. Though her words had bite, her features didn't—she was pale and trembling. Reyker and Brokk ran to her, taking hold of her arms and lifting her onto the ship.

The jarl ground her teeth, her fingers digging into them, unwilling to cry out. Blood soaked through her tunic. They eased her to the deck and Brokk unbuckled her armor, tossing it aside. The wound was deep, a gouge just below her rib cage.

"Bastard caught me with a talon," Solvei said, shutting her eyes.

Brokk pressed his hands to the wound and Bronagh ripped a dead Renegade's tunic from the broken body it covered. She handed the cloth to Brokk, who wrapped the makeshift bandage around the jarl's torso. Brokk looked to the bone-healer. "Can you help her?"

Keeva shook her head. "I can't fix this. She needs a blood-healer."

Reyker scanned the fjord. So many ships were sunk or buried in poison, so many bodies lay on the decks or floated in the water. They had come to make a stand together—warriors from different tribes, different nations. Now they were dying together.

Solvei was going to die with them. The Dragon flew back and forth overhead, as if daring them to move. If any of the healers were left alive, there was no way to get to them without attracting the Dragon's attention.

"Eathalin," Reyker said. She was on the cliff with Lira. With the Fallen Ones' blood in her, she'd become a better healer than Lira had ever been. "If the three of you can get the jarl there"—he pointed to the shore at the bottom of the cliffs—"you can fetch Eathalin to help her."

"What about you?" Bronagh asked.

The mast was broken, the stake gone. Their plan had been flimsy at best, and it had come undone just as he'd feared. "Someone has to keep the Dragon occupied."

"No." Brokk grabbed his arm. "You aren't facing him alone. Not again."

"We can take Solvei," Keeva said, sharing a look with Bronagh. The sea-farer was already nodding. "She's our jarl too."

Brokk rubbed a hand across his mouth. "I don't—"

"Yes." Solvei's eyes opened. "Bronagh. Keeva. You are Renegades. No matter where you came from, now you are warriors of the Frozen Sun. Just as Mabyn, Alane, and Sursha were. I place my life in your hands."

To Reyker, the names of the dead were daggers, each one driving deeper than the last.

Brokk moved to help Solvei to her feet, and Reyker ducked beneath the jarl's other arm. "The cage *did* work," she said, just before her body went limp. They carried her, half conscious, to the railing, waiting as the magiskas dropped into the icy water and grabbed a floating piece of wreckage from one of the ships.

Reyker and Brokk lowered Solvei so that all but her legs were lying atop the wooden plank. Bronagh used her sea gift to propel the plank through the bodies bobbing on the swells.

The Dragon was on the other side of the fjord, trampling a ship full of Aukians, but its head arched sideways at the motion on the water. It stretched its wings and took to the air, eyes on the three figures making their way toward shore. Before Reyker could move, a shout rose from Garreth's ship. Zabelle was perched on the railing. "Over here, you ugly bastard!"

The nomads stomped their feet and drummed their hands, hurling insults in languages Reyker didn't understand.

Mercenaries on another ship had hauled out a ceremonial drum, Bog Men chanting and dancing to the pound of its rhythm. War cries went up from one of the Dunian ships. An Aukian crew burst into some sort of boisterous drinking song.

The Dragon's head swiveled from one ship to the next, as if the commotion had scrambled its mind. As if it wanted to attack every ship at once and was trying to figure out how.

Brokk raised his voice, belting out an Iseneldish song he and Reyker had learned as boys when they'd snuck into Vaknavangur's mead house. Reyker joined him, and the fjord overflowed with the noise of the last few hundred warriors left alive.

The magiskas made it to shore with Solvei.

Reyker felt as he had in the Mist, like nothing could break him. The Dragon roared, and the warriors answered with roars of their own, drowning out the monster.

Then something happened. Something changed.

Light burst from the cliff. The spell Lira held vanished just as an answering light crackled under the Dragon's scales. The creature shuddered, jerking its head side to side, shrieking loud enough Reyker thought his ears would bleed.

A wind-wafter on Garreth's ship raised her palm. The wind howled as she harnessed it, threw it like a weapon. It hit the Dragon and pushed him. It was only a nudge, barely anything, but more than nothing. More than any magiska had ever moved him before.

A fire-sweeper hurled flames at the beast, and though its skin did not burn, the Dragon screeched.

"Arrows!" Reyker shouted, and he heard Garreth calling the nomad archers, saw Zabelle draw and shoot before any other. The arrow did not splinter. It did not dissolve. It stuck between the Dragon's scales—no blood, no wound, but a victory all the same.

More blades flew at the Dragon, spears and arrows from warriors, knives and swords thrown by metal-gifted magiskas. Some bounced off, but others got stuck as the first arrow had, and the Dragon shook itself, biting at the shafts and hilts wedged in its scales. Magiskas coated the beast with fire, knocked it about with wind and hail, soaked it with waves, surrounded it with gulls and gyrfalcons that pecked at its eyes.

Two magiskas hefted a piece of the broken cage from where it lay upon the half-sunken ship and slammed it into the Dragon's hind leg.

From around the bar jutting into its scales, a bead of red rose to the surface.

The Dragon's wings beat the air as it fought to stay upright amid the onslaught, and it crashed into the cog. The ship rolled hard, nomads scrabbling to hold on. Garreth slid toward Zabelle, who dangled from the railing.

The nomad warrior. The Ghost Prince. They meant as much to Lira as Solvei and Brokk did to him.

It wasn't battle-madness that sent Reyker into a run. It was fear and guilt and love, combining into a different sort of madness, fueling his rash decision. He ignored Brokk's shout, climbing the railing and leaping off it, onto the Dragon's back. He would rip one of the bars from the section of cage stuck in the Dragon's scales and stab the beast. He would end this, once and for all.

The scales were slicker than they appeared. Reyker slid as the dragon thrashed, and he grabbed on to the section of cage to keep from falling.

The Dragon's tail lashed to the side, whipping across the cog's deck, and the tip caught Garreth's torso, a blow that knocked him clear off his feet, sending him flying away from the ship, into the water.

Reyker looked at the sea where Garreth had vanished. Looked at the Dragon. *A choice that is not a choice.*

No. He was done with that.

He released his grip on the cage to go after Lira's brother.

The Dragon's leg snatched him back, claws closing around Reyker's shoulders, keeping him in place. The beast arched its neck, and that giant head swung toward him, nostrils twitching. Sniffing at its own blood, then at Reyker's blood—trickles of it on his palms from a splintered shard of bone affixed to the cage. The Dragon's pupils widened, recognizing something in his scent. It carried Reyker away, fleeing the battle, heading inland. The fjord gave way to snow-dusted hills, and still the Dragon's claws did not loosen.

Reyker watched the sea, but Garreth didn't resurface.

The last thing he saw before the Dragon turned and the mountains blocked his view was Lira, jumping from the cliff.

CHAPTER 40

LIRA

The drop from the fjord's cliff was half the height of Glasnith's bluffs, but my veins were no longer full of the gods' blood. The fall knocked most of the breath from my lungs, and the cold stole the rest. I surfaced with a gasp, keenly aware of the deficiencies in my vision.

I drifted in darkness. The only light came from the souls on the ships, prismatic lanterns hovering in the distance. And one solitary light, sinking under the waves. I swam for that light, briny water stinging my eyes, but the cold slowed me, weariness slowed me. Garreth was drowning, and I could scarcely keep myself afloat. How would I find the strength to dive down and pull him to the surface?

Another soul plunged into the water—its shape like the roots of a tree, thick and steadfast—swimming toward my brother.

My arms bumped something solid, something I couldn't see. I surfaced for a breath and was blocked by another object. Reaching out, I felt bones and skin. A body without a soul. I pushed away from it, but as my head emerged and my arms and legs kicked, more bodies touched me, closing in on all sides. With no lights in them to guide me, I couldn't see how to get around them. When I tried to swim, I found myself surrounded by the dead.

My breaths were too shallow, too fast. My limbs were numb.

"Lira." Brokk's voice was calm. I followed it to where his soul floated, not far, but not close either. Garreth's soul shimmered beside his—he was alive, yet silent. "Swim. This way."

"You hate me." My mind was as sluggish as the rest of me, and this was all I could think to say.

Brokk didn't deny it. "Swim," he said again. "Your brother needs you."

That penetrated the fog that had paralyzed me. I forced my arms to sweep through the water, forced my legs to kick. The dead were every-where, touching me, barring my path, but I focused on those two souls, on Brokk's voice as he said, "Keep going. Almost there."

Then I was past the corpses, nothing but empty waves lapping at me. Brokk towed Garreth to shore, and I followed. When we reached land, Brokk dragged Garreth from the water. I climbed out on hands and knees, crouching beside my brother. "Is he breathing?"

"Barely."

We rolled Garreth onto his side, and I felt him shudder, heard him retch.

"That's it," Brokk said, and there was the thump of the warrior slapping Garreth's back. "Get it all out, princeling."

"Thank you for saving him, Brokk."

"Don't thank me yet. He needs a healer."

After another minute of retching and wheezing, Garreth's breaths steadied. I took his hand, and he squeezed it. "Gods, it feels like a horse trampled me. What happened?"

"You got walloped by a giant tail and nearly drowned in a fjord," Brokk said. "Fairly ordinary occurrences as of late. It likely jarred your head and cracked a few of your ribs." His tone was too light. There was something he wasn't saying.

The lights in Garreth's soul were dimmer than they'd been a minute ago.

Brokk left us as Zabelle swam ashore. Her steps were heavy, water-logged, and she crashed to her knees across from me. "Garreth!" she said. "I promised my allegiance to every god and devil from every corner of the world in exchange for your life, so we have a great many temples to build upon our return to Glasnith." There were tears in her voice, though I doubted she'd let any slip down her face.

"I love you," Garreth said. From the quiet that followed, I gathered it was the first time he'd told her. As the silence stretched out, Garreth cleared his throat. "Should I not have said it?"

"No, you arse. You should have said it a long time ago." Zabelle's soul bent over his. Next came the sound of lips meeting, but only for a moment before Zabelle said, "Garreth? Can you hear me? Garreth, wake up!"

"Move, both of you." I recognized Keeva's soul just as she shoved at me, ordering us out of the way so she could check Garreth's injuries. We scooted back, and that was when I noticed where Brokk had gone. He was with Bronagh just a few paces up the shore from us, the two of them tending to Solvei. I could tell by the dimming in her soul and the tang of blood on the wind that the jarl was dying. Just as Garreth was.

Behind me, footsteps and hooves crunched over gravel at the bottom of the cliff. Eathalin, riding atop Victory. Dismounting, she stood between Solvei and Garreth. "Tell me their conditions."

Bronagh answered first. "The jarl is bleeding out. She won't last much longer."

"I mended the prince's broken bones," Keeva said, "but he has injuries inside his body, wounds I cannot fix."

I was the only one who had been with Eathalin at the top of the cliff. I'd watched her pour every bit of her power into that spell. Her soul wavered between the jarl and the prince; she had served under them both, cared for them both. She was too young to bear such burdens, too innocent to make the choices that had to be made.

I wasn't.

I took her hands. "Do you have the strength to heal them both?"

"No," she said softly.

"To heal one of them?"

"Maybe."

I could have made the decision for her. She would do as I asked. *Save my brother*—the plea pressed against my throat, rattled my tongue. I choked it back down. "Whose wounds will be easier for you to heal?"

She hesitated. "The jarl's."

Of course. Even a deep outer wound was less challenging than patching what could not be seen with the eyes. I had known it, and still it made my chest constrict as I said, "Then there is no choice. You cannot risk losing them both. You must save who you can."

Her hands slipped from mine.

I moved to Garreth's side, taking his hand again.

Zabelle was on his other side. The sun in her soul crackled, its rays weeping across the hills and dunes, setting them aflame. "What have you done, Lira? Garreth is your country's leader. He is your *brother*."

Yes. That was why I had chosen Alane instead of him when Seffra demanded a sacrifice. At the time, I'd convinced myself the choice was not selfish, but rational. A lie—I'd dismissed him as a possibility, allowing myself to pick someone whose loss hurt me a little less.

The scream building in my lungs faded to a whisper as I answered Zabelle. "That doesn't make Garreth's life worth more than Solvei's."

Or Alane's.

I watched the green lights of Glasnith dwindle in Garreth's soul. The orange shades that represented duty. The lavender shades that signified love. They guttered, winking out, until love was the only luminary left. And then it extinguished too.

Garreth. My brother. The last of my family.

"He's gone," I said.

Zabelle slapped me. Not as hard as she could have, but hard enough to push some of that pain drenching her soul on to me. I let go of Garreth's hand and walked away, to where Victory waited at the bottom of the cliffs. Footsteps approached from behind me.

"You're going after Reyker?" Brokk asked.

I glanced over my shoulder, saw the red pulse in his soul. Anger. Hatred. "Yes."

"That was decent of you, the choice you made." His voice was strained—from worry over Solvei, or from showing appreciation to his love's murderer. "To be reasonable instead of selfish."

What did it say about me that I would destroy Alane to save Reyker, but wouldn't let Solvei die to save my brother?

"Why did you help me, Brokk? You could have left me to drown."

He paused, and I heard the squelch of his fists, sticky with Solvei's blood. "Because I want you to live. You're here, and Alane is not, and you deserve to live with that guilt. You deserve your blindness. You deserve your brother's death. That's why I helped you. I want you to live a long, mournful life."

The world got louder for an instant, the waves, the cries of gulls, the crunch of rocks. Solvei's wheezing. Zabelle's hushed sobs.

I could only stand there, stunned, like I was still caught in that pool of bodies.

When Victory nudged me, I grabbed her mane and pulled myself up. The mare picked her way along the shore until we were on even ground. "Go," I said, and Victory ran.

I was running away as much as I was chasing after Reyker, running from my dead brother's body and my fear that Brokk was right. Maybe drowning slowly instead of quickly, in a sea of the corpses I'd made, was all I deserved.

CHAPTER 41

REYKER

The Dragon seemed to be aiming for the castle, but before reaching it, the claws holding Reyker began to shrink. The beast shed its scales like it was molting, the armored coat giving way to skin, the elongated fangs to human teeth. The weapons and section of cage stuck in its body fell away. Its wings thinned to flimsy membranes that disintegrated, and there was nothing left to keep them aloft. Reyker fell over a copse of trees, smacking into brittle branches, which broke beneath him and slowed his fall.

He lay on a patch of soft snow, breathing hard, staring up at the broken branches above. And then, a voice. That voice he hated more than any other.

"Reyker?"

Reyker scrambled backward, his body protesting with every movement. There was Draki, hunched over, wearing flesh and bone and nothing else. The wound on his leg, where the cage had stuck him, clotted and healed.

Reyker stood and drew his sword.

"Put that away," Draki said. "Don't point a blade unless you mean to use it." It was one of their father's rules, spoken with no trace of mockery. Draki rubbed the bridge of his nose. "How much did we drink? I feel like I blacked out for a century. And why in Sjaf's name am I naked?"

The sword shook in Reyker's hand. "What are you playing at, Draki?"

"Draki? Is that some wench's pet name for me? Is that who stole my clothes and gave me these?" He examined the tattoos curling along his body with raised brows.

Reyker swallowed and tried again. "Aldrik?"

"Who else would I be? You must still be drunk. Father is going to murder me for tarnishing his golden lordling."

Reyker's mouth went dry. The spell. Eathalin's spell had worked.

He had to be certain. "Who is your mother?"

Aldrik knocked the sword from his hand and pushed him against a tree. "Drunk or not, if you bring up my volva ancestry, you will pay for it. When did you get so big?" He sized Reyker up, and his gaze stumbled over Reyker's chest—the top half of the scar over his heart was exposed by his torn tunic.

"Who did this to you?" Aldrik asked. His features twitched, and the tic was so familiar. Though he'd hidden it well, in his own sick way, Aldrik had cared about Reyker.

"Gods," Reyker said. "You were always a prick, Aldrik, but you didn't have to be a monster."

"Monster? Is that what you think of me?"

"Yes! And you made me one too!" He shoved Aldrik off him, and his brother stumbled.

Draki never stumbled.

"When I was a boy," Reyker said, "all I wanted was to make you proud. To make you look at me like I mattered, like you were glad I was your brother."

"That's all you ever want from anyone. *Look at me, the great Reyker Lagorsson! See how clever I am, how noble and respectful, how strong and swift and brave! Behold the trueborn son of Lord Lagor!*" Aldrik spread his arms and made use of his nakedness with an obscene gesture. Reyker pulled off his coat and threw it at his brother. Smirking, Aldrik tied it around his waist. "Everyone falls all over themselves to get close to you. It makes you weak."

"You were jealous."

"I am many things, and jealous is the least of them!" Aldrik grimaced, pressing a hand to his stomach. "No one can hurt me because of my gift. No one wants to hurt me because I bear no influence, I will not inherit Vaknavangur. But you—you are a symbol of Iseneld's future. You think they are raising you to be a lord, but they are grooming you to be a jarl. I see it. So do Father's enemies. Do you know how many men have been caught sneaking around Vaknavangur with orders to execute Lagor and his heir? I've killed ten myself, and they weren't all enemies. Even Father's allies, overlords who want their own sons to be jarls, plot ways for you to have an accident—a fall off a horse, or drowning in a spring." Aldrik paused, coughing into his hand.

Draki never coughed.

His fingers came away dark and wet. He stared at them. "It hurts." The words were small, and it broke something in Reyker. "Why does it hurt?"

Aldrik's knees gave out.

Reyker couldn't stop himself from stepping closer, crouching in front of Aldrik. His brother wheezed, pounding his fist against his chest. He smiled at Reyker. "Is this how it feels to be an ordinary mortal? It's appalling."

Something jutted from beneath Aldrik's skin, sharp and white, sliding out from between his ribs. A shard of bone that didn't seem to be Aldrik's. A jagged spear of ice pushed through his stomach. Liquid oozed from the wounds, seeped through his pores like sweat. Not blood. It was thick and stringy, blacker than night. The poison the Dragon had retched onto the ships.

The black river.

Aldrik slumped, and Reyker caught him, settling him on the ground. Black skeins leaked from his lips. "I didn't mean to be a monster," Aldrik rasped. "If I was cruel, it's because you were all I had. I wanted you to be strong. I needed to keep you alive."

Reyker heard the echo, Lira ripping away his memories, telling him, *I only wanted to save you.*

Draki deserved to die. But this was not Draki. This was one piece of the man who had become Draki. Callous, vindictive Aldrik. Abandoned, mistreated Aldrik. The elder son forced to wither in his younger brother's shadow. What might he have been if their father had nurtured him, their village respected him, as they had Reyker?

He could not tell Aldrik it would be all right, would not say he was forgiven. Yet, in spite of everything, Reyker could not purge the regret festering in his belly. He could not change the fact that he had loved Aldrik, that some gods-forsaken splinter of his heart loved him still and wanted him to know he was not alone. "I'm here," Reyker said.

Reyker held his brother as skewers of ice and bone impaled him from within, as Aldrik's lungs and throat filled with the black river and he choked and seized. Aldrik clung to him, his eyes never leaving Reyker's.

It took a moment for Reyker to realize the onyx-tinted night had paled to blue. The distant horizon glimmered with promise. The insects quieted. The birds began to sing.

Aldrik's hands had slipped from Reyker's shoulders. His eyes shone like glass.

At the edge of the woods, two figures appeared. Lira slid from Vengeance's back and walked toward him. He had an idea of what she saw—the shape of a man molded by smoke and steel, holding on to nothing, because the dead had no souls.

She pointed at where the first sliver of sun mounted the sea. "Is that what I think it is?"

"Yes. My brother is gone."

"So is mine." Lira sat down in the frosted dirt, as if her legs couldn't hold her anymore, drawing her knees in to her chest. Reyker let go of Aldrik and crawled to her. He wanted to touch her, but he didn't dare, not when the black river—poisonous to anyone but him—soaked his clothes, glazed his skin.

She leaned her head closer to his. "Is it over?"

He closed his eyes. He did not lie. "It will never be over."

CHAPTER 42

DRAKI

It was bitter, his brother's heart, when he'd placed it in his mouth. As bitter on the tongue as it had been inside Reyker's chest, pumping hate, hate, hate for him all those years.

You do not know what I have done for you. What I have made myself to protect you.

For nothing. For this—

Power slammed into him, a torrent effused, and—oh, mother of demons, it was divine, it was ice in his veins shocking him awake, it was honey on his lips, it was a lover bowing between his legs, it was, it was—

A thing. Dark and viscous, wrapping him in tentacles, pulling him under.

His skin itched, burned. He erupted.

Becoming.

It hurt. He did not like to be hurt, it had been so long since he'd last felt pain—six years since the volvur hearts had rendered him invulnerable—and it was worse, far worse than he remembered, his body ripping and tearing and reshaping into, into . . .

Into a beast.

The irony. He wanted to laugh, to scream, but more than anything he wanted out out out. The near-god he had been, the parts of his mind and flesh that resembled a mortal, were buried underneath scales and wings.

He thought the pain would end when his transformation was complete.

It did not.

The gift he'd stolen from his brother was a curse, a weapon, cutting him to pieces, and he saw what he had done and had the sense to admit his folly. The gods had known. They had sent someone to love him as his mother never could, as his father never could. And they had known Draki would kill the boy anyway, that destruction was all a son of Ildja was capable of. He had played right into their hands.

This, he'd realized. *This is how it ends.*

He saw everything, trapped inside himself, as the beast he'd become ravaged and raged, as an army sailed to his doorstep.

As his brother, resurrected, stood before him.

As his death-bringer plundered his soul and it all slipped away from him. A life of blood and fire, always reaching higher, always taking more because even if the world was his, it would not be enough, not until he was a god—*the* god, the only deity left, because once the world belonged to him he would have stormed into the realms of gods and eaten their hearts, or the semblances of them, wherever their power resided. Every last one. Even his mother. Yes, he'd have eaten the soul-eater and siphoned her power. How could he not? It was what she had made him, a creature of want, of hunger, of consumption, taking stealing feeding but never. Ever. Sated.

A memory tumbled past him. That night in Glasnith's forest, when he and Reyker had first seen the girl, small and frightened and glowing with magic. Draki had hungered for that magic, to make it his own. When he saw how Reyker looked at the girl, softening those hard edges Draki had worked to sculpt, a different sort of craving overtook him.

Oh, the possibilities. He could use the girl. He could bend and break and mold her. And, through her, Reyker as well.

As the memory faded, as the god known as Draki vanished with it, a final thought:

This. This was where the end began.

CHAPTER 43

LIRA

We walked side by side as the sun scraped higher, high enough for me to feel its warmth on my skin, the first time its rays had grazed the earth in months. Victory plodded behind us, the Dragon's corpse slung across the mare's back. Reyker and I didn't speak, both of us stunned, mired in our own thoughts. Nothing felt real—Garreth's death, Draki's death, the end of the war that seemed as much a defeat as a triumph—and this dreamlike state served as a dam, a buffer keeping out the pain. I feared when it crumbled, I would collapse with it.

Reyker drew his sword, and I knew we must be near the castle, but there were no souls. We passed the unmanned ramparts, and a nest in the center of the castle grounds—Reyker described it as a large bed made from straw and leaves, with bones around it. Animals. Humans. The Dragon's meals.

As a man and a beast, everywhere Draki had gone, he'd left a trail of bones.

Together, Reyker and I entered the silent halls of Dragon's Domain. It still felt familiar, and I navigated the keep easily, finding my old rooms. The consort's quarters. Reyker went into the bathing room to rinse the poison from his skin, and I went to Draki's rooms to search for clothes.

It smelled like Draki. Even though his corpse was outside, lying in the stables, it was hard not to feel his presence saturating every corner. A ghost, a nightmare—staining the air, hovering over my shoulder, whispering threats and promises.

"You're dead," I said. "You can't hurt us anymore."

There was nothing, no sound, no movement. But the quiet grew, stretching out, filling the space, until the lack of sound *was* a sound, until nothing seemed to be something. Until no answer was an answer unto itself. I grabbed a tunic and trousers from the wardrobe and hurried out of his chambers, slamming the door.

I barged into the bathing room. "You're leaving, aren't you?"

Water sloshed onto the floor as Reyker stepped from the bath. "If I don't take his body away, the Renegades will desecrate it. Even though he deserves it, I can't . . ."

"I understand." This was less about Draki—Aldrik—and more about Reyker's need for closure. That didn't make it turn my stomach any less.

"I'll be back in a week," he said. "You could come with me."

The offer was tempting. Time alone with him in the wilds of Iseneld. Putting off the consequences of my choice to save Solvei instead of Garreth. Keeping my dam intact for a little while longer.

I shook my head. "I can't run away from this."

I heard the scratch of Reyker's hands rubbing across the stubble on his jaw. "Will you be here when I return?" There was hesitation in the way he asked. He'd said he needed time—time away from me, whether he'd put it that way or not—yet here he was, imploring me to stay.

I longed to stay. I just wasn't sure I should. "Do you really want me to?"

"I'll always want you, Lira."

I dropped the clothes balled in my arms and took a step, then another, until I was in front of him. Unable to see anything but the shining lights of his soul. I reached up, tracing the shape of his face with my fingertips, seeing his features in my mind. His breaths came faster, but he remained still. My hands slipped down his neck, over the planes of his back, his chest, his stomach, mapping every inch of his body, spurring memories so vivid, so visual, of all the times I'd looked at him, all the times I'd taken the sight of him for granted. My hands moved lower, and though I couldn't see Reyker's body, I could see the sharp blue streaks of desire I'd stoked, pulsing through his soul.

Here was another buffer, a balm against the grief.

"Always is a long time," I said, kicking off my boots. Tossing aside my tunic. Unlacing my trousers.

Fate had forced us together, had chased and corralled us since we'd met. Reyker loved me. I loved him. But without fate tying us to each other, would we have made different choices? Would we make different choices now that our fates had been fulfilled?

Reyker gripped my waist and lifted me, my back pressing against the wall, my legs wrapping around his hips. "My soul is fused to yours," he said. "My heart, no matter who it once belonged to, is yours. Have I not made this clear?"

"You have." My lips found his neck, tasting soap and skin and that unnameable spice that was his alone. "But I need you to show me again."

So he did.

⸻⊹⸻

We were silent on our walk from my old chambers to the courtyard, both of us dreading another goodbye, and dreading what would come after, the business of mourning those we'd lost, those we'd helped kill. There were cracks forming in my dam, and I didn't know how much longer it would be before it broke. Much was left unsaid and unsettled between Reyker and me, things that would have to wait until we'd sorted through the Dragon's ruins.

"You're certain you'll be all right?" Reyker asked.

I gripped his collar and pulled him close. "I'm in a castle, not dancing on the edge of a cliff. I'll be fine."

"Please, no more cliffs for you."

I kissed him hard, then let him go. "Hurry back."

I could hear his smile as he said, "Yes, my wolf."

Standing just outside the stables, I watched Reyker throw Draki's body across Victory's back before climbing on himself. I knew the corpse only by the dark channel obscuring the lower half of Reyker's soul, the upper half of the horse's. It was a void cutting through them, an absence where there had once been a demigod who almost destroyed the world.

He would not be missed.

Once they were gone, I walked back inside the castle. I only made it a few steps before the dam gave way to a wave of grief that slammed me to the floor. I curled up on the cold stones, wracked with sobs, tears dripping down my cheeks, my neck, slipping into my ears. I dug my hands into my hair, screamed Garreth's name into my palms, cried so hard I retched.

When it was over, I mopped my face, caught my breath, and got up. Shaky, but standing. I was still standing. "I'm all right," I told the empty castle. "I'm all right."

If I said it enough times, I might start to believe it.

Reyker had taken a spear from the armory for me to use like a cane. I left the castle, surveying the ground in front of me with the spear to avoid rocks and crevices. Moving carefully, I followed the smudge in my vision—all I could see of the sun—to find the fjord. I hadn't made it far when I came across a line of souls marching up from the shore. A soul approached me, a nomad whose name I couldn't remember. "Is the Dragon dead?" she asked.

"Dead."

She ran, shouting it, and others joined her. The light of those souls that had been dulled by loss and pain began to brighten, to sharpen. "The Dragon is dead!" They chanted and cheered and screamed it, with relief, with vindication, with unbridled joy. "The Dragon is dead!"

I was looking for Eathalin, but Zabelle found me first. "Come with me," she said.

A tiny part of me wondered if she meant to harm me. That same part wondered if I should try to stop her.

She led me up a stairway onto the castle ramparts. In my memory, the view from up here was beautiful. Draki used to walk me around the ramparts, pointing out at the sea, explaining all the fortifications that made the castle impregnable with the enthusiasm of a child with a new toy.

"Tomorrow," Zabelle said, "I will sail home to Glasnith with every nomad warrior who is willing and able. You will accompany us."

A laugh stuck in my throat. It came out sounding more like a sob. "I let their prince die. I doubt I'll be welcome there."

"You were the death-bringer. You're not welcome anywhere. But the Ghost Prince is dead. I am the closest thing to a leader in Glasnith, and I aim to pick up where he left off, rebuilding our nation. I don't know who to trust. I need an advisor. Your gift could help us." Zabelle gripped my arm. "You owe him this, Lira."

I knocked her hand away with my spear, searching for a fitting rebuttal. Coming up empty. My stomach sank, not stopping until it hit my feet.

Zabelle was right. The Green Gods had given the Daughters of Aillira gifts to better Glasnith. I had a duty, not just to my brother's memory, but to my country and its people. With the threat of the Dragon removed, there was only one reason to remain in Iseneld.

I had much to atone for. The time for selfish choices was over.

"Yes," I said, bowing my head. "Yes, I will go with you."

And that meant I had a promise to break.

CHAPTER 44

REYKER

The snow had mostly melted under the early spring sun by the time he found an adequate spot. When he'd set out three days ago, he'd not known exactly where he was going. Torn over the identity of the dead body he traveled with, he'd considered dragging the corpse to the Mountain of Fire and throwing it in, but even with them both dead, that felt too much like a victory for Ildja. She'd taken enough. She could not have his brother's body.

His brother. His gods-damned brother.

Reyker had gotten off the horse at least once a day, thrown the corpse down, ripped away the blanket he'd rolled it in. Though the wounds where ice and bone stuck through skin were ripe with rot, the rest of the body was pristine. Reyker had wiped away the film of poison, and without it, the face was a mask of beautiful arrogance. Mocking Reyker, who screamed at that body, at that face, sometimes calling it Draki, other times Aldrik.

Reyker had wept and punched the ground next to the corpse's head, spit on the corpse's face, almost pulled his trousers down to piss on it. Almost turned around and taken the corpse back to the Renegades and nomads to defile as they saw fit. Every time, Vengeance eyed him with waning patience, until he wrapped the corpse up and slung it over the mare's back and they were moving again.

Now he arrived in Vaknavangur, his father's lands. *His* lands. He'd seen no Dragonmen on his journey, and the buildings Draki's men had taken over stood empty. His father's bones were here somewhere, in the place Lagor had fallen after Draki put a sword through him.

He rode to the outskirts of the village. This was where he'd followed Aldrik that day, nearly eleven years ago, and watched him ride away. Where his world had ended, though he'd not yet known it. Reyker laid Aldrik on the ground, on that demarcation between who his brother had been and what he'd become, and lit a fire.

Even in death, the body would not burn.

So Reyker dug at the frozen earth, with his axe, with his hands. It had to be deep. He would not risk the body being discovered, exhumed, desecrated. Or worse, enshrined by those who'd worshipped Draki, those who might hear the legends and worship him in years to come. It took hours, dusk burnishing the fields by the time he was satisfied with the depth of the pit. There was nothing left to say, no prayers that felt right. He set his brother in the grave and covered it with earth.

He was tired, his fingernails cracked and bloody and caked with dirt, but he didn't want to stay in Vaknavangur, in his dead family's empty house, alone. He rode a few leagues away and made camp in the dark, sleeping fitfully, dreaming that his brother was alive, trapped in the grave, crying out for him.

No. It would never be over.

He rode into Fjullthorp three days later, filthy, weary, afraid of what was waiting for him, the uncertainty of what came next. But tangled with the fear was hope—that he could be a better man without the black river whispering in his veins, that he could help build a better Iseneld without Draki's presence looming over the country. That whatever happened, he and Lira would face it together, dredging something good out of the wreckage.

There were Renegades standing guard at the gatehouse. Reyker dropped the hood of his cloak, and the warriors saluted as if he were still high commander. "The jarl wants to see you," one told him. "She's in the feasting hall."

He nodded, pulling his hood up and keeping his head down. He wasn't ready for more salutes, for questions and celebrations and pretending to feel nothing but joy over Draki's death.

The castle grounds were crowded with Renegades and nomads, with Aukians and Dunians and Savannans, and even a few former Dragonmen, all sharing ale and food, communicating with stilted words and elaborate gestures. A strange sight for Iseneld, isolated for so long by distance, by the island-serpent, by fearsome legends and leaders loath to welcome foreigners to its shores. Maybe that would change, and the alliance between their nations would continue past the war's end.

After settling Vengeance in the stables, he entered the keep. The hallways and rooms inside were piled with blankets and clothes and food sacks people were using as beds. He wandered past Lira's chambers, finding them empty, before heading to the feasting hall at the castle's center.

Solvei and Brokk sat at the long wooden table, sorting through stacks of parchment. They looked up as he walked in.

Reyker nodded to Brokk, bowed his head to Solvei. "You look well, my jarl. Are you healed?"

"I am."

"What's all this?" Reyker waved a hand at the mess on the table.

"Land claims. We're giving back parcels Draki took from our citizens. The first of his many misdeeds I intend to rectify. Where is the Dragon's body?"

He cleared his throat. "Buried well away from here, where no one will find it."

She splayed her palms on the table and rose. "You endanger our alliances and our island by taking away proof of the Dragon's demise. How can we lay to rest rumors that Draki did not die—*cannot* die—without a body to show them? His legend will persist, when I could be hanging his corpse from the walls of his own castle to symbolize what happens to tyrants. Tell us where you buried him, and I'll overlook your treasonous offense."

"With all due respect, my jarl, that isn't going to happen. I accept any punishment you wish to enact for my actions."

Brokk cursed under his breath. Solvei pursed her lips. She grabbed a claim from the top of the pile. "Your punishment is that I'm offering you the title of lord of Vaknavangur. Track down the displaced descendants of the men Draki killed and give them back their family homes. Choose the strongest among them and train them to protect the village, and be ready to serve in my army, should I call upon you."

Reyker's hand shook as he accepted the claim and scanned it. This was his birthright, what his parents always wanted for him, his stolen legacy returned. "How is this a punishment?"

The jarl drew a sealed envelope from her coat. "Because if you serve as lord, you will do it alone."

A cold fist tightened inside him as he tore open the envelope and a small silver object dropped to the floor. He picked up his mother's ring and read the letter—words that were clearly Lira's, though someone else had written them for her, not only because she could not see, but because she couldn't write Iseneldish and he couldn't read Glasnithian. Why had he never learned? Who had she told such things? Apologies and pleas for forgiveness and declarations of love all circling back to the same thing: she would not stay, not even for him.

The jarl was watching him. "You wrote this for her?" he asked.

"At her insistence. I told Lira I could find a place for her, as I have for Bronagh and Keeva, but . . ."

But. Lira had chosen to leave Iseneld for Glasnith, to serve Zabelle rather than Solvei. Abandoning him. Leaving without a goodbye because, according to her, she feared she would never have the strength to face him and walk away. Instead, she'd slunk off like a coward.

He lifted the letter, read part of it again.

We have been selfish, putting each other before our countries and our people, for far too long. The time has come to atone—to do our duties, help our kin and our nations heal, at the expense of our hearts.

He glared at her words, hating them all the more because she was right, and his expendable heart didn't know what to make of that. What good was it to gain Vaknavangur yet lose his wife?

Maybe he should have thought about it longer, but it wouldn't have mattered. There was only one way for him to atone. He tucked the letter and the ring into his cloak and put the land claim back on the table. "I can't take this. Give Vaknavangur to Brokk."

"What?" Brokk had sat quietly, not daring to interrupt their exchange, but now he stood. "My father was a foreigner. My mother was a low-level warrior. I'm no lord."

"You are my brother. Isn't that what you said? And you are older than me by two months. That makes you heir."

"You're being stupid and rash."

"I'm not. You earned this. I haven't signed my name to this claim, which means the village belongs to our jarl. She can give it to whomever she chooses. I nominate you."

Solvei drummed her fingers on the table. "I was a fisherman's daughter, and now I am high jarl. Under my rule, titles will not be awarded by birth, but by deeds." She pushed the claim at Brokk. "Do you accept, commander?"

"I . . ." Brokk's mouth hung open. He looked at Solvei, then at Reyker. "Are you certain about this?"

Reyker could feel Lira's letter burning him like a brand. He scratched at the triad of swords on the side of his neck. "Completely."

Even so, there was a twinge in his chest as Brokk took the document.

"I accept," Brokk said. "On the condition that if the rightful heir ever wishes to reclaim it, Vaknavangur is his."

"Agreed," Reyker said, even though he would never do such a thing. March into the village he still thought of as home and take it from his family? Even without bloodshed, it was too much like what Draki had done.

Brokk hugged him, slapping his back. "I'll do my best to make them proud," he whispered. Reyker's parents. Brokk's mother and brothers. All those who died that day, years ago, and all those who lived and carried on their family names. There were tears in both their eyes when they let go.

"With that settled," Solvei said, "there's still the matter of what to do with you, Lagorsson. I suppose you're going to beg leave from my service to chase your woman to Glasnith."

Gods aflame, how he wanted to. But her letter had forbidden it.

We need time. Time to do our duties without distraction. Time on our own to figure out who we are in a world without Draki, before we try to figure out who we are together. Though I meant every vow I made to you, I will not hold you to yours.

He rubbed the stump of his phantom finger. The loss of it, and the absence of the metal ring he'd worn there for little more than a day, made his hand feel insubstantial, as if it might vanish along with his finger at any moment.

It doesn't count, he'd told her. Without a priest, without a witness. And now, without rings. Beyond the memory of it, their marriage might as well not have happened. Was she goading him, or did she really know him so little that she thought he could move on after everything they had shared? Either way, Lira was going to get an earful next time he saw her.

And he would see her again. Just not yet.

"Actually, my jarl," Reyker said, "based on Iseneld's new alliances with the eastern nations, I believe you're in need of an ambassador."

CHAPTER 45

LIRA

I woke at dawn to the sound of hammering and pulled the pillow over my head in vain, knowing it wouldn't be enough to drown out the construction noise. Knowing that no matter how tired I was, no matter how late I'd been up last night talking with Eathalin, I'd be rising with the sun. Just as I had every day for the last seven months.

I splashed water on my face from the basin, threw on trousers and a tunic, and grabbed my cane before making my way out of the dormitory. It was the first structure of the old temple that had been rebuilt, and I'd memorized its layout—the bedchambers, the bathing room, the kitchens and dining hall. It was half-empty now, but one day it would be filled with teachers and apprentices. At least, that was Eathalin's hope.

I lived with Eathalin and twenty other Daughters of Aillira. Those of us who'd developed our gifts—many of us veterans of the Dragon's War— taught and trained the younger pledges. We still used the term *pledge*, though there was no longer a required commitment. That had been the first rule I made when I decided to help Eathalin rebuild Aillira's Temple.

My cane clacked across the wooden floor as I entered the kitchens and grabbed the mug of tea Eathalin had waiting for me. "Good morrow," she said, her voice and her soul far too bright this early in the morning.

"Hmm," was all I could manage. The tea was strong, and after a few sips I felt more human. "What have you planned for lessons today?"

"I thought I'd take the pledges into the village to help with winter preparations. The harvest-reapers will collect the last of the crops, the tract-seeker will locate game for the hunters, the storm-spinners and wind-wafter will shield the builders from the weather while they finish repairs on the last of the cottages."

There had been storms nearly every day for the last week, and it had hindered construction. Taloorah was in far better shape than it had been when I came here looking for Ildja's key, but there was still work to be done.

Not like in Stony Harbor, which Zabelle had up and running not long after we returned from Iseneld. I'd stayed with her there for a while because she needed me. There were chieftains who refused to meet with her, but they would treat with Torin's daughter, blessed Daughter of Aillira and hero of the Dragon's War. They didn't know I could see their souls, that I knew who was noble and who was wicked, black clouds of deception spilling out whenever they lied to me.

It didn't make up for my lost vision, but these new aspects of my gift did come in handy.

I'd remained in Stony Harbor until I could no longer stand being haunted by the past, by memories of everyone I'd loved—Garreth, Rhys, Mother, Father, Quinlan. And Reyker, who'd haunted me no less than the dead. I had to get away. I had to find a place where I could continue to be useful. Eathalin suggested I help her with the pledges in Taloorah, and I'd been here since.

I'd come to think of this place as home. Or as close to a home as I was willing to accept.

"And you?" Eathalin asked, pulling me from my thoughts. "What are you up to?"

"Practicing with Orla later." Orla was twelve, and the only other soul-reader I'd ever met besides my mother. She reminded me of Ishleen— quiet and clever, a good listener, a girl who popped right out of her shell if you pushed her hard enough.

I finished my tea and set the mug down. "There's a shipment coming in from Stony Harbor that should arrive this morning. Weapons and livestock, whatever Zabelle could spare. I'll get a few rooms ready for the nomads."

"Do you think Zabelle will come with them? Or any of the Daughters of Aillira?"

"Not with winter on its way. They'll be making their own preparations in Stony Harbor. Maybe in the spring."

"I miss them," Eathalin said.

I reached out, squeezing her shoulder. She was growing up fast. Too fast, because of the gods' blood flowing through her. No one but us understood what it was like to carry that sort of power. It weighed on her, isolated her. "Let's make a feast tonight," I said, "to celebrate the start of winter and thank the nomads who come. I bet Zabelle sent along some wine or ale."

"Oh, that would be lovely! I'll tell the others." Eathalin took off down the hall, giggling and shouting, banging on doors, acting as a fourteen-year-old girl should.

In the spare rooms, I filled the basins with water, tossed clean blankets on the beds, and stacked wood beside the hearths. I checked the room beside mine, and upon finding it empty, grabbed another mug of tea and went to the end of a long hallway, opening the door to the root cellar, descending the stairs.

Ishleen was curled up in the corner like a cat, humming to herself.

When the Fallen Ones were set free, so was she. The grove had become an ordinary forest, and the loch had dried up. The decay in Ishleen's flesh had healed, but her burned-out eyes hadn't. Though she'd retained her mystic gifts, seeing beyond what ordinary mortals could, she was fully blind, with no souls to light her way. Worse than that was the touch of madness that remained. It punctured her soul, spots of green and brown, spreading like mold.

I'd found her wandering through the Tangled Forest, brought her back to Stony Harbor. But she didn't belong there any more than I did, so when I came to Taloorah, there was no choice but to bring her along.

"Good morrow, Ishleen." I crouched before her, passing her the tea.

"It will be for you," she said.

I didn't bother asking what she meant. Ishleen spent half her life functioning almost normally, and the other half being plagued by visions, speaking cryptically. When her gift overwhelmed her, she hid in the cellar, sometimes for days on end, not bathing or sleeping, only eating if I coaxed her.

I took an apple from one of the cellar crates and put it in her hand, waiting until I heard her teeth sink into its skin. "Do you need anything?" I asked.

"The Dragon is dead."

I went still. "He is," I said.

"That doesn't make us safe. There are other villains in this world. No peace lasts forever. War will reach our shores again one day."

"Maybe." I tilted my head toward the ceiling, to the noise of the Daughters of Aillira bathing and dressing and helping themselves to tea. "But when it does, we will be ready."

She held my wrist as I tried to rise, tracing a triangle and a heart across my palm. Two symbols that, together, created a word from our secret, long-ago language.

Sister.

I drew the same symbol over her palm with my finger, following it with another—three circles, intersecting.

Always.

⚔

With daily chores out of the way, I left the dormitory and made my way across the courtyard, to the sanctuary.

Eathalin and I had debated what to do about the dead thorntree with the other Daughters of Aillira, and ultimately agreed it felt wrong to remove it. Though I could no longer see it, the image stuck with me. Even on its side, slowly rotting, with its roots sticking up like a giant petrified anemone, it had been majestic. The bark was peeling, its crimson hues fading to coral, but it remained a testament to Aillira and Veronis and the love that had sparked a war between gods. We'd left the tree where it was and built the sanctuary around it, with walls but no roof, like the one in Stony Harbor.

I came here every morning, even when it rained, and kneeled before the thorntree, hands clasped together. Whispering the names of the dead.

I never asked for forgiveness; I simply did it to remember. Sometimes I prayed to Eyvor, the soul-keeper. Usually I did not pray to the gods, but to the woman who lost everything, whose name remained a curse among some Glasnithians, hated and revered. My namesake, who dismantled the Halls of Suffering and killed the god of death.

May you burn brightly, Aillira, I prayed. *May you love fiercely.*

May I be granted the strength and the chance to do the same.

The sounds of horses and carts drifted to my ears. The nomads had arrived with their supplies, and I'd been too absorbed in meditation to notice. Footsteps entered the sanctuary.

"Sorry," I said, getting to my feet, brushing dirt from my trousers. "You must be tired after your journey. Let me show you to your—"

"Hey."

I spun toward his voice. Against the black scrim of my vision, his familiar soul shimmered, smoke and steel dancing across its landscape in soft blues and cool grays. Calm. Harmonious.

We'd had no contact since I'd left Iseneld, but Glasnith's new alliances meant I'd heard things, sometimes from emissaries and ambassadors, other times from nomad envoys or foreign sailors. Like how Solvei and the youngest of three Dunian princesses—the one who'd fought with us in Iseneld, a warrior even Zabelle seemed to be in awe of—had been spending a great deal of time together. How the Frozen Sun was thriving under its new high jarl, bestowed with the nickname Jarl Dragoncatcher, who had restored a semblance of peace in the wake of the Dragon's death. How, with no body to display, rumors persisted that Draki had merely gone into hiding and would rise again, some devotees still worshiping the god-man.

And I'd heard that the former Sword of the Dragon had forfeited his right to his title and lands, opting to serve as the high jarl's ambassador, bringing aid to the places he'd once helped destroy. It started with Skerrey, where Reyker had worked alongside Brayen, the boy who nearly killed him with a venomous arrow, to rebuild the villages. Since then, the Dragon's brother had sailed to one island after another, trying to undo some of the damage he'd caused. Every update I'd gotten had made my chest swell with pride.

Gods, how I'd missed him.

"Hey," I said back.

We stood frozen, him staring at me, me staring into his soul—there were still cracks and holes, scars that would never heal, shadows that the light couldn't banish, but they were fewer and smaller. He was as close to whole as he would ever be.

"Zabelle told me you could use an extra set of hands in Taloorah to help finish construction before the winter," he said. Speaking with the formality of an ambassador.

"Any help you can provide would be much appreciated." Damn, now I sounded like an ambassador too. "Is Victory here?" I asked.

"Do you think she'd let me come without her?"

I wanted to laugh, but I couldn't. There was so much I was dying to say, months' worth of words bottled up rushing to escape all at once, getting stuck. Only one sentence made it to my lips. "I had to leave." A fumbling, inadequate apology.

"I know." He took a step closer. Not nearly close enough. "It was cruel."

"I know." In the pause that followed, my pulse thundered. I braced myself, wondering if he came here to berate me for being faithless, for not believing in him, in us, as I should have.

"But it was necessary," he said finally. There was a jangle of metal as Reyker pulled something from around his neck and slipped it over mine. "This is for you. I found a silversmith in the Auk Isles. I sketched the design as best I could. I've been learning to read Glasnithian, but not to write it yet, so I had to trust a Glasnithian warrior I met to get the translation right."

I held the replica of my mother's medallion, tracing the engraving of the thorntree with my thumb. And then on the back, the verse. My prayer.

"It's not as meaningful as the one you lost," he said. "The one I threw away."

"Things break, Reyker. Things get lost. We replace and rebuild. We give them new meaning." That was a lesson I'd spent the last months learning; since he'd returned, it was a lesson Reyker must have learned too. He was closer now, close enough to breathe him in. He smelled like horse and the dust of roads and the salt of the sea. "How long are you here for?" I asked.

"As long as you need me."

It was the offer of an ambassador with the question of a man buried beneath. I recognized it for what it was, taking a moment to gather my thoughts, to ask myself if I was ready. He shifted nervously, the lights inside him flickering, until I took another step, standing right in front of him, hating that I couldn't see the arch of his brows, the curve of his mouth. Loving that I could see the warm spheres glowing in his soul.

I didn't tell him I was sorry or ask him to forgive me for leaving.

He already knew. He already had.

I brushed my smooth fingertips against his calloused ones, drawing three circles in the center of his palm. He lifted his hand like an offering, and I accepted, our fingers twining, linking my body to his.

For all else is dust.

"So," he said, a little breathless. "Tell me what I've missed."

"Nothing." I smiled. "Everything."

We sat down in the dirt, holding each other's hands. Nothing more—there would be time for more later, for tears and anger, apologies traced across each other's skin and promises forged in steel. But for now, we proceeded slowly. Sharing our stories, talking, listening. Rebuilding. The remnants of Aillira's thorntree lay beside us, the only witness to our rebirth.

ACKNOWLEDGMENTS

Eight years ago, I made my first attempt at writing a fantasy book. It was a great big sloppy disaster. But with a lot of work, and a lot of help from some kind and generous people, that disaster was broken down, remade, painted and polished, polished again, and again, and . . . finally, it became the first book in the Frozen Sun Saga. After a long, rough road, the book found a home. I was thrilled to get the chance to continue Reyker and Lira's story in a second book, and end it in this one. What you hold in your hands is the conclusion of a story that consumed several years of my life, many of my thoughts, and a small piece of my soul.

I want to start by thanking every reader who stuck with Lira and Reyker from the beginning to the end, especially the ones who took the time to contact me or show up at book events and tell me how much they enjoyed the books and to demand to know when the next one would be out. An extra special thank-you to all the bloggers and bookstagrammers who reviewed and recommended this series (you know who you are, and you're awesome). Connecting with people who care about my characters as much as I do has been the most amazing part of being published.

I want to thank Blackstone, my fantastic publisher, for all the ways they've supported this series. To Rick Bleiweiss, without whom my book might still be wandering in publishing purgatory—you are a dream-maker. To my editor, Madeline Hopkins, who helped me tone down all the heart ripping (seriously—there used to be more) and find my characters' humanity, even when all seemed lost. To my copyeditor, Ember Hood, who sorts through my tangled web of words to find the knots of meaning. To Alex Cruz and Kurt Jones, who turned my vague visions into gorgeous realities with their mind-blowing cover designs. To Sean Thomas, because I still get chills when I watch my book trailer. To Alana Kerr Collins and Tim Campbell, whose narrations of the audiobooks in this series are absolute perfection. To Stephanie Stanton and Ananda Finwall, who make sure my book is beautiful inside and out. To Mandy Earles and Greg Boguslawski, for all their hard work and dedication. And to Lauren Maturo, Jeff Yamaguchi, Roger Cox, Josie Woodbridge, Craig and Michelle Black, Josh Stanton, Stephanie Hall, Bryan Green, Jesse Bickford, Tom Williamson, Kathryn English, Keith McFarland, and everyone else at Blackstone—a thousand thank-yous for everything you do.

To Juliet Marillier, Erin Beaty, and Jessica Leake, for their beautiful blurbs. To all the booksellers and librarians who have recommended my books to readers or organized my author events—especially Spartanburg County Library and Hub City Bookshop, my local spots. Also, to Genevieve Gagne-Hawkes and Beth Miller of Writers House—without you, I'd still be floundering.

To all my friends and family who have supported me over the years and helped spread the word about these books, you guys are the best. Lastly, but most importantly, to Katla and Brock—you are my rocks, and without you, I would probably just live inside my own head. Thank you for sharing the good times and the bad. Thank you for loving me. You are my greatest adventure.